Dear Reader,

The editors at Harlequin and Silhouette are thrilled to be able to bring you a brand-new featured author program beginning in 2005! Signature Select aims to single out outstanding stories, contemporary themes and oft-requested classics by some of your favorite series authors and present them to you in a variety of formats bound by truly striking covers.

We plan to provide several different types of reading experiences in the new Signature Select program. The Spotlight books will offer a single "big read" by a talented series author, the Collections will present three novellas on a selected theme in one volume, the Sagas will contain sprawling, sometimes multi-generational family tales (often related to a favorite family first introduced in series) and the Miniseries will feature requested, previously published books, with two or, occasionally, three complete stories in one volume. The Signature Select program will offer one book in each of these categories per month, and fans of limited continuity series will also find these continuing stories under the Signature Select umbrella.

In addition, these volumes will bring you bonus features...different in every single book! You may learn more about the author in an extended interview, more about the setting or inspiration for the book, more about subjects related to the theme and, often, a bonus short read will be included.

Watch for new stories from Janelle Denison, Donna Kauffman, Leslie Kelly, Marie Ferrarella, Suzanne Forster, Stephanie Bond, Christine Rimmer and scores more of the brightest talents in romance fiction!

We have an exciting year ahead!

Warm wishes for happy reading,

Marsha Zinberg

Marsha Zinberg
Executive Editor
The Signature Select Program

Signature Select™
COLLECTION

smokescreen

Doranna Durgin
Meredith Fletcher
Vicki Hinze

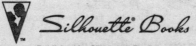

Published by Silhouette Books
America's Publisher of Contemporary Romance

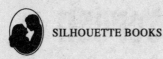 **SILHOUETTE BOOKS**

ISBN 0-373-28522-1

SMOKESCREEN

CONTENTS

Dedicated to the one
with whom I can be my true self, good and bad!

CHAMELEON

Doranna Durgin

Greetings, all!

When I started to write this story, I took it as a fun opportunity to write about a heroine with something extra. But in my fantasy novels I've always had to have a deep understanding of the magic involved, and here, with this new kind of "magic," I felt myself searching for that same understanding. And since the cool idea of having Sam bitten by a radioactive creature had already been taken, I had to dig a little deeper.

Turns out that for a superheroine, Sam isn't so different from you or me. Many of us present a different face to the world than that of our true selves; many of us hide something of ourselves away from others. Sam (whose story was initially called "Sam I Am" just because I'm a smarty-pants) just happens to have the talent to truly keep herself hidden away...which makes it twice as hard for her to peel away the layers. I came to appreciate her strength more than I expected as I learned more about her through the writing...I hope you see that something special in her as well!

Doranna Durgin

Chapter 1

Yup. He's definitely going to be a problem.

Sam Fredericks stuck her hands deep in the pockets of her baggy cargo boarder pants, fully decked out as Punk Boarder Chick—blocky black and red long-sleeved Burly Girl shirt, skater beanie pulled down over jet-black hair with electric blue streaks. Stud in her nose and tongue, hoop at her brow, tiny hoops climbing the outside rim of her ear. Battered ice-blue Fiberlight skateboard at her side.

Only Sam knew she wasn't really as she seemed. Oh, the accessories were real enough, as was the practiced sneer of youthful attitude. But underneath this assumed appearance, the real Sam had thick, wavy copper hair in need of a trim, a flaring jaw, and a chin with a little notch she didn't much like. The real Sam had only two earrings per ear, and her nose...

Nuh-uh. Her nose had only the original number of holes in it.

But the Boarder Chick guise served her well, hiding her in plain sight—unlike the man making his too-casual way down the street. *Does he really think no one's going to notice him?*

Tonight she hung under the corner streetlight and

exchanged boasts and insults with the kids who'd gathered to eye the liquor store halfway down the block. Down the block in the opposite direction, a scarred residential area still clung to life. The houses were small, the yards nonexistent and the paint peeling. One of those houses provided rooms for the streetwalkers hanging off the curb not far from here—sometimes Sam pretended to be one of them. Nearby, a recently closed-down crack house had already crept back to activity. And in the middle, the quiet gray duplex with the clean yard, a single hanging flowerpot on the front porch, and the very many excellent locks on the door….

That was the house Sam protected.

It was a refuge, camouflaged as neatly as Sam herself. Battered and desperate women fled to this place, this new version of the underground railroad. They started their long journey here, moving from house to house until they could emerge in another city, in another state, as another person.

Sam spent her days and some of her nights tailing subjects for a local P.I., but she filled her free time here. Taking advantage of her unusual skills—her ability to make people see her as she wished, as whatever she wished—to do what others couldn't. It was only ever in their heads, but it was enough. At first she'd only done it because she knew she could…and because it also filled time that might otherwise feel suspiciously empty. But after seeing some of the refugees…

Now she protected them with a fulfilling passion, completely aware of the irony of it all. A woman of a thousand identities but no real personal life, helping protect countless women who risked everything to find new lives.

And as long as she didn't run into anyone watching the world through a camera, her endless guises hid her from the world, let her move through it unnoticed, blending in wherever she happened to be—as whoever she wanted to be. Unnoticed, and ultimately, unknown. Sam I Am, ever unseen.

The women who passed through this refuge remained just as anonymous. Even, theoretically, the high-profile woman who'd recently moved to deeper hiding places. The woman had been terrified of her husband, and she'd warned the Captain—the only name Sam had for the ex-cop who ran this house—that he would cause trouble any way he could. That he would rampage through this city in a temper tantrum of Godzillan proportions, flinging threats and blowing through women's shelters hunting for her.

And he had. He still did.

Wary and unwelcoming, Sam eyed the out-of-place lurker as he moved closer to the refuge.

The threats had spread until the woman's identity became obvious by who made them, and Sam didn't blame her for running deep. Even she'd heard of the man, a gangster with old world ties and godfather aspirations. Carl Scalpucci. The East Coast had proven too challenging, so he'd moved to the western part of New York state—here where the shadow of the coastal players landed darkly enough to give him power, and yet left him independent.

He was cruel. Ruthless. And not the least bit reluctant to show it.

Scalpucci was hunting hard enough that he just might end up here; he couldn't know that his wife had already moved on to a secondary house. That made the refuge and everyone in it vulnerable to one evil man's threats—and it left Sam the perfect person to keep an eye on things, night after night, without giving away the fact that anyone watched it at all. One day her disguise was of a slight young man of color, the next this pale goth boarder.

It left her in the perfect place to watch this man cruise down the sidewalk, holding something at chest level. As he came into the light of a streetlamp, she suddenly recognized the object as a camera.

Dammit, he's been taking pictures all this time.

She eased away from her corner gang, dropping the skateboard to rest one foot on it. Considering him.

On closer examination, she doubted he was one of the outraged hubbie's evil henchmen after all. The evil henchmen would be better than this—if they even bothered with surveillance. And this man definitely didn't have the knack for going unnoticed. There was something about the way he held himself—an unconscious presence, an awareness of self. He had no cockiness in his walk, just a forthright manner that made Sam doubt he could fade into the background if his life depended on it.

Which it might, if he got himself mixed up in the business of this street. Not necessarily a bad thing. If he wasn't one of Scalpucci's people, then he was hunting his own wife or girlfriend. Bad timing for someone to get this close, *now*—he could lead Scalpucci straight to the refuge. He had to go.

He discovered her attention; he eyed her for a moment, and decided he didn't care. Which was, of course, the whole point to the Boarder Chick guise. She got to stare sullenly at him, and she didn't need any more excuse than his presence on her turf. She got to study him, from the subdued black cross-trainers to the chinos defining his butt to the lightweight bomber jacket outlining his shoulders. Physically, he could have done the job—could have been sent to intimidate. And even emotionally—there was something to the set of his jaw under that thick, dark mustache, and the way a slight frown shadowed his eyes in the streetlight. This man had a mission.

Sam wasn't much for mustaches, but this one suited him. So did the stubble darkening his jaw, but neither would stop her from chasing him away. Husband on the hunt or reporter on the prowl, the refuge didn't need him and his camera.

She pushed off against the sidewalk, a lazy kick that took her exactly as far as she'd meant to go. He looked at her as she arrived, and she flipped the board up without looking, catching it against her thigh. "You taking pictures of the crack house or the whorehouse?"

"Neither," he said, which both surprised her—she'd expected a lie—and dismayed her. Yep, he was trying to zero in on the refuge house.

"Doesn't matter." She shrugged. "They'll both figure you've got them on film. The beeper boys really take offense at that sort of thing."

He raised an eyebrow. It, too, was dark and thick. Expressive. He looked down at the camera and said, "It's not film, it's digital."

"Even better." Sam snorted. "The crunch of a digital camera against asphalt…mmm, yeah." She crossed her arms. "They like the crunch of breaking bones, too."

This time he took a closer look at her, studying her with an acuity of gaze that made her wonder if he somehow saw through her guise. No one ever had, but she'd always known someone *might*. She hadn't expected the rush of adrenaline that came with the possibility…or the startling hint of anticipation. She fought an unexpected impulse to be herself, to show him Sam I Am and see how he looked at her then. But she stared back at him, bluffing it out.

He shook his head, barely perceptibly. She thought he smiled slightly, but the corners of his mouth hid in the shadow of his mustache. "You're trying to scare me off."

It sounded like a question, leaving the unspoken matter of why.

She didn't let his bluntness throw her. "Yeah," she said. "You don't belong here. You come around taking pictures, someone's going to get upset at you. That'll cause trouble. Then everyone's on edge and it's not so safe for us to hang out here. We like hanging out here. We don't like watching nervous cops scrape dead losers off the street."

"Loser," he repeated flatly.

She shrugged. "You want I should go with the word I was actually thinking?"

"Don't go to any trouble."

"Not as long as you go away."

He shook his head, once, his gaze back out on the street. Already distracted. "Can't. Maybe if you skate yourself back to the corner, no one else will bother with me." He looked over her head to the corner and nodded at it. "Your friends seem to have the right idea."

Sam glanced over her shoulder. Off to the liquor store they'd gone, joshing and roughing each other up along the way, hoping to scam some beer. "I can catch up. You been listening to me at all? The part about dead losers?" She let a little desperation into her voice. Totally unfeigned, too, because if he didn't get smart she'd have to pull out her secret weapon: getting loud enough so the unsociable neighbors did indeed notice their intruder.

And she didn't want to do that. In spite of the implications of his presence, he hadn't yet set off her abuser alarm bells. He hadn't gotten loud or rude with this pushy young boarder…he'd just been entirely undeterred. And now he tipped his head, pondering her; the motion let the streetlight illuminate thoughtful dark gray eyes. "You're worried."

She snorted. "Hell, yes. Things get messy around here, cops hang around for weeks."

He looked back over at the houses, clearly not sure just which one was his target. Reluctant.

"Messy," Sam told him. "Messy, messy, messy. Any minute now. Whatever you're looking for, mister, you won't find it here."

"Actually," he said lightly, turning that perceptive gray gaze back on Sam, "I think I will. But not tonight. You've already drawn too much attention my way. Then again, you knew that when you came over, didn't you?"

She offered him a knowing little smile, a no-regrets smart-ass kind of smile. "Yeah," she said. "Maybe I did."

The next night Sam was a streetwalker. Vinyl thigh-high boots, a leopard-print tube top under a red bolero jacket, snug shorts a size or two too small. Long lank hair, heroin skinny, her face full of sharp features and her teeth stained beyond redemption. Unlike the night before, the clothes were as illusionary as her face and knobby limbs; Sam didn't intend to go half-dressed on a cool fall evening. Instead of the apparent leopard print,

Sam actually wore a snug black turtleneck and low-riding jeans. The real Sam. Sam I Am.

Only Sam herself knew Sam I Am.

The other girls knew her in this guise, though if their "agent" ever came around, she contrived to be *unseen.* From here she could watch the house; she could flirt with the drivers who had no intention of stopping, and she could fade back when a real john pulled up. Just short of going *unseen* she could also go *unnoticed,* and she never used it more than when she strolled the length of this block and back again.

Tonight she struggled to keep up appearances. Not the guise—she never used a guise on the job that she hadn't practiced to perfection until it became second nature—but the attitude. For today she'd gotten a call from the Captain. A warning.

"You need to know," the woman had said in her graveled, cigarette-damaged voice, "that there have been threats."

Sam had been at home, rubbing her toes in the soft fur of her sprawling cat's exposed belly and ready to snatch them away the moment Miss Kitty got that evil look in her eye. Somewhat baffled, she'd said, "I knew that."

"Escalation," the woman said, her voice holding a terseness she'd never revealed to Sam before. "He's beginning to understand she's already slipped through his fingers. And we've got someone new coming in. Couldn't be helped. I can really use you out there—but I won't think less of you if you don't want to chance it."

Sam laughed. "Chance what? I'm the one in disguise. I'm the one who's not really taking chances at all." Not that the Captain knew the extent of her disguises—that they were more than wigs and costumes and makeup, that they came as a literal change of appearance. No, she couldn't pull off a six-foot gymbound hulk, but she could do a wiry, cocky kind of guy. She couldn't clothe herself in the body of a three-hundred-pound woman, but she could pack on a few pounds and curves.

Samantha Fredericks: nine years old, sobbing her pillow wet at the latest brutal honesty from her parents. You'll never be pretty, so get used to it. You're not smart enough to aim high, so get used to going low. Samantha Fredericks, escaping into her own mind. She imagined she was a princess.

She didn't ever imagine she could actually make it so.

The birth of a chameleon.

No, the Captain had no idea. But her relief at Sam's willingness had been clear enough. "Good. If we can get through the next couple of days, I think he'll quit looking for how she escaped and start looking for who she's become—and by then it'll be too late."

"Are you setting up alternate locations?" Sam had asked, not even sure if the Captain would answer. Secrecy and compartmentalization kept the underground railroad safe. The only ones who knew the entire route through this city were the Captain and the women who'd been through the system, and by the time they reemerged from that underground, the women were in new cities and new states, assuming new identities. To talk would only reveal their past and jeopardize their present.

No one ever talked.

The Captain hesitated, and Sam was on the verge of

a *never mind* when the woman said, "Yes. If it happens, I'll be in touch."

And that's when Sam had understood how dire the threats, and how close Scalpucci had come to unearthing the refuge.

It's what she considered as she stood under the streetlight on the corner across from that she'd occupied the night before, strutting her apparently exposed skin for the benefit of those around her and admiring the condom collections the other ladies had brought out for show and tell. Wow, colors.

When she looked up, she saw him. In jeans this evening, and damned if they didn't hug his backside just as well as the chinos had. Even abusers could have a great ass. Yeah, black jeans, black hooded sweatshirt. Lurking a little more successfully than the evening before, but still obvious enough.

She bet he had the camera again.

"Ladies," she murmured, excusing herself. "I think I see a live one."

They might have contested her claim—traffic had been light this evening—but she was already sauntering down the cracked sidewalk, expertly avoiding the rough spots in footwear that appeared to include three-inch heels but in truth consisted of worn running shoes.

He greeted her with resignation, tucking the camera into the roomy, sagging pockets of the sweatshirt.

"Why, honey," she said, stopping to cock one hip and rest her hand on it. "If I didn't know better, I'd say you weren't glad to see me."

"Sorry." He shrugged. "I'm busy."

She made a show of looking up and down the street, and then up and down his body. "You don't look busy."

Another slow assessment, this time obviously tipping her head to get a better look at his behind. "You look like fun."

He hesitated—and just like the evening before, he narrowed his eyes slightly, taking the moment to look at her, really look at her. She astonished herself by blushing, relieved that he wouldn't see it. And she tipped her head to put her eyes in deeper night shadow, all too aware that they were the one thing she'd never been able to change. Her eyes were always Sam's eyes, honey-brown and dark-lashed. Not waiting for his response, she lowered her voice. "If you're not buying, bud, best you move on. My man is in that house," she nodded at the refuge, "and if he sees you out here with that camera, he'll bust it—and then he'll bust your ass."

"So I've been told." He didn't look like he doubted her. He looked as though it didn't matter enough to deter him from finding the one he'd lost. His attention went inward…it went sad. Thinking of her. Ex-girlfriend, ex-wife? Odd. Usually the look was anger. Frustration. Not sadness.

Sam reminded herself that someone had run from this man, or he wouldn't be looking. "You've got a bad case of not listening."

"Yes." His gaze sharpened, returned to her. That same dark gray…giving her that same certainty from the night before, that he could see right through her to Sam I Am. But she held fast against the suddenly rapid beating of her heart, and released her breath in surreptitious relief when he gave an abrupt shake of his head. "No, I guess I don't."

"You better," she advised him. A battered van turned onto the street…the refuge vehicle, an old plumber's

van with the fading logo still splashed across the sides
and a convenient paucity of windows. She circled him,
pulling out the stops on her strutty walk, tossing back
her hair…and coming to a stop in just the right spot to
block his view of the van when it stopped. "You really
better."

Gently but firmly, he put his hands on her shoulders and
moved her aside. "I've got someone I need to talk to—"

"You don't belong here!" She put herself right back
in his path and went so far as to shove his chest. Hard
muscle under that sweatshirt; she'd have to hustle in an
entirely different way if he got rough with her—and she
fully expected that he was capable and inclined.

"Easy." He backed off with his hands raised in pla-
cation, contrasting with the annoyance on his face. "This
is none of your—"

She heard the van door opening. Knew a shrouded
woman would be headed for the house, under escort by
the Captain.

She shoved him again.

"Hey!" He spoke more sharply this time—and this
time she figured she'd see his temper; she braced herself.

Angry voices rang out from across the street. From
the very whorehouse with which she'd been threatening him, except that neither of them needed that confrontation—not when she wasn't really one of the
house girls, and yet she was here working house turf.
He jerked in response, as quick as Sam to see the figure emerging from the whorehouse. When he reached
for her she felt a flash of irritation—now she was
going to have to deal with both of them—but something in his face made her hesitate to reach for the
pepper spray waiting in her outlandishly pink little

purse, and this time when he put his hands on her shoulders, he moved her aside just enough so the next step put him directly between Sam and the approaching threat.

Chivalry. Imagine that. Totally unexpected from any man who'd driven a woman underground, but chivalry nonetheless.

Totally in her way.

"Go." She dropped her voice low, injecting intensity and even a little pleading, and this time when she pushed him—from behind—it was more of a request. "Please. I can handle this. It'll be easier for both of us."

His long, searching look made his reaction plain enough. *And leave you here with him?*

"I can handle this—*if* you're not here to piss him off. Don't make it any harder." He wouldn't know she didn't belong here—wouldn't know she'd be in more trouble than he if they faced the man together. "Will you just get the hell out of here?"

His expression changed, the meaning clear enough as he glanced at the van—at his chance to confront the Captain. *I don't want to, but I will. You owe me.*

Actually, she very much thought it was the other way around. But there would be no telling him such a thing. As he turned, jogging away at a pace that made his retreat perfectly clear to anyone watching, Sam discovered the house "agent" much closer than she realized, coming fast with long, powerful strides. The man in charge. He focused on her, his frowning anger making it perfectly clear he'd recognized her as an interloper.

Sam muttered the baddest of words and managed to stay frozen on the spot like a rabbit in shock, drawing him in.

"Who the hell—" he started, close enough to reach for her—and doing it.

Sam darted around the thick elm on the sidewalk subway and went *unseen* as it stood between them in the darkness, running back up the sidewalk. Fifteen feet away from him she stopped short, standing silent, breathing shallowly in spite of the sudden burst of activity.

He did what they always did. He stormed around the tree not once but twice. He searched up and down the street, muted fury hardening his already hard features and the mercury streetlight harsh against his anger-flushed skin. Sam outwaited him, knowing herself safe as long as she made no noise that might send him bumbling right into her. Inevitably, he cursed under his breath; just as inevitably, he shouted out threats. "Stay away from here! Unless you work under me, you don't work here at all!"

Sam knew well enough that he meant the statement literally.

And, thinking of the look in her persistent interloper's eyes as he made that forced, reluctant decision to retreat, she knew well enough he'd be back.

There in the ragged light of the streetlamp, going unseen as the pimp stalked down the street to harass the hookers about bringing in more tricks, it took her a moment to realize she was smiling.

He'd been chased off again, dammit. Different woman, same game. *You don't belong here.*

Of course, they'd both been right. He didn't belong in that neighborhood—but he still intended to go back. He couldn't—and wouldn't—fake an attempt to blend in; he was who he was. But he understood the need for discretion. It was why he'd brought the camera—so he could take the pictures and run. It was why he'd left when he'd inevitably drawn attention.

Though tonight…he wasn't so sure he'd done the right thing. He shouldn't have left the hooker to deal with her pimp, not even if she so emphatically thought it was best that way. And if he'd stayed, he might have been able to grab a moment with the woman who ran the underground—and to get the information he needed. Right now, she was his only chance. He'd have convinced her, whatever it took.

But instead he'd walked away—no, *run* away—leaving the Captain, leaving the hooker to face her fate.

But that didn't mean he wasn't going back.

In fact, he'd only retreated so far as this little late-night diner, a charming place just the other side of whatever invisible line turned one neighborhood respectable and another not worthy of sidewalks. He'd gotten enough pictures so he didn't mind the chance to look them over—time-stamped digital pictures to show him who spent time on the street, the ebb and flow of the activity in the houses…things he hadn't had a chance to take in because he'd opted for snapping the pictures rather than lingering.

No lingering because he'd never been good at playing games and taking on roles and telling little white lies. Jethro Sheridan was WYSIWYG…*what you see is what you get.* Generally, the WYSIWYG worked for him. People knew what to expect from him; they could depend on him.

It had taken him far too long to learn that he couldn't count on the same. When he assumed the truth from the people in his life, they didn't have to work terribly hard to hide their lies. Mariska and her casual flings and her financial scheming…he'd been lucky he hadn't lost the silkscreen shop, though he'd lost his heart and a certain amount of innocence. And now Lizbet…she'd lied to him. She'd run, leaving him behind.

He wasn't about to take it quietly. He'd find her, whatever it took. Starting with this refuge. And starting with these pictures.

He propped the camera on the table beside his coffee—hot, black and straight, steaming hard enough to tickle his nose—and flicked on the display. In spite of adjustments for the low light, he expected the pictures to be dark; it was one reason he'd taken so many. But just maybe he'd gotten photos of someone who'd been hanging around both nights, someone he could question. That is, someone he could question without any ensuing mayhem. If he had to, he'd buy a hooker's time. Maybe that woman from tonight. Skinny, drug-damaged…but quick enough of wit. Unlike his first informant, a mentally challenged young woman with a sweet and far-too-trusting nature. He'd found her hanging around outside a battered woman's shelter, and a few moments of discussion revealed that she, too, had hidden in the underground. Except she'd gone in at the urging of friends who'd been too optimistic about her ability to adapt, and she'd soon found her way back to her comfort zone on the streets. But "I don't see Bobby anymore," she'd told him, very wisely. And then she'd been glad to talk about the Captain, who'd been so nice to her. What a nice lady. And did you know she was an ex-cop?

He hadn't. He hadn't known much at all, except that Lizbet had gone to a shelter, and that before the night was over she'd disappeared. He'd gone for her right away, and he'd still been too late.

And now…now he needed that someone to talk to next. He cycled quickly through the pictures, looking for the hooker—he'd become very good at taking waist-shot photos. He didn't think she even suspected he'd gotten a picture of her, when in fact he had several.

Except he didn't.

He cycled through the photos more carefully, picking out the houses, following his own recorded progress down the street. There, a spot between buildings across the street from the shelter—he thought he might be able to return and watch things from there, maybe even find another chance to talk to the Captain. There, the streetwalkers, gathered near the corner, the angle a little awkward from that distance—what Hollywood would call creative cinematography but was really only badly framed. There, hooker headquarters—"Holy prostitution!" Robin would say to Batman, profoundly contradictory as usual.

And here. Right here, he should have pictures of the bony little hooker dressed in skin and heels. Standing up to him, warning him off…getting in his way. *So* getting in his way. Keeping him from Lizbet.

Instead he looked into the shadowed glare of an entirely different woman. Black turtleneck curving around a torso toned but not too thin. Jeans riding low on hips with the kind of flare that would catch his eye over and over again. Her feet weren't in the picture but he would bet on something sensible, something very far from heels. Her shaggy hair caught the mercury streetlight in an inhuman color that spoke of copper coloring, and it tried to obscure a strongly heart-shaped face. A frowning face. The face of someone talking to Jethro.

Except he hadn't spoken to her. He hadn't seen her. And it's not as if he was trying to remember last year. This had happened within the *hour*.

The next picture—there she was again. Turning to look across the street, the light catching her eye. They couldn't be quite that color—not as they looked under the streetlight—but he'd bet they had the same odd sense of glow-from-within.

"Holy who-the-hell-are-you?" he muttered at the camera image, staring at it a moment longer. He took a fortifying sip of surprisingly good coffee and set the mug back without looking. After a moment of frown, he cycled quickly through the rest of the night's pictures. No sign of the hooker. But...didn't that woman look familiar...?

With deft movements, he pulled out the camera's memory card and replaced it with the one he'd filled the previous evening. Again he followed his progress down the street—a shorter journey, photo-wise, because it'd been his first pass through and he'd been moving a little too fast, a little too worried about being spotted...knowing he stuck out like a sore thumb and didn't have the nature to do otherwise. And at the end the attitudinal young woman had come gliding up on her skateboard to chase him off.

The display on the back of his camera wasn't huge. Generous, yes. Good enough, yes. But not huge. So he hesitated when he found the skateboarder, recognizing the clothes, the stance, the attitude. Not so sure of himself when he looked at the woman herself. Disbelieving what he thought he saw, wishing he had a better shot. Maybe when he got home, he could put it up on his computer and manipulate it in Photoshop.

Because he thought it was the same woman. The

same shaggy, coppery hair. The distinctive little notch in her chin. The same emphasis of expression. The light caught those same eyes, fired from within.

But he distinctly remembered a nose ring. He remembered that the boarder had been young, still growing into herself and all soft around the edges. And the hooker—thin as a rail, bony and used up.

This woman was neither. Vibrant and determined and self-confident as opposed to arrogant....

Too bad she hadn't actually ever been there.

Digital cameras don't lie, Jethro.

Or so he'd believed. Now he wasn't so certain. Nor could he imagine who would go to the trouble of deleting specific photos and replacing them with ringers. It seemed far too subtle for an underground organization, not to mention pointless.

Unless the point was to convince Jethro he was crazy. *Okay, that could work.* He was already half-crazy with Lizbet's disappearance.

Crazy enough to go back there tonight and get another photo of that hooker. Crazy enough to hide out in that little niche revealed by his photos this evening. Just crazy enough to watch that street for another chance at the Captain—hookers, skateboarders and big angry pimps notwithstanding.

Chapter 2

Sam couldn't believe her eyes. She, who spent all her time feeding illusion to the rest of the world, and secure in her quiet knowledge of what was and what wasn't, stared at the dark figure crouched in the dirty little not-even-an-alley where half the street girls took their quickies and couldn't believe what she saw.

She tried closing her eyes, squinching them shut hard, and then looking again.

Nope. He was still there. Persistent in his stupidity. She didn't know whether to admire him or go give him a good kick. It was hard to think of him as someone who'd driven a woman into hiding, in spite of his current oblivious persistence. She kept remembering the way he'd put himself between her and the danger from the hookers' "agent." She'd just pushed him to the limit and she'd been expecting a blow, not a noble gesture. Contradictory, for sure.

Oh. My. God. He couldn't be leaving that scant safety for another less-than-stealthy approach of the house, could he? Not really. Sam closed her eyes, pinched the bridge of her nose, and muttered an especially foul string of words reserved for moments like this. Whatever his motivations, he risked the security of the underground railroad every time he drew attention to it.

Which would be every time he showed his face.

Oh, look. How inconspicuous was that, crouching at the back bumper of an old van? She frowned at the van a moment—it wasn't one she'd recognized, and though she had the plate memorized to give to her P.I. boss if it became necessary, she already knew it didn't belong here. The vehicles that parked here regularly, she knew. The ones she didn't know—customers of this sort or that—never hung around long enough to become noteworthy.

Please don't tell me he's going to take pictures from there.

She should have let him get into trouble with the pimp earlier in the evening. They didn't need him here, not when they had the infamous ex-husband spreading threats and intimidation so indiscriminately that he actually had a chance of locating the refuge. This man wasn't the ex's style in thugs, but he could still inadvertently put this place on Scalpucci's radar.

Oh, things just kept getting better. The Captain's sturdy silhouette appeared in the first-floor window. She'd spotted the interloper. No doubt she'd seen him earlier, too—once the local pimp had joined in the party, no doubt *every*one on the block had seen them. Any moment the Captain would be out to deal with Sam's oblivious if chivalrous interloper, filling her own reputation as a bad-ass lady cop who'd retired young with the cloud of controversy over her head. Excessive force, intimidation, planting evidence…

None of that was true, but it helped to set the scene. And it spoke of the woman's dedication to her refuge. Sam's interloper didn't have a clue what would soon be headed his way. But it was Sam's job to spare the Captain this kind of confrontation, especially when she already had her hands full. Sam's job—her personal commitment—was to keep the impending moment from happening.

Sam made herself unnoticed—an instant of concentration, a twinge of feeling from deep inside to tell her she'd done it right—and went to intervene. The Captain still lingered at the door and if Sam moved fast enough, she could head off the whole mess.

She reached the van and grabbed the man's shirt collar, hauling him back and yanking him off balance so he could only backpedal in an effort to regain his feet. His stifled yelp gave her grim satisfaction; she'd meant to startle him, and she'd succeeded.

But he recovered more quickly than she ever expected. His back up against the van, he didn't even give her a chance to speak. "Back the hell off, lady—I'm here for a reason and I'm not leaving."

"You're *trying* to piss her off?" Sam nodded toward the house. "It hasn't occurred to you that she must damn well be able to take care of herself or she wouldn't be living here?"

"She's *not* living here, she's—"

Sam scoffed. "Of course she lives there." And the Captain did. Always on hand to look out for her refugees. "If she sees you she's going to come out and—"

His fingers, held to her lips, came as a great surprise. They were too gentle to be part of this confrontation. "Exactly," he said, and his voice matched the gesture. "This is exactly where I want to be."

"No," Sam said firmly, "it's not." Clever. Really clever. That would be sure to convince him. So she backed her words with action, and grabbed him by the arm and got him several steps down the street before he managed to disengage himself.

"Holy freaking—" something. He muttered it to himself and Sam couldn't catch the words, but she understood the allusion well enough.

"Batman?" she said. "I'm trying to save your butt *again* and you're quoting Batman at me?"

He gave her a funny look. Almost a wounded look. "Robin," he corrected her. "And it wasn't a quote. It was just…along those lines."

"Great," she said. "Just great." But she prodded him a few more steps down the street while she was at it. A glance told her that the Captain was on the house stoop, knowing Sam was out here, hesitating long enough to see if she would handle things. "Whatever you want, whoever you're here to find, you're only causing trouble for the rest of us. *We've* got to survive here. When the bullets fly, they don't exactly have laser-guidance systems."

"Well, isn't that fancy talk for a lady of the night."

She would have kicked him in the knee if it wouldn't have stopped their halting progress. "You jerk! Every time you show up here, you mess with the balance. The peace. All that lurking? That camera? You think anyone here likes that?"

"Every time?" he said, and his look turned sharp. "You act as though we've met before this evening."

She looked twice at him that time, and didn't like the speculation in his eye.

Doesn't matter. Just get him out of here.

"As if I would remember," she snapped at him, giving him another little shove. "You all look the same to me. Now will you just get the hell out of here before we all pay for your interference?"

The explosion came without warning. The noise, the light, the huge hand smacking her down just as the pavement came up to meet her. The night turned inside out, swallowed them, and spat them out again.

The pavement smelled faintly like aftershave.

But only, Sam realized, because while her knees and palms still stung from impact, she lay crookedly over her annoying interloper, spanning the hard muscle of his back. *Impact.* Ringing ears. Dark whirling world with the glow of fire in the corner of her eye.

The van.

No, what used to be the van. *Bomb.* Flames licked into the night, someone's car alarm went off in what seemed like the distance but who could tell with ears still recoiling in shock. *Bomb.* Okay, she still had a brain cell or two at work. She did a quick repair to her guise, hunting for the image in her head, absorbing herself in it. There'd been a bomb, and it had been more than a little pop-off of a warning. Any closer, and she would have been more than stunned. She'd have been—

He wasn't moving yet.

Was he even breathing? Surely he hadn't hit the ground that hard, even if she *had* landed on top of him—

"Sam!" A low voice in the night—or what seemed like a low voice. The Captain! Sam pushed herself away from the man beneath her and quickly dropped her guise. She never showed her exact personas to the Captain; she never showed them to anyone. They knew she was on the job, they knew she had an uncanny ability to blend in. That's all they needed to know.

"Over here," Sam answered, and she thought she pitched her voice correctly. She pushed herself off the pavement, resting her hand on the black-clad back beneath her just long enough to reassure herself he did indeed breathe. Just stunned, she hoped, from the double whammy of being hit by asphalt from the front and by Sam from the back. She climbed painfully to her feet and met the Captain in the tree-shadowed edge of the yard not far away.

"You're okay?" the Captain asked, her hard mouth set in a thin line.

"Okay enough." Sam nodded at the new pavement decoration. "I'll say the same for him in a moment or two."

"Good. Then get him out of here. Get both of you out of here. There's no way to avoid official attention this time, and you can't afford it. *I* can't afford for you to have it, either—if we have to move the primary house on short notice, I'll need you lurking around on watch as much as possible, can't have you on anyone's list." She rubbed her forehead; she'd probably had a headache even before the van went sky-high. "That bastard must have tracked us down—but he's got to know she's not here. He's just putting us on notice."

Sam looked at her abraded palms and frowned. No amount of Nu-Skin would handle this one. "This guy's not in on it," she said, the words coming out before she even truly thought about it.

"I don't think so either." The Captain looked over at the man, who'd come around enough to mutter a bleary, succinct and heartfelt word of badness. "He's too…"

"Nice," Sam finished for her. "Doesn't belong here and can't even fake it. Somewhere he's got a nice little house with a dog—golden retriever, wanna bet?—a little picket fence, a green lawn and a cat in the window. And maybe his mom lives with him."

The Captain's tight mouth skewed into something resembling a smile. "*Nice*. He's after someone who came through here, remember that. But get him out of here all the same, and find out how he tracked us down." She cocked her head. "Sirens. Move yourself, dammit. I've got panicked ladies to deal with."

Sam couldn't hear the sirens. The explosion must have affected her hearing. Damn. But she didn't doubt. She returned to the interloper and crouched down. Many parts of her body instantly suggested she would never rise from that position again, and she ignored them. She took the moment to turn herself back into her hooker self, and then she prodded his shoulder. "I know you're in there," she said. "Let's go. We've got to get out of here."

He pushed himself to his hands and knees and looked over at her, his dazed expression making way for a trickle of anger. "What the hell—"

"Holy freaking *boom*," she informed him. "That's what the hell. Now let's go."

"I don't have anything to hide." He put fingers to the darkness gleaming on his mustache and looked at the resulting smear of blood. "I'm not going anywhere. Maybe the cops can get some information about this place for me."

Sam bit back her exasperation. "Oh, really? You don't think they'll be interested in the way you've been hanging around here for days…or how you were hanging around by the van before it went up in itty-bitty pieces?"

"What?" He frowned, not so much at her words but at what she guessed to be the discovery that his hearing was as affected as hers.

"Or how about I tell them about the threats you've been making?" She was getting creative now.

He heard enough of that to react strongly, sitting back on his heels to look at her. "I haven't been—"

She shrugged. "It's all enough to put you on the wrong side of them. So come on. Run away now and you're alive to come back and lurk another day."

He gave the house an odd, sad gaze. "I'm probably too late already. Madonna said the Captain didn't keep people here for long."

Madonna. His informant. Sam needed to know more, so the Captain could change those things that had been compromised. She held out a sore hand. "Come *on*. Before they get here."

"I don't hear anything."

Sam made a face at him. "Neither do I. But you better believe they're on the way."

He must have. He rose unsteadily to his feet, smeared the blood under his nose around with his sleeve, and gestured at her to lead the way.

Lead she did, grabbing his hand to pull him around not one corner but two, where she stashed him between a New Age herb shop and a Chinese take-out storefront. "Stay," she told him, in the same commanding tones she might have used with his fictional golden retriever in his fictional picket fence-enclosed yard. He bristled—not that she could blame him—and she relented enough to add, "One of the Captain's people wants to talk to you. That's what you wanted, right?"

After a hesitation, he nodded. A careful nod, one that meant his head probably still rang as much as hers. He leaned against the brick of the New Age shop and crossed his arms and raised an eyebrow at her, and she headed off to "get" his new keeper. Herself, of course. She couldn't keep up the hooker guise, not and do what she needed this night. She needed something more flexible.

Plain old Sam I Am.

Well, almost. Because no one ever saw that part of her. But as close as anyone ever got.

She took herself down the block to the run-down gas station across from the liquor store and let herself into the nasty little unisex bathroom at the side of the building. The door didn't actually close all the way and there wasn't any toilet paper, but all she needed was the flickering light, the mirror below it and a trickle of water. She cleaned her face of dirt and blood, and carefully washed her abraded hands. No way to get around the fact that she'd been near the explosion, but that didn't matter—as one of the Captain's people she had reason to be there. She'd just have to hope her semicaptive interloper hadn't noticed the exact nature of her injuries, because she hadn't thought to hide them.

Her clean face made a big difference, although even in the bad light Sam could tell she was pale. She left herself that way—no reason she shouldn't be, given the circumstances. She sleeked her hair, faded her freckles, and eased the flaring angle of her jaw. Her hair lost the bright edge of its copper sheen, grew sleeker. She hesitated, looking at herself, her torn turtleneck, her wary eyes…fighting the impulse to change herself to someone else entirely rather than face this man so close to her real self. But she didn't hesitate long. She'd best stick to a guise she could hold even under the greatest duress. This one, she could hold even through sleep.

Someone pounded on the door. "C'mon, bitch, go to the Y if you want personal time."

Sam shoved her way out, responding with casual

crudity and a sneer that made the waiting woman step back, well-versed in the ways of *don't tread on me* here on the streets. The woman was frightened…probably looking for a way to hide from the cops who must be streaming into the area by now.

On the other hand, Sam had heard her through the door clearly enough. Maybe she'd be able to count on her hearing after all. She struck out for her stashed interloper, her game face in place, her purpose clear. *Learn what he knows.*

And after that, get rid of him.

Jethro leaned against the cold brick wall and waited for his ears to stop ringing. They didn't.

This is what people do to one another. Lies and running and hurting one another, leaving tangled trails like the one Jethro now tried to follow. What had Lizbet gotten herself into? And dammit, how much simpler it would have been if she'd just been honest about it. Until now, he'd been hoping—foolishly and futilely enough—that he'd somehow been fast enough to find her in that first refuge, the entry station of the underground railroad.

Now he hoped she wasn't anywhere near. A car bomb, for God's sake.

His head pounded and he avoided focusing on the dark features of the alley around him; it only made his vision swim and there wasn't anything worth looking at anyway. But his nosebleed had stopped and he'd been in enough rugby wrecks to know his head would clear soon enough.

She came around the corner at a fast clip, stopping short when she saw he stood right where the hooker had left him, her body language full of relief.

And he recognized her right away.

Except then he didn't. Then she didn't quite look like the woman in his pictures at all. That woman had been full of spark and eye-catching features; this woman was blander. More boring. Pasteurized and processed. Even the flare of her hip and rounded curve of her bottom had somehow gone…less so. He barely stopped himself from reaching out to touch her, hunting tactile proof of those differences.

A sister, perhaps. Or maybe just his unsteady vision.

He gestured at himself two-handed. *See? I waited. Now I want something for it.*

She said, "I need to know how you learned about the Captain's house."

"Hi," he said. "Nice to meet you. I'm Jethro Sheridan."

Not, it should be said, that he truly cared about an introduction. But it made a point.

She got it, too. "Jeth," she said. "I'm Sam. And I'm afraid what's going on here tonight is too important to dance around with conversational niceties."

"Jethro," he corrected her. "And I wouldn't be here if this weren't important to me, too. I expect to get something out of this encounter. I even think I want that particular payment up front."

She took a sharp breath, holding it for an instant before letting it out with enough force to reveal her exasperation. Then she took another, and seemed calmer. "Do you have any idea what happened here tonight?"

"As near as I can tell," he said dryly, "a van blew up and almost took me with it."

"That was a warning." She shot the words back at him with anger. "Someone who doesn't like what we're doing. Someone who penetrated enough of our security to leave a warning of that magnitude. We need to know what else he knows—how many of us are in danger. How many of our…clients…are in danger. And that means I need to know how *you* found your way here, so I can go back and check out your source."

He hesitated, taken by surprise at the ring of truth in those words. She'd put her cards on the table…he hadn't expected it. Some bullying, perhaps, and lies and evasion. That's what these people were good at. And still…he needed what he needed from her. "I'm looking for someone. I want to know where she's gone."

Sam—if that was her name—snorted. "What makes you think I know? The whole system works to make sure I *don't*. I do my little job and I don't know anything or anyone else involved."

"Then you'll have to find out."

This time he got a rude noise. "Do you have any idea what we risk to protect these women? If someone ran from you, she had a reason. I'm not going to betray her, and I'm not going to endanger everyone else in the system."

"Ran from me?" He repeated the words blankly. "What are you talking about, *ran from me?* Don't you do your homework?"

She crossed her arms, revealing a flash of pale skin behind a rip in her clingy black turtleneck. "I guess you haven't been listening. My *homework* is to avoid doing homework. At least the kind you're talking about."

"So you think I—" He stopped short on those words, took a hold of his temper and his gut-deep horror, and said as distinctly as possible, "I'm Lizbet's *brother.* I came to help her—to keep her from ruining her life."

"Uh-huh." She gave him a bored look. "I don't think she's the one who ruined her life, do you?"

It took him a moment. A long moment, after which he was flatly speechless. No one in his life ever doubted his word, simply because everyone in his life knew better. "You don't believe me. You think *I'm* the one she's running from."

She shrugged. The rip in her turtleneck grew with the gesture, shrinking again as her shoulders settled into place. "Maybe."

He wasn't used to it; helpless anger rushed through him, tightening every muscle. She must have seen it; her eyes narrowed. But she held her ground and after a moment he put a coherent thought or two together. "Then why ask me anything? I might make it all up on the spot."

"Sure," she agreed. "I might go off and check into things and learn you were lying. But I know your name. I know the name of the woman you were looking for. It's enough. I can find you if I need to."

He hesitated, hunting for rancor in her voice and face and finding none. Just matter-of-fact, as though this were simply the world she was used to, so different from his. He ran his thumb over the spot where his little finger used to reside. That misbegotten firecracker prank had happened so long ago that the scar tissue wasn't even sensitive anymore. It could have been the finger that never was, instead of lost in the culmination of a series of mean childhood tricks and fibs. Instead of being the thing that opened his eyes to how false words and careless action trapped even those who loved one another in layers of misery. His father and his affairs, his mother and her drinking.

So Jethro had learned to tell the truth, to avoid the misery—even if it meant never quite trusting others to do the same.

And his sister had learned to close her eyes, pretending her world was peachy keen even as it closed around her. Hiding the bruises...believing the promises it would never happen again.

Sam stood in the mouth of the alley, waiting. She appeared relaxed enough; Jethro forced himself to do the same, wincing at all the tender places he found in the process. *And what,* he wondered, *are her truths?* What brought her out into this dark night, watching over a system that took women away from their own lives?

And she said, "Just tell me. And then I'll go away."

"No," he said, quite suddenly certain of his only remaining chance to find Lizbet. "I'll show you."

He couldn't be serious.

Sam's hands landed on her hips of their own volition, disbelieving defiance shouting out through posture. Her palms stung fiercely. "You can't be serious."

He pointed at himself. Clothes disheveled, hair disheveled—hell, even that mustache was disheveled. "Do I look serious?"

She wrinkled her nose. He looked serious.

"You're wasting time," he told her. "Holy Oleo, what have you got to lose? It's not like you're going to learn anything I don't already know—that's the whole point, isn't it? That I'm the one who can help you follow the trail backwards?"

"Holy Oleo," she said flatly, her thoughts going a hidden ninety miles an hour. To a certain point, he was right. He'd only be revisiting someone to whom he'd already spoken. "You took that whole Batman thing a little too seriously when you were growing up, didn't you?"

"Easily," he admitted, and in that moment, in that little self-aware dip of his head, that wry twist of his mouth, he charmed her.

And is that how Lizbet had started?

Of course, there was no telling. Maybe he was, against all amazing odds, actually the woman's brother. She didn't exactly have time to check him out. "And if you come along, you probably figure you'll ride me the whole time. You really think I'll let some little juicy tidbit slip?"

"No. I think you'll figure out I'm telling the truth and you'll give me some juicy tidbit on purpose."

She let out a long breath through her nose. "Were you listening when I already told you I don't know anything?"

"Listening," he said. "But believing's got to go both ways."

Stubborn jerk.

"Excuse me?"

Aurgh, had she said that out loud? "I said," she repeated, "you're a stubborn jerk."

His eyes gleamed briefly in the darkness; she thought he'd smiled. Somehow she'd actually just made points with that too-blunt honesty. "Okay, then. Shall we go?"

Not so fast. But still, she felt the time slipping away; the Captain's trust made her shoulders ache with impossible responsibility. She had to find Jethro Sheridan's source, to see if that same source had spoken to Scalpucci—and then what else had been said. What else of the railroad had been compromised.

"Besides," he added, in a casual tone that gave her no warning he had a trump card to play, "you need someone to drive. Unless you *want* to handle a steering wheel with that road rash on your palms?"

Ah, damn. There was that. She lifted her hands, gave them a rueful glance. "You've got good eyes."

"And a good camera," he said, but didn't make any effort to explain the comment, not even when she frowned at him and fairly demanded it. He just moved on with the conversation. "You choose. I'll take you back to where I got my information. You let me hang around. Maybe I can convince you I'm Lizbet's brother, maybe I can't. I figure I'll learn something either way."

He thought he knew something about her. He thought he'd talked her into a corner, thought she couldn't drive easily, thought she'd been bowed down by his superior logic. Given that camera crack, he might even think he had a clue about who she was. Who she *really* was.

Not a chance. No one knew who really lived behind her ever-changing exterior. No one ever had—not since those early years when she'd learned to hide her true self and to give her parents what they wanted to see and hear in a daughter, all to get a glimpse of approval—that kiss on the cheek, that simple caress on her arm. A parental smile of pride. Oh, she'd learned all right. And after a while the real Sam never came out to anyone. Never risked that disapproval.

"All right," she said, mind made up. She could ditch him any time she pleased—so it was, for a chameleon. And she had no worries about spilling information to him…he might not believe she didn't have any, but it would be his problem when he learned she'd been straight about that. "My car is a couple blocks from here. I hope you can drive a stick."

Sam shouldn't have been surprised when he pulled to the curb a mere block from Sheltering Arms, the women's shelter that sent the Captain the most referrals. She shouldn't have been, but she was. This whole system ran on secrecy, and their contact at Sheltering Arms was no less dedicated than anyone else. There's no way anyone here would have talked—not unless she'd been threatened somehow—and threatened badly. Those here were used to dealing with domestic violence, with how quickly it ratcheted out of control and with how deeply the aftermath scarred its battered victims.

Threatened. Threatened badly.

Sam shot Jethro Sheridan a sideways look.

She wished she had more than just her mousegun with her this evening. The Kel-Tec snugged nicely into her back pocket, but it wasn't a gun that could be brandished. It was a gun to be used from point-blank range, before its target even knew the threat existed. It wasn't a gun that offered second chances.

And nonetheless, it was what she had. She gave Jeth a warning look—one he certainly wouldn't be able to interpret, and if he actually needed the warning then she was a fool to give it. But she did, and then she sighed and fumbled in the backseat for her lined windbreaker, holding her hand out for her keys at the same time. And though she winced inwardly in anticipation of that cold metal hitting her abraded palms, it didn't happen. Jeth carefully hung the keyring off the end of her undamaged pinky so she could slide the keys into her pocket.

Well. All right, then.

They got out of the car at the same time, hit the locks, and stood up to regard one another over the roof. He looked like he might have something to say and she felt words hovering on her own lips—unformed words of further warning, words looking for reassurance that he might actually be telling the truth about Lizbet being his sister.

Then again, even if that were the case…it meant he knew his sister had been beaten, knew and hadn't given her the safe harbor or support she needed to resolve the situation without going underground.

That's probably not fair.

No, of course not. And exactly how fair was anything about this situation?

Sam nodded at the shelter. Her breath gusted a light cloud against the sharpening chill in the night air. Snow, maybe, even this early in the season. Whatever. She said, "Lead on."

He surprised her then. He pulled a pair of gloves from his sweatshirt pocket, fine deerskin half-finger gloves with slightly padded palms. "My biking gloves," he said, holding them out to her. "They're probably big, but they might help."

She hesitated, looking up at him. Searching his eyes for signs of a man who might have threatened someone at this shelter into talking.

He smiled crookedly at her. "Not the gesture you expected from a man who takes his problems out on women?"

She was supposed to be embarrassed, but she didn't look away. She took the gloves and murmured, "Just for the record, Jeth, I'm not personally worried about it."

He took the warning for what it was. "No," he said, "I don't suppose you are."

Chapter 3

He led her not to the shelter itself, but to the dark empty lot beside it—a burned-out shop torn down but not completely removed, making for piles of old construction material, piles of garbage and piles of people. Veteran street people, mostly, those who conformed so poorly to society that living this way had turned into a default choice. They were angry tonight, huddled by their carts and beneath their cardboard and eyeing Jethro balefully from beneath prodigious layers of clothing. Sam came in behind him, making herself *unnoticed*—letting him draw all the attention and watching the results with sharp eyes.

These were not hateful people; their community had its own sort of unspoken order. But they didn't like Jethro. They didn't want him here. Several of them pulled their own disappearing acts, sliding completely into their makeshift shelters—or simply closing their eyes to pretend they weren't there.

Sam knew that trick, too. It was the first guise she'd learned.

"Over here somewhere," Jethro murmured, heading for the back of the lot. The night had turned sour, carrying the smell of old alcohol and rotten garbage and the accumulation of the unwashed, but he didn't seem to notice.

That, Sam decided, putting the fingers of one hand over her mouth and nose, must be what the mustache was for. Air filter. Fingers in place, she smelled nothing but the faint scent of her own blood and the leather of the glove. Used, worn leather, imbued faintly with the scent of aftershave.

"Here," he said, and then he frowned. He crouched down by a cart that had been filled with old flip-flops—outrageous colors, sequined thongs, giant flowers hanging limply from the toes. "This is hers," he said, and looked around at the various nearby lumps of sleeping humanity. "She seemed pretty possessive of it. I wouldn't have thought she'd—"

"There are two of you!" someone said, an accusing tone.

Whoops. Someone who could see Sam. Someone who could not only see her, but who could perceive she'd made an effort to go unnoticed. It happened now and then, most often under circumstances just like these. Someone not well. Someone off their meds—or someone on someone *else's* meds. Sam dropped the guise, such as it was, and by the time Jethro turned around, raised her eyebrows at him in question. "Your source is *here?*"

"That's better," said the voice, muffled by whatever concealed its owner. "Now take care of her."

"She *was* here," Jethro said. "And this cart is hers…"

"*Stupidstupidstupid,*" said the voice.

Sam was beginning to think the same…and yet she also couldn't ignore the little frisson of warning that tightened her shoulders. She gestured at the lumps of sheltering humanity. "Then we'd better start knocking on doors."

He winced. "I hate to bother them."

"Bother them," Sam said flatly. "There's plenty at stake." And she stood back and crossed her arms, because there was no point in bothering them with two strange faces when only one would recognize their quarry.

Jethro took a deep breath. His determination—that which had been so obvious when Sam had accosted him on the street these two past nights—returned, squaring his shoulders in the darkness. He lifted a flap of cardboard here, pulled aside the corner of an old blanket there. And in a moment he muttered, "Damn." A spare, short word so grim that Sam instantly came to join him.

He moved aside so the faintly available streetlight crept across the woman he'd found. At first Sam thought her old; then she realized the woman was merely worn. And beaten. Oh, yes, quite thoroughly beaten. Both eyes too puffy to open, tears of blood and salt mixing with the grime on her skin, her nose misshapen and her lips no longer apparently human. Her hands, cradled at her breast, displayed the lumpy asymmetry of broken bones. She muttered something defiant.

Sam shot Jethro an instant look of accusation, a look brimming with fury.

"Hey!" he said instantly. "I didn't do this! When I need a hobby, I go for rugby, or I go for my bike."

Sam said nothing, her lips tight as she bent over the beaten woman.

"Dammit, not every man who crosses your path is the kind of man who—"

"Shut up." Sam didn't care how sharp and short her

words came out; she cared only that he shut up. "This isn't about you right now. It's about getting help for her. Do you have a cell phone?"

"Yes," he said, and to his credit he switched mental gears quickly enough. "But maybe we should just take her. To the hospital, I mean. It might be faster."

"Agreed," she said. And they'd have a chance to talk to her…if she could talk at all. She quickly removed the tattered blankets, stuffing them into the shopping cart with the flip-flops. "This is Madonna?"

"You caught that?" He shrugged when Sam glanced up, and nodded. "She answers to it, anyway."

So Sam spoke to her, and reassured her, and Madonna—when she got to her feet—turned out to be a plump young woman whose shoes and clothes were still decently new. She muttered constantly, twitching her head in motions that seemed ingrained, but her swollen lips made her words incomprehensible.

"She told me about the house," Jethro said, delaying them long enough to tuck the shopping cart away in a dark corner and to warn the silent lot that these were Madonna's things. He came back to help Sam guide Madonna to the car. "She said the ladies at the shelter were nice to her when she didn't know where to go, and that they got her into the underground. I gather her boyfriend wasn't really a boyfriend after all, but someone looking to beat her down into prostitution."

Sam used the remote to unlock the doors to her battered Civic. "It doesn't make sense. If she was in the underground, what the hell is she doing here?"

Jethro carefully folded the woman down into the backseat and closed the door. "I didn't get the impression she was very good at staying on her medicine. And

how she's just as happy living on the street as living everybody else's life."

Sam slid into the driver's seat, hands still tender on
the wheel but nicely protected by the gloves. "The Captain's runaways practically swear on their own lives that
they'll never reveal a single word about the underground. And then she covers her tracks by getting everyone out of the city ASAP. If they let anything slip, at
least they won't be in our backyard." She started the car,
glancing over at Jethro with a meaningful tilt to her
head. "That means your *sister* is probably long gone."

Her words were sharp as an elbow jab, but he let them
go for the matter at hand as he took the passenger seat
and buckled himself in. "Well, this one never made it
out of the city. And she was happy to talk to me. She's
quite concerned that I was separated from Lizbet. She
told me enough to get me to the right street, where some
very interesting individuals kept chasing me away."

From the backseat, the woman cried softly, "Won't
tell! Bad bad bad…"

"You don't have to tell," Sam reassured her, glancing in the rearview mirror to find their battered informant curled up on the seat. She pulled away from the
curb and onto the deserted night street. "We're taking
you to a hospital."

And by the time they got there, she hoped to have
pried her own information from this woman. She'd feel
like heartless scum in the process simply for questioning someone who needed nothing but comforting, but
she'd do it anyway. Because this woman hadn't been
beaten by coincidence. Someone had come to her looking for the same information she'd given Jethro—and
had been willing to beat the information out of her. If

she'd somehow told them more than she'd said to Jethro...

Then everyone in the city network was already in trouble.

"Jeth."

Jethro spun away from the lure of the hospital vending machine, so certain he'd been alone...and yet there she was. Leaning against the corner, one ankle hooked over the other. Still looking not quite as he kept expecting, no matter how many times he saw her. His eyes kept looking for details and edges that simply weren't there.

But they were on his camera.

"It's Jethro," he said, correcting her yet one more time.

"Sure," she said, but there was something in those honey-amber eyes of hers that failed to convince him she'd heed that detail. The eyes, now...those were the same. He hadn't known for sure until they'd reached the hospital and he'd seen her blinking under the well-lit emergency entrance.

Twins, he decided. Identical twins, without quite being identical at all. That could explain two women so similar. Explaining how one of those twins had shown up in his pictures instead of the young woman and the hooker to whom he'd actually spoken...that was something else altogether. He wished he had the camera here right now—the temptation to take a picture of Sam was overwhelming.

He suspected she wouldn't allow it.

And in the end, it didn't matter. Other than satisfying his natural compulsion to dig down to the truth of things, it didn't matter.

What mattered was finding his sister...and with

every moment that passed, he felt her slipping away. Madonna had told him how quickly they moved through the system. Sam had confirmed it any number of times. Lizbet had been gone only a matter of days, but for all Jethro knew, those days had been plenty of time to send her along her way. To her new life. Away from the scum of a husband who'd beaten her.

Jethro had tried to help. He'd given Lizbet a place to stay, the name of a good divorce lawyer. He drove her to support meetings when she was afraid to go by herself.

No doubt someone at one of those meetings had first spoken to her of the underground. And now—after her husband had tried to get her back, failed and gone out and killed someone on a raging spree of drunken anger; after Lizbet and Jethro had both thought her finally, truly, safe; after the trial had been delayed and that son of a bitch had somehow come up with the considerable bail—

Now she was gone.

I hadn't given up, he thought at her, wherever she was. *I would have seen it through with you.*

"Jeth?" There Sam still stood, still silhouetted in black against a worn desert sand wall, the same casual pose—this time with a tilt to her head and concern in those eyes.

"Jethro," he said without thinking. "Where'd you go? I turned around and *poof,* I was alone."

"Thought I'd run out on you, did you? That explains the vending machine. There's solace to be found in junk food." She unhooked her ankles and leaned back against the wall. "You might try bribing me with a Milky Way."

He didn't *want* to bribe her. He wanted answers. Any answer that would get him closer to Lizbet with the clock tick-tick-ticking away. But he saw the fatigue in her eyes and counted up the time they'd been together and surmised that they could both use food. They weren't likely to find any such thing in this machine, only a close approximation thereof....

He bought her a Milky Way.

She took the first bite and closed her eyes as if heaven had descended upon her, chewing with obvious delight. Shoot, if that's what candy did for her, what would she do if he—

He blinked. He hadn't expected that thought. Not in the middle of this particular night and this particular crisis. He quickly thumbed change into the machine and pushed the keypad to drop another candy bar into his waiting hand.

Sam swallowed. She didn't open her eyes when she said, "Madonna sang a pretty song to the creeps who beat her. She wasn't going to tell them anything—not even as much as she told you. She said she liked you but they were mean even before they quit pretending to be nice."

"You talked to her?" Jethro stopped his hand just before the candy reached his mouth. "How did you—they won't even let me ask about her."

Sam didn't answer his question. "She told them pretty much everything. I'm not even sure how she knew that much—but then, I haven't been through the system, so I have no idea what you learn on the way through. Too much, apparently. That car bomb came from our mean guys…and I know who it was. I know who he's looking for. And I bet he's counting on the disruption of that bomb to keep anyone from stopping him." She sighed, and when she opened her eyes it was with renewed determination. Amazing what chocolate could do. "I've got to warn the Captain."

She pushed away from the wall, popping the last of the candy into her mouth and tossing the wrapper in a trash can on the way by. Jethro hastened to catch up. "You haven't told me a thing."

"Haven't I?" She glanced back, affecting surprise.

"Nothing I didn't already know—or that I *need* to know. Don't forget I've got my own reasons for helping out."

She stopped short, pivoting slowly and pinning her gaze on his. Sunshine through honey. "I don't need your help," she said. "I never did. You invited yourself along because you thought I'd get careless and feed you useful secrets, and it didn't happen. Time to give it up. I've got work to do." And she left him standing there, heading for the bank of phones on the other side of the Emergency reception desk.

He stared after her a moment, then blew a gust of air through his mustache. "Holy freakin' iceberg."

"*Waaay* too seriously with the whole Batman thing," she informed him over her shoulder.

"Hey!" He ran a few steps to catch up with her, turning to put himself in front of her and then walking backward toward the phones when she didn't hesitate. Only when one of the phones pressed into his back did she stop, fishing in her pocket with an annoyed expression and little success. He dropped a few quarters into her hand. "Didn't *you* ever want to be a superhero?"

She pulled her brows together in a faintly puzzled, newly annoyed expression. "I never *wanted* it…" and then she pressed her lips together and dropped the change into the phone, quickly tapping out a number.

Jethro waited while she did, easing around to the side so she couldn't take off on him so quickly. After an endless number of rings, Sam slammed the phone back down on the hook and stared at it with an expression that should have melted it. Then she gave him a hard, dismissive glance. "I don't have time for this," she said, and what she meant was that she didn't have time for *him*.

"Make time," he told her. "Or I've got some photos to share with the police."

He hadn't expected it to stop her so short. And then she seemed to realize she'd given too much away and she turned away from him—but stopped short at that, too, and finally turned to face him. "You're full of crap. The police don't care about me."

He shrugged. "Maybe not. Maybe I should just show those photos around the street and see what people have to say."

She informed him what they'd have to say in one succinct, anatomically impossible suggestion.

Unperturbed, he crossed his arms over his chest, leaned against the phone beside him, and said, "You all have the same eyes."

You all have the same eyes.

Dammit all anyway. She didn't need this. Not with the Captain out of touch and no one else to contact and the fair certainty that Scalpucci would move on the other houses in the local underground, hunting his wife. He'd not only likely find her, but he'd go through everyone in his way to get her. Other women on the run, other house guardians...

And what did it matter, anyway? So Jethro had photos. It didn't matter who he showed them to. He was the one who would seem crazy, claiming that the woman in the photos—her true appearance, so carefully hidden until now—had actually been different in person.

Except she'd taken too long to respond to him…
given herself away. He might not know just what those
photos meant to her, but he knew they meant *something*.

Didn't mean she couldn't still fake it. She narrowed
her eyes at him. "You're still full of crap." She pushed
past him, headed for the exit and her sloppily parked car.

Damned if he didn't follow—making no bones about
it, right on her heels. The kind of persistence she'd want
on *her* side if she needed help. From a man who—despite the way he'd nearly been blown up, despite the
way Sam the hooker had dragged him around and
Sam—almost—I Am had bossed him and resisted him,
despite the way he'd so far been thwarted at every
turn—didn't show any of the classic signs of frightening temper or inter-gender control issues. Persistent,
yes. He wanted what he wanted, all right. But even in
these strange circumstances, he'd been willing to work
with her to get it.

And he'd kept enough of his wits about him to catch
a glimpse of her most closely guarded secret.

But just a glimpse. He couldn't truly understand. He
was fishing.

He had to be.

She unlocked the car door with one stab at the remote
button—driver's side only. And when she looked up
she found Jethro on the other side of the car, his hand
at the door. Waiting. Looking at her with an interesting
combination of trust and demand. He'd cleaned up
somewhat while she'd been questioning Madonna under
the guise of a young nurse's aide. His mustache looked
soft and groomed; his hair no longer entirely disheveled,
but obviously finger-combed. No dried blood in sight,

just a few fresh-looking cuts and a bruised bump on the side of his nose.

Waiting.

She unlocked the door. Dammit.

The car shifted under his weight as he joined her. "Thanks."

"I just don't have time to argue with you," she muttered, starting the car.

"No, you could have simply driven off and left me there. I know you wanted to." He tipped his head at her. "Although you *do* still have my gloves."

"And I like them," she said, putting the car into reverse and threading her way out of the parking aisle. "It's a good look. Very chick warrior. Just what I need right now."

"Do you?" He turned in the seat, putting his back to the door and straining the seat belt, so he could regard her more fully. "Now that I'm in the car and headed into chick warrior turf with you, is there anything more you'd like to tell me about your little talk with Madonna? Aside from how you got in there—in case you think I didn't notice the way you glossed over that part the first time."

She made a face without thinking, and quickly smoothed it away. "I don't care if you noticed. You don't need to know."

He blew air through his mustache. "Strictly speaking, that's true enough." But he didn't let her off the hook, not with his gaze riveted to her face as it was. He showed no concern for the fast corner she took. "But I *want* to know."

And again, she ignored it. Glossed it over with other answers he wanted—answers she might as well give him. At this point, the refuge houses were blown. "Madonna spent time in three houses before she hit the streets again. The first, you know about." She slowed to take a red light, and glanced over at him. "This strikes me as a good time to mention again that too much time has passed for your sister to have been at the entry house, and that you're far, far better off now than if you'd spoken to the Captain about finding her."

Jethro snorted, unconvinced about that latter.

"Not kidding," Sam told him, and hit the accelerator for the green, abruptly enough to rock his head back.

"Moot point, don't you think?"

"Only if you don't try to find Lizbet again."

Silence. Then he cleared his throat. "Am I that transparent?"

"More than. Besides, if you do happen to find her again, it'll be long after your sister is out of this city. Once that happens, even the Captain doesn't know where they go."

Another silence, while Sam took a short exit ramp to the city's inner loop, four constantly shifting lanes of left- and right-hand exits that took great familiarity to navigate with any efficiency even with the paucity of cars on the road at this time of night. Then Jethro said, "That's twice now. My sister. You believe me now?"

"I'm staking my work with the underground on it." The Captain would shun her if Jethro turned out to be Lizbet's ex.

The Captain might well shun her anyway. She should have left him in that hospital parking lot to call himself a cab and spend the rest of his life wondering where Lizbet had gone.

"Why do you do it?" he asked abruptly. "Help them?"

She looked at him in surprise. Why? Maybe because these women were doing what she'd never really been able to do—risk everything to find themselves. True, they had incentive she'd never encountered. She'd always been a little too comfortable with her life, even when she felt she never truly knew herself or what she wanted. She'd never quite found the wherewithal to leave behind what she knew in an effort to find out what she *didn't.*

As if she was going to say those words to this man. So she said simply, "Because I can," which was also true—and also what she often told herself.

"Why's that?"

She glanced at him, a truly bemused look. "You never give up, do you? Are you sure you're not a reporter?"

He grinned, an engaging combination with that mustache. "Just a humble silk-screening man," he said. "A curious one. Why can you? What is it you can bring to them that no one else does?"

"What would you do if the answer was 'nothing'?"

He gave it a moment's thought. "I wouldn't believe it."

"Why not?" She turned the tables on him just to be doing it.

"Because of the way your voice sounded when you said that. *Because I can.* That meant something."

Chapter 4

Sam almost stopped the car to look at him, surprised at the depth of his perception. Instead she found the exit she wanted and shot onto a street full of blinking construction sawhorses and signs, taking the curves of the rerouted street at a speed much faster than the posted limit. "Okay," she said. "I'll give you that. I work with a private investigator. I have the training to keep an eye on that house and to know who and what might be trouble. I can't *believe* I missed that van." And she could hardly tell him why. She could hardly say she'd been distracted by him, that she'd been the one dogging his footsteps these past two nights. She didn't give him the time to ask. More turning the tables. "Now you tell *me*. We hardly ever get family members hunting up our refugees. Husbands and boyfriends, yes. Brothers, no. Why are you so determined to find your sister?"

He hesitated, and she sensed it wasn't out of reluctance, but in an effort to find the right words. Then he shrugged and said, "Because I *should*."

She looked at him, a quick glance as a streetlight flashed overhead. He meant it. And she might push for details, but for now she had what was important. The worry in his voice. The sense of connection behind those words. Maybe she'd done the right thing after all, opening that car door for him.

Or maybe not. But she'd done it, and now they headed straight for one of the very secrets she wasn't supposed to know, and certainly wasn't ever supposed to tell. She glanced at him again, found him watching her…suppressed that frisson of awareness that he could somehow see through her. Literally, right through her guises.

He couldn't. No one ever had. But there was his camera, snugged against the seat and the center console of the car, and while she'd been caught on the fringes of a camera field-of-view once or twice, no one had been perceptive enough to notice the discrepancies—or they'd chalked it up to a processing mix-up. But this was a digital, and he'd already noticed the discrepancies.

She'd have to find a moment to erase those pictures—turn them into a puzzling memory instead of damning evidence.

A final turn and she cruised to the curb of a residential street. A few years of following people for her boss had built a detailed map of this city in her head; as soon as Madonna had given her the refuge house addresses, she'd known the neighborhoods, the fastest way to get there, the hindrances they might encounter. This particular neighborhood offered tree-lined sidewalks, maple trees in the yards, sparse fall landscaping around the houses. Nothing too fancy, just close-set homes with deceptively long backyards—and, if she remembered correctly, an active neighborhood watch program.

"This one?" Jeth asked, looking intently out the window at the house in front of which they parked.

"Two down," she told him. "And you're staying here."

He gave her his complete attention, mouth tugging to the side in dry amusement, dark gray-blue gaze riveted on her face.

And there it was again, that unfamiliar feeling that he could truly see her. If anyone could, it would be this man. A terrifying thought, and a beguiling one. To be touched by someone who knew the real Sam....

Except he was saying, "What makes you think so?"

And in exasperation she responded, "You won't find her here, Jeth. She's *gone*. You've got to let her go."

He blinked in total lack of comprehension. "Let her go? This is my *sister*. I'm just supposed to forget she ever existed?"

Typical. "It's not about *you*. You're supposed to accept that this was her choice, not yours."

"To leave her whole family behind? To spend the rest of her life living a lie? You must be kidding."

She unfastened her seat belt with more of a snap than she'd meant to, hand on the door latch. "Yes. Just exactly that. And I'm not kidding."

He shook his head, mirroring her actions and ready to get out of the car. "I'm not going to stop looking." He pushed the door open; the overhead light came on.

She grabbed the tough material of his jacket and yanked, catching him off balance. The door closed enough to turn out the light, but enough streetlight remained to see him, only inches away now, incredulous and furious.

His hand closed over hers on his jacket. "You do this to people," he said, grinding the words out in accusation. "You take them from their families. You turn their lives into a game of deceit."

"That's right!" She snapped the words back at him,

not trying to escape his grasp—just as he didn't fight hers. Face-to-face, glare-to-glare. She whose whole life was nothing but one big game of deceit and the man who knew nothing but honesty. "By the time they reach us they're desperate and some of them are one step away from dead. By the time they get to us, *everyone else has failed them.*"

He jerked as though slapped; the anger turned to miserable guilt. Not a man who could hide his feelings any more than he could hide his nature. "I *tried,*" he said, and seemed to realize how tightly he held her injured hand, releasing his grip slowly to turn the contact into a lighter, more apologetic touch. "Dammit, I—"

He looked away, took a shaky breath. She gave him the moment, and then said quietly, "I guess you probably did. But it wasn't enough. For whatever reason it just wasn't enough. She wouldn't have come to us if it had been." She uncrimped her fingers from his jacket, suppressing a wince, and then, after an uncertain hesitation, let them land on his arm in a more comforting touch, however briefly. "Now she's gone, Jeth. You don't have to understand or accept it to make it so. But…I think you'd be a lot happier if you could."

He took another deep breath, looked back into her eyes, and said firmly, "Jethro."

She sat back. "You could be named an unpronounceable symbol—the man formerly known as Jethro—and you still wouldn't come to that door with me."

He snorted as he, too, sat back, and then he gave his mustache a quick one-fingered stroke and said, "I'm not going to just sit here."

"Fine," she said promptly, totally resisting the urge to let her fingers follow in the path of his. "I could use someone to watch the street. It's the middle of the night—there shouldn't be anyone else out here. So if there is, you can let me know."

"And who are we expecting?"

She stumbled over telling him, but the word was already out on the street. No longer a secret of any kind. "Does the name Scalpucci sound familiar?"

She'd succeeded in surprising him—she wasn't sure if it was because of the name or simply because she'd answered his question. She nodded and said, "We've helped his wife. We're pretty sure he's behind the van bomb—he knew his wife wasn't there, but it's just like him to punish us for resisting him—and I bet his people are the ones who found Madonna. If *you* could find her—"

"Gee. Thanks."

"Don't even try to guilt me out on that one. You're out of your league and you know it. I think that's why—" *why you make such an impact on me.* But somehow she didn't say it, even though she just that suddenly recognized it. He was out of his league and he wasn't giving up. Unlike those in her early life who'd never made the effort to search out the real Sam—who were satisfied with the facade she gave them—he cared enough to keep trying.

He waited.

She pulled herself together and said, "The point is, Madonna told Scalpucci's people—or someone's people—about two of our houses. This is one of them. I'm not sure why it's still so peaceful and quiet here…they should have been able to beat us here."

Jeth nodded at the house, two doors down. "Maybe they did."

Yeah. Point to him. Maybe she and Jeth had wasted

all this time in the car while those in the refuge house were hurt or even dead. Sam hoped Gretchen Scalpucci had been moved out of the city by this point, but she didn't know. The woman might well be inside that house. "Let's go," she told him. "But don't come up the drive. You understand that if you alarm the woman who runs this house, she'll close the door and we won't learn anything one way or the other."

He nodded, and she reached for her door handle— but didn't quite open it before reminding him, "Either way, you won't find your sister here. And that woman won't tell you anything even if she knows it. She won't tell *me,* either. That's the way we work."

His jaw tightened at that; she saw the resistance in his expression. He wouldn't argue, but he still didn't quite believe it.

He'd learn.

They exited the car together; Sam stood in the crisp night air a moment, feeling out all the aches and pains that had settled in after the inactivity of driving. Nothing more than pavement bruises and of course her hands; she flexed them inside the gloves and reaccustomed herself to the sting of it. "The sidewalk," she reminded him, and strode off toward the house.

Just another home on the street, complete with late-season marigolds in the front landscaping and a lawn ornament or two against the bushes lining the house. She approached the three-step landing, a little concrete number with a short wrought iron railing; the house looked dark inside, showing only a diffuse glow from some interior night-light. A glance back at Jethro showed him slowly strolling away down the sidewalk, as obvious as ever. She bit her lip on a grin, surprised by the sudden affection the sight gave her. And it didn't matter how obvious he was—if Scalpucci's men were here, then all the better if they thought the underground had put a watch on this place.

And then she looked up into a silent rush of darkness and realized that oh, yeah, Scalpucci's men were here. At least one of them. *This* one. He loomed up from the bushes and grabbed her before she truly registered his presence, one hand clamping tightly on her wrist. Way too tightly—it hurt, dammit. She gave an involuntary hiss of anger and protest, jerking her hand within the grip and giving herself a good hard internal kick. It simply hadn't occurred to her that Scalpucci would send anyone to *lurk*. To bully and break in and cause havoc, yes. But to lurk?

Unless he'd already been inside and she'd merely interrupted his departure. She gave the house a wild glance, hunting for hidden signs of distress and disturbance within. Its implacable exterior stared back at her, telling her nothing.

Her knee-jerk reaction to break free had gained her nothing; he hadn't even readjusted his hold. Damned gorilla. She'd barely gotten started—

He gave her a little shake. "You're one of them." It wasn't a question.

"And you're one of *them*," she retorted, glaring at him through the darkness. She couldn't pin down so much as a single feature; she might recognize him again from his movement, but not from his face.

He gave her another shake, rattling her from wrist to shoulder to neck and jaw. "Where's Gretchen Scalpucci?"

She shrugged ever so slightly, deliberately not thinking about the moment—not thinking about escape. If she thought about it, if she tried to plan her move, she'd only stumble over herself. But if she just waited, if she just *was,* then when the right moment came she'd take it.

She only hoped Jethro didn't turn around and notice them before then.

"Listen, you little bitch—you give me what I need and I won't have to throw you through that window to get the attention of the women in that house. They can sleep right on through the night."

"What makes you think they're sleeping now?" she asked. "What makes you think anyone's there at all, after what you people pulled in the west end?"

"A bitch who thinks she's cute. Just what I need."

She got only a glimpse of his scowl, but it was enough. And his shift of weight—enough. *He's going to do it, the son of a bitch—right through the window—*

He pulled her in closer, bent to pick her up; he lifted her off the ground with no apparent effort and she let him, snarling inside at his carelessly rude touch and managing what sounded like a startled and helpless squeak. He didn't straighten, but repositioned himself, preparing to toss her like a discus. *Right through the window—*

The instant he started to unwind, Sam took advantage of the energy and movement he supplied, flipping herself backward out of his arms.

In a perfect world, she would have landed on her toes, maybe with a little support from her fingertips. In this world, this night, she fell heavily forward, hitting her knees and sprawling onto her hands. The abraded skin lit like fire within her borrowed gloves, tearing open scabs and tipping off her temper. She snarled, abandoned any thought of tackling this ape on her own, and twisted to leap for escape and those front steps. It wouldn't take much to alert whoever stood vigil here, even a good scream—

Maybe he read her mind. He threw himself after her, belly-flopping atop her hard enough to knock every bit of air from her lungs. Son of a— She might as well have left the Kel-Tec at home. It might be meant for just this kind of encounter, but there was no way she'd reach it, not with her hips grinding into the thin lawn and the holstered Kel-Tec trapped in her back pocket between them. She flailed around the edges of the landscaping, hunting something, *anything,* that she might use against him.

That's when she realized he'd done more than flattened her; he shoved his distinctly hardened anatomy against her bottom with discovery and purpose. "You!" she spat, hunting air. "You—*disgusting*—"

He lowered his face to her ear, his hands braced against the ground on either side of her head. "Two orders," he said, as though whispering sweet nothings. "Find Gretchen Scalpucci. Leave the rest of you humiliated. I'd had other plans for the house, but this—" he grunted slightly, pushing against her, intrusive even through their clothing. "This is good, too."

"*Not* good!" she panted, what little air she had disappearing under his increasing weight. "Wasn't Madonna enough fun for the night?"

He laughed, an ugly sound as good as a confession.

"That's—*it!*" She slammed her head back into his nose, too restricted to do much damage but not expecting to, because her real goal—

Her real goal gleamed palely at ground level next to her own nose, and she went for it. She sunk her teeth into the strip of skin exposed by his ridden-up jacket sleeves and this time she got a surprised bellow, and then everything happened pretty much at once. House lights came on, Jethro shouted her name from what seemed a very long distance and Sam's flailing hands found a flat cut-out lawn ornament jammed into the ground on a thick piece of rebar. She yanked it out, spat out the flesh of his arm, and laid into him with the lawn ornament, awkward but unrelenting as he jerked his arm out of range. She shot forward, rose to her knees and cocked the flat, heavy wood back like a bat, swinging to the bleachers just as he sent a big ham fist in her direction. She ducked.

He didn't.

He reeled backward, barely catching himself with one hand, and Sam surged to her feet, throwing so much energy into her next blow that the impact lifted her feet off the ground by a grass blade or two.

"Sam!"

And suddenly Jethro was right there, rolling the stunned heavyweight to his stomach and cranking an arm up behind the man in a way those beefy muscles barely allowed. He yanked a couple of stout Velcro tie-downs from his pocket as Sam watched in disbelief, wavering slightly on her feet. Dammit, she felt like she'd been trampled by a whole herd of gorillas and not just this one and it made her seriously cranky. "What the hell are those?"

"My geek straps," Jethro said, intent on his task; the effort it took left her with no doubt that the Velcro would hold. His words came in little rushes between his movements. "For my pants. When I'm biking."

"Perfect," she said numbly. In the light from the refuge house windows she got her first good glimpse of her own improvised weapon and discovered a little old lady bending over to weed, her petticoats and undies bared to the world. Okay, there was something appropriate about *that*. She gave a little laugh and threw the wooden figure on top of the trussed man. As Jethro stood, the man rolled partway to his back, stopped there by his own beefy arms behind him, and Sam prodded his soft groin with her toe. "All gone," she noted with satisfaction. "I hope you'll think of your current stunning performance any time you get a notion to use *this* again."

Jethro made a strangled noise. And then he said, "Why didn't you call me? You think I wouldn't have been of any help? You and my sister—"

"Shut up," she told him, blunt and unable to muster any kinder words for him as she nursed all her new owies. "What makes you think I had a chance?"

"I—"

"Shut up," said an entirely new voice. "And drag that trash off my lawn. Who the hell are you and what are you doing here? Better talk fast, because the cops are on their way."

"No, they're not," Sam said, calm enough as she finally caught her breath. She looked up at the woman on the front stoop, finding an African-American version of the Captain. Short, stout and damned tough. "Not unless someone else called them, and I don't see any other house lights on down the street. You don't want them here any more than I do."

The woman grunted something uncomplimentary and held up a cell phone. "Got my finger on 9-1-1."

"Sure," Sam agreed. "But let's talk before you use it. I've come from the Captain's end of town. You're gonna want to hear this."

For the first time, the woman hesitated; in the darkness she nodded at Jethro. "And him?"

"He's going to stand out here and make sure this guy doesn't have any pals trying to finish what he started." Sam rubbed her hip where it had hit the cold, hard ground.

Jethro leaned in close to her. "Why *wouldn't* there be?" He glanced at the house as if he weren't sure he wanted her to overhear. "If Scalpucci is behind this trouble, why would he send only one man? Why not send a posse?"

"Huh. Good point." The bomb had been more Scalpucci's style—unmistakable, in your face, getting the job done with a bang. She looked down at the conquered mound of muscle and asked it, "How about that?" But she didn't wait for the answer she knew wouldn't be forthcoming. "I think we'd better get out to that other house. But I've got to talk to her first." Sam nodded at the house. "I mean it about staying out here. I need her to trust me."

"And I'm not part of your little organization."

Sam gave him a sweet smile. "You're a man. That's enough." She patted his cheek, counting on the gesture to put him off long enough so she could make her getaway without further discussion—and though she couldn't quite decipher the startled look on his face, she made her getaway nonetheless.

Whew. Just in time. Traitors, those fingers of hers, wanting to linger. Pure and simple traitors.

The house guardian met her with hands impatiently propped on her square hips. "What the hell is going on? Who are you? I've already asked once and by my way of thinking you've had far too long to answer."

"My name is Sam." Sam stood at the bottom step of the tiny porch, one hand on the rail, knowing she wouldn't be invited inside. "I watch the Captain's house. Earlier this evening a van blew up in front of it."

The woman stiffened. She hadn't heard. Sam wasn't surprised. The Captain was probably still dealing with the cops and no one else had the contact info—and wouldn't, not unless the Captain's death set into motion the events that would bring her successor up to speed. But for now…

The woman's voice turned quiet. "And she's all right?"

"She's tied up with things. But we think your location has been compromised. That's what I came to tell you—to warn you—and given what we found…" She nodded at the dark lump on the grass that had so recently been trying to hurt her.

"She gave you this location?" the woman asked suspiciously.

"No," Sam said dryly. "That's the point. I got it from the same person who was beaten into revealing it to Scalpucci's people. I don't suppose you have Gretchen Scalpucci here."

The guardian snorted. "I don't suppose I'll tell you. And what's *his* story?"

"He's looking for someone."

"And you brought him *here?*"

Sam shook her head, somewhat bemused herself. "That I did. Of course, I don't believe his sister's even in the city anymore, and your location is blown anyway—you need to pack up and get out of here even if Gretchen Scalpucci never got anywhere near you. She wasn't at the refuge, either, and Scalpucci still left us a bomb to make sure we know he's peeved at us. My guess is that he'll try to take out the entire underground. I hope you've got a fallback."

The woman snorted again. "Of course. We started evacuation procedures as soon as you got noisy out here. Another half hour and no one will ever know anyone was here."

Sam looked at their prisoner. Jethro had left him in an ungainly huddle on the grass to return to the sidewalk, somewhat more vigilant than he'd been the first time. "I've got another house to warn. I'd rather not stick around to deal with him."

"Not a problem. The cops can get a tip once we're outta here. I'll make sure they know he beat on someone once already tonight."

Sam nodded, gave her the quick details of Madonna's situation, and saw the first signs of sadness in the woman's eyes. "I remember her. I had hoped she would make it. She was taking her meds when she was here, and she's really quite a smart young lady."

Sam felt the same twinge of regret, thinking of the vacant lot where Madonna had set up house. "I guess she just has to make it her own way."

"And him?"

Jethro, that's who the woman meant. And Sam didn't blame her for the hard note that came into her voice. "His sister came through. He can't let go. He's been helpful this evening." She hadn't realized it until she said it…so used to being on her own, so used to simply handling things as they happened.

"Do you believe him?" the woman asked abruptly.

"You know, I do." That, too, came as a surprise. At first she'd easily assumed Jethro had been lying, that he'd been the abuser behind one of their refugees. But Sam was a people watcher by nature...and by profession. And in spite of the violence of this evening, she'd never seen anything of it reflected in Jethro. Nothing but honesty and persistence and more than a dab of deliberate blindness when it came to his sister's decision. "I don't agree with him, but I do believe him."

Another snort. And a hard directive. "Don't compromise us."

And that raised Sam's hackles but good. "The whole system is already compromised. He's not learning anything that will hold true within fifteen minutes after we walk away from here." She felt her own surprise at the strength of her response, saw it reflected in the other woman's face. She grasped for annoyance to cover the moment. "Don't worry about us. But see if you can reach the Captain. She doesn't know Madonna talked." And as she stepped away from the landing, her thoughts went unbidden to Jeth's earlier question...why only one man? Why hadn't she run into a whole group? They could have bulldozed through her and right into the house.

Unless they were otherwise occupied.

Unless they already knew the other house held Gretchen, and had sent this one man here to deliver the same kind of message Scalpucci had given the Captain.

Great. The thought put spring back into her step; she broke into a run as she headed for the car, swooping up behind Jethro to grab his arm. He hesitated, gaze on the house, thoughts on his sister. Sam shook her head, more sharply than she truly felt. "I told you it wouldn't happen. She's not there—and if she was that woman would shoot you and put you out to the curb before she let you in." Not quite. Stun guns were just as effective and not as problematic. But he didn't need to know that. "Now let's *go*."

He still hesitated, hope lingering. And then he visibly steeled himself. "You're sure—"

"*Yes*. Now get in or get out of the way."

He finally caught her urgency. He finally tore himself away from the house, even if not quite convinced. "What's the big hurry?" he said as they slid into the car on their respective sides.

"You said it," she said. "Only one man. So where are the others?"

He snapped the seat belt buckle together, a noise somehow made grim by the circumstances. "One step ahead of us."

"Exactly."

Chapter 5

"How far?" Jethro asked, but it wasn't the thing foremost on his mind. *Had he just walked away from Lizbet? Would he ever have another chance?*

Or maybe she was just ahead. So hard to know…so hard to trust.

"Ten minutes," she said shortly. "More or less."

He watched her profile, still expecting to see something other than the moderate and unremarkable nose…something with a bump just below the bridge and more expressive nostrils. And the mouth…the lower lip should be fuller and distinctly undercut, the chin below more stubborn.

But it wasn't. And he couldn't figure out how he thought it could or should be. "Holy Velcro handcuffs," he said. It wasn't what he was really thinking or what he really wanted to say, but for once Jethro Sheridan didn't *know* how to say all the things on his mind. "Looks like you pulled a real superhero trick—leaving the bad guy trussed up at the scene of the crime."

She took the exit from the inner to the outer loop and didn't respond. But she must have felt him watching, because she finally gave him a hard glance and said, "I didn't ask about your sister. She wouldn't have told me anything if I had. I don't even know that woman's *name*—that should tell you something."

He tried to absorb her words, found himself stuck on the fact that she hadn't even asked, that these people kept so very much from each other. "You could have tried."

"No," she said flatly. "I couldn't have. I told you from the start that you wouldn't learn anything this evening and I meant it. I told you not to come. You seem to think you're the only one of the two of us who tells the truth about things large and small, so I guess you didn't want to believe me."

"That's not it," he protested, loudly enough to cover the stab of guilt that meant she was, at least to some extent, right in what she said. "I thought maybe you were wrong, not that you were putting me on."

"Wrong," she repeated, taking her eyes from the road long enough for a sideways glance at him. "Yeah, sure. Whatever."

"Sam—"

"Forget it. You've got your eye on your goal. That's what matters, right?"

He rubbed a knuckle over his mustache and made himself stop. "Yes," he muttered, and then, "Not only," but if she heard him she didn't respond.

For a moment he half expected her to pull over by the side of the deserted four-lane commuter loop, but she gave him another of those looks—this one with more challenge in it. "Tell me about your sister."

"Is this a test?" he found himself asking dryly.

"If you want." The thought seemed to amuse her. "It won't change anything."

"Then what's the point?" God, he'd had his fill of this

dark underground world with its intractable members and its secrets and the way it stood so firmly between himself and Lizbet.

Her hands tightened on the steering wheel; she winced and carefully relaxed them back to fingertip driving. "The point is…I want to know."

"It makes a difference to you," he clarified, unwilling to let it go unsaid. Too many things went unsaid in this woman's life…even things he thought she probably needed to say. Or to hear.

She took a deep breath, drumming her fingertips against the wheel. "Okay. Yeah. It makes a difference to me."

Okay. Yeah.

Jethro smiled. He could afford to; she was checking the side-view mirror and wouldn't see. She wouldn't guess he'd gotten a warm rumble of feeling from her admission. And to keep her from guessing, he answered her question. "Her husband—Craig, though I prefer to keep things simple and just call him 'that asshole'—started hitting her a couple of years ago. She hid it from us all." He shook his head. "I just can't believe we didn't guess it."

"When a woman wants to protect something, she finds a way."

"Spoken like an expert."

She ignored him. "Lizbet was protecting the only life she thought she could live. That she thought she deserved. It's common."

"Well, it sucks. Because *that asshole* made her life miserable. And it finally got bad enough that we realized what was going on."

"We?"

"I had a girlfriend. She—" She'd rifled his bank accounts and almost lost him the business, and then she'd disappeared. He hadn't made any real effort to find her. "She's gone. But at the time, she was the first to notice that Lizbet was hiding something. It hadn't gotten too bad, not yet. So I went to discuss the situation with him."

Sam snorted. "I'll bet *that* worked." But she sounded sympathetic, too—enough to take the edge off her words.

"I know better, now," he said. "At the time…he seemed sincere enough. Cowed enough."

"He probably was. And then he started to resent your interference, and then he told himself no one could control him, and then he started in on her again."

He laughed, and it felt painful even to his own ears. "You've heard this before."

"I wouldn't be doing this work if there wasn't a need for it."

Right. "It gets better. This time when I went over there, it was to pack Lizbet up to stay with me for a while." His girlfriend hadn't liked the idea…that's when she'd had her way with his bank accounts. "Except he was there, and he tried to stop me."

"Ah." She navigated through the narrow streets of some dignified old brick homes not far from one of the most exclusive areas of town. "And you had a manly confrontation?"

"I broke his nose," Jethro said sheepishly. He hadn't expected the meeting to escalate so suddenly. "He wasn't used to someone who hit back. And Lizbet came with me. She called a lawyer that very afternoon. She'd had enough."

"Not something *that asshole* would have taken well."

Jethro rubbed his fingers over his eyes, suddenly

overcome by the absurdity of the whole situation—of his role in events. The words on the tip of his tongue sounded so dramatic, so *melodramatic,* that he almost couldn't believe them himself. "In fact, he went out, drank himself cocky, and found a seventeen-year-old kid to take offense at. Killed him."

"Damn," she said, and he realized she had no trouble believing it. Believing it could happen just like that. Believing that Jethro wasn't just spinning a story.

"So he ended up in jail waiting trial—couldn't raise the bail—and Lizbet went back home."

"That's not the end."

"Or I wouldn't be here," he said, finishing her thought; he saw it in the glance she gave him as she picked out the next street in the dark. "No, that's not the end. He raised the bail. He got out. I went to Lizbet's as soon as I heard, but…it was too late." He closed his eyes, unable to keep the images away. Blood on the wall, overturned furniture. No sign of Lizbet *or* the asshole. He'd checked the hospitals, he'd checked with police….

She was gone. And that asshole had established himself in a rent-by-the-week apartment on the other side of the city, an apparent low-life poster child.

"And you're sure—" She didn't finish her sentence; she took a twisting turn that made him believe she was bringing him into this neighborhood the back way.

"I know she was at Sheltering Arms. I know that's where she fell off the map."

And Sam pulled over to the curb, put the car in Park and pocketed the keys. Thumping bass filled the neighborhood from the only house on the street lit from within; the driveway was crammed with cars, and more cars littered the curb around it. Sam looked at him—not the Sam he kept expecting to see, the one he wanted to touch and verify, but this blander version. She nodded. "Yeah," she said. "You *did* try. You did a lot of the wrong things, but so does everyone. Don't feel bad that she hid things from you so well. It happens all the time."

It shouldn't have happened to me. And even so, he found himself needing her acceptance…relieved by it. A little surprised by it. She struck him as hard, as matter-of-fact…as often distant. And yet every now and then a little heart would come peeking out and grab at him. "You're not so different than she," he said, thinking out loud when he shouldn't have. "So much of you is hidden. The question is why. And somehow…what."

She gave an unexpected start; a flicker of panic crossed her face and disappeared into complete composure. "Anything I want to," she told him. "For as long as I want to."

I'm hidden. He can't see me.

Not *really* see her.

Sam swallowed her bolt of panic and remembered the face she wore over her own. The not quite Sam face. The safe face. She exited the car without any further hesitation, leaving Jethro scrambling to catch up. "It's the same deal," she told him, meeting him at the grill of the car and speaking louder than she'd have preferred so he could hear her over the gut-rumbling music of the local homecoming party. The party parking filled the curbs around the refuge; she'd had to pull in half a block down. "You've got to stay back. If you want to help, keep an eye out for Scalpucci's people. If not, then just wait here."

"Of course I want to help." The tilt of his head was

enough for Sam to imagine his puzzled, troubled expression. She knew he'd been affected by their discussion of his sister, knew he didn't understand her abrupt change.

No. I don't know him that well. And he doesn't know me.

Dammit. Get your head together.

Sam struck out for the refuge house with long, firm strides. She wouldn't linger here; she'd warn the occupants off and if all went well, they'd be gone before Scalpucci's people arrived.

The Captain would clean up the mess, the backup houses would swing into gear, and Sam would ply her guises wherever she was needed.

Caught up in her thoughts, she'd steamed on ahead of Jethro on the sidewalk—and then stopped short. He caught up with her quickly enough—and just as quick, saw what had stopped her. "They're already here."

A full-size van filled the refuge driveway, parked crookedly so as to block both lanes of the two-car garage—no windows, no markings. Hopefully no bombs.

She exchanged a glance with Jethro, discovered that like her he'd instantly shed the baggage from their conversation; like her, he'd focused directly on the situation before them. "Looks like 9-1-1 time."

Sam didn't hesitate. She was the Captain's voice here; she was the one who understood the ramifications of involving the police. "No," she said, lowering her voice so he had to move closer, to tip his head down. She drew him aside, onto the strip of grass and under the tree between the curb and the sidewalk—over where a lookout on the other side of the van wouldn't see. "These women are on the run. We can't call the police.

We might as well call the men they're running from. The men who *beat* them."

"They'd be *alive*," Jeth said, just as urgently.

"You'd really call that living?" she shot back at him. "And we can't! It would expose the entire underground to the authorities. It would affect these women, and the ones waiting for the chance to join us. We'd have to start all over again, and even then we might not manage— not once the cops have been forced to take official notice of us."

He looked at her, stumped. "You told that woman to have the cops pick up the guy you clobbered at the last place."

"*After* she evacuates everyone, with no plans to return." Sam peered around him to eye the van and shook her head. "We might well do the same here…it all depends. I need to get a closer look. Gotta understand just what's going down here."

"It doesn't seem like the same thing." Jeth twisted to look behind himself. "One guy lurking compared to a whole van right out there in the open."

Exactly. "I need to get a closer look," she repeated, and then when he looked askance, held up a hand—sore, covered by his gloves, but assertive nonetheless. "Listen. This is what I do. And I only get paid by the job, so I must be pretty good at it. I'm neither dead or broke."

"And I'm supposed to just hang back here and watch." Couldn't get any more skeptical than that.

"It's not your cause, is it? It's my thing. I'll handle it."

But he still had that stubborn look, and she caught her hair up in one hand, sweeping the bangs back. "I'll come back, okay? I'll take a look and I'll come back and tell you what I see. Maybe we'll end up calling the police after all—but I won't make that decision until I can scope out how things stand in there."

After a long moment, he nodded. "Then I'll wait. But I won't wait long, so don't take your time."

She said, struck by a sudden congruence of inspiration, "How about I take your camera instead? I can take a few pictures through the windows, give you an idea what's going down."

A slow smile spread beneath that mustache. "Good idea."

Oh, man, that was almost too easy. Guilt nibbled at her as he retrieved the camera, downright took chunks out of her as he handed it over and gave her quick directions about the manual use mode that she didn't need. She already knew. She knew enough to take the new photos over the old ones, too. Including any pictures of the real Sam, the ones he'd alluded to having.

"Hey," he said, misreading her distraction as nerves. "You don't have to—"

"I do," she assured him. "Try to stay inconspicuous. Go hide in the front seat if it comes to that. I won't be gone long."

Long enough to make a casual approach to the trio of evergreen shrubs at the corner of the refuge yard; long enough to duck down behind them and flip through the digital's menu and the existing photos, aided by the light of a red-tinted flashlight. Long enough to erase them all.

And then, still crouching there, she gathered her concentration and hunted for the unique hum of thought that would take her *unseen*.

There.

She did a quick circuit of the van, then of the backyard perimeter—finding both spots empty. And then she reckoned that she'd been gone too long; she'd lost too much time in erasing the images of Sam I Am. *He never said he wouldn't follow.* In fact, he'd specifically said he wouldn't wait long. She'd have to go back and reassure him, then make another pass. As it was she could only peek in the windows, enough to assure her that the women were there, to snap a few quickie pictures that probably wouldn't even be in focus. Enough to see that two angry-looking men had them under not only a watchful gaze, but the threat of a gun.

And one of the men was Scalpucci.

What the devil?

Sam trotted back to the bushes, counting on the nearby party to cover any sound she might make. Gretchen Scalpucci. She had to be at this house. Scalpucci's little spy had found her and called in Scalpucci, and that's why Sam and Jeth had made it here before everything was over. Preoccupied, her ears filled with the thump of excessive party bass and her mind's eye with the bare glimpse of bullying men and frightened women, she crouched behind the cover and dropped her *unseen* guise.

And Jeth's voice blurted, "Holy freakin' crap!"

There he knelt, right at the edge of the bushes, blending into the dark shadows so he'd simply looked like part of the foliage itself.

Sam closed her eyes, ducked her head, pressed the heel of her hand to her forehead. *No, no, NO. Not now. Not ever.* "Ah," she said, finding no words to suit the situation, "Holy freakin' *fuck*."

The shadows lined his anger, sharpening the angles of his face and hiding his eyes. "I hope," he said tightly, "you can find a way to convince me I was seeing things just now. That you didn't actually just…appear."

"I didn't." Earnest words, a little desperate…because the truth was even harder. She dropped down to her knees in the cold grass, desperately hunting some way to handle this moment—to get past it and back to work. Saving women. Saving the underground.

He stared at her, aghast even in shadow. "My God." If anything, the anger built. "Those photos…you can *change*. You can *disappear*." Then he scrubbed his hands across his face, roughly enough to make Sam wince. Then again, her whole being was set to *wince* just this moment. "No. I didn't say that. Holy Batman redux, I did *not* say that."

"I can't disappear, though," she said. Helpfully, she thought.

His head swung up to pin her with that shadowed gaze. "No," he said. "No more lies. That's all you do, isn't it? Lie? Who you are, *what* you are?"

Sam stiffened. *Self-righteous*— But she didn't even give herself time to finish the thought. "I *wasn't* lying," she informed him, reaching deeply into the acerbic tone that worked so well to cover hurt she wouldn't even admit to herself. "I *don't* disappear. Any camera can tell you as much. People just can't see me. It's in their heads, not my body."

"Camera," he repeated. He looked at the digital in her hands. "It doesn't work for cameras. Whatever the hell you do, it doesn't work for them. And I saw your images. The *real* you. You're the one who's been chasing me off—"

"It didn't work," Sam said dryly.

"Everything about you…is *any* of it true?"

She couldn't keep the snap out of her voice. "Everything that matters."

"And you really think you're some sort of hero, using the ultimate lie to lead these women off into a life of their own deception? Don't you think that's the blind leading the blind?"

"I can see perfectly fine." Sam glared at him, no longer sunk in the horror of being discovered, no longer thinking of the shivery feeling he'd sometimes given her. "I see a damned lot better than you. These women need help—that's what this is about. Not about me. Not about you."

He snorted. "Get real. If you ditched this charade and called the cops on Scalpucci *right now,* his wife would be safe."

She snorted back, and then aimed below the belt. "Like your sister was *safe.*"

He flinched. Hard. "She could have come to me. She *should* have come to me."

The night music filled the air around them, thumping its way through the conversation, filling in the gaps with angry noise. She took a breath. "Look, Jeth, I admire your faith in the system—"

He scoffed. "Naiveté, don't you mean?"

Sam peered behind her, checking the driveway and the van and finding the house just as it had been. No telling what was happening on the inside. She reached past all her hurt and defensiveness, trying to see him just as clearly as he wanted to see her. "Maybe some of that," she admitted, hunting honesty of a sort she didn't often need to tap. "But I'm not sure it's bad to look at life that way. It gives the rest of us something to aim for."

Silence. Even the music, for that instant, was silent.

His voice was low and crystal clear against that back-drop, his face still hidden by shadows. "That's not...I wasn't expecting you to say that."

"Look," Sam told him, sitting back on her heels when she realized she'd somehow ended up leaning toward him, almost off balance in her need to convince him— to *reach* him. "I do what I need to. I do the things no one else can do, in a way no one else can do them. But I'm not the one who makes this underground either possible or necessary. And I did my best to keep you out of it."

"You were trying to protect the underground." His voice had grown subdued, almost hidden in the renewed music.

She inched closer on her knees, checking the house again, feeling the pressure from all sides. "That's why I'm here. To protect them." She was losing time she couldn't afford...she should just walk away from Jeth and do what needed to be done.

But she needed him. She needed his help, and she needed the understanding of the one person who'd finally been so damned bulldoggedly persistent that he'd found her deeply hidden truths. "That's why I'm here," she repeated, and this close she could see his face, see the furl of his brow as he struggled to deal with what he'd witnessed and what she was. "But I never lied to you about what this night would bring for you."

After a long moment, he nodded. "No," he said. "You never did."

She inched closer yet. No more time to waste. He had to *listen.* "I can't talk about this. I've got to go back there." She handed him the camera, the images queued up on the LCD display on the back. "Scalpucci is here. Not just his errand boys, but Scalpucci himself. I can't think of anything that would bring him out in the open like this—except for his wife. That would explain their delay in reaching this place—they had to pick up Scalpucci. And Gretchen's got to be here, too."

He looked up at her with the grimmest of expressions, his mouth thinned to a line in the shadow of his mustache and his eyes gone from a struggling frown to a new type of anguish. "She's not the only one." He turned the camera so she could see. "The woman in the middle…that's my sister."

Sam's mouth dropped open. "No," she said, unthinking words straight from her stunned brain to her mouth. "She can't still be here. It's been *days*. Unless—" No, she wasn't going to say that out loud. She wasn't.

Except he looked at her, and she knew that now of all times, the only thing keeping the thin twist of connection between them was the truth. So she took a deep breath and said, low enough so maybe he just wouldn't hear it after all, "Unless she had to recover before she could travel."

He heard her. His face tightened down and his breath came short and sharp and only after all that was he finally able to mutter, "Son of a *bitch*." And then he looked up at her and said, "But you can help her. You can help them all. You can use your…your what, your superhero powers?—and get them out of there."

She laughed, more than a little bitter. "There's no superhero here. Just one very normal person with a few tricks up her sleeve." A million different ways to be someone other than who she really was, at least as far as anyone could perceive. Just…not really. Not ever really.

"Then use those tricks," he said, suddenly and unexpectedly fierce. "Everything I said…I was wrong. About all of it. Just use *them*."

She nodded. Slowly. "I will," she said. "But not because I think you believe what you just said. I don't. But…it's *what I do*."

"Because you can."

"Yes. Because I can."

And he nodded, as much to himself as to her. "I'll help. Whatever that takes. But first—"

She knew what was coming. What he needed to trust her. She lifted her chin, looking straight into his shadowed eyes. For a moment they hesitated, knee-to-knee, behind the bushes with the night air pounding around them and action looming close. The sparse streetlight fell on his eyes—not enough to see color, but enough to reveal expression. *Impatience. Expectation.*

She took a deep breath and let her guise fall away. Not just like that, but only after a long moment of struggle—a moment in which she thought she might not be able to do it at all. To reveal herself—her *real* self—for the first time since childhood.

She might as well be naked.

She wanted to run. But she forced herself to stay right where she was, sitting on her heels on the cold ground, Jeth so close—closer than she'd thought somehow. Her heart beat the quick, flighty rhythm of a cornered wild thing and she wondered just how much of her feelings showed on her face.

Her real face.

"Ah," Jeth said, and his hand came up to brush her cheek with the back of his knuckles. "There you are." His hand wasn't entirely steady as a fingertip followed the bridge of her nose and over one eyebrow. Sam leaned into his touch without thinking, and then blinked when she realized it.

"Here I am," she said. Shaky. Naked and vulnerable and real. Looking back at the first man who'd ever seen through her, and finding him still riveted to her. *Don't think about it. Don't try to plan it. Just find the moment.*

Now. *This* moment. This instant of clarity before the world rushed in and Sam I Am leaped into action and then Jeth walked away with his sister.

She took his whiskery nighttime face in her own hands and drew him close. He accepted the invitation without hesitation, kissing her with an assurance that was just as honest as the rest of him. More than just a simple kiss, no matter how sweet and thrilling.

Affirmation.

He pulled back slightly, his hands tightening at her waist for a final, deeper kiss. When he broke away it was to look her in the eye. "Just so you know."

Sam shook her head, dazed and trying to pull herself back to the moment. *Hiding in the yard, Scalpucci's men inside the house, women in danger, Sam on her own—*

No, not so much on her own.

She took a deep breath. "Look, I've got to…I can't go in there like this. I've got to—"

"Hide," he said, a familiar note of dryness in his voice—except this time she could hear the affection that went with it.

"Yes," she agreed. "I've got to hide."

There she was. The Sam he'd been looking for and she was about to go away.

Jethro wanted to go bang his head on the smooth bark of the nearby maple tree, or to fling himself back on the cold ground with an arm over his face, long enough to absorb the events of this strangest day of his life. Until he could truly believe what he'd seen in these last few moments—and what he'd felt. Manly reactions all.

He found he still had his hands on Sam's hips, those glorious curvy hips that seemed so unlikely on a woman so slender. He tightened his hold, knowing that Sam—*this* Sam—was about to go away. That her strong chin and wide jaw and fierce eyebrows would blend into the less noticeable public-faced Sam, leaving him only her sunlight-honey eyes.

So he took one last look, baffled by this sudden surge of feeling for a woman who not only deceived others freely—had deceived *him*—but who lived her whole life this way. Somehow. Fooling people but not cameras…she turned herself into a product of her own mind, and made others believe it.

Holy freakin' superhero.

And that was the whole point, wasn't it? Hadn't he always wanted to believe in a superhero who could and would stand up for the way things should be? And here she was. She just happened to get the job done with a frighteningly effective mask of lies.

But she was *doing* it. She was helping women like his sister…doing what Jethro himself hadn't been able to get done.

"Okay," he said, drinking in one long, last look at her. Shaggy hair in need of a cut, copper undertones visible even in this light. A smattering of freckles to go with it. He held her gaze, and he nodded. And when he let his focus widen, she was back to what she'd been. Attractive but less remarkable. More conventional and less noticeable. Even the feel of her changed, the angle between waist and hip easing. She'd put on her disguise, and accomplished it so thoroughly that his mind believed it down to every sense.

She'd hidden her vulnerability just as neatly. When she looked at him her face was tough and her expression impenetrable…all business. "I think I can get in the back," she told him. "They won't see me, that's for sure. But it could get noisy. I need some cover."

And Jethro, never having called on himself to be devious, said blankly, "How?"

She grinned. "It's not so hard. Come knocking at the door as a neighbor because you've seen their lights on, assume they've been kept up by the party, and rant and rave about young kids these days and how the police have been called."

"Hey," he said, uncertain. "I don't think I'm old enough to rant and rave."

She saw his doubt, grew sharp at the sight. "Still too noble to lie?"

"No!" Well, maybe. "I mean…I just don't think I *can*."

"Jeth," she said, a little too patiently, "we're running out of time. We might be too late already. We don't know what's going on in there. I can do this, but everyone in that house will be safer if I have your help."

And she was right, too. "The van," he blurted. "Maybe it's got an alarm. I can set it off. Or if it doesn't have an alarm, it must have a horn. Even if they don't come out to check, it should give you cover."

"Why, Jeth," Sam said, and batted her eyelashes at him in the darkness. "How sly you can be when you put your mind to it." And then, more seriously, "At least one of them will probably come out to check. Don't hang around." She dug into her pocket and pulled out a tiny gun, an automatic in a tailored holster; she held it out to him.

He took it in disbelief, fingers running over the leather. "Is this *real?*"

"It's real enough. It's a mousegun. It's got eight rounds and there's one already in the chamber. There's no safety—that's why the holster." She tapped the trigger through the holster. "Pull the trigger, and you're going to get a bang. And if you need it, don't screw around. Jam it right up close before they even know you have it and empty the damn thing. Don't expect some-one the size of the guy we put down at the last house to take an instant dive—depending how the shots are placed, he'll still be able to do plenty of damage to you if you stick around and let him."

He held it back out to her. "Maybe you should just—"

"Take it. You're going to be out here alone. Once I get inside, I'll have the house guardian on my side." She looked at the house, at the van…back at Jethro. "We've got to move. You ready?"

"For this? Never." He shook his head, barely able to believe what he was about to do. "I guess I'll just fake it."

"Exactly," she said with satisfaction, and quite abruptly disappeared. Abruptly and literally. Sam in the bushes…Sam gone. He thought he felt the touch of her hand on his; he definitely heard her murmur that he should give her a moment to reach the house before he started his noise.

Holy freakin' fakin' it.

Chapter 6

Sam only hoped Jeth could bring himself to join her world long enough to provide the distraction she'd need.

Of course, she also hoped that they hadn't delayed too long, that Scalpucci was so cocky he hadn't brought the manpower he'd need once Sam got into the middle of things....

She had no illusions about her ability to tackle these men. She was scrappy in a fight and she knew all the street moves she'd ever need, but she was small and even regular workouts didn't provide her with the upper body strength to match the steroid-enhanced creatures with whom Scalpucci surrounded himself.

On the other hand, she wasn't above cheating. Hell, she didn't think twice about cheating. And the men in that house would find it almost impossible to hit a moving, invisible target. If she took out the lights, they might not even realize she was anything more—or less—than a quick opponent in the dark.

But before that, she wanted the women out of there—both the refugees and the house guardian. And even then...if she got them out cleanly, then she could avoid the whole confrontational thing altogether.

Sam found the back door, a closed and locked half-glass door that she could have picked had she brought her tools but would instead sacrifice to the cause as soon as Jeth made his noise. The backyard spread out behind her, fully landscaped and crammed with the foliage of a mature neighborhood in a city full of green space. Plenty of places for the women to take cover on the way out. Sheers covered the half-glass door, giving her only a fuzzy view of the interior. Lights blazed in the kitchen directly beyond this door, but no one occupied it. Beyond that stood a small dining room—the same room she'd seen from the window beside the house.

There the women had been gathered, though Sam could only see glimpses—the flash of movement, a faint shriek of protest.

Bad men. You deserve whatever happens here tonight.

It made her want to glide up to them unseen and exact the kind of revenge that would put her in jail if anyone ever identified her. To use her skills in exactly the way that would horrify Jeth, so genuine and naive in his black-and-white world where bad things didn't happen if you tried hard enough to stop them simply because that's the way it *should* be.

A chameleon she might be, but stupid…not quite. Criminal…not quite.

Sometimes Jeth's way was right. She could lie to everyone else, but to herself she had to tell the truth.

So the revenge…another day, maybe. Or a different kind of revenge. For now she'd get these women out as fast as she could, and if it meant scrapping, it meant scrapping. But no side trips. No distractions. Just a pure break-out and run.

Come on, Jeth. Sam waited poised by the back door,

her elbow cocked and ready to take out the bottom corner pane of glass. *Fake it if you have to, but fake it* now.

And finally, a car alarm split through the subliminal
thump of music…oddly, not quite close enough to be
the van. Sam took the moment anyway, tapping the
glass with her elbow just hard enough to crack it, then
sliding her hand back up in her jacket sleeve to pick at
the shards with her already tender hands. Just enough
to reach in and—

Another car alarm went off. And he must have been
getting the hang of it, for almost immediately a third
alarm joined in—and then another. Sam grinned to herself as she flipped the deadbolt and slid the chain lock
out of place and then released the doorknob lock. No one
came rushing at her—as near as she could tell, at least
two men had gone to the front door, and though Scalpucci
still stood in the dining room with Gretchen in a cruel
hold, he'd also turned toward the front of the house.

Sam slid inside, clothed in her *unseen* guise, reas-
sessing the situation with every step. They were all big,
like the man at the last house. Too big for her to handle
in numbers, though if Scalpucci had been there alone…

But he wasn't. And she didn't have the leeway to try
for cleverness; best strategy would be to go in fast, come
out fast. *Run away.* After that she could call the police,
holding out a faint hope that Scalpucci would in some
way pay for his actions.

The house guardian sat at the end of the dining room
table. With no finesse and nothing to lose, Sam waited
until Scalpucci shouted something at the front of the
house and then reached in to pluck at the woman's
sleeve from behind, hissing a warning. The woman startled and then froze, and Sam had to speak up against the

fifth whooping car alarm when she said, "Help's here.
Grab them up and go out the back—it's open."

The refuge guardians weren't chosen for their looks
or their sweet dispositions. This woman may or may not
have suspected there'd been no visible movement behind
her, but she knew how to prioritize her reactions. She
kicked one woman under the table—Jeth's sister?—and
snapped her fingers at the other. The frightened women
only stared stupidly at her as the guardian gestured over
her shoulder to the freedom of the open back door.

But the first woman…Jeth's sister had his hair and his
nose and though she also had a hell of a bruise on her
face and an arm in a restrictive sling, she still had some
of his determination. She quite matter-of-factly pushed
her chair back and walked out of the room, and the car
alarms covered every step of her movement. Sam
stepped aside undetected to let her pass and then returned to her spot by the door. Scalpucci and another
man bellowed a few terse words at each other across the
house and through the front door. Suspicious, oh yes. But
Sam had her eye on the light switches, and thank good-
ness for that. For while the second woman still stared at
the rising house guardian in catatonic fright, Scalpucci
turned to look at both women with instant fury.

Sam hit the switch, plunging the kitchen into darkness and bursting out from cover without her *unseen*
guise—a guise that was of no use when she needed to
interact with people. She darted into the lighted dining
room and grabbed the guardian, a woman older and of
a size with Sam, to propel her back into the kitchen.
"Run, dammit!" She hunted and found the dining room
light switch, slapping it off even as she dragged the
frightened, frozen refugee from her place at the table.

Finally, the woman ran, shrieking all the way out as if the noise alone propelled her; it created an excruciating dissonance with the car alarms and finally faded.

That left Sam and Scalpucci and his thoroughly—and freshly—battered wife. Even in the darkness, Scalpucci pinned his gaze on Sam. "It won't work," he said, nearly shouting to overcome the car alarms. "I have what I want—and I'm going to do what I want."

Sam hovered at the edge of action, ready to grab any opportunity to free Gretchen. All but one of the alarms abruptly stopped; soon enough Scalpucci's two men would return. "Let me guess," she said flatly. "You want to wreck the underground so badly that there's no chance it'll rebuild."

"Something like that." He aimed a cocky sneer of a grin her way. "I think I've got a pretty good start, don't you?"

"Actually, I think you've already failed." Sam gathered herself in the darkness, aiming to go *unseen* and launch for Gretchen at the same time—no finesse, just a snatch and run. Scalpucci would know she was on the move, but he'd convince himself he'd lost her in the darkness and then she'd be waiting to take him down with a simple foot stuck in his path. More *Three Stooges* material than superhero stuff...but just as effective.

Except...

Light flooded the room, making her blink. Scalpucci gave her a smug, superior look. "Dumb bitch. Did you think I couldn't find the other light switch?"

The other light switch. Of course there would be one. "No," Sam said, "I didn't. I figured you for a real dim bulb."

"*I'm* the one in control!" he snarled at her, and it involved spittle.

Sam kept herself from flinching at the sudden verbal violence, knowing it was just what he wanted. "Not anymore. I left one of your men trussed up over on the south side, and the cops have probably found him by now. They've been called here as well. So what I *think* is that you should cut your losses and quietly leave."

His face—heavy features heading fast toward jowly, a handsome mouth constantly distorted with emotion—turned ugly with anger, bringing up a heavy red flush. He spat something uncomplimentary, punctuating it with a shove to Gretchen, the only woman within reach. Sam bit her lip, cursed the light switch, and weighed her chances of breaking his killer grip on his wife so they could both bolt to freedom.

One of the men returned from the front of the house, stopping short in surprise at the doorway opposite Sam. "What the hell?"

Dammit. Two of them now.

"Never mind that," Scalpucci said, suddenly calm now that his employee had returned. "And never mind finding the others. We've spent too much time here. Grab her and let's go. Be sure to leave one of your special gifts behind."

"Already set," the man said, eyeing Sam; his .38 revolver looked small in his hand. "We can trigger it any time."

Scalpucci looked straight at Sam and said, "This is your doing. All of you dumb bitches and your oh-so-clever underground. And now everyone in the city will know what happens to those who defy me." He gave his wife a hard shake, his hand clamped so tightly on her slender arm that his fingers met. She, too, found Sam's gaze, a hopeless expression; she mouthed *I'm sorry.*

"Seems like a good time to scream," Sam told her, and meant it. A cry for help in the night—Jeth should hear it if no one else. And she frantically hunted other options, knowing she couldn't take both these men, that Jeth had her gun and she couldn't go *unseen* under this spotlight.

"You keep your mouth shut," Scalpucci said, giving Gretchen another good shake as the other man headed for Sam, one hammy hand extended to gesture her into his clutches.

"Holy freakin' *jerk*." Sam scowled at Scalpucci from the other side of the dining room table. Options. Who needed options? She'd just make a few of her own. She whirled to the light switch, flicked it off—and ducked, going *unseen* just that fast. Just barely fast enough, for the revolver discharged with a giant smack of noise; the bullet slammed into the wall above Sam's head.

She leaped up, flinging a chair hard at the gun-toting minion and leaving him to wrestle with it while she charged right up onto the sturdy dining table and skidded across to launch onto Scalpucci from above.

And still Scalpucci managed to grab her arm and her shoulder and slam her into the wall beside him.

Hard.

Her guise flickered away, leaving her reeling, sinking to the floor. Visible and vulnerable and alone.

All wrong. This was going all wrong. Jethro had made his noise, he'd done what she'd asked; he'd drawn them off. He'd managed to do it in a way he *could* do it, with a veritable chorus of car alarms. And yet Sam stayed within the house, where the lights flicked on and off without apparent reason and screaming resonated and a certain amount of crashing and thumping made its way out the open front door, audible even above the party music and the huddle of angry young men who'd come outside to shut up their vehicles.

Sam.

Something had gone wrong. In spite of her mind-boggling ability to wear other faces and other bodies and to go unseen altogether…something had gone wrong. And here he crouched behind a car, a tiny gun he wasn't even willing to use filling the palm of his hand. He curled his fingers around it in frustration, making an awkward fist…and then he looked down at the fist with dawning determination.

Something had gone wrong, and it was time to move.

He stood up from behind the car. Scalpucci's man was still on the lawn, looming to disapprove of the recent noise and keeping an eye on the angry young men who spat brags and threats from several houses down. Jethro moved along the street side of the parked cars and approached the van from the far side. He didn't hesitate or lurk or try to keep himself unnoticed; he was good at none of those things. He just walked up like he belonged. He fumbled the safety off, pushed the tiny gun up against the van tire and pulled the trigger.

The combined noise of the discharging gun and exploding tire made a hugely satisfying sound, carrying across to the party, grabbing the attention of the angry young men. Jethro jumped in spite of himself, but as the lookout cursed and hesitated on the lawn, uncertain whether to check the van or prepare for the attention of the angry young men, Jethro went for the front door at rugby speed. He could only hope that sheer audacity counted for something.

Apparently, sheer audacity had its moments.

Jethro burst through the open front door unimpeded as the confrontation outside escalated. Accusation, protest, demands...until finally a querulous voice shouted from next door, "I've called the police!"

No telling when they'd get here.

Unless...Jethro helped them along.

No more the truth than what Sam had asked him to do in the first place, but suddenly somehow he didn't think twice. He put his back to the wall, tightened his hold on the tiny gun, and prepared to do battle on a level new to Jethro Sheridan.

"*Police!* Drop your weapons and come out with your hands on your heads."

Jeth. Jeth's voice. It penetrated Sam's daze.

"Bullshit!" Scalpucci yelled back, not buying the authority—or lack thereof—in Jeth's voice. The complete lack of flashing light bars might have had something to do with it, too.

"Not for long," Jeth said steadily. "And meanwhile your getaway van is limping off on three tires. Who'd have thought a big tough-looking guy like that could be chased off by a bunch of kids?"

And Sam marveled, for even she had no idea if Jethro's words were true.

She didn't need to know. All she had to do was take advantage of the moment—

She lunged to her feet, still unable to focus and not bothering to try. She was better off than the man who'd taken her chair in his face, and all she had to do was free Gretchen—for Scalpucci had her again—and they could run. All of them, run far and hard and leave this mess behind. The cleanup would be something else again…but cleanup was for survivors, and first they all had to be survivors.

She had to free Gretchen…

So she put herself in the position to be grabbed. Lunged at Scalpucci so he'd *have* to grab her just to keep his florid face intact. He thought one hand would do, as it did for his deeply conditioned wife.

He thought wrong. Sam twisted, bringing the ball of her foot up against the side of his knee. He cried out, more anger at her defiance than pain—she didn't have the room to land a solid blow.

But neither did he. He tried slamming her against the wall one-handed, and it gave her time to land a fist on his ear, imagining her target to be the other ear and her fist going all the way through. This time his yowl sounded heartfelt, and more so when she pulled back to do it again, both feet finally solidly on the floor.

"In here, Officer!" Jethro yelled, a convincing note of desperation in his voice.

Are they really—?

Damn, too soon, gotta get out of here—

And finally, Scalpucci released Gretchen to aim a one-handed blow at Sam, a blow Sam ducked, flickering *unseen* in his grip in a guise she'd never tried before, enough to startle him and not enough to convince him he wasn't simply seeing stars after the two solid, fist-aching hits she'd landed at the side of his head. He froze, just for an instant—

And then froze for real at the spectacular return of the older woman, the guardian. She reappeared briefly in the doorway and then charged forward at full shriek, and damned if she wasn't followed by the woman who'd been frozen in fear and even by Jeth's sister, who held a weapon of the frypan persuasion. As Scalpucci's minion finally threw off the chair and climbed up as far as his knees, they descended upon him—and Gretchen, rather than running, flung herself into the action boiling around the second man.

"No!" Scalpucci bellowed, his florid color inching toward purple. "You fool! We've got to get out of here—"

"Too late," Jeth said, appearing around the corner behind Scalpucci—and from Scalpucci's sudden stiff hollow-backed posture, Sam surmised the little Kel-Tec was firmly jammed into his spine. Jeth tossed a pilfered extension cord on the dining room table and said most amiably, "Suppose you release her."

Scalpucci glared down at Sam, his hand still clamped around her forearm tightly enough to make bone ache. She'd taken nothing for granted; she stood half-crouched and ready to deliver hurt from half a dozen directions. But when she looked back up at him, she smiled sweetly and she gave him the flicker effect again.

The blood drained from his face even as Jeth grinned behind him. And slowly, so slowly, he peeled his fingers away from her arm.

Free, Sam wasted not an instant. She grabbed up the cord and hog-tied Scalpucci in short order, kicking his knees out from beneath him and accepting Jeth's wordless help to finish the job as Jeth handed over the little gun. She turned to check the women; between belts and torn curtains and yes, the frypan, they had the other man well under control.

The guardian stood, dusted off the knees of her jeans, and handed Sam a kitchen hand towel split lengthwise.

"You might need this," she said, indicating the similar gag around the dazed man beside her.

"Yeah," said Jeth. "Especially when he learns the cops aren't really here."

Sam only grinned at him as Scalpucci said, *"What?"* and took breath for more. Sam got there with the towel first, tapping Scalpucci sharply on the forehead with the pistol to get his attention, indicating with a cock of her head and a significant look at the weapon that she'd do it again—and harder—if he gave her reason.

Jeth said, "The van's gone, though. The third guy took off just now."

"But not," Sam verified, yanking the gag tight and then yanking the knot even tighter, "when you said he did."

Jeth's mustache twitched. He shook his head, then ducked it. From there he said, "The cops *have* been called."

"Then there's no time to waste." The house guardian nudged the closest woman toward the door—but she didn't move. She stood rooted to the spot, her eyes on Jeth as if she'd just now seen him. And Jeth returned the look, totally flummoxed, his work of the past moments quite obviously forgotten.

Sam reached out to tug him forward, a giant step over Scalpucci—who, fully trussed, now lay on his side on the floor. *"Outside,"* she said. "Out back. Do this *away from here.*"

The guardian wasn't slow to realize the relationship between the two, and wasn't about to let it interfere with their safety. She shoved Lizbet and pulled Jeth, and then suddenly the sound of an approaching siren cut the air and they all scrambled for the back door. Only Jeth hesitated, looking back at Sam…for Sam hadn't moved.

She waved him on, and when he didn't leave, repeated herself more vigorously—"Go!"—until he turned away.

But first, a conversation.

She crouched by Scalpucci, forearms propped on her thighs. The arm he'd grabbed throbbed in warning—the very least of the things for which she owed him. His eyes bulged above the gag and she followed the gaze to her hands—to the Kel-Tec. She laughed. "Oh, no," she said. "This is the least of your problems."

Her words left him visibly puzzled; he worked his hands behind his back, trying to loosen the cords. The siren closed in on the street—on the house. Sam didn't move. Didn't worry. "You thought you'd shut us down," she said. "Looks like it was the other way around. Carl Scalpucci, defeated by a bunch of battered women—including his wife. Is that what you're going to tell the police when they ask?" She glanced at the red and blue lights now reflecting through the windows and open front door to paint the walls. "And when they ask how, are you going to tell them about this?" She let herself flicker between guises—only briefly, for as discomfiting as Scalpucci found the sight, the effect from the inside left her dizzy with shifting energies. She leaned a little closer to Scalpucci. He tried—unsuccessfully—to cringe back through the wall. "You probably think I'd prefer you kept certain things as our little secret. Well, guess what. You are *so* wrong. When that first cop walks through the door, I think you should tell him everything. Tell him how we beat you two up, and how your loyal associate ran from the scene. Tell him that I flicker like a bad fluorescent lightbulb. Hell, tell him that I can *disappear.* Tell him all of that." She stood, looming over him. "Try not to babble too much, though. And watch your blood pressure, okay? I didn't even know a man could turn that color and live."

An authoritative knock pounded against the open front door. "Police! Come to the door!"

Sam went *unseen*. Such a relief to slide into the guise and hold it without the flicker; so satisfying to see the look on Scalpucci's face. "Go ahead," she said. "Tell him. All of it."

She wanted to stick around to see it. To see Scalpucci, tied and gagged and surrounded by evidence, snarling demands and absurdities about a woman who flickered and who had then disappeared to walk right out from under the cops' own noses. But she couldn't take the chance of being caught in the house, and she couldn't take the chance that a K-9 unit might roll on this one. She gave him one last long look as the cops finally, cautiously, entered the house, and painted him into her memory.

The Captain would be glad of his capture. Tied to the car bomb, to the break-in here, to the explosives this man had planted...he'd be jailed not for his crimes against this city as a whole, but for his personal beastliness. Like nailing a mafia don on tax evasion, only better.

She hesitated in the kitchen, tucking herself aside so the cop who'd covered the back door could enter; the woman declared the kitchen clear and cautiously moved into the dining room, regarding Scalpucci with dawning recognition.

It was enough.

Sam smiled, and she walked unseen into the night.

Chapter 7

"You're still leaving?" Jethro stood stunned in darkness that would soon turn to the predawn hours. Several blocks away from the refuge with the guardian leading the way and they'd finally stopped...and she'd said that he couldn't come any farther. That he had to just stand here and watch as Lizbet walked away.

Until that moment it hadn't occurred to him that she might still consider her flight. The loss of her established life. The loss of their family.

And now she looked at him and nodded. "It's the only way for me."

"It's *not* the only way," he said, taking a step forward, voice raising enough so the guardian narrowed her eyes in warning.

"It's okay," Lizbet told her. "He really is my brother. He's not the problem."

Or the solution, apparently. "Lizbet, let me help—"

"You *tried* to help," she said, and her voice sharpened. Tried. Right. And there she stood, catching her breath with one arm in a sling and her face still bruised and asymmetrically puffy. *Tried.* But hadn't done enough.

"I'm sorry," he said, miserable. "I should have done

better—I should have scared his sad ass right out of the state. I should have—"

Should have...

Sam stopped short at the curb of the residential street, still *unseen,* only feet away from the refugees. Only feet away from Jeth, who stood with an awkward combination of guilt and defiance, as startled as Sam by the guardian's brusque interruption. "Bullshit!" she snapped. "There is no *should have,* because there's no *could have.* Not with a man like that one. Nothing stops his kind but bars or death."

"Lizbet—"

"It's not forever, Jethro." She sent him a pleading look, and Sam could well understand its meaning. *Make this moment easier, not harder.* "He *is* guilty, and he *will* go to jail. His lawyer even tried to get him to plead out, but that would be admitting he'd been wrong, and don't you know it but his victims always—" Her voice broke, but she took a breath and went on. "His victims always *deserve* it."

The woman behind her startled Sam when she punctuated Lizbet's words by spitting on the lawn beside them, and Gretchen put an understanding hand on Lizbet's arm.

"Anyway," Lizbet said, "I'm lucky. Once everything's settled, I can come back. Or if I like my new life, I can let you know where I am. You can visit."

"Lizbet," Jeth said, his voice thick, "you still could have come to me. You could have at least told me—"

Lizbet lifted her head sharply, cutting off his words with that simple gesture. "No," she said, "I couldn't. Because you would have tried to do something. You would have tried to fix the unfixable. And that son of a bitch told me he'd kill you this time."

Sam winced at the shock on Jeth's face, the transition to the realization of why she'd made her choices…the very choices for which he'd blamed her. If she hadn't been *unseen,* she'd have put a hand on his arm…taken a step closer…at least given him an understanding look. But she'd made her own choices; this was the way she lived her life. She had an extraordinary talent and she used it, and it affected every facet of her life—from the way she looked at things to the pieces of her true self which she chose to show others. For every price that talent exacted, it also gave her a gift—allowing her to blend where she wanted to, to help where she wanted to. To experience things that might otherwise be denied her.

And now and then, she could choose just to be Sam I Am.

This time, this moment, she'd been *unseen* so as not to endanger the refugees as she tracked them down, following the murmured directives, panting breath and occasional scuff of foot as behind her, the party music cut off and another siren ground to a stop. Now she stayed that way, letting Jeth and Lizbet play out their goodbye. Watching Jeth, speechless as he drew his sister in for the most cautious of hugs and then separated to brush a gentle thumb across her cheek. She'd been ready for more arguing; no doubt she knew him well.

What she couldn't know was the things Jeth had learned this night by Sam's side, seeing a world in which he'd never before been involved. So her eyes widened at his understanding. She took an unwilling step backward at the urging of the restless guardian; Gretchen tugged her hand, murmured something to her.

And Jeth said simply, "Call me when you can." He stood on the sidewalk, hands jammed into his back pockets, and watched Lizbet go. *Let* her go.

Sam gave him a moment. A long moment. And then she switched guises and quietly cleared her throat.

He whirled, alarmed; his face cleared when he saw her—and then turned rueful. "I suppose you were there all along."

"A few moments," she agreed.

He stuck his hands back into his back pockets, and fatigue washed over his features. Yeah, it'd been a long night.

"You didn't fail, you know," she told him.

"What, you read minds, too?"

She moved up to him, off the grass and onto the sidewalk. She, too, was tired, and achy in too many places to count. Her hands had stiffened up in his gloves, skinned and tender and now puffy around the knuckles from the most recent action. "Expressions," she said. "Body language. It takes more than new faces to pull off my guises, you know." She moved closer yet. "The point is, your sister is safe. That's what you really wanted, isn't it?"

He looked away from her, putting his face in total shadow. "Yeah. It is."

"I passed the van on my way here…the cops will have all the pieces to tie Scalpucci up for a long time." She cleared her throat again, looked directly at his shadowed face. "You should know that I erased the existing pictures on your camera. What's left should go to the police, one way or the other. Just wipe my prints, will you?"

"Sure." He finally turned back to her, his expression not what she'd expected—fierce enough to make her blink. "This is it, then? What you do? And you're fine with all this hiding and skulking."

She laughed. "I *excel* at all this hiding and skulking. I even earn a very good living while I'm at it." She took a step back, held her hands out in a *take-a-look* gesture. "This is me." She changed from her standard public guise to a young woman with mocha skin and a free-form Afro. "And this." A man—slight of stature, but with a mustache that mirrored Jeth's. "And this." And back to the public Sam again. "*This* is what I do." And then, finally, she dropped the guises altogether. His eyes widened slightly; she knew what he saw. Sam with the shaggy, copper-touched hair, Sam with the gold-brown eyes and the strong flare of jaw and the stubborn chin. Wiry, with the high, narrow waist that would have looked so much better under a bigger cup size. *Sam I Am.* "I had hoped," she said, "that with all you've seen tonight, you could understand why."

A twitch of his mustache gave away his small smile. "Holy freakin' chameleon," he said. "Damned if I don't."

She looked at him a moment, holding his night-shadowed gaze and startled by the realization that this night was over. That if they walked away now, with nothing more said between them…

She didn't want that. She surprised herself, but she didn't want that. She didn't want to lose the honesty she'd seen and felt and offered here tonight. She didn't want to lose—so quickly—the man who had shared it with her.

"I had *hoped*," she said, "that with all you've seen tonight…you might want more."

"Holy freakin' *me*," he said. "Damned if I—"

Sam cut him short the best way she knew how—up close and personal with that mustache after all.

UPGRADE
Meredith Fletcher

Dear Reader,

I find technology so fascinating! In this world we live in, you really can't escape it. (Well, I suppose you could, but it would mean giving up electricity and other necessary comforts.) And who would want to?

I engage new software applications all the time (which has made me one of the greatest computer virus hunters in the world!) and pick up computer hardware that I can find the slightest excuse for (and a way to write it off on taxes!).

With all of these changes taking place in our everyday lives, with the medical leaps we've made in rebuilding the human body, adjusting the brain, and fabricating organs and limbs, I can't help but ask myself when the technology becomes available to rebuild ourselves in the image we want, will we? And what will happen then?

That was one of the questions I posed to myself when I wrote "Upgrade." If we have the ability to integrate the human body with computer systems, when will we stop? What will be left?

When I was younger, I loved watching *The Six Million Dollar Man*. Steve Austin (Lee Majors) was just so yummy. He was the kind of guy you wanted to rescue you and "upgrade your security clearance." But when *The Bionic Woman* spun out of that series, I wanted to be Jaime Sommers. Her stories, although with the same kind of bionic action, somehow came across as more human, more *real*. I really love the escapist action blended with human dynamics.

Hopefully, that's what you'll find in "Upgrade" as Enhanced FBI Special Agent Christie Chace squares off against military bodyguard Dalton Geller are in a no-holds fight for what they both believe in. Both are dedicated to their cause, compelled to do their best. Poor them. Of course, you see, they're doomed to fall in love. But that's not so bad, is it?

If you like this story and would like to see more set in the Enhanced universe, please let Harlequin and myself know. I can be reached at MFletcher1216@aol.com.

Happy reading!

Meredith Fletcher

Chapter 1

Washington, D.C. 2052
10:57 p.m.

Above the big barrel of the Colt .45 semiautomatic pistol pressed against Christie Chace's forehead, the man's sea-green eyes stirred like clouds in a sudden summer storm. *He's excited,* she thought.

She logged that fact in a nanosecond as she held her own Glock forty-caliber pistol where she thought his nose was. She couldn't really be sure since he wore a flesh-tone electrostatic-cling face mask that covered everything but his eyes.

"I hope that you're as professional as you seem. If you're not," Christie said, holding her fear in check and reminding herself that he hadn't fired yet and they might both get out of the situation alive, "I'm going to be embarrassed."

That caught the man's attention. Interest flared in his gaze.

Christie kept her breathing quiet and as relaxed as she could. After all, this wasn't the first time that she'd had a gun pointed in her direction. She'd even been shot twice before, once in the line of duty and once during a private matter that had spiraled out of control. Of course, if things went badly tonight, it would be the first time she'd ever been shot in the head. And, at this range with the caliber of weapon the no-faced man held, it would probably also be the last time.

She stared at the man, trying to make sense of his presence there. She couldn't. In her capacity as an agent of the Federal Bureau of Investigation, she'd been assigned to shadow Arturo Gennady. Gennady was a major developer in the Enhanced program, which drastically augmented the human body for military and law enforcement purposes. Some of that technology was filtering into the private sector.

A few days ago, Gennady had been contacted by blackmailers who threatened to expose one of his assistants if Gennady didn't turn over copies of the project he was currently finishing up. Unwilling to sacrifice his assistant or knuckle under to the blackmailers, Gennady had turned to the FBI. Christie's director of operations had turned to her.

The Enhanced program was of personal interest to Christie. She'd been one of the first FBI volunteers to undergo the extensive two years of surgeries to augment her speed, strength, hearing and vision, and implant cutting-edge communications devices inside her body. Her father had been a police officer, so a career in law enforcement had more or less been in her blood. But her interest in technology stemmed from her own love of it.

Plus, volunteering for the program fast-tracked her career in the FBI.

Covering the assignment, Christie had helped Gennady leverage the meeting place. Then she'd put her team in place, covering the warehouse area where the drop was supposed to go down. The plan was for the blackmailers to make contact, then FBI agents would take them into custody.

The no-faced man dropping out of the darkness in the warehouse where she'd taken up an observation post like he did was a wrinkle Christie hadn't planned on. The action had been supposed to take place out on the dockyards fronting the Potomac River.

"I mean, it's one thing to sneak up on me like you did," Christie stated coolly, "and major style points for that because I don't usually get caught off-guard, but I don't see how you think you're just going to walk away now. As a professional, I think you would agree that we have something of a standoff."

The sea-green eyes never blinked.

"We can try to discuss this," Christie suggested, "or we can shoot each other. Because I guarantee you I'm not going to back down." She waited. "I think we could talk."

He said nothing.

Okay, tough guy, she thought. *Let's dance.*

"We'll go on three," she said in a calm voice. "One, two…"

"What?" Surprise echoed in his voice.

"We'll shoot each other. On three. I don't see any other way out of this, do you?"

His eyes tightened and she knew beneath the electro-static-cling mask he was frowning, possibly irritated. She hoped like hell he was irritated. At least as irritated as she was. She hated surprises. Especially during an operation she'd planned for days.

"And don't think about shooting early," she told him, "because I promise you I'll still shoot. In case you haven't noticed, I'm fast." He hadn't counted on her speed when he'd sneaked up behind her. When she'd turned around and pushed her own pistol into his face, he'd been caught off-guard just as badly as she had. His eyes had gone wide with surprise.

"Faster than anything I've ever seen," the man admitted.

He's not afraid either. That fact irked Christie. If she were facing a scared perp, there was no telling what the outcome would be. With a professional, she was certain the man would know when to cut his losses or strike a deal. But his fearlessness of her was insulting.

"One, two…" she began again.

"Just like that?" the man asked, his voice tight with displeasure. "That's how you want to do it? One, two…" He caught himself before he said *three* and stopped. "Then we just shoot each other?"

"You have a favorite number?" Christie asked. "I'm amenable as hell, but I have to warn you—I get bored easily. If we have to count up to a three-digit number, I can't promise I won't pull the trigger early. Ten would be a real stretch, but if you want to go to ten, I'll try."

She took a deep breath, drawing in his scent. Few criminals thought to change scents or deodorant after committing a crime. And interfering with an FBI agent during a stakeout was definitely a criminal action. From the smell of him, he bought expensive. Match the physical description she had of the guy—he was six-three at least, with broad shoulders and narrow hips encased in a black turtleneck, black jeans and black running shoes— and the scent, and she might have a case that would stick.

Plus, the man didn't know she was recording the encounter on audio and video, or that Operations Support had already been alerted to the situation.

"*Special Agent Chace,*" the com-officer said smoothly, "*at this time we can't move any agents into your area without compromising the operation. Dr. Gennady's blackmailers have arrived. I'm running the visual you're sending through the identification databases. I haven't gotten a positive ID yet.*"

The man standing in front of Christie didn't hear the exchange because contact came over the telecom/recording unit in her right jawbone. The unit's presence was undetectable except by CAT scan, part of the overall cutting-edge Enhanced cyberbundle hardwired into her body that accounted for the incredible display of speed that had caught her would-be captor standing flat-footed.

Christie stared into his eyes, knowing she was on her own. *Terrific. The blackmailers had to show up three minutes early, didn't they?*

Billions of dollars were on the line, all of it government investments in national defense. This was also a presidential election year. No way was the director of operations going to let go of all that for the life of one special agent in the field. And, she had to admit, the fact that the no-faced man hadn't shot her outright spoke volumes about restraint. Her D.O. wanted to take down the blackmailers at the stakeout. Grabbing No-Face for interference would be a side dish.

"I have a favorite number," the no-faced man said, and Christie couldn't help noticing that his low baritone was sexy despite the muffling effect of the cling mask. "But I'm not too happy with shooting each other."

"Shooting each other?" Christie asked. "Or getting shot?"

His eyes crinkled and she knew he was getting even

more irritated. "Are you really as tough as you make yourself out to be?"

"At gunpoint," Christie replied, "do I have a choice?"

"Chace." The deep growl over the telecom/recording unit belonged to Stuart Fielding, the D.O. over her present assignment. *"Don't antagonize this man. I don't want your mission blown."*

"Yes, sir," Christie said. "I can see how my getting shot would complicate things. I'll do my best to see that it doesn't happen."

No-Face's eyes widened a little.

Okay, so now he knew she had a com-unit on her. He should be more worried.

"He's not going to shoot you," Fielding said. In his fifties, the D.O. was a coldly pragmatic man, supremely confident of his abilities and his judgment. He'd weathered terrorist action in the field inside the United States and its protectorates, as well as political meltdowns.

What makes you so sure? Christie wondered. She felt panic hammering around in the back of her mind, but she held her service weapon in a loose, relaxed grip the way she'd been trained.

"If he was going to shoot you, he'd already have done it," Fielding went on.

"Excuse me, sir," Christie said, "but maybe he's part of this."

"If he was, don't you think he would have warned his buddies off by now?"

"If I was part of anything," No-Face said, "don't you think I'd have called for reinforcements by now?"

Okay, Christie thought. *The votes are in.*

"I'll get agents over to your position as soon as I can," Fielding said. *"Until then, sit on this guy."*

Lovely, Christie thought. Despite her precarious situation, she couldn't sit by while the stakeout played out without her. Dr. Gennady had believed in her and had put his life on the line to get to the people attempting to blackmail him over one of his research assistants who had a juvenile record for cracking into secure corporate technology development sites that the government hadn't caught.

Christie had worked with Dr. Arturo Gennady after the blackmailers had contacted him, and she'd gotten to know him. She'd promised him she would take care of him. No-Face was keeping her from doing that.

She liked Gennady. He was in his seventies, his mind as sharp as his humor. The whole time he'd been with her, he'd been a complete gentleman, always kind and considerate.

Gennady was also one of the foremost authorities on nanotechnology involving Enhanced musculature.

Enhancement covered the vast array of cyberware that had been developed for implantation into the human body. After a long history of cosmetic surgeries and artificial organs and joint replacements, the development of Enhanced—the term agreed upon by the various corporations who had started developing and selling product lines—features designed for the human body was a natural progression. Gennady's expertise was why the government had placed him under contract and safeguarded his lab in Washington, D.C.

He'd been scared when he'd come forward to let the Bureau know he'd been contacted by blackmailers trying to get their hands on research he was conducting.

Mentally accessing the small computer at the back of her brain, Christie activated the video pickup programming. The live satellite feed juiced through the microfilaments connected to her left optic nerve, taking over the feed from eye to brain and basically opening a simulated video screen in the back of her head. Vision in her left eye went to black, then filled again with the primary digital camcorder view of the blackmailers' drop site outside.

Getting used to having two images in her head at once—one from her natural vision, if it could still be called that after all the vision enhancements she'd had done, and the other from the electronic programming—had taken time and effort. That feature alone had gotten a lot of agents released from the Bureau's Enhanced pilot program when they hadn't learned to adapt to the simultaneous feeds. Less than three months after the two-year-long period of Enhanced surgical operations to reconfigure her mind and body, she switched from one view to the other inside her head as naturally as breathing.

She felt the man's weight at the other end of her pistol. If that moved, she intended to start shooting.

The warehouse she'd chosen as her observation point was seventy-three yards from the drop point. Nine other Bureau agents lurked in the shadows around the commercial docks of the Potomac River. She was the only Enhanced agent. If No-Face had come after one of them, chances were they would never have known about it. No-Face was damn good at skulking, and those men had purely human reflexes. Even being Enhanced, she'd barely brought the situation to a stalemate.

Out on the deserted street in front of the warehouse, Dr. Arturo Gennady's burgundy luxury sedan looked about as conspicuous as a pink flamingo in a desert. At the end of the block, along the street that fronted the Potomac River and the glitter of the capital city on the north side, a van turned and came toward Gennady's vehicle.

Christie's stomach tightened. It was strange how seeing the van close in on Gennady's car was more frightening than the pistol pressed against her forehead.

Christie flipped through the seven camera views open for her perusal and selected the one that showed Gennady sitting in his car. The camera was equipped with a low-light multiplier that stripped the night's shadows from the car and left images as clear as they would be in daylight.

Tall and thin, Gennady wore an elegant suit with a flower in the lapel. He'd just come from a granddaughter's violin recital in Georgetown. He pulled nervously at his goatee, and then adjusted his spectacles. He hadn't had his eyesight Enhanced, which was an anomaly for someone working in the enhancement field. His attention was fully on the approaching van.

"Do you see them?" Gennady asked nervously over the com-channel they'd encrypted for him. He couldn't hear their conversations except when they cut him in. He didn't know about the situation with Christie.

"We have them, Professor," Dwight Yeager said before Christie could reply. Dwight was Christie's partner, a young agent with political connections that would probably see him advance through the Bureau ranks in record time.

"Ms. Chace," Gennady said. *"Are you there?"*

"I'm right here," Christie said. "Everything's going to be all right. Just hang in there."

In the car, Gennady nodded slightly. "I will. Thank you."

The masked man's voice drew Christie back into the warehouse. She let go of the camera feed and resumed her normal vision. No-Face was looking at her with renewed interest.

"Who are you?" he asked.

"Who are you?" she countered.

He shook his head slowly. "I didn't come here to kill you, and I didn't come here to interfere with your op."

Op? Christie filed that away. The offhand use of that term told her that No-Face had a military or law enforcement background, or at least was familiar with one or both of those areas. Of course, a lot of the "security" divisions owned by the large international corporations had those kinds of backgrounds. Many of those corporate "security" divisions handled the same kind of blackmail as the people squeezing Dr. Gennady. There was some speculation that the people behind the blackmailing were one of the huge conglomerates hoping to acquire the government-regulated weapons technology.

"Then why are you here?" Christie divided her attention between the scene in the warehouse and the van approaching Gennady's car, flipping back and forth between her normal vision and the camera feeds. The van moved slowly, like a shark cruising through the ocean.

"Came to peep the hostiles," No-Face said.

Peep. Another military or law enforcement term, meaning to check out. Christie noticed how he held the pistol: as nice and relaxed as she did.

"Didn't expect you to be here," he admitted.

"You were already here," Christie accused.

"Guilty. I also thought maybe you were one of the bad guys."

That was why she hadn't noticed him. Remembering how she'd walked around and assumed the warehouse was clear made her feel vulnerable.

"You're lucky we didn't have a thermographic satellite link," she said. "You wouldn't have been able to hide so easily." A thermographic scan would have revealed his heat signature even up on the second-floor landing that protruded partway over the first floor. He'd obviously found a good hiding place, otherwise she'd have found him when she did her preliminary reconnaissance two hours ago.

So he'd been in place for at least two hours. And she had been in the warehouse. Either she was getting sloppy or he was damn good. Remembering how he'd come up out of the darkness, she knew he was damn good. She'd never been sloppy.

"What's your part in this?" she asked.

"Uh-uh," he replied.

"We can discuss it here or in lockup."

"I'm not sticking around for the debrief."

Military, Christie thought at his use of the term. *Definitely military.*

"You got a plan for getting away from here?" she taunted.

"I'm working on it."

No way, No-Face. You're mine. Christie flipped her vision back to the external cameras.

The van was even with Gennady's sedan. Per the orders he'd gotten from the blackmailers, Gennady got out and stood by the car. The van stopped.

"Nobody's in the van," Dwight Yeager reported. *"What the hell is going on?"*

Christie flipped through the cameras available to her and found the one focused on the van's interior. No one was at the wheel. She switched through the views again, looking for a wide-angle view of the contact site. Out on the river, a fast speedboat drifted with the sluggish current. A bright light dawned onboard the boat, then it was gone, but it was enough to let her know that something nasty had been launched.

"Get him out of there!" Christie commanded, knowing it was already too late. "Get him out of—"

The artillery round plowed into the sedan, which exploded in a ball of white-hot flame, causing it to leap high into the air and flip over. A secondary explosion caused by the fuel tank detonating from the heat of the first blast occurred while the vehicle was plummeting back toward the street. Arturo Gennady's body dropped out on the street nearly fifty yards from where he'd been standing.

The sonic wave from the artillery round fired from the boat out on the river and the explosion slammed into the warehouse window. Vibrations shook the floor beneath Christie's feet. She turned her head, momentarily losing the electronic connections to the cameras, and stared through the window in disbelief.

You gave Gennady your word, Christie thought as she continued the standoff with the no-faced man. She held her pistol tightly. *You gave him your word that he would be all right, that you would take care of him.*

In the next instant, an executive-style helicopter dropped out of the sky and drew level with the warehouse window. Automatically, Christie triggered the telescopic function of her Enhanced vision, locking in the light multiplier function as well. In a split second, she could see through the night as clearly as day.

The side door of the helicopter slid back, revealing

a man sitting behind a belt-fed Heckler & Koch fifty-caliber machine gun. The man aimed at the warehouse window and opened fire.

Chapter 2

Instinct and experience drove Dalton Geller into action. The beautiful blonde holding the pistol to his head hadn't expected the attack from the river or the helicopter dropping from the sky with the machine gunner onboard. Neither had he, but he'd at least had it happen a few times in the past.

Until tonight, he'd thought those days were over. After the death of his best friend, Mac Reynolds, Dalton—and the U.S. Army—had been persuaded by Grace Reynolds that she needed more security than she had been getting at that time. Dr. Grace Reynolds was one of the top cybernetics integration people in the world and was currently involved in a radical upgrade on the implant surgeries for the military Enhanced program.

For the last few years, Dalton had shepherded Dr. Reynolds and her son Michael. Technically on loan from the U.S. Army, Dalton provided bodyguard services as well as security assessment. Only a few days ago, he had spotted Dr. Reynolds conversing with a known organized crime figure. Grace had been upset by the encounter, and she'd later refused to talk about it.

Dalton, however, hadn't been able to let it go. His investigation of the Chinese Triad had led him here to this warehouse. He hadn't figured on the woman, though.

And he definitely hadn't figured on the Triad attacking and killing without warning. Now, as confident and able as she seemed, he was certain the young woman who had moved so inhumanly quick was about to die under the withering hail of machine-gun fire. He leaped for her, intending to knock her down before the withering hail of fifty-caliber rounds that chewed through the window frame could reach her.

Instead, the woman fisted his shirt in one hand, stopped his forward momentum like it was nothing and drove him backward. His breath left his body in a whoosh and he felt like a truck had hit him. He crashed to the floor fifteen feet back from where he'd been standing. She landed astride him like a bronc rider, thighs on either side of his hips, fisting his shirt to keep his head from hitting the floor. He felt the lean hardness of her body layered in soft feminine flesh pressed against his. Under other circumstances, Dalton would have welcomed the experience.

However, her pistol was still securely against his forehead. Somehow he'd managed to wedge his up under that pretty little chin. They were still at a stalemate.

She glared at him with her milk chocolate-brown eyes, as if he was to blame for the bullets that ripped out the window and tracked down the side of the warehouse wall. The machine gunner was good. He laid down a fairly straight line. The armor-piercing bullets provided plenty of punch to go entirely through the warehouse and exit on the other side.

"Duck!" Dalton yelled over the cacophony of ripping metal and machine-gun fire. It was hard to force the word out with the remaining bit of air left in his lungs.

She leaned down over him, flattening her body against his. Her breasts pillowed against his chest. The sensation was a hell of a lot more distracting than Dalton wanted it to be. His breath, when it returned, was ragged and filled with her scent—heady and sweet, a mixture of perfume and pure woman.

The line of fifty-caliber bullets blasted through the warehouse wall only inches above her head. The deafening noise pummeled them with a physical presence. He roped his free hand behind the woman's neck, pulling her down close to him, hoping to hell she didn't fire her pistol at him.

Frankly, he was surprised when she didn't because he'd seen a lot of trained soldiers lose their cool under that kind of fire, but it had been a gamble he'd had to take. He'd inadvertently bumped into her op and hadn't had the good sense to leave when the leaving was good.

She pushed up off him and glared down again. The distraction in those brown eyes told him she was listening to something he couldn't hear. He figured she wore a small radio, maybe even a com-implant because he couldn't see the device. She was a cop, but she didn't look like any cop Dalton had ever seen. Even the female MPs he'd gotten to know on more than a casual basis during his career around the world hadn't come across as forcefully and as quickly as this woman.

Her blond hair hung down to her shoulders. She was at least five-eight, maybe five-nine, with an athletic build that still didn't explain how she'd been able to pick him up and throw him fifteen feet with one hand. A moon-shaped scar showed under the left side of her chin. Her lips were thin but interesting, and her nose between those milk chocolate eyes offered challenge and impertinence. She wore a black Kevlar duster over a black sweater and slacks. Like him, she'd chosen a good pair of running shoes for the night.

The machine-gun fire continued out on the street, as did the *whump* of the artillery rounds. Splashes of light and twisting shadows lapped at the shattered remnants of the warehouse window. More light blasted in through the ragged line of bullet holes in the warehouse wall.

Dalton looked at her and spoke loud enough to be heard over the gunfire and explosions, "I can't stay and you've got to go. If you've got a team out there, and I'm sure you do, they need your help. Somebody's determined to send a message tonight." He paused to let that sink in. "So either we shoot each other or we let each other go. Me, I'm all in favor of letting go."

She cursed with an effortless fluency and gusto that would have done a drill sergeant proud. Then she said, "We let go." Her voice hardened as she made her threat. "But I'm going to remember you."

Likewise, lady, Dalton thought. He had the uneasy feeling he'd be seeing her again all too soon. He didn't know how to protect Grace and Michael from the woman and that bothered him. She represented as great a threat to Grace and her son as the men he'd come to the warehouse to find out about.

Listening to the familiar sounds of explosions and gunfire on the street outside, Dalton wondered how deep Grace had gotten in with the Triad killers before he'd found out about it. And he had no clue how he was going to confront her about it.

When the woman moved, it was with that same incredible speed she'd shown earlier. She had the grace of a dancer, every move effortless and sure. Before Dalton could get up, she was at the window. She held her pistol in both hands.

For a moment, the woman's beauty distracted Dalton. The glow of the explosions and the fires that had evidently caught below on the first floor drew her face out of the darkness. She wasn't the most beautiful woman Dalton had ever seen, but she was certainly the most memorable he'd met in years. Except for Grace.

Thinking that galvanized him. He put his hands behind his shoulders, drew his feet up and kicked them out, and flipped to his feet. His chest felt bruised and ached with the exertion.

Movement caught by his peripheral vision drew his attention down to the first floor at the back of the warehouse. He'd entered the building through there before hiding on the second-story landing above.

The eight men who now entered the door all wore field gear—Kevlar body armor and helmets, combat harnesses and bandoliers supporting extra magazines, and assault rifles as their lead weapons.

Definitely a scorched-earth campaign, he thought, knowing the attackers meant to kill everyone and destroy everything. *They hadn't come to take prisoners.*

"Hey, blondie," Dalton called as he dropped into a kneeling position, and cupped the pistol butt with his supporting hand. Wheeling instantly, the woman took him in, then followed his line of sight as he aimed at the first man in the group of new arrivals.

Hoping the woman was as good as he thought she was and didn't shoot him by mistake, he squeezed off two rounds as the first four men lifted their rifles and aimed at her.

The harsh reports of his Colt banged inside the warehouse, as he drew a bead on the next man's face. There was no hope of cutting through the invaders' bulletproof armor with the subsonic rounds the .45s were loaded with. The most he could do was split their attention.

His first two rounds had caught the lead man in the chest, punching him backward. Dalton had hoped for a head shot, but shooting down and into the darkness as he was made that difficult.

Five of the men fired at the woman. Bullets smacked into the wall behind her, striking sparks from the metal surface.

Standing on the second floor, which only covered half the first floor, she was exposed. Dalton expected her to go to ground; that move was the most sensible thing to do under the circumstances, but it would have left her trapped. Two of the enemy gunners ran for the stairs leading up to the second floor, obviously intending to flank her while she was pinned down.

Instead of going to cover, though, the woman ran for the second-floor railing. Her speed was incredible, her legs moved in a blur.

She's Enhanced, Dalton realized. That explained the speed she'd used earlier when she'd almost turned the tables on him. It also explained her strength. He was lucky he was as good as he was. Otherwise, she would have killed him.

The insight struck a sour chord within Dalton and brought back bitter memories. A lot of soldiers in Special Ops had been offered a chance at getting Enhanced. He'd turned down the opportunity. Flat. He believed that the technology, and the false sense of security the Enhancement had provided, had gotten a lot of men killed. A number of them had been his friends. One of them had been his best friend, Mac. He still remembered Grace's face when he'd given her the news about her husband's death. He shoved those memories away and concentrated on getting the woman and himself out of danger.

When the woman reached the railing, she hurled herself outward like an Olympic diver, bringing both hands in front of her on the pistol. She performed a half gainer with a twist, firing with pinpoint accuracy even while she was upside down in the air. Her rounds caught the lead gunner on the floor in the face, knocking his head back and pitching his body backward. The other gunmen had to duck back for cover as she emptied her pistol in a rapid staccato.

Finishing the dive, she landed on her feet and was already running for cover a heartbeat later. The gunmen fired, too, tracking her behind a line of crates, not able to keep up with the inhuman speed she exhibited.

Deciding he was seriously outgunned and knowing he couldn't dive down to the first floor with the same assurance that he would survive the twenty-foot drop as the woman had, Dalton turned his attention to the two men coming up the stairs. He stayed low and ran, holding his pistol in both hands.

The first man topped the stairs and stepped onto the second-floor deck just as Dalton threw his body into a baseball slide across the slick floor. One foot caught the gunman in the ankles while the other took out the guy's knees. Kevlar body armor or not, the joints weren't protected.

Something in the gunman's leg snapped and he screamed loud enough to be heard over the rapid fire roaring in the first-floor area.

Dalton came to a sudden stop as the gunman smashed against the wall beside the stairs. Rolling to his left but staying low, avoiding the instinctive impulse to rise up, Dalton shoved his pistol forward and targeted the second man's face.

Beneath the Kevlar helmet and night-vision goggles, the man's face showed Asian ancestry and hard features marred by a wicked scar on his right cheek.

Okay, that checks out with what Katsumi said, Dalton thought. Katsumi Shan had been the informant Dalton had used to find out about the drop site and Arturo Gennady. According to Katsumi, the people blackmailing Gennady consisted of Chinese gang members called the Bronze Tigers.

The gunman's night-vision goggles swiveled and targeted Dalton. From less than three feet away, Dalton fired. The muzzle flashes screamed green images across the night-vision goggle lenses and the man jerked backward. Even as the dead man fell, Dalton wheeled back to face the gunman he'd trapped up against the wall. Dalton fired his last two rounds into that man's face as well, then rolled into a crouch.

The dead man's arm slewed around and Dalton caught a glimpse of the protective plastic pocket sewn into the sleeve of the leather jacket. He looked closer. The pocket held a compact video unit that displayed two images of the beautiful blonde that had held him at gunpoint, one full face and one profile.

Damn it! They had this planned from the onset!

Dalton dumped the Colt's empty magazine on the floor, shoved a fresh one in from his pockets and picked up the empty. He didn't want to leave any fingerprints behind. He'd used gloves to load the magazines so no partial prints existed on the empty brass, either.

Hurrying, knowing firsthand that even though the woman was Enhanced she wasn't invincible, Dalton leathered his sidearm in the pancake holster belted at his back. He picked up the first dead man's assault rifle, dumped the partially used clip, and fed in a new one from the combat harness the man wore.

Sitting on the stairs, left leg folded up under him like he was back on the range at Fort Benning in Georgia, Dalton pulled the assault rifle to his shoulder and took aim at one of the two men circling around behind the crates. He dropped the sights over the back of the first gunman's neck, over the top of where the Kevlar vest would end, and squeezed the trigger. The man dropped like a puppet with its strings cut.

With both eyes open like the drill instructor in Ranger school had taught him, Dalton searched for his next target, catching the gunman as he turned around to see what had happened to his buddy. Dalton fired twice, a quick double-tap that caught the man at the base of the throat then again in his chin. He pirouetted and fell in a twisted shamble of limbs.

By then some of the gunners had figured out where Dalton was. With the heat turned up and bullets blazing his way, he figured it was time to go. He stripped a bandolier of magazines for the assault rifle from the dead man on the stairs and threw himself to the first floor. Bullets smacked the metal stairs and the dead man in his wake.

Dalton landed and rolled, moving quick and staying low, then got to his feet and ran for the nearest stack of crates. He slid into place behind the crates and listened, holding the assault rifle in an upright position with both hands so he could drop it quickly into target acquisition. He pushed the fire-selector to three-round bursts. Sniping wasn't going to cut it in the tight alleys between the cargo stacks.

Perspiration streaked his face under the electrostatic-cling mask. The cloth over his mouth restricted his breathing. But there was no way he was going to take the mask off and risk getting identified. He had to protect Grace and Michael. He'd given Mac his word on that.

Dalton was looking back to his right, watching out for pursuit, when he caught movement to his left in his peripheral vision. He turned his head, bringing the assault rifle around and down, and saw the gunman tight in against a stack of crates across the alley from him.

Not gonna make it this time, Dalton thought. But he didn't quit. He never had.

Hunkered down on a short stack of crates between two smaller ones on the first floor, Christie spotted No-Face as he slammed into place in the alley ahead of her. He'd taken out the men climbing the stairs, as well as two of them who had been hot on her tail.

She waited for just a moment, wondering what to do about him. She still couldn't believe how hard the gunmen had come after her, or how they'd known she was there. Dead silence echoed in her head, reminding her how used to the conversations channeling through her communications unit she was and how they were now missing.

The communications had been cut off almost immediately after the machine gunner in the helicopter had opened fire. She felt certain the signals were being shut down with a nearby frequency generator, an umbrella of disruption that had killed digital communications of all kinds. The encrypted frequencies used by the Bureau were even better than Washington, D.C. police and fire departments. However, before the shutdown had happened, she'd heard the yells of the men in her unit, screaming that they'd been hit or that they were under fire. She had no doubt that some of them were now dead.

Suddenly she spotted the gunman sneaking up on No-Face and bringing his rifle to bear. *The enemy of my enemy is my friend,* she told herself. It was an old axiom from Sun Tzu's *The Art of War.* Soundlessly, she leaped from the top of the crate, kicking out at the man's head and making solid contact.

The Kevlar helmet cracked the wooden crate beside the man. He went down in a loose-limbed sprawl. Christie landed on her feet just as No-Face pointed the assault rifle at the center of her chest.

They stared at each other, and Christie didn't know what the man was going to do.

"Nice save," No-Face said in a hoarse voice. He lifted the rifle to his side once more. "He had me cold. Keep your head up. You and I are getting out of here."

"Just like that?" Christie asked bitterly.

The face beneath the electrostatic mask moved and she bet he'd smiled. How the hell he could smile at a time like this she didn't know. *He didn't lose his team out there,* she told herself. *His friends and fellow agents aren't dead.*

"Close enough," he replied. "Do you know how to use an assault rifle?"

"Yes." That was part of Bureau training for field ops these days. Everybody else had assault weapons, so the FBI agents had to have them as well.

He stripped the assault rifle from the gunman's hands and tossed it to her. She slid her pistol into her shoulder holster beneath the Kevlar duster and worked the rifle's action.

"Check the magazine," he said as he stripped spare magazines from the unconscious man.

Christie did. The capacity indication holes showed twenty-five rounds were stored in the staggered magazine. "Full."

Without a word, he tossed her the bandolier of extra magazines. She caught it and stood there.

"Move," he said. "His two buddies are running a little scared right now, but you can bet they're regrouping. This is a scorched-earth mission designed to deliver a lot of casualties. Somebody's sending a message."

Christie hung the bandolier over her shoulder.

No-Face drew the unconscious man's silenced pistol, shot the man through the head twice, and dropped the weapon before she had any indication of what he was going to do. He turned to go like what he'd just done was nothing. The blank mask suited him to a *T* in that moment.

"Move out," he ordered.

Move out? The hell she would. She launched herself at him, letting free the dark anger that blossomed inside her.

Chapter 3

Christie slammed the rifle across No-Face's chest and knocked him back into the stack of crates. "What the hell did you just do?" she demanded.

She'd hit him so hard she'd knocked the wind out of him and he couldn't answer immediately. He hung against the crate with his feet inches off the ground.

"He was unconscious," Christie said. "You didn't have to kill him."

No-Face struggled to free himself and couldn't. He finally sucked in a deep, shuddering breath that rasped wetly. The mask section over his mouth hollowed, then pushed out as he managed to inhale then exhale. "You don't leave…a pissed off individual…behind when you're…executing a strategic retreat," he gasped. "Not if you…might have to…cover the same…territory. And that guy would…definitely have been… pissed off."

Horror and denial coursed through Christie. He wasn't going to ignore what he'd done, or try to call it anything other than what it was. "That was murder."

"That was survival," he countered, getting his breath back. "You don't leave an enemy alive unless you know you can leave him behind." He sucked in a deep breath.

"Do you plan on hanging around here till the rest of the group finds us?"

Men's voices drifted to her ears, calling out in Chinese as they cleared the warehouse section by section. They were getting close.

Reluctantly, Christie let him drop. He remained on his feet with effort.

"They were after you." He crossed to the dead man and yanked the corpse's arm into view. "Look."

Christie looked, spotting the video display in the protective plastic pocket on the sleeve. The screen showed her twice, full face and profile.

"They were hunting you," he said. "They knew you were here. You and your team were set up."

"How did they know?"

He let the arm drop. "I don't know. I'm still working that out."

"Who are you?"

He shook his head. "No. We had this conversation."

Christie started to square up with him. She needed answers and she needed them fast.

Lunging forward, he put a hand against her face, painfully squashing her nose with his palm, and shoved. She only thought about resisting for a moment, knowing she could have overpowered him with her Enhanced strength. The pain in her nose was too much. Her eyes watered. She went backward reluctantly.

"Move!" he shouted as he kept driving her. An instant later, bullets ripped into the crates they'd been standing in front of. He turned and fired the assault rifle one-handed, unleashing a stream of bullets that sprayed back into the alley he'd come through.

Knowing it would be foolish to fight against him,

Christie let herself be driven, turning and keeping her footing with difficulty.

They raced in a zigzag pattern through the stacks. Without access to her onboard computer and GPS mapping program, which continuously downloaded global positioning satellite information and let her know where she was, Christie was uncertain about the direction to take.

No-Face showed no hesitation at all. He moved through the maze of cargo like he'd lived there all his life, only doubling back twice when they inadvertently encountered enemy reinforcements. He knew the battlefield as if he'd laid it out.

He fired short, controlled bursts once they were moving, chasing the gunmen back and putting one of them down. Christie relaxed and fell into the same groove, drawing confidence from the way he moved and the way he led.

The last turn put her in view of the back warehouse doors. No-Face pulled her in against the line of crates without the three guards stationed at the door spotting them. The sea-green eyes regarded her.

"You're strong," he whispered.

Figuring he was looking for a response, Christie nodded. She wasn't breathing as hard as he was. Her lungs had been Enhanced as well, adding tiny micro oxygen scrubbers that kicked in when her adrenaline was pumping near max.

"Can you get me up there?" He pointed to the top crate twelve feet above.

Putting her assault rifle aside, Christie made a cradle of her hands and bent at the waist. "Can you land on your feet?"

"Usually do," he said, stepping into her hands and hanging on to his captured assault rifle with both hands.

Christie threw him at once, aiming him for the top of the stack. He flew up two feet past it, twisted in the air, and came down on his feet. He knelt and brought his rifle to his shoulder even as Christie reclaimed her own.

The guards had been watching for people on the ground. They hadn't looked up. No-Face fired quickly, aiming for the weak spots between the helmet and the shoulder pads of the body armor. From the height, his bullets struck home in two of the gunmen's lungs and spinal cords, killing them within seconds.

The third man ducked back and brought up his weapon, firing a torrent of bullets that drove No-Face to cover. He was carrying a SAW, a military M-249 5.56 mm machine gun designated as a Squad Automatic Weapon used for team support. It generally carried a two-hundred-round magazine. The Bureau had trained all agents working against gangs and hostile foreign corp security—which sometimes amounted to the same people—in heavy firepower.

We've got to get out of here before reinforcements arrive, Christie thought. They'd left the last gunman only a short distance behind, but by now the gang leaders must know the mission was in trouble.

She triggered the adrenal pump within her chest that flooded her system with adrenaline. The fight/flight chemical concoction Nature had invented had been refined in labs. For a few minutes, she was faster and stronger than ever.

Dashing around the corner of the cargo, she sped for the third gunman. Crouched down as he was, she knew shooting him would be almost impossible. In her adrenaline-laced condition, the man seemed to be moving in slow motion, the bullets individually spaced instead of a blur of muzzle flashes.

She'd crossed half of the fifty feet separating her from the gunman when he noticed her. He swiveled, trying desperately to bring the M-249 around. She heard No-Face's voice even over the hammering booms of the machine gun.

"Noooooooo!"

From the corner of her eye, she saw No-Face stand up atop the crates and try to pull the rifle into line. She was in the way, though, blocking the shot even if he had time to make it. The crate he was on was shot to hell.

Christie leaped, easily pulling her body up into a flying kick, poised perfectly. Her left foot smacked into the gunman's Kevlar-masked face just as a line of bullets cut the air beneath her. Her forward momentum drove the gunman into the wall behind him. He was unconscious before he slumped to the ground.

With her Enhanced sense of balance, a small amplification of the inner ear, Christie whirled in midair and landed on her feet facing back toward the center of the warehouse. She lifted the assault rifle and scanned the area with her night vision.

"Are you waiting for an invitation?" she asked. She knew her words came out fast, strung together by the adrenaline bouncing through her nervous system.

No-Face leaped from the top of the crates, dropped to the floor in a roll that brought him back to his feet and ran to her. She stood in front of the man she'd kicked unconscious, not giving him a chance to kill the fallen enemy. No-Face opened the door, shoved through and dropped into a crouch as he scanned the outside of the building.

"Clear," he shouted, and his voice seemed to come from a long way off.

Christie turned and bolted for the door, watching as the last gunman came into view. Bullets chased Christie outside. No-Face had already run to the end of the alley and taken up a defensive position.

She ran to him. *Safety in numbers. At least he hasn't tried to kill me yet.* And if he screwed up and got careless, she intended to put him in handcuffs despite the fact that he'd saved her ass a couple of times.

Before she reached him, he darted around the corner, legging up the alley to the front of the warehouse. She followed him, eating up the distance between them easily with the adrenaline in her system.

He was about to settle into position at the corner of the warehouse when machine-gun fire tore through the metal. Tracer rounds chewed craters in the street. The helicopter cut the sky above them like a shark slicing through a dark ocean.

Beyond the alley's mouth, Arturo Gennady's car continued to burn and that was just the centerpiece of hellish wrath that had descended on the immediate vicinity. All of the buildings had been hit. A cannon from the speedboat had razed all of the observation and camera points her team had taken up.

Pinned down in the alley, Christie watched helplessly as a second helicopter dropped out of the sky and hovered in the street near the burning car. The black-clad gunmen evacuated the warehouse on the double. Some of them carried bodies over their shoulders.

"Taking away their dead," No-Face said. "So you can't identify them."

Christie cursed, knowing he was right. In seconds, both helicopters vanished into the night sky.

"Can you contact your team?" No-Face asked.

Christie tried. Only silence echoed inside her head. "No."

"Your support team?"

"Nothing," she said.

Sirens screamed across the Potomac, coming closer. *You're already too late,* Christie thought bitterly, watching the flames twist and spiral in the gutted hollows of the buildings where her team had been.

She looked at No-Face, studying those sea-green eyes. A thin slice under his left eye wept blood and soaked the cloth of his mask. "Do you know who they are?" she asked.

He hesitated, then answered, "Not yet." He stood.

"Where are you going?" Christie stood as well. She felt vaguely nauseous and she cursed the adrenaline side effects she was about to go through. Her arms and legs and head felt heavy and her coordination was rapidly going. Flooding her body with adrenaline enabled her to do superhuman things, but the payback her system demanded was equally devastating.

"I'm going to take care of some business." He looked at her. "You took an adrenal pump with the Enhanced package?"

Stubbornly, Christie didn't answer him. She tried to lift the rifle.

"That was a mistake. The pump leaves you nothing." He moved too fast for her, knocking the rifle out of her hands. She reached for her pistol. He took that away and emptied it, flicking the bullets over the ground at his feet. He dropped the empty magazine and the weapon on the ground.

Christie leaned forward to pick them up and fell drunkenly to her hands and knees. She could barely hold her head up. An adrenaline pump was used only as a last resort, enabling the possessor one last frantic chance in a live-or-die situation. Using it during an on-going situation with no sign of relief meant being weak as a kitten if that situation continued past the pump's window. She'd had no choice back at the warehouse, and she had no choice now.

No-Face turned and gazed at the battle zone the docks had turned into. "I doubt any of your team made it out alive." He turned back to her. "There was nothing you could do about that. It wasn't your fault." He sounded like he felt sorry for her.

"Bastard." The epithet came out weak, with nowhere near the force she'd intended. If she could just keep him talking a few more minutes, gloating or feeling sorry for her or whatever the hell it was, either Fielding would have units available to take him down or she'd catch her second wind. She hoped it would be the second wind.

"Save it for the guys that did this." He started to walk away from her, then stopped as if he was unsure of what he was doing. "It was the Bronze Tigers Triad. I saw a tattoo on one of the men inside the warehouse. You want to vent some hostility or arrange a little payback, start there."

"I'm just supposed to believe you?"

"Yeah," he said. "I saved your ass up there—"

"I saved yours, too."

"Yeah, you did. So I owe you this one. It's always nice to know who your enemies are. Saves on a lot of confusion." He started walking away.

Trembling, trying hard not to throw up, Christie threatened, "I'm going to find you."

"Don't waste your time," he said. "Save it for the Tigers." Then he turned the corner and was gone.

Raising her head, fighting the vertigo that spun cease-
lessly inside her senses, Christie looked at Arturo Gennady's dead body lying out in the street. Tears filled her
eyes but she held them back. She wouldn't cry now, not
with Fielding's reinforcements on the way. But later, when
she was alone and no one was watching, she'd let go.

"Chace! *Chace!*"

Looking up, not believing she'd heard the voice,
Christie spotted Dwight Yeager stumbling through the
rubble toward her. Two other agents from the team
stumbled along in his wake.

Thank God, Christie thought. *Someone survived.* But
her thoughts turned dark at once. There was no getting
around the fact that they had walked into an ambush. All
the survivors were going to be suspect.

Including her.

Chapter 4

Dalton skillfully drove the motorcycle through downtown Washington, D.C. traffic on Wisconsin Avenue NW until he spotted the Adonis Club on the corner. Weaving through the traffic, he headed onto the side road that led to the parking area behind the club.

Three stories tall and covered with neon images of male strippers, the Adonis Club fit the urban decay that had settled over that area of the city. Other bars and sex clubs offering adult entertainment lined both sides of the street for blocks. Domestic and international politicians and corporation execs enjoyed partying in the red-light district, and the fixes were in with the metro law enforcement to make certain their activities were protected.

Dalton didn't care for the club or the area. It reminded him too much of the demilitarized zones where he'd spent time. Red-light districts didn't change much from Hong Kong to Singapore to Korea to Czechoslovakia. They all thrived on illicit commerce and weathered the constant fear of sudden death.

Hot, sluggish wind stirred through the city, spinning trash in miniature tornadoes. A mixture of music—rock and roll, blues, country and techno—slammed the neighborhood. The time was 12:32 a.m. and the red-light district was just getting its second wind.

Dalton wore wraparound sunglasses equipped with night-vision capability that stripped away the shadows hunkered in the alley. After leaving the Potomac commercial docks, he'd retreated to the rooftop of an abandoned building where he'd cached a change of clothes. Once he'd dressed in jeans, a dark green T-shirt, square-toed motorcycle boots and a leather riding jacket, he'd walked back to the parking garage where he'd left the motorcycle.

A huge video screen showed a nearly nude male gyrating on a polished onyx stage in front of offset mirrors that rendered shadowy echoes of the dancer. Purple lights pulsed over the sweat-slick body in motion.

Dalton paid at the front door, waving a disposable cash card with an equally disposable ID through the reader. One of the steroid giants working the door waved a wand over Dalton.

"No fighting, no rude behavior," the other bouncer stated. "The ladies are here to have a good time, not to be hassled by a guy figuring he's shooting fish in a barrel. You want to party, we have professionals upstairs to take care of that."

Dalton took no offense. The Adonis Club pandered to the female execs, diplomatic attachés and government assistants that sought out sex on the wild side. And to men looking for men.

"Sure," Dalton said.

"The reason I say that," the bouncer continued, "you don't look like a regular or a street hustler."

"I'll take that as a compliment."

The bouncer picked up a tattooing laser that issued

temporary imprints that faded out of the skin within hours. "Hand stamp."

Dalton shook his head. "Not going to be in that long."

Nodding, the bouncer lifted his left arm and spoke into the microphone concealed there. "One. Male. He's clean."

The front door led to a short passageway. A locked door at the end opened and thumping bass filled the hall. Two more bouncers greeted Dalton before they allowed him in.

The main room was filled with screaming women cheering on the naked men working three stages. Club scrip, paper money issued by the Adonis Club and paid for through debit and credit cards, littered the stage floors. Women, and the few men in evidence, paid for the privilege of having paper scrip to lure their favorite dancers over to them. Other men worked table dances and more amenable arrangements in the deep chairs on the right side of the club.

Monitors above the stages showed magnified views of the dancers so the attendees in the back wouldn't miss anything. The music was dirty blues, a low and throbbing beat that lent itself to suggestive movements and grinding.

Dalton turned to one of the bouncers. "I'm here to see Katsumi. Is she around?"

"She's in her office," the guy said. "If she wants to see you, she will."

Dalton walked toward the stairwell to the right that led to the second-story offices the club's owners used or leased out to businesses that fed off the club scene. Masseurs, escort services, tattoo artists and photography studios worked club hours and more.

Katsumi Shan kept an office there as well, but it was generally manned by automated services. Dalton had met her while he'd served in the military. Katsumi had been with the Central Intelligence Agency as a freelance information specialist and had functioned as a liaison for missions Dalton and his team had undertaken.

For a while, Katsumi and Dalton had been lovers, joined by similar interests in history and culture. Unfortunately, Katsumi had learned how to play both sides of the street and had sold almost as many secrets as she'd kept.

After she'd gotten bounced from the CIA, who hadn't wanted to deal with the grief she could bring to them if they tried to jail her or kill her, Katsumi had ended up going into business for herself. She'd bought—some said *blackmailed*—her way into a part ownership of the Adonis Club in Washington, D.C., gradually ending up there after knocking around Asia and Europe. The nation's capital, as she'd told Dalton, offered a number of intrigues. Katsumi lived for intrigues and secrets and behind-the-scenes power plays. That was why the CIA had enlisted her.

In addition to the income she derived from the Adonis Club, she also performed other services that tapped into her spy skills, working with some of the same people she'd gotten to know while liaising in other countries. From what Dalton had been able to learn, Katsumi dealt in security, spying and murder. None of that had been confirmed.

Dalton had met Katsumi again when, shortly after taking the security assignment with Grace and Michael, it had become clear that she'd been employed to spy on Grace's cybernetics work. Dalton had convinced her to pursue other assignments, though she'd never said who hired her. For a while, they'd renewed the physical relationship because they'd been good in bed together, but after Katsumi had offered to cut Dalton in on her business, bringing to the forefront the basic differences between their values, he'd found reasons to stay away from her.

Until he'd met with her three days ago and found out about the Bronze Tigers, Dalton hadn't seen Katsumi in over a year. He knew the only reason she'd given him the information that had led him to the scene at the warehouse tonight had been because it was no business of hers.

Now Dalton needed more information. He wanted to know why the Bronze Tigers had escalated the blackmail scheme to an assassination.

At the top of the stairs, Dalton buzzed Katsumi's door and waited. Dalton buzzed again. He grew impatient. Whoever the blonde was that he'd met back at the warehouse, she was both in trouble and was going to be trouble. But he hadn't been able to walk away without telling her about the Bronze Tigers. She'd deserved that.

And maybe it'll keep her busy enough to stay away from Grace and Michael, Dalton thought. But he couldn't help thinking about her. She'd been easy on the eyes and she'd impressed the hell out of him with her abilities.

He buzzed again.

No answer.

Apprehension crept into Dalton's mind. He opened the LokTek security pad to reveal the alphanumeric keypad. Katsumi had given him the current access code three days ago, stating that she hoped to see him again on something other than business.

He coded the door and it slid back soundlessly. The door closed behind him when he stepped into the large office lit by recessed lighting that left the interior dim.

Japanese decor, red betel nut finish mixed with ebony, replete with dragons and tigers, furnished the office. One wall was covered with a large aquarium that concealed the recording equipment Katsumi sometimes used to record prospective clients' eyes to use on optical locks. Large colorful koi swam slowly through the water. With the fourteen-foot ceilings in the room, the aquarium was as impressive as hell.

Katsumi kept private living quarters in the back that were equally as impressive.

"Katsumi," Dalton called over the low volume of the video screen pumping a twenty-four-hour news channel on the holograph at the center of the kidney-shaped desk. The scene showed the destroyed buildings in the Potomac commercial docks. An FBI spokesperson answered a reporter's questions. In the background, a picture of the blonde showed, listing her name as Special Agent Christie Chace. She looked young in the picture.

Dalton raised his voice and called for Katsumi again.

Silence answered him.

The apprehensive ball in Dalton's stomach coiled more tightly. Katsumi had been cagey while giving him the information about Arturo Gennady, telling him that just knowing about the blackmail plans was potentially lethal. He'd brought her a picture of Sammy Bao, one of the Bronze Tigers' chief enforcers and she'd immediately known who he was.

She'd called him that afternoon and let him know about the drop. Even though he'd asked, Katsumi hadn't told him how she'd found out about it. But she'd known about Gennady, too. Having a part ownership of the Adonis Club created a pipeline of information about corporate and political activity. Katsumi had a group of regulars in that club as well as in other sex-for-hire agencies that she employed to ferret out secrets.

Dalton wished he'd brought his pistol, but he knew he'd never have gotten it past the club security. Cautiously, he advanced on the open door leading to Katsumi's private quarters.

She hung nude from the large ceiling fan, a belt around her neck and her body slack in death. In life, she'd been petite, only an inch or two above five feet, with a slender figure that hinted at curves. She'd been thirty, two years younger than Dalton, but she could easily pass for half that. In her way, she'd been ageless. Her hair was cut spiky short and currently colored reddish-orange with gold tips. She was a gifted chameleon, could change her looks and her demeanor with the addition of a wig or a change of clothes. She'd loved fooling people.

That was over.

Grief hit Dalton hard. He hadn't been in love with Katsumi, hadn't even completely trusted her except for those times when he knew they had similar interests or when she had no reason to lie to him. But she'd been one of the ties to his past, one of the ties to Mac and the Ranger team. He was losing all of those.

And with Katsumi dead, Dalton knew the danger to Grace and Michael had multiplied. He focused on that and put his grief and anger away for the moment. He couldn't do anything for Katsumi, but he could protect Mac's family.

Blood hadn't yet pooled in Katsumi's lower body, so

she'd been killed in the last couple of hours. Bruises, cuts and scrapes covered her arms and legs, mute testimony that she hadn't gone without a fight.

Crossing over to the floor-to-ceiling video screen that covered the wall and pulling on his leather gloves, Dalton punched the keypad to blank the outside feed and keyed the code that activated the security system. The screen filled with snow, telling him the vid-capture program was off-line. Already knowing what he was going to find, he searched anyway, searching back through the vid-log.

The first image didn't show till 10:32 p.m. that night. Katsumi had been practicing her martial arts in the open space in front of the big circular bed in the middle of the room. The vid-feed turned to snow abruptly at 10:34.

She'd been killed shortly after that, maybe at the same time Dalton had been fighting for his life.

Damn, Katsumi. Was this connected to what you told me? Or was this something you got into on your own? Not knowing was potentially dangerous.

Dalton checked the video memory to see if the security system had recorded his arrival, intending to erase it if it had. Katsumi's system offered radical file purging. Not even an expert in computer forensics could recover files she'd erased. Only blank snow filled the screen. The system was still off-line. Maybe it would even look like it had failed out when police lab techs investigated later.

He took a last look at Katsumi and hated leaving her like that. But cutting her down would interfere with any chance the forensics team might have at discovering who had killed her. She'd fought. There might be physical evidence. He hoped so.

But Dalton's cynical nature told him a crime-scene team would find nothing. The Bronze Tigers hadn't left bodies of their own men behind at the warehouse. He doubted whoever killed Katsumi had been careless enough to leave evidence behind.

He turned and left. With Katsumi dead and the scorched-earth tactics at the warehouse, he knew the danger to Grace and Michael had grown. It was time to get home and batten down the hatches, maybe even see if he could talk some sense into Grace.

Chapter 5

"So you don't know who this guy was?" Director of Operations Stuart Fielding demanded.

"No," Christie replied as she watched the fire department rescue teams carry another body from one of the bombed-out buildings. Four of them had survived the attack. Bill Cather's injuries were going to put him out of the Bureau, though, and Jerry Templeton was going to be sidelined for a month working out rehab.

She and Fielding stood at the edge of the battle zone. Yellow police crime-scene tape surrounded the area. The D.O. had called in the metro units to work scene security and the fire departments to work search and rescue, but the Bureau forensics teams were going to process the scene.

Out in the river, police boats kept curious mariners away. The red and blue lights whipped through the darkness, layering bright slashes across the dark water and through the night. More gawkers lined the crime-scene tape but there weren't many of them. The commercial docks were a dangerous place to be at night, and sometimes during the day.

Scattered fires still hollowed the night out in three buildings. Three fire department pumping units had laid hose to the river, using the water there to extinguish the fires.

Two Bureau helicopters circled overhead, keeping the media copters from hovering. That didn't stop the long-range lenses, though. The D.O. monitored the live news releases on a video screen in the site command vehicle only a short distance away.

"This guy just comes out of nowhere and drops in on your stakeout?" Fielding said.

"He was already here when I got here," Christie said.

"My question is why was he here?"

Christie hesitated, then looked at her supervisor. "He was peeping them."

"Peeping them?" Fielding's interest showed. "Why?"

"He didn't say."

"Then guess."

"He was protecting someone."

"Who?"

"If I knew that, I'd know who he was."

Fielding craned his head. Vertebrae cracked and popped. "What makes you say that?"

"Because he tried to protect me. That's his nature."

Fielding didn't say anything.

"He could have cut and run when everything hit the fan," Christie said. "Instead, he stuck. His first instinct when the helicopter arrived with the machine gunner was to pull me to safety." She didn't tell Fielding that she'd knocked No-Face to the ground. "He backed every play I made inside that warehouse."

"That doesn't give us a lot."

"He was a pro," Christie said. "You'd have had to see this guy move." She saw him again in her mind, the diving and sliding, the way he'd handled both his pistol and the assault rifle. The quiet calm he'd radiated even in the heat of battle stayed with her. Even though she didn't know who he was, she was certain she'd met very few men like him. The only thing that jarred was the way he'd cold-bloodedly killed the man she'd knocked unconscious. "I had trouble keeping up with him and I'm Enhanced.

"When we find out who he is, we're going to find out he's had military service," Christie said. "Or maybe he's still in it."

"Corp security?" Fielding asked.

"Spying on Gennady?" Christie experienced a pang as she thought about the kindly old scientist again. He'd taken his life in his hands by reporting the blackmail attempt.

He put his life in my hands, Christie thought bitterly. *I failed him.*

I failed my team, too.

"Maybe spying on Gennady," Fielding explained. "If the blackmailers succeeded in getting the prototype from Gennady, maybe one of the corps figured on taking the prototype from the blackmailers. You could have run into the point man for an interception team."

"Then where were his buddies?" Christie asked.

"I don't know."

"They weren't there."

"Maybe they had orders not to interfere if things went sour. A lot of the independent teams work like that."

Christie knew that. Nearly half of her work with the Bureau had been engaged in following up on international industrial espionage cases in the United States and occasionally in military bases where government research was being done.

"I didn't get that feeling," Christie said.

Fielding was silent for a moment. "That may be, Special Agent Chace, but I can't very well follow up on this debacle going on your feelings."

"No, sir." Chastened, Christie barely restrained an angry retort. Fielding was right, but she was, too. "What about the Bronze Tigers?"

"All I have is your word on that. The video download from your onboard systems were down."

"We can explore the Bronze Tiger angle."

Fielding hesitated. "The Triads in the D.C. area usually manage protection, gambling and the sex rackets. They don't pursue industrial espionage."

Grimly, Christie looked out at the battle zone. "No disrespect, sir, but this wasn't a case of botched blackmail." She remembered No-Face's declaration that the attack had been a scorched-earth strike. "This was murder. The Bronze Tigers have been involved in several of those. We've managed to deport several of their enforcers and crime bosses for that."

Fielding rubbed his chin, then sighed. "Get a handle on one of them. You can try to shake something out of him. But I'm betting you won't get far." He paused. "I don't like sitting still any more than you do."

"No, sir."

"Let me know if you need anything from me."

"Yes, sir."

Fielding excused himself and walked over to the media representatives.

Christie didn't envy the D.O. the job of handling the media people. The task required more patience and tact than she was willing to invest. She forced herself to stay and watch the search-and-rescue effort even though

Fielding had cleared her to leave. Two bodies of team members had yet to be recovered. She wasn't leaving until they were all going home.

Some nights, Christie, her dad used to tell her when she started talking to him about going into law enforcement, *you're gonna just wish you could chuck it and walk away. Maybe you got it in your head now that you can do something to save lives, and—God willing—you will. But you'll see a lot of lives lost out there, too. Strangers, mostly. But you're going to lose some friends along the way, too.*

Her father had told her that the first time she'd ever mentioned following in his footsteps and being a cop. And he'd told her again the night she'd shown him the acceptance letter she'd received from the FBI. Reaction in the Chace household had been mixed. Her mom hadn't liked the idea of police work at all, and liked the idea of the FBI even less.

And when Christie had mentioned her interest in the Enhanced program, things had really gotten tense. Even though he didn't care for the new program, her dad had supported her decision in every way he could, but she had known he was afraid for her.

Christie took a deep breath. With all the media people around, she knew she was going to end up on several newscasts. Maybe for days to come. The murders tonight—and she refused to call them anything else— were the biggest news to hit the Washington, D.C. area in weeks. Once the Triad was linked to this, as she knew they doubtless would be, the story would receive even more interest and exposure.

Gennady's family would blame her for his death. Christie knew she had to accept that. Moreover, she didn't blame them.

She wished she could go home, to her parents' home, and talk to her dad in the kitchen the way they always did when the subject matter was something involving his past and her present professions. She didn't want to have to face the idea of returning to her apartment and spending the night alone.

When you can't do anything about the past, her dad had always told her, *concentrate on what you can do about the future. See if you can find a way to turn it around.*

Christie concentrated on that, finding a way she could turn Gennady's death around. Someone was going to pay for the man's murder. And she intended to hold No-Face accountable, too.

"C'mon, Dalton, show me the heat!"

Despite the tension and all the unresolved issues regarding last night's action and Katsumi's murder that still filled him, Dalton couldn't help but smile a little as he faced the confident young batter guarding the plate. For nearly three years, he'd helped guide and nurture Michael Reynolds, watched him grow from a seven-year-old boy shattered by his father's death into a confident and articulate ten-year-old. Dalton felt good knowing he was part of that change.

"C'mon!" Michael crowed, waving his bat to show that he was ready. "Show me that stinky cheese!"

Well, Dalton amended, *articulate most of the time.* He scuffed the rubber with his baseball cleat, dug in, then put the ball behind his back. He leaned forward and squinted at Michael.

The boy's smile grew wider in anticipation. An Atlanta Braves batting helmet covered his normally unruly chestnut hair. He was average-size for a boy his age, but he was built lanky, already handsome and the spitting image of Captain Mackenzie Reynolds. Summer had sprinkled freckles across the bridge of Michael's nose.

"Here it comes." Dalton moved his fingers over the baseball behind his back, tracing the seams by touch till he got the grip he wanted. Then he brought his hands together, covering the ball with the glove, stepped into the pitch and threw.

Michael lifted his left leg, drove forward, set and swung, twisting his hips and following through the swing naturally. Dalton took pride in the boy's abilities. He'd taught him not only the mechanics of the game, but the love of it as well.

The bat met the ball with a metallic crack. Immediately, the ball came back at Dalton but well out of his reach. He lifted his glove and watched it go over. The sheer power of the hit carried the ball into the deep grass beyond the baseball diamond carved out of the surrounding forest.

"Home run!" Michael yelled. "Out to the grass is a home run!" He tossed the bat to the ground then jogged around the bases, whooping and hollering with glee.

Smiling, Dalton watched the boy. They'd created the baseball field themselves, mowing and removing trees and stumps and rocks a few months after Dalton had signed on as security for Dr. Grace Reynolds. The first few weeks, there had only been the batter's boxes and a pitching mound, and little involvement from the boy. But Dalton had stayed at it, hoping to lure Michael out of his grief. Ultimately, the field had healed his own as much as it had the boy's. As Michael's interest in the game grew, so did the field. Now they had sixty-foot baselines and a deep outfield.

"Enjoy it while you can, kid," Dalton threatened. "Next year the baselines are gonna be ninety feet. The outfield is gonna be farther out."

"Just like the pros," Michael whooped as he rounded third.

Next year. The words echoed in Dalton's head, underscoring the images of the violence at the warehouse and Katsumi hanging in her own bedroom. Next year would have to wait. They hadn't gotten through this year yet.

"Give me another one," Michael shouted as he picked up the bat and stepped into the box.

"Ten more," Dalton said, "then break's over and we get back inside and hit the books."

"Awww, Dalton." Michael frowned.

"Them's the rules, kid." Dalton had learned to be firm despite Michael's best wheedling. That had been one of the hardest skills he'd ever had to learn.

After batting practice—and only token pleading on Michael's part—they picked up the baseball gear, packed it in the big equipment bag and headed back to the cottage next to the main lab.

The compound consisted of seven buildings: the lab, Grace's cottage, Dr. Lance Watterson's cottage, an apartment complex for the lab assistants, a barracks for the security teams, a cafeteria and the garage for the vehicles. A twelve-foot fence, electrified and topped with razor wire, surrounded the complex.

Thick forest walled the lab from the rest of the world, part of Virginia's Jefferson National Forest only a few miles from Roanoke. Grace had insisted on a place of her own to work after Michael had been born, a place where her son could grow in at least a semblance of normal life. Her work was important enough that the government had agreed in the end. They'd moved Grace to the complex nine years ago, once the resident researcher had finished his contracts.

Even before she'd married Mackenzie Reynolds fourteen years ago, Grace had been an up-and-coming cyberneticist who had caught the eye of the Defense Advanced Research Projects Agency and the National Security Agency. DARPA and the NSA had jointly recruited her and paid for the research and development she did from combined funding.

By the time she'd agreed to the government contract, Grace had already introduced several radical concepts for integrating cyberware into the human body. With dual degrees in biology and cybertechnology, coupled with genius and vision, she would have been in demand in dozens of places. She'd chosen to serve her country's interests. She strove to reach a full marriage of the tech and the flesh so that an Enhanced individual was no longer a composite but was a true hybrid.

Mac had met Grace fifteen years ago, when he and other Rangers posted at Fort Benning had volunteered for the aggressive military Enhanced program only then in its infancy. The systems at that time had primarily been aimed at installing vision and hearing enhancements, as well as encrypted communications systems inside the body. The Enhanced musculature and reflexes had still been in the conception stage because they were much more invasive.

Dalton followed Michael into the small kitchen Grace maintained in the Reynoldses' cottage. As Grace and Michael's primary bodyguard, Dalton had his own quarters in the cottage. By no means spacious, the three of them would have been tripping over each other had Grace not spent as much time in the lab as she did.

Michael dropped his gear on the kitchen floor and opened the refrigerator. Before Dalton could tell the boy to pick it up, a hologram formed above the surface of the breakfast bar.

"Michael Christopher Reynolds, do not litter that kitchen with your baseball gear."

Sheepishly, Michael picked up his bat bag and cleats. "Hi, Mom," he said. "I just forgot for a minute. It's no biggie."

Grace Reynolds's holographic image looked just like her, but it was only a foot tall. She wore her dark hair down to her shoulders but usually kept it pulled back. With her work consuming so much of her life, she adhered to a strict regimen when it came to her son and her health. She worked out three days a week, and she never missed breakfast or dinner with Michael. Sometimes she was up at four and back to the cottage by seven to prepare her son's breakfast, and sometimes she returned to the lab after dinner and whatever extracurricular activity she and Michael had decided on, but she never missed those family times.

She was a beautiful woman, though she never gave more than passing attention to her appearance these days. As usual, she wore a white lab coat over a white sweatshirt and black sweatpants. Losing Mac had taken a lot out of her, and Dalton was convinced that she'd never found a way to truly let go.

Maybe I haven't either, Dalton thought. Work consumed most of Grace's life these days, and Dalton had been surprised to learn how much time a growing boy could take up. Neither of them had moved on from

Mac's death. Even Katsumi's attentions had only lasted as a short diversion.

When Mac had still been alive, Dalton had sometimes accompanied his commanding officer home on leave. They'd hunted and fished together, bringing Michael along when the boy was old enough. Occasionally, work and guilt permitting, Grace had joined them, though she'd never been far from her computer and communications with her lab. During those times, Dalton had gotten to know Mac's family. When Mac had been killed, Dalton had arranged for temporary leave to help the family through their loss.

Dalton's own family was gone. The death of his father when he was seventeen had sent Dalton to the U.S. Army recruiting offices. The Army had taken him three months before his eighteenth birthday. If Dalton hadn't joined the Army, he'd have been made a ward of the court, taken from the job he'd had for two years, then turned out on his own.

The few months Dalton had intended to stay with Grace and Michael had become nearly three years. The Army had bridged his service, assigning him as Grace and Michael's chief bodyguard. Grace had seen how Michael was responding to Dalton's attentions and had taken steps to have that adjustment made. She had considerable pull with the government due to the breakthrough work she was doing.

"It is a biggie, young man," Grace admonished.

"Okay, Mom," Michael said.

"How did baseball practice go?" The holographic view showed part of the cybernetics lab behind Grace.

"Baseball practice was great," Michael declared. "Dalton's turning into a real rag-arm."

"Rag-arm?" Grace's eyebrows lifted.

"A baseball term," Dalton said quickly. Language was an important thing with Grace. "It means he thinks I'm becoming substandard."

"Yeah," Michael said. "His fastball has lost its zip. His curve doesn't have as much movement on it."

"I see." Grace smiled. "Perhaps it's time we had Dalton into the lab for an upgrade."

Dalton didn't say anything. Grace pursed her lips quickly, realizing her mistake. Dalton hadn't cared for the Enhanced program in the beginning. He cared even less for it after Mac and most of the team had been wiped out.

"Nah," Michael said. "I think I'm just seeing the ball better." He flexed an arm, making his bicep pop up a little. "And I'm getting stronger. Dalton's just not a professional pitcher. Those guys could probably still smoke 'em by me."

"I'm glad to hear that you two are enjoying yourselves," Grace said. "But I don't want you to neglect your studies."

"I won't. I'm about to head over." Michael had a professional teacher every day.

"See you later, slugger," Grace called.

"Bye, Mom." Michael trotted off to his room to drop off his gear.

Hesitant, but knowing he couldn't put it off any longer, Dalton said, "Grace, you got a minute?"

Grace looked at him. Dalton seldom interrupted her routine.

"A minute," she agreed. "We're getting ready for the prototype we're supposed to get a week from Friday."

"I know." Dalton had upped the security for the arrival. Grace had acted nervous about the event for a week. Three days ago, Dalton had figured out why.

"I need to talk to you soon," Dalton said.

"About what?"

"I'd rather go into it later." Dalton heard approaching footsteps in the living room. "And I'd rather we were alone."

Grace shook her head and looked troubled. "I don't know. Things right now…" She took a deep breath. "Things right now are very hectic. There have been some complications with the delivery."

Yeah, Dalton thought, *I can see where Arturo Gennady getting himself dead could be a problem.* So far, though, Grace hadn't brought that up to him. Since he'd gotten in early this morning, she'd been in the lab. There were days that she did without sleep.

"As soon as you can," Dalton said. He knew better than to press her while she was in the lab. Only Michael could deflect her from her work. "It's important, Grace."

One of the lab techs behind Grace called for her attention.

"All right," Grace acquiesced. "After dinner tonight."

Dalton took it because he knew it was all he could get.

As Grace's holograph faded, Dalton thought about the attack last night that had left Dr. Arturo Gennady and five FBI agents dead. He wondered what Special Agent Christie Chace was doing. He was convinced that Chace wasn't the kind of woman that would walk away from something just because the going got rough.

He'd thought about her a lot during the sleepless hours after he'd arrived back at the compound. He remembered how she'd felt atop him, and he knew how much trouble she could be if she ever figured out who he was. The push/pull of caution and attraction warred within him. He wouldn't mind seeing the FBI agent again, but not when it was going to threaten everyone he was trying to protect. And he was sure that trouble was what Special Agent Chace would bring.

Chapter 6

"Sammy Bao." Christie put steel in her voice, talking over the noise of the restaurant conversations. Since she also carried a 12-gauge automatic shotgun across her heavy Kevlar vest, attention came quickly and silence followed.

A dozen FBI agents followed her on the takedown. All of them were similarly attired and carried military weapons.

The Bronze Tiger Triad owned the Hong Kong Noodle Restaurant. Of course, the ownership was concealed by a chain of shell companies and documents filled with enough legalese to occupy a phalanx of attorneys. The restaurant was also, unofficially, off-limits for any kind of criminal or law enforcement activity. It was a no-man's-land where the local police and the Triad could work out differences and agree on who was going to take the fall for an agreed-upon degree of infraction of the law.

Everyone in the restaurant froze as the clientele drew in a collective breath.

A fat man in a black business suit stood up in the back. He made a production out of folding his red napkin and throwing it onto his table in disgust. He approached Christie, looking angry.

"Who are you?" the man demanded.

"Special Agent Chace of the Federal Bureau of Investigation." Christie tapped the photo ID hanging from a stainless steel necklace around her neck. She didn't lower the shotgun. She wore camel-colored slacks, boots and a Kelly green poplin blouse. Her shoulder holster showed prominently because she'd left her jacket in the car outside. She'd pulled her hair back in a twist. Wraparound sunglasses hid and protected her eyes but didn't interfere with her Enhanced vision. "I've got a warrant for Sammy Bao. That's him sitting at the table you just left."

At the table, Sammy Bao showed no sign of being concerned. He had jet-black hair and a matching gunfighter mustache. According to his file, he was in his late twenties and was suspected of several heinous crimes in addition to nine unsolved murders. No witnesses had ever shown up to testify against him. He wore a neon-blue jacket over a black turtleneck, black slacks and shiny black shoes. He steepled his hands in front of him. A casual observer might have thought he was praying. Christie knew that he was bored. The sleeve fell down enough to reveal the gold Rolex on his left wrist.

"Nonsense," the fat man said. "This kind of thing is not done here."

"It is today," Christie told him.

"I am Wo Fat, the owner of this place. I will allow no disrespect to be shown to any of my guests. We have an agreement with—"

"You don't have an agreement with me," Christie said.

The man barked commands in Chinese. "Do not allow this to happen in my place of business. I will not tolerate this insult."

Half a dozen men at the back of the restaurant stood up. Sammy Bao remained seated, smiling slightly in amusement.

From the cut of their jackets, Christie knew the men were armed.

Wo Fat faced her and smiled unpleasantly. "As you can see, Special Agent Chace, you are not welcome here. Now you need to leave before—"

Moving with Enhanced speed, Christie shifted the shotgun up and planted the muzzle over Wo Fat's nose while she grabbed the man's shirtfront with her free hand. She'd spent last night and most of the morning and afternoon talking with the husbands, wives and significant others of those of her team who had been killed last night. And she'd been racking her brain trying to find a way to track down the man with sea-green eyes and commando moves.

"Sammy Bao is coming with me," Christie said in Chinese. "That's nonnegotiable. If you do one more thing to stop me, I'll arrest you for interference. Do you understand?"

The fat man's eyes narrowed in anger, but there was a lot of fear in there, too. "You are making a big mistake." His flat eyes cut to her ID. "Special Agent Christina Chace."

"If your little entourage doesn't take their seats," Christie said in a cool voice, "it'll be the last mistake you get to watch me make."

"You would shoot me?" Surprise sent Wo Fat's eyebrows climbing and his mouth made a shocked *O*. Maybe his position in the Bronze Tigers meant he hadn't been personally threatened in so long he'd forgotten what the experience was like.

"In a heartbeat," Christie said, never taking her eyes

off the man. She told herself the situation was different than the one No-Face acted on. Wo Fat wasn't unconscious, and he was definitely a threat.

"Stay!" Wo Fat barked, throwing out a hand to the advancing men.

His men froze.

Christie showed him a cold smile even though her stomach was queasy. In less than twenty-four hours, she'd stepped into two life-threatening situations.

"You've got them trained well," Christie said. "Now tell them to sit."

Wo Fat issued the command. The men returned to their seats.

"Sammy Bao," Christie called.

Bao laughed and applauded. He got up from his seat and walked over to her. "It's all right," he told Wo Fat. "Please keep my meal warm. I won't be long."

"Hands," Christie ordered.

Bao thrust his hands out. Christie had one of the agents cuff Bao's hands behind his back. A quick frisk turned up two 9 mm pistols in a double shoulder rig under the neon-blue jacket.

"Do you have a permit for these?" Christie asked.

Bao smiled confidently at her. "Sure. My mother said I could bring them."

"Let's go," Christie said to the agent holding on to Bao. "Take him. I'll be right behind you." Once her team had cleared the restaurant, she walked out backward, keeping Wo Fat at the business end of the shotgun. She'd upped the ante. Now it remained to see how the hand played out.

After dinner, when the dishes had been washed, dried and put away, and Michael had been sent off to bed,

Grace asked Dalton what he wanted to talk about over coffee at the breakfast bar.

Dalton hesitated. He was about to step onto the most dangerous ground he'd ever been on in his relationship with Grace and Michael. It *was* a relationship, too. He'd acknowledged that some time ago, though he couldn't point to a date on a calendar or an hour on a clock.

"Dalton?" Grace looked at him with concern. She was tired and on edge. She'd been that way for days. Looking back on events, Dalton realized she'd been in that state for longer than he could recall.

He tried to open his mouth and couldn't. He took a deep breath instead.

"Maybe I can make this easier for you," Grace suggested. "You've been here almost three years. That's a long time. You're a young man. You've got your whole life ahead of you. If you've been offered another position, or if you just want to move on, trust me when I say that I understand."

God, she's making this hard. Dalton hated what he was about to do.

Grace hurried on, looking more agitated than before. "After Mac was..." She stopped. "After Mac *died,* I think we needed each other. Michael needed you, too. Having you here, Dalton, it's been a godsend. Truly. I don't know how we would have managed. Every morning when I walk to the lab and I see that baseball field you and Michael built, or I hear about the baseball games you guys have managed to get up with the people here, I realize how much of a difference you've made in his life." She paused. "How much of a difference you've made in *our* lives. But I won't stop you from getting on with your life. I'll give you the best recommendation possible and you'll go with my blessings."

"Grace," Dalton said softly, dreading what he had to do.

She looked up at him.

"I'm not leaving," Dalton said.

She took a deep breath, appearing confused and relieved all at the same time. "All right."

"What do you know about a man named Sammy Bao?" Dalton's stomach flipped like he'd just stepped off into a free fall. Only he was used to free-falling from Ranger jump school. This was something totally new and it scared the hell out of him.

Grace's answer came instantly and with a little puzzlement. "I don't know anyone by that name."

Dalton opened his phone/PDA, opened the razor-thin leaves that unfolded into an eight-by-ten digital screen and activated the image storage function that pulsed a static charge to smooth the image. Only a fraction of an inch thick, the leaves smoothed out instantly, pixelating into a solid, seamless image with an Atlanta Braves screensaver. He pressed both thumbs against the upper corners of the screen, letting the scan function read his prints. The device was military issue. If anyone got hold of the PDA, no one would guess at the hidden features, and even if someone found them, they couldn't be reached without Dalton's permission.

Or at least both thumbs.

The device accessed the off-site intel dump he'd set up and brought it forward. He tapped the screen and a picture of Sammy Bao filled the viewing surface. The image was a head and shoulders shot Dalton had gotten from an information source still within the Rangers who had raided the National Crime Information Center for background materials on the man. Katsumi hadn't been Dalton's only resource, but she had initially identified the Bronze Tiger lieutenant.

"Where did you get that?" Grace demanded.

Dalton watched her, feeling scared and guilty at the same time. Grace was his friend. She was his best friend's widow.

And she was Michael's mom.

"This man," Dalton said, "is a Triad member. Do you know what that is?"

"Where did you get that?" Grace's voice turned hard and cold.

Despite the fearful reluctance that thrummed within him, Dalton pressed on. "Chinese Triads are crime families. This man, Sammy Bao, is one of the most dangerous men working for the Bronze Tigers. He's a murderer several times over."

"Dalton." Grace slid off her stool and stood facing him, her arms wrapped tightly around herself.

Dalton recognized the tone in her voice immediately. It was the one she used with Michael when she wasn't about to put up with one more excuse or continued evasion. He tapped the screen again and pulled up another image.

This one showed Grace in front of the ice-cream shop down the street from the virtual reality arcade where Michael liked to play games during their monthly sojourn into Roanoke, Virginia. The government contractors provided everything Grace wanted or needed, but she still took Michael into town for a movie and shopping once a month so he wasn't totally cut off from civilization. Bao stood talking to Grace beside a dark sedan whose license plates had led Dalton to a dead end.

Other images followed, showing Grace talking to Bao. She clearly hadn't been happy about the encounter.

On that day, Dalton had started down the street, leaving Michael with the secondary security man. By the time Dalton had gotten to where Grace stood, Bao and the sedan had gone. Grace had merely said Bao had been someone asking for directions.

"Grace," Dalton said gently. "I need to know what's going on."

"Don't," Grace said. She held a hand over her mouth and looked sick.

"Let me help," Dalton said. "Please, Grace. Let me help with this."

She shook her head, unable to speak for a long time. "You can't help."

"Did Bao threaten you?" Dalton knew that Grace would never sell out her work or her country.

Tears spilled down Grace's cheeks. The sight hurt Dalton. It was the first time he'd seen her cry since Mac's funeral.

"That man told me that he would…" Grace stopped. Her hands shook as she tried to hold herself.

"He threatened you?" Dalton asked.

She shook her head and whispered hoarsely, "Michael! He threatened to hurt my baby!"

The sick feeling that flooded through Dalton took the edge off his anger. His knees felt weak and he was glad he was sitting. He made himself speak but he hated the strained note in his voice. "They can't hurt Michael." He tried to make himself sound confident and knew he was failing. "He's safe here, Grace. Both of you are safe."

She looked at him and the tears stopped. Anger filled her eyes. "This man—Bao, whatever his name is—had pictures. Of you, Dalton. And Michael. In the baseball field. He told me a sniper in the forest could kill my son or leave him paralyzed. Whichever he told them to do."

Dalton felt the world tilt. The compound had been designed to keep people *out,* not as a fortress to keep people inside from being hurt. "That's not as easy to do as he makes it sound, Grace. Believe me. Michael is—"

She cut him off angrily. "Damn you! Don't you dare tell me my son is safe!"

"We can leave," Dalton said. "We can go right now."

"They have people watching," Grace moaned. "They have people watching all the time. Even if I left, this man said they would track us down—he insisted they had ways of finding us—and they would kill Michael anyway. He said they had given their word that they would do this."

The hopelessness in Grace's eyes crushed Dalton.

"You've heard me talk about Arturo Gennady?" Grace asked.

Dalton nodded. Over the past several weeks, Gennady's work had been showcased in the media. "Yes." And Dalton knew immediately where she was going.

"He was killed last night," Grace said. "Bao and his men, the Bronze Tigers or whatever they are, they killed Arturo because he tried to set them up for the FBI."

"You don't know that." Dalton knew his argument was weak, but it was all he had. "Bao could have been lying."

"He wasn't lying!" Grace struggled to control herself. "I received digital images of Arturo standing beside his car in Washington, D.C. last night. At the docks where he was killed."

"Gennady played it wrong. He shouldn't have been

there. The FBI should never have asked Gennady to be there." Dalton was angry with the young woman, Special Agent Christina Chace, because her botched operation made convincing Grace even harder now. Gennady *shouldn't* have been there, but Dalton also knew it was the only way Chace could have pulled off the sting. "We shouldn't be talking. We should be getting Michael out to the car and getting the hell out of here."

"No." Grace's voice was firm. "That man meant what he said—he will have Michael killed or harmed. I can't bear that. Not after losing Mac." She shook her head. "I can't leave. We can't leave."

"That's not true," Dalton told her. "Grace, believe me—"

"Believe you?" Grace stared at him. "You once told me you'd bring my husband back. Don't you remember that?"

Dalton had. That had been years ago, battles ago. He'd been young and cocky at the time. He didn't know that Grace had even remembered him promising that. Since Mac had been killed, that promise had haunted him every day.

"Safe and sound, you said." Tears flowed down Grace's cheeks again. "You didn't."

The accusation was damning.

"You failed me once," Grace told him. "I won't let you fail me again."

Dalton didn't know what to say, didn't even know if he could speak past the lump in his throat. Grace had never before blamed him for Mac's death in that firefight, never before even questioned why he had lived and Mac hadn't.

"You are not going to do anything about this," Grace told him. "Do you hear me?"

Dalton nodded.

Grace took a deep breath. "And if you do anything, anything at all to jeopardize this situation—" She stepped toward him. "—I swear to God that you will never see Michael again. Is that clear?"

Dalton looked at her. "Yes." There was no other answer he could give. He knew she meant what she said.

Without another word, Grace turned and left.

Sitting at the table, not knowing what he was supposed to do, Dalton felt as hurt and helpless as the night Mac had died in his arms.

Chapter 7

Christie stood at the one-way glass in the observation room looking into the interview room she'd taken at Bureau headquarters. A chill filled the dark observation room and the coffee she sipped didn't relieve much of it.

On the other side of the one-way mirror, Sammy Bao sat at a small metal table surrounded by blank walls. Digital and audio equipment staggered all around the room recorded everything. He affected a relaxed, even bored, attitude. For all Christie knew, that was how he felt. Sammy Bao was a stone killer, one of the few that Christie had met personally during her time with the FBI.

D.O. Fielding entered through the side door. He looked at Christie, then at Bao. "Crack him yet?"

"Haven't even been in to see him yet," Christie admitted. "I thought maybe he needed some time alone."

"Looks like he's fine with that."

"I know."

Bao yawned and went back to staring at the one-way mirror.

"I'm beginning to think that he likes looking at himself," Christie said.

"You didn't arrest him?"

"No. Brought him in as a material witness. That's why he's not shackled and in an orange jumpsuit."

"Material witness for what?"

"Two of the murders he probably committed crossed state lines. He had connections to the victims. I thought I would explore that with him."

"The D.C. district attorney's office has already explored those murders with him."

"The Bureau hasn't."

"We let D.C., Maryland and Texas take the leads on those murders as I recall."

Christie knew that Fielding had reviewed Bao's files before coming down to the observation room. He was thorough. "Yes, sir."

"They couldn't make their murder cases," Fielding said.

"No, sir."

"Investigating the murders at this point could be construed as harassment if we're not careful."

By *we,* Christie knew he was talking about her. "Yes, sir. But I'm not investigating the murders."

Fielding looked at her.

"Those two murder victims were transported across state lines against their will," Christie explained. "That's kidnapping. Kidnapping is totally within the Bureau's purview."

"Yes," the D.O. said with a slight smile. "Yes, it is, Agent Chace. And you think Mr. Bao might have some information to share regarding that matter."

"I also feel someone might have threatened him. That's why he's reticent about coming forward with information about those two murders."

"Carry on, Agent Chace. But be warned—Bao's attorney is cooling his heels in my office right now. You've got maybe twenty minutes with Bao before we have to charge him or let him go. As I recall, we don't have any evidence to hold him."

"Yes, sir." Christie threw her coffee cup in the trash and followed Fielding out into the narrow, sterile hallway. Fielding went left, back toward his office, and Christie nodded to Agent Perez, who was working as her second on the interview.

Christie led the way into the room. Her shoulder holster hung empty because she'd checked her service pistol as per standard operating procedure. S.O.P. was designed to protect all the agents in the holding area.

Bao didn't look up. He stated flatly, "I suppose my attorney is here and this little charade is at an end."

Tossing the files onto the interview table, Christie remained standing. Bao started to stand as well. She stuck a leg behind his, put her hand to his chest and shoved him back into his chair.

"Class isn't dismissed yet," Christie said.

Bao laughed, but anger glinted in his eyes. "What do you want, Agent Chace?"

She questioned him for forty-seven minutes, straight and without finesse, hammering him with question after question. She covered the two murder cases, stated her convictions that Bao was part of the kidnapping and probably part of the later murders.

Bao denied all of it. He admitted to knowing both the victims, seeming to take pride in the fact that she could come that close to him but no closer. He never once asked for his lawyer.

Someone rapped on the door.

"Come in," Christie said, feeling frustrated but working hard not to show it.

Agent Osborn, one of the newbies, stuck his head in the door. "D.O. says time's up with this one. His lawyer is here making noise. Charge him or let him go."

Bao stood and smiled. "Well then, Agent Chace. This has been…interesting." He shrugged. "Maybe next time we can do this at my convenience. At a place of my choosing. A lawyer will be of no use to you then or there, I assure you."

Christie intercepted Bao before he reached the door, stepping in front of him and going nose to nose with him. They were the same height so she stared him in the eyes.

"Why did you kill Arturo Gennady?" Christie demanded. "He was an old man."

Bao returned her level gaze. "I don't know what you're talking about."

"You knew it was a sting," Christie went on. "All you had to do was not show up."

Bao looked at the other two FBI agents as if wondering if they knew what she was talking about.

Thinking about the dead agents and all the phone time she'd logged that morning and afternoon talking to grieving loved ones, Christie barely resisted punching Bao in the face when he turned back to her and shrugged. "You made a mistake. If you hadn't tried to cowboy that stakeout and kill my people, we'd never have known who you were," she said.

"What makes you think it was me or my family?"

"I saw the Bronze Tiger chops tattooed on one of the men." It was the same lie Christie had told Fielding. And she was basing it all on No-Face's word.

"Other men wear such tattoos," Bao replied.

"No they don't. Bronze Tigers don't let anyone wear

their chops. And if anyone tries to leave your *family,* you kill him."

"You must like fairy tales, Agent Chace."

"Only the ones where the good guys win."

"I'm surprised that you believe in bogeymen."

"They believe in you, too. I'm sure your soldiers told you about the masked man that was with me."

Bao's eyes narrowed, showing the first sign of interest Christie had seen.

"You don't know who he is, do you?" Christie taunted. "But he knows who you are. And he doesn't strike me as the kind of man who goes away until he's finished with something." *Not at all,* she thought, remembering those sea-green eyes and obvious combat experience. "I'm pretty sure he's not finished with you."

"Mr. Bao, you don't have to stay in there any longer." The speaker was a young man in an expensive suit who stood out in the hallway holding on to an expensive PDA that he carried like a badge of office.

Bao waved the young attorney away. He kept his eyes fixed on Christie. "You're inventing another myth."

Christie gave him a cold look. "Am I? Your soldiers had us wired. I saw my picture on a vid-flash on the sleeve of one of them. You knew Gennady wasn't giving in to the blackmail pressure from the Bronze Tigers. You knew my team would be there. You intended for all of us to die."

"Again, Agent Chace, I don't know what you're talking about. If you should feel inclined to talk to me about this matter in the future, arrange it through my attorney. I'll make sure he leaves you his information." Bao turned to go, then stopped himself. "One other bit of advice I would like to give you. Because you have been so charitable to me."

Christie waited. *Every time he opens his smug mouth, he's giving you information. Just remember that. Let him talk. Make sure you learn.*

"I heard about a woman in the media," Bao said. "Her name was Katsumi Shan. Perhaps you've heard of her."

Christie waited.

"I was told she was a very inquisitive woman, too. Always sticking her nose into business that was not hers. She was found hanging." Bao smiled. "Evidently someone didn't like her attentions. It is something to keep in mind."

"I won't stop," Christie said defiantly. "I don't scare." She tried to tell herself she wasn't scared now, but she knew she was and accepted it. Her father had taught her to deal with fear. *When you're a cop, that's one of the things that will be with you every day of your career. You want to know when to start worrying, Christie? The day you stop being afraid.*

"Good," Bao said. "But you realize these men, who-ever they are, that murdered your team probably would like nothing better than another chance at you."

Christie watched him walk away. She steeled herself until she was certain Bao was out of earshot. Then she cursed. That was something her father didn't teach her and didn't approve.

When she had control of herself, she left the inter-view room and returned to her office. Seated at her clut-tered desk, she breathed out. Then she closed her eyes, accessed the computer in the back of her head and started searching for information about Katsumi Shan. There had to be a tie. Bao had meant the information to be a lure.

* * *

"I need one of the back rooms," Dalton said to the young clerk behind the counter of the Internet café. He thought he spoke clearly, but it was possible that he hadn't. He wasn't at his best.

"The back room?" the clerk repeated, acting like he didn't know what Dalton was talking about.

Dalton tried to control his anger. It wasn't easy. He'd left the lab compound three hours ago with the intention of getting a handle on the can of worms he'd opened as well as the one that had already been opened.

You should have just kept your damn mouth shut, he told himself. *Maybe if you'd gotten some information from Grace things would have been different. But you didn't. You should have known going in that Grace isn't the kind of woman to crumble under pressure.*

As it was now, he still didn't know anything, and Grace wasn't talking to him. She'd gone to the lab and showed no signs of coming out anytime soon.

Check that, Dalton told himself. *You do know something. Bao and the Bronze Tigers threatened Michael. Not Grace. Michael.*

Once he'd been certain Michael was asleep, Dalton had assigned two men he trusted on the cottage, then had gone into Roanoke. He'd spent some time in the taverns, drowning his anger and fear and frustration the way he had back in the military. Drinking to excess was something he hadn't done in almost three years. Then, half in the bag and royally pissed, he'd decided to take action.

At the moment, he knew about Bao and the Bronze Tigers. But they were a known quantity. The offensive front that he didn't know, and was certain would involve her at some point, was the FBI agent, Christie Chace.

Since he'd met her in the warehouse last night, she'd seldom been far from his thoughts. Drinking put a curve
in his thoughts that he couldn't shake. The warrior part
of him remembered that she was going to be a stubborn
adversary, while the male part of him couldn't forget
what her lean, hard body had felt like against his.

*Maybe if you were sober she wouldn't seem so damn
attractive,* he groused at himself. Emotions and whiskey were a bad combination. He'd gotten angry at the
last bar he'd been in, almost let himself get sucked into
a fight—which would have pleased him to no end for
the moment, but would have upped the complications
with Grace in geometric proportions—and had chosen
to come to the Internet café.

Now the young Internet café clerk was leaving himself wide-open to attack.

"Hey, Euclid," a deep basso voice called. "I'll deal with
this one." Kirk Brandt, the ex-Navy intelligence officer
that ran the café, limped out from behind the bar. He was
short and wide, built like a fireplug. His face was broad
and friendly, even with the burn scarring that tracked his
right cheek and chin and pulled at his right eye.

Kirk had served as a submariner for twelve years before his boat had taken a direct hit from a pirate in the
Indian Ocean. Nearly every man aboard the sub was
lost. Few of them had escaped damage. Kirk had mus-
tered out with a full pension, a background in encrypted
communications and one leg short.

These days he ran the Internet café for a straight job
and contracted out for security testing for big corporations. The wounds he'd suffered had left his right leg a
twisted mess of scarring and prosthetic from the knee
down, but his mind was as agile as ever. Dalton had met

Kirk at the arcades with Michael. They'd found similar interests in military strategy games, then progressed to sharing stories about their experiences in the service. By the time they'd finished that, they had a solid if casual friendship.

Kirk had also let Dalton know that he kept back rooms at the twenty-four-hour café that were heavily encrypted. Most of the front room computers were used by dedicated gamers who wanted to handle more machine than they could easily afford at home. Few used them for research or business, though there were some.

"You, my friend," Kirk said, "have been drinking like a man with a woman on his mind."

"It shows?" Dalton brushed at his chin, feeling stubble and the familiar creeping numbness that told him he was half-drunk.

"Big time." Kirk patted him on the shoulder. "C'mon back and let's see what you need."

Dalton followed the ex-Navy man into the back room. Four sleek machines sat in the darkness. The walls were blank, devoid of distractions. Kirk gestured Dalton to one of the consoles, typed in a series of commands and brought the computer up.

"I designed the search engine myself," Kirk said. "You don't use Google for anything back in this room. Too much spyware on the Net. My engine ducks it or kills it all."

Focusing on the screen with effort, Dalton looked for the keyboard.

"Way behind the times, my friend." Kirk slipped a wireless microphone over Dalton's head. "You just have to talk to my babies."

Dalton frowned. "I don't care for tech that much."

Kirk grinned sympathetically. "I heard there were a few people like you left in the world. Problem is, you'd still be writing on stone tablets if you had your way."

Probably be a lot safer, Dalton thought.

"And you wouldn't be able to do what you're about to do," Kirk said as if reading his thoughts. "You want me to leave?"

"No." Dalton wasn't sure he could operate the computer by himself and get the most out of it. And there wasn't anything in Special Agent Christie Chace's background that he was afraid for Kirk to know.

They started searching, saving files that Kirk promised to copy over to a memory wafer for Dalton later. Dalton was surprised at how much the FBI agent had been in the media. On the other hand, after seeing how she'd handled herself during the warehouse firefight last night, he had expected it. She'd been a key player in several operations against international gang members and foreign corporate espionage.

"She's Enhanced," Kirk said when they came to a *Viewpoint* story about Chace's joining the pilot FBI program for intensive immersion in the cybersystems. "That's one thing I wish I'd been able to get while I was in the Navy. Of course, Command was only offering the systems to special ops guys serving on the front line, not to a guy wearing dolphins and working miles out."

"Where it was safe, right?" Dalton asked wryly.

"Oh yeah. Couldn't have been much safer." Kirk unconsciously touched the burn scarring on his face. "You were a Ranger, Dalton? Didn't they ever offer the Enhanced program to you?"

"I turned it down," Dalton replied. "Most of my squad didn't." For a moment, with the liquor working in him, the ghosts of those final days with the team haunted him. He held Mac again, his friend's body riddled with bullets from a heavy-caliber machine gun, almost torn apart. "They died. All of them. Most of the rest of us that weren't Enhanced got killed, too."

"Sorry to hear that," Kirk said. That had been one of the stories that Dalton hadn't shared with the ex-Navy man.

"Have you talked to the military guys who are Enhanced?" Dalton asked.

"A few of them," Kirk replied.

"Ever notice how they seem…different?"

"What do you mean?"

With the whiskey in him, loosening him up, Dalton couldn't seem to stay quiet. Or maybe Grace's accusation had hurt him more than he was willing to admit to himself.

"The guys who got Enhanced," Dalton said, "didn't think they could die or get hurt. Like they could stand there and the bullet would bounce off them, or like they could dodge out of the way of the ones with their name on them."

Kirk hesitated. "I don't know that I would say that was true."

"You ever fought with guys who were Enhanced?"

"No. Never saw any hands-on engagement action."

"Well," Dalton said, "they are different. Not all the time. But sometimes when a firefight got at its worst and the squad needed to deliver the most, I'd see all the fear go out of them. Like someone had turned off a switch. During those times, our casualties ran high. They didn't stop till they were dead." He paused, remembering. "I'm not sure some of them stopped then."

Memories washed over him, filled with visions of bursting artillery, shrill cries of wounded and dying men, the acrid stink of blood and gunpowder, the heat of mortars slamming the ground and the taste of dirt and smoke in the air.

"My team's last op was like that," Dalton said. "We were hard up against it and should have pulled back to our last position. Instead, my commanding officer ordered us to take the site."

"Did you?"

"Yeah," Dalton said bitterly. "For about five minutes. We had enough time to evac our dead and wounded. It took that long because we had so many dead." He'd carried Mac's body to the evac helicopter himself.

"Man," Kirk said soberly, "that's harsh."

"I lost my best friend there."

"That's where you lost Mac?"

At that point, Dalton knew he'd been talking about Mac, and he knew Kirk had been listening. "Yeah."

They stayed silent together, both of them struggling with their own demons and nightmares, but they continued to prowl the Internet for information about FBI Special Agent Christie Chace.

"She's a hotdogger," Kirk said when they both agreed they'd exhausted the information pipeline three hours later. "She likes the action. And she's good at it."

Dalton silently agreed. All the files in the FBI databases they'd ferreted out about the FBI agent had agreed on that score.

"But she's a total babe," Kirk added, unconsciously shifting through the file he'd created on Christie Chace and stopping at one of the photos of Chace walking the perimeter of a terrorist bombing in downtown Washington, D.C.

Dalton looked at the digital image and remembered again how the woman had moved with superhuman speed, how coolly she'd acted under fire. Bruising had already spread across his chest despite the Kevlar vest he'd worn.

"You didn't say where you'd met her," Kirk said.

"In D.C."

"I didn't know you got up there much."

"I don't."

Kirk shrugged. "You ask me, she's a good reason to go back."

"I'm a loner. And my job takes up a lot of my time."

"Yeah." Kirk gave Dalton a sidelong glance. "I can see that. How's Michael?"

"Michael's good." A sudden stab of fear raced through Dalton. He heard Grace's threat again—*And if you do anything, anything at all to jeopardize this situation I swear to God that you will never see Michael again.* He closed his eyes for a moment, centering himself. He couldn't imagine not being able to be there for the boy, couldn't imagine a time when he'd have to ask, *How's Michael?*

The computer pinged for attention, jarring Dalton out of his dark thoughts.

"Late arrival," Kirk said, then called the media file into view.

The piece came with digital images, showing FBI Special Agent Christie Chace taking alleged Bronze Tiger Triad gang member Sammy Bao from the Hong Kong Noodle earlier that day. In one of the images, she held a shotgun to a man's nose as Bao was placed in handcuffs.

"Damn," Kirk said. "The woman's got brass, you got to give her that."

"Yeah, but if she goes around acting like that, she's gonna get her head blown off."

"I know. You don't jack around with the Tigers unless you've already scheduled a trip to the crematorium." Kirk gave Dalton a serious look. "Look, total babe or not, this could be one to stay away from, pal."

"Yeah." Dalton realized that the effects of the alcohol he'd consumed were diminishing and it was almost 4:00 a.m. If he left now, he could get a couple hours sleep before Michael got up and started his day.

He paid Kirk and thanked the man for his time, then headed up the street for his motorcycle. His thoughts raced inside his head. Somehow he had to make peace with Grace, and he had to pray that FBI Special Agent Christie Chace never found the trail that led to the lab compound.

But he knew that was a vain hope. From everything he'd seen in the media files, Chace was as intelligent and driven as she was quick.

Chapter 8

"Christie."

Startled, Christie looked up at her father as he rummaged through the refrigerator at the family home where she'd grown up. The Chace family lived in a residential area in Georgetown. She'd attended Georgetown University, always staying close to family although she'd traveled a lot for her job at the Bureau. There was no place like home.

At six feet four inches, Wallace Chace was a big man who had just turned sixty. He'd been a Washington, D.C. policeman for thirty-seven of those years, twenty-four of them spent in a patrol car, nine as a shift commander and the last four in Internal Affairs. After retiring two years ago, he continued working part-time in a civilian capacity with Internal Affairs, but his wife often suspected that it was just Wallace's excuse for riding around in a patrol car from time to time.

"You gonna cut that onion or memorize it?" her father asked. His voice was gruff, but there was a twinkle in his hazel eyes.

Christie looked down at the onion on the cutting board in front of her. She even had a knife in her hand.

"I got the bratwurst coming off the grill in ten minutes." Wallace took a serving tray of deviled eggs and a large bowl of Caesar salad from the refrigerator. "It ain't gonna be the same without onions."

"Oh," Christie teased. "You wouldn't want to miss the chance at heartburn."

"Nah. I got new medication from the doc. I'll get through this just fine."

Christie tuned into her Enhanced speed, looked at the onion for a moment, then chopped. The knife blade was a blur, moving with superhuman precision, and the onion turned into a heap of perfectly diced pieces.

"Done," Christie announced.

Wallace shook his head. "I'm never gonna get used to that Enhanced stuff."

Christie used the knife to scrape the diced onions into a serving dish and added tongs. Her father had been wary when she'd volunteered for the Enhanced pilot program, but he'd been wary when she'd applied for the Bureau as well. In both cases, once he'd seen she was committed, he'd stood solidly behind her. When she'd been recovering after the Enhanced surgeries, learning to walk all over again, he'd regularly dropped in for visits to check on her and bring homemade soups and stews her mother had prepared.

"The tech is all coming, Dad." Christie reached into the open refrigerator for the salad dressing her mother had made fresh that morning. "You had your vision corrected when your eyes started to change. Mom had a little *work* done on her cheekbones and eyes when she went in to have her vision and hearing enhanced."

Wallace put a finger to his lips. When he spoke, his voice was low. "We don't talk about your mother's *work*."

"Everybody's doing cosmetic surgery," Christie protested. "That's one of the first enhancements people choose. As well as a phone implant. It's no big deal."

"Yeah, well *everybody* isn't your mother. Around here, we just talk about her vision and hearing enhancements. If we talk about that at all. And maybe I've had my vision enhanced, but I can't see bacteria at a hundred yards."

"Neither can I." Christie paused. "Ugh. And why would you want to?"

"I was just saying…"

"I know."

Wallace looked at her.

Christie knew that look. He was concerned. She was his youngest daughter, and the only one that had chosen to follow his career in law enforcement.

"So what's occupying your mind so much?"

Christie leaned a hip against the kitchen sink. Wallace took up position against the island. The kitchen had long been a place where business had been conducted in the Chace family. Milestones had been celebrated, plans had been firmed up, weddings had been arranged and bad news had been shared in that little room decorated with her mother's collection of frontier cooking and baking utensils.

"You know about my team?" Christie asked.

"Of course I know. I just don't ask."

That was one of the unwritten rules they had between them. When Wallace had been a policeman, no one was allowed to question him about homicides or robberies or anything else that he worked on or around unless he brought it up first.

"It's been tough," Christie said.

"Losing people is always hard. God forbid it should ever get easy."

"I know. This thing has gotten complicated."

"Want to talk about it?"

Christie considered the offer. "I don't want to wreck the family day."

Wallace waved the worry away. "Your mom knows how we are. If you think I can help, I'd be glad to."

Over the years, Christie had discovered her father was a great sounding board. He could listen for hours, then help her distill the main problems she faced each time, and helped her support her reasoning for the course of action she'd already chosen to pursue.

She started in, laying out the foundation for the story by telling her father about Arturo Gennady and how the scientist was getting blackmailed.

Christie was just getting into the details of the stakeout when the back door opened and her oldest sister, Pam, entered. Pam was dark-haired like their mother, and tended toward a full figure, which was made even more full by her current pregnancy.

"Ah, you two," Pam said, shaking her head. She stuck her head out the door. "They're doing cop talk, Mom. You were right."

"The bratwurst?" Wallace asked.

"Burnt to a crisp," Pam said. "Mom's phoning for pizza now."

"Don't even joke about that," Wallace cautioned.

"They're fine, Dad. Russell pulled them off the grill." Pam took the eggs, salad and diced onions and headed back outside.

"And that would be our cue," Wallace said. "We can talk while we eat."

And they did, managing to hold down one end of the long family table amid the flower gardens that Christie's mom worked on year-round. They conversed in shorthand, the way they'd learned to do around the rest of the family, and tuned out the other conversations taking place around them.

As economical and concise as she could be, knowing her father could read reams between the lines, Christie finished up with her confrontation with Bao and the murder of the Katsumi Shan woman.

"No one knows who killed this woman?" Wallace asked when she finished.

"If they do, no one's saying."

Wallace pushed his empty plate away. "Bao figures this woman means something to you."

"Why?"

"Because he mentioned her to you. Have you ever used her as a snitch?"

"No."

"But she has a history of dealing information," Wallace said.

Christie nodded. She'd talked to Washington, D.C. police detectives who had worked with Shan.

"Maybe Bao thinks she gave you information."

"Why would he think that?"

"Because the Shan woman had dug into Bronze Tiger business and got noticed."

"Why?"

"Because someone asked her to."

"Who?"

"Your wild card. The mysterious commando with the sea-green eyes."

"You think there's a connection?"

"You think there isn't?"

Christie picked at her salad and thought about it. Her

dad was right. The connection was there. She just hadn't seen it.

"Any further thoughts about your mysterious guy?" Wallace asked.

Aside from the little fantasy issues I've been having? Christie thought. The way he'd moved and the way he'd looked, even with no face and only those incredible eyes, her mind had insisted on pushing the button on her libido. She flushed a little and hoped her dad didn't notice.

"I told Fielding I thought he was protecting someone," Christie said.

"Did Fielding buy into it?"

"Fielding's not a theory-based guy. He likes dealing in facts. If I'm going to mention that, I have to prove it."

"We know the guy wasn't there to protect Gennady."

"Because he gave me the Bronze Tigers."

"Yeah. But why did he do that?"

Christie followed the chain of logic, realizing that she'd had it all along. "Because he's trying to protect someone else."

"Who?" Wallace waited patiently.

"Someone else the Bronze Tigers would go after."

"What project was Gennady working on?"

"A radical redesign of an automatic targeting system that's going to be layered into the spinal cord," Christie said. "When it's finished, special ops warriors are supposed to be able to leave the targeting to their on-board computers. It will ping an IFF—Identify Friend or Foe—signature off enemy troops faster than the human mind can recognize and shoot."

Wallace sighed and crossed his arms. "What about civilians that happen to be in the area? They're not going to ping the IFF signature either."

"Civilians aren't supposed to be in the battle zones."

Wallace shook his head. "I know you can do amazing things with the Enhanced hardware you've received, Christie, but you can't remove the human factor. We make value judgments. Machines—computer programs—don't."

"I don't think the government is trying to turn out flesh-and-blood robots, Dad."

"It's starting to sound like it to me." Wallace waved. "That's a discussion for another time. Let's look at your problem. The Bronze Tigers chose to kill Arturo Gennady and your team."

"To send a message."

"But they'd still want to do business, right?"

"They were sending a message to the FBI."

"At the cost of losing their cyberwidget? C'mon, Christie, you can think straighter than that. They wouldn't kill the goose that lays the golden eggs."

"Meaning they wouldn't kill Gennady without another way to get the programming."

Wallace nodded. "So what other way did they have?"

"Gennady's team."

Shaking his head, Wallace said, "Too easy," at the same time that Christie realized the same thing.

"The Tigers would know DARPA would be all over Gennady's team," Christie said.

"Are they?"

"Yes." Christie thought about what her father was pushing her toward. "Gennady's design was going to be handed off to another scientist. Dr. Grace Reynolds."

"What does she do?"

"Gennady handled the hardware side of things. The design issues and programming. Dr. Reynolds is working on the biological end of things—making sure the invasive surgery and hardware links to the human central nervous system without causing paralysis and other problems."

"So everything Gennady knew or worked out—"

"Is going to be in Dr. Reynolds's hands." Christie felt elated. The answer had been there, but it was all conjecture, something that Fielding would demand proof of.

"If the Bronze Tigers killed Gennady to send a message," Wallace said, "it wasn't a message to the FBI. It was to someone else."

"Grace Reynolds," Christie said, smiling as the pieces fell together in her head. "They knew Gennady wouldn't roll over, and they knew Gennady's designs would be turned over to Dr. Reynolds. The message was for her."

"How vulnerable is she?"

Christie had seen Grace Reynolds's file when she'd been working with Arturo Gennady to set up the sting. Gennady had also talked about Dr. Reynolds, saying she was one of the brightest minds he'd ever encountered.

"She has a son," Christie answered. "Ten years old. Dr. Gennady mentioned having met him. There's a baseball field at the lab that the boy built with someone's help."

"Is there a father?"

"You figure him for No-Face?"

"That would be my first guess. A man alone in the warehouse, my immediate impression is that he was a guy working to protect his family. With the way you moved, I'll bet he's military."

Christie closed her eyes, accessed the computer in the back of her skull and opened the files she had on Gennady. She found the information on Dr. Reynolds in a subdirectory, then opened it as well. Digital and video images took shape in her mind. Dr. Reynolds's personal data expanded automatically.

"Mackenzie Reynolds," Christie said. "Captain. United States Army Rangers."

Wallace smiled. "Well, there you go. Mystery solved."

A pang twisted through Christie's stomach. *The man who owns those eyes can't be married. There can't be a Mrs. Sea-Green Eyes.* Then she noticed another notation.

"Not Captain Reynolds," Christie said. "He's dead. Killed in action almost three years ago."

Wallace thought for a moment. "Then it has to be someone close to him. Someone who has an interest in Dr. Reynolds and her son."

"Let me run a correlation check." Still with her eyes closed, she ran a search through Captain Reynolds's past and Dr. Reynolds's present. One name appeared on both lists: Master Sergeant Dalton Anthony Geller.

Using her FBI credentials, she pulled up a military ID image, front and profile. She didn't recognize the face, but the eyes were a dead giveaway.

Opening her eyes and shutting down video access to her onboard computer, she grinned at her father.

"Well?" Wallace asked.

"I got him."

Chapter 9

"No, Special Agent Chace, I did not know Dalton was going to that warehouse that night. Furthermore, I am not convinced that you know he was there."

Sitting in Grace's office in the main lab, Dalton was impressed with the way Grace lied. Of course, technically she wasn't lying because she was carefully phrasing her responses and avoiding some questions altogether. And every chance she got, she put the pressure back on Christie.

The FBI agent was just as cool and tactful. She wasn't intimidated by Grace's office, which was staged for the occasional video conferences she did with the DARPA section heads that she was accountable to, nor did Grace's authority intimidate her.

"I'm satisfied that Sergeant Geller was there," Christie said.

"Young lady," Grace said, "there is a world of difference between satisfaction and proof. I work with theory every day, and I'm going to tell you now that the people who employ me don't reward me for creative thinking. They reward me for results."

Dalton sat quietly in a chair beside Christie. The *young woman* address stung Christie. Although Grace wasn't quite old enough to be Christie's parent, the superior tone obviously struck home.

"Yes, ma'am," Christie responded, and Dalton knew that the *ma'am* was a politely concealed rebuttal about Grace's position as an elder. "But Sergeant Geller was also at a club where a woman connected to this investigation was found murdered," Christie said. She reached forward and tapped the holographic projector control with her forefinger. "May I?"

Grace folded her arms and leaned back in her chair. "If you feel you must."

At Christie's touch, the holograph sprang to life. 3-D images hung in the air a few inches above the desktop, evidently fed through some Enhanced function layered into Christie's data pack.

Dalton stayed still with effort. A scene from the Adonis Club took shape in front of him. *How the hell did she make that connection?*

"The murdered woman, Katsumi Shan, worked with your husband and Sergeant Geller in their overseas postings," Christie said. A picture of Katsumi Shan took the place of the bar scene. "I checked back through the security vids of the night the woman was killed." Katsumi melted away and was replaced by a scene of Dalton walking through the club. "As you can see, Sergeant Geller was there the night the woman was found hanging in her office/apartment."

Grace waved a hand over the control pad. The image disappeared. "You're suggesting Sergeant Geller killed that woman?"

"No. The time-date stamp on the vid and the medical examiner's report make it impossible for Sergeant Geller to be the killer." Christie glanced at Dalton. "Unless he killed her earlier, managed to spoof the security vid recorders—which was done—then went back."

"Whatever for?" Grace demanded.

"I don't know."

"Surely not to expose himself to that club's security system again," Grace pointed out.

"No." Christie didn't appear to admit defeat, but she settled back into the chair.

"Why are you telling me this?" Grace asked.

"I thought you should know."

"Why?"

"Because I believe the people who killed Arturo Gennady will come for you next." Christie paused. "If they haven't already."

Grace's facade cracked a little then, but Dalton doubted that anyone who didn't know her extremely well would have noticed.

"If they do," Grace said, "I'd be happy to notify your office."

"That's not how it's going to work," Christie said. "My team and I are going to stay here for a while."

"Why?"

"Additional security."

"Nonsense," Grace said belligerently. She tossed an accusatory glance at Dalton.

"Dr. Reynolds," Christie said, "you don't have a choice in the matter."

"Young lady, I assure you that as project leader for this—"

"That you deserve the additional security," Christie interrupted. "Section Chief Alonzo Graves, of DARPA and the man you report to, agrees with that assessment in light of what has happened to Dr. Gennady. Appar-

ently your project is highly thought of. Since I'm connected with the Bronze Tigers and am familiar with
their activities in the Washington area, Chief Graves
agreed that my team and I would be an ideal short-term
addition to Sergeant Geller's on-site rotation. I've got a
few weeks to render a threat assessment in the matter."
She cut her gaze to Dalton. "We won't be operating
under Sergeant Geller as your present security teams do.
We'll be independent."

"We'll see about that," Grace snapped. "The last
thing I need at this juncture of the project is someone
new to my routines that gets underfoot."

"Yes, ma'am. I appreciate that. But your safety, and
that of your son, is paramount at this point. As well as
the integrity of Project Seek-n-Fire." Christie leaned
forward and touched the holograph control again.
"Here's the document from Chief Graves. He said he
will be in touch with you by end of day Monday to discuss the matter with you."

Turning coldly impersonal as she regarded the document that printed out on the holograph, Grace said,
"Well, it seems that I have no choice in the matter."

"No, ma'am," Christie agreed.

Grace stood. "Since this appears to be a security matter and nothing I can exert any control over, I'll leave
you with Sergeant Geller." She turned and left the room.

Christie looked at Dalton. "*That* was not a happy
woman."

"She doesn't like to have her routine disrupted."

"I'm not here to cause disruption."

"You already have." Dalton wanted to talk to Grace,
to let her know that the FBI team's presence there was
not his doing. But he knew that Grace wouldn't talk

to him. And he wasn't about to talk to Grace about anything until he had Special Agent Christie Chace dealt with.

"Maybe you want to tell me about that night at the warehouse," Christie said.

Dalton stood and walked toward the door. "You said you thought I shot a man in cold blood."

"You did." Christie stood and joined him.

"Then, if I was there, why would I want to admit anything?"

"There's no body. I couldn't bring charges if I wanted to."

Dalton found himself all too aware of how close she stood to him. The heat from her body pressed against him. The delicate fragrance she wore tickled his nose. He wanted her. The knowledge struck him with a savagery he'd never known before. Even the carnal relationship he'd shared with Katsumi Shan paled by comparison. The brown eyes seemed to drink him in. His throat felt dry and he experienced a sexual response that would have been embarrassing if she'd noticed.

Unexpectedly, she reached out and touched the small straight scab under his eye. He'd gotten the scratch during the firefight in the warehouse. Her soft fingertips trailed electrical sparks across his skin that seemed to fire inside his brain.

"I know you were there, Sergeant Geller," she said in a soft voice that sent thrills along his spine.

Dalton had to make himself speak, and had to try twice to get the job done. "What do you need from me, Special Agent Chace?"

"A bed," she said. Then, as if realizing what she'd inadvertently said, she took her hand back and slipped her sunglasses back on. "Three bedrooms if you can manage it. My team and I are prepared to double-bunk."

"Sure," Dalton said. The idea of double-bunking was just as tantalizing. He turned and walked down the hallway. Special Agent Christie Chace had trapped him between a rock and a hard place. Yet, at the same time—if things didn't blow up in his face, she'd brought enough pressure to bear that maybe Grace would listen to him.

The safest thing for Grace to do would be to admit Sammy Bao's contact and go into hiding. Trusting the FBI when it came to Grace and Michael was the last thing he wanted to do.

"So what's your take on Sergeant Tall-Dark-And-Moody?" Lorna Saunders asked. She was the other female agent on Christie's team. Tall and full-figured, her mocha-with-cream complexion flawless, her dark hair cropped short, Lorna was thirty, also Enhanced and often intimidated the male of the species with her brusque attitude and physical presence. She'd only been with the Bureau for four years but was already getting noticed by the Director of Operations. Christie had had to work hard to get Lorna assigned to her task force.

"I don't have a take," Christie said as she unpacked in the small bedroom she was sharing with the other agent.

Dalton had come up with three rooms by packing two of his team in with other security guards. None of the on-site security people had been happy about the FBI's invasion.

"You're the only one of us who's met him before today," Lorna said.

"I wouldn't call a gun battle much of a chance to meet somebody."

"Sometimes you get to know more about a person durin' a tough situation."

"We didn't even get to introductions."

"Don't hide what you're thinkin' from me, honey," Lorna said with her rich Alabama drawl. "You don't need Enhanced vision to see that man gets under your skin. But I think your little secret is safe from the male agents on this team because they won't see things like I will."

"I don't know what you're talking about, Agent Saunders." Christie put her underwear into one of the small chests of drawers. Before she could close it, Lorna had snagged a wispy pair of bikini panties from the stack that Christie could have sworn she'd carefully hidden.

"Uh-huh," Lorna said triumphantly, dangling the panties by one manicured finger.

"I don't know how those got in there," Christie growled. "Must have been a mistake."

"A mistake." Lorna snorted. "You keep tellin' that one and your nose is gonna grow."

Christie grabbed the panties and stuffed them into the drawer. But it was too late. She could already feel her cheeks flaming.

"And it would be a shame," Lorna said, "doin' that to a nose as pretty as the one you got." Despite her accent, she had a college degree and was one of the smartest people Christie knew. The accent was just the way she was, and it was also a tool she used to allow people she dealt with to underestimate her.

"Maybe we could stay focused," Christie suggested.

"Oh, you had him focused all right," Lorna said as she put her own clothes away. "The way you got that jacket cut so it shows your backside off in those tailored slacks, he was noticin' plenty. But I suppose that was a mistake, too."

Christie glared at her fellow agent defiantly. "It's just a suit."

Lorna laughed.

Sighing, Christie said, "Okay. So maybe I'm a *little* interested in him. But this is hardly the time and place, is it?"

"One thing my auntie used to tell me," Lorna said, "love makes its own time and place. Don't mean that everything's gonna be okay. Just that it's gonna grab ahold of your attention."

I sincerely hope not, Christie thought. *That would be about the last thing I needed right now.*

"I'm going to take a shower," she announced, grabbing a change of clothes and heading for the bath. *A cold shower. And if it doesn't help, I'm going to take another.*

"Special Agent Chace is going to be trouble," Grace said.

Turning around, Dalton spotted the holograph in the kitchen taking shape. "I didn't call her in."

Grace just stared at him. The accusation was naked in her eyes. "I told you what would happen if you chose to ignore my warning. I will discontinue your services, and I will make it so that you won't see Michael again."

"Calling the FBI in at this moment would be a big mistake," Dalton told her. He felt tense. The idea of losing Michael and not being able to do anything about it hurt. "They try to take things over. The only reason Chace isn't doing that now is because she has no proof that Sammy Bao has contacted you. She's weaseled her way in for a look, but she doesn't know anything. If the fact that Bao has talked to you becomes known, the FBI will take over completely."

A pained look filled Grace's face. "I can't allow that."

Dalton didn't know how to respond.

"Those…those people may think I went to the FBI," Grace said. "And they may take their ire out on my son. I need you to stay close to Michael. Don't let anything happen to him." She paused and some of the hardness in her face cracked. "Please."

Dalton wanted to promise her. That was his first instinct. He wanted to promise her that nothing would happen to Michael on his watch. He barely stopped himself. The last thing she wanted was a promise from him. "I will, Grace. What are you going to do about the situation?"

"I don't know. Maybe you're right, maybe with the FBI involved now and with Agent Chace already making her suspicions known to Sammy Bao, maybe there won't be any further trouble."

"The Bronze Tigers aren't the kind of people who just walk away from a situation," Dalton said. "Don't just stick your head in the sand, Grace."

"Keep my son safe. That's all I'm asking you to do. If Bao comes around again, I'll deal with him." Grace faded from view.

Dalton cursed as he stared at the empty space where the image had been. He felt like he was on a collision course with a nightmare. How the hell was he supposed to keep Grace and Michael safe from the Bronze Tigers *and* the FBI?

Chapter 10

By Thursday, Christie's respect for the security work Dalton did at the lab site had grown immeasurably. Security ran like a Swiss watch. Nobody went in or out without being checked and supervised, and all the grids were solid, human security backed by electronic systems and redundant electronic systems.

Her respect for Dalton had grown, too. There was no denying the love that existed between Dalton and Michael Reynolds.

The time Dalton and Michael spent at the baseball field, both in practice and in upkeeping the grounds, showed the commitment between them. They talked all the time when Michael wasn't with his private school-teacher, and Christie had yet to see when Dalton wasn't with the boy when Michael was free. Dalton actually spent more one-on-one time with the boy than the mother.

The relationship Dalton had with Christie was professional, but she'd noticed him looking at her with more than passing interest on several occasions. Unfortunately, he'd caught her doing the same thing. That attraction was interfering with her concentration. Not her job performance, because she wouldn't let it come to that, but it was definitely throwing her game off.

Grace Reynolds kept her distance, never talking to Christie except on the two opportunities that had presented themselves regarding Enhanced upgrades that were coming for law enforcement. Both times, Grace had made it apparent that she didn't want to talk to Christie.

Through it all, though, Dalton and Grace had some kind of secret communication going on between them. Christie could feel it even though she couldn't point to a concrete example. Whatever the secret was, it was also the source of conflict that Christie noticed between them.

She stood behind the backstop at the baseball field. Dalton was throwing Michael batting practice as he did every morning except Sunday, when they had a weekly game between the Lab Rats, who were made up of some of Grace's assistants, and the Braves, made up of the security team.

Dalton wore a gray T-shirt with the sleeves hacked off and a pair of athletic shorts that showed off his tight butt and bronze legs. The Braves baseball hat shadowed his face and the wraparound sunglasses hid his eyes. He pitched to the boy with a smooth, economical precision that Christie had seen in baseball games broadcast on video screen.

Michael hit a ball out to deep center, over Dalton's head.

"Hey, Christie," Michael said, as he stepped back and saw her. Over the past four days, she had gotten to know him and they were on a first-name basis. He was a neat kid and reminded her of her older brothers when they were younger.

"Way to swing, Michael," Christie congratulated.

"Want to try a couple?" the boy asked.

"Agent Chace is probably really busy now," Dalton said. He stared at Christie in irritation.

"Actually," Christie said, looking at the boy, "I'm on break at the moment. I just finished up my morning run." She looked at Dalton. "I'd love to hit a few balls."

Dalton dropped his gaze to the ground and shook his head.

"We've got extra bats over here." Michael gestured to the wooden bats in the cubbies inside the batting cage.

"Thanks." Christie sized up the bats and made her selection.

"You ever played before?" Michael asked.

"A little." Christie stepped into the box and drew the bat back.

Michael stepped behind the backstop. "Take it easy on her, Dalton. She's a girl."

"Yeah," Dalton replied. "I noticed."

And what exactly is that supposed to mean, Sergeant Geller? Christie squared herself in the box, locked the bat behind her, and looked at Dalton. "Let's see that smoke, Sergeant Geller."

"Yeah. Go get her, Dalton!" Michael cheered.

Dalton lobbed the ball over the plate. Christie swung easily, smacking the ball down third baseline.

"That all you got?" Christie asked.

Dalton reached into the five-gallon bucket beside him for another ball. He went into his windup and threw. The ball came straight at Christie's head. She dodged, dropping into the box.

Michael laughed uproariously, hooting and cheering for Dalton.

"Sorry," Dalton said. "You were crowding the plate."

Okay, Sergeant Geller, let's play your little game.

Christie stood and brushed the dirt off her T-shirt and shorts. She picked up the bat and stepped back into the box. Dalton threw again and she drove the ball into deep left.

He looked more irritated as he reached into the bucket again. This time the ball came in faster. Christie hit it again, driving right back at him. He got his glove up in time to save his face.

"Wow, Dalton, she can really hit," Michael crowed.

"We'll see." Dalton's pitching became increasingly aggressive. Christie hit ten in a row, missed one, then hit five more. All of them went into the outfield, and all of them were decent base hits with a couple of possible doubles.

"Okay, let's make this more fair," Dalton said. "This mound is too close for me to heat up all the way."

"More fair for who?" Christie asked, enjoying the challenge she'd stepped into. It felt great to meet Dalton on equal ground—and blow his mind by beating him.

"You," Dalton growled. "It's not going to be easy because I'm going to throw with everything I've got." He walked back to the regulation distance played by the major leagues.

Then the contest began in earnest. Dalton threw fifteen pitches, all of them screamers. Christie hit fourteen of them, all deep enough that Michael screamed, "Home run!" each time. She got hold of the fifteenth pitch, but it fouled off behind the backstop.

Michael began cheering for her.

Christie couldn't help grinning. "When do you plan on heating up, Sergeant?"

He frowned at her, right hand holding a ball in his fingertips against his thigh. "This isn't really fair, is it?"

"What do you mean?" Christie stepped back out of the box so Dalton couldn't jam her on a pitch.

"I mean you're using your Enhanced abilities."

"You think that was Enhanced skills?" Anger surged through Christie. "What that was, Sergeant Geller, was the product of hundreds of Sunday afternoons my father spent with me so I could play on the high school and college baseball teams. What you just saw was the result of hard work and dedication. From me and my dad." She couldn't believe it. "You want to see Enhanced abilities, throw me another ball." She stepped back into the box and drew the bat back. "C'mon. Don't hold back because I'm a girl."

"This is stupid," Dalton said, frowning.

"Put it over," Christie challenged.

"C'mon, Dalton," Michael said. "Show her your real heat."

Dalton hesitated for a moment, then took the mound, picked up a ball and went into his windup. When he released the ball, the pitch came faster than anything she'd seen so far.

But Christie used her Enhanced skills and time slowed. She centered on the ball, could have counted the seams as it hurtled toward her. Stepping into the ball, she brought the bat around in a blur. The crack sounded like a gunshot.

The ball arced up, shot out of the ballpark and went over the tall security fence around the outside of the compound. It hit a long way from the fence line.

"Wow!" Michael yelled, running out around the backstop. "That must have gone four hundred feet."

Accessing the GPS coordinates through her onboard computer, Christie said, "Eleven hundred and forty-two feet, nine point two three inches." She pulled the bat apart where it had split with the impact. "With a broken bat." She dropped the halves in the trash bin by the home dugout.

"Hey," Michael said excitedly. "Would you like to play baseball with us Sunday?"

Enjoying the disgusted look Dalton was giving her, Christie ran a hand through Michael's unruly hair. "I'd love to play baseball with you guys."

"Great. You can be on our team."

"You might have to talk Sergeant Geller into that. He doesn't look real happy with the idea." Christie smiled at Michael. "I'll tell you what, if Sergeant Geller doesn't want me to play for your team, I'll play for the other team. That way we can still play together."

That set Michael off in a frenzy. He launched into a major recruitment sales pitch to Dalton. Christie excused herself, saying she had to go relieve someone on duty. But she smiled to herself all the way back.

Now she just needed to figure out what Dalton was hiding.

"Man, you should have seen her, Mom," Michael said excitedly at the Reynoldses' dinner table. He mimed holding a baseball bat. "*Whack!* It was *incredible.* I never saw a ball go so far in my life! And she hit *everything.*"

Personally, Dalton was hearing more about Christie's batting display than he would have liked. He could tell from Grace's distracted interest that she was, too. Michael hadn't caught on; he was too involved in the story.

"And she's going to play for my team Sunday," Michael went on. "Dalton wasn't too happy about it at first, but he's coming around."

Grace looked at Dalton. "He wasn't happy about it?"

"No, but I think he knows we're really going to clobber the Lab Rats now."

Dalton thought he'd never seen Grace appear more tired. Suddenly, his radar went off. *I missed it.* He cursed himself, knowing that Sammy Bao or one of the other Bronze Tigers had gotten a message to her. That was why she was so fatigued. She was worn out with worry.

He sat frozen at the table, waiting for Michael to wind down and for Grace to send him to get dressed for bed.

Finally dinner was over and Michael went off to bathe and change into his sleepwear.

At the sink, washing because it was his turn in their rotation, Dalton wondered how to bring it up. Long minutes of uncomfortable silence passed.

Then Grace broke the tension. "Yes. They did."

"Contact you?" Dalton asked.

"Yes."

Dalton's throat was tight. He didn't dare look at her. "Who?"

"I don't know. I didn't recognize the voice."

"How did they call?"

"I found a satellite phone in my desk this morning. It wasn't my phone. It rang at 9:13 a.m."

Dalton took that in. "There's only one way that phone could have gotten into your desk. Someone at the site is working with them. One of our people."

"Or one of the FBI agents," Grace replied.

"I've kept them out of your office."

"You think you have anyway." She sighed. "I don't know who left the phone and you can't guess. This is Michael's life we're talking about here."

Dalton continued washing. His mind raced like a rat

in a wheel, and like a rat in a wheel, he got nowhere. "What are you going to do?"

"Whatever I have to." Grace looked at him. "I'm telling you this now because I knew you'd figure it out on your own. Or guess. You know me too well. I don't want you poking around in this. Not with Michael…" Tears slid down her cheeks.

"I know," Dalton said hoarsely. "But you can't live in fear, Grace."

"Haven't you noticed?" she asked with a sad smile. "I have been. For years. Ever since they told me Mac was dead. I've been living scared that I wouldn't be smart enough or strong enough to take care of Michael, that I wouldn't know how to raise him, or love him enough. Or a million other things, Dalton." Her voice caught. "I just can't shake the fear. It's too much. And now this." Her voice broke. "I can't lose him, Dalton. I *won't* lose him. And I won't let you lose him for me."

Dalton was quiet.

"Don't betray me," Grace pleaded. "I'm telling you this because I knew you would figure it out, but also because I trust…" She hesitated. "Because I *want* to trust you."

Because you have *to,* Dalton told himself. The realization brought a sharp pain that cut through him. She trusted him because she *had* to after all these years. Not because she felt like she could. That fact hurt even worse when he admitted to himself what he had to do.

The phone rang in the middle of the night.

Christie reached for it out of habit till she remembered the phone was inside her head. She rolled over in the bed and said, "Yes." She accessed the phone information and found out it was Dalton Geller's personal mobile number.

"Special Agent Chace, are you awake?"

Recognizing Dalton's voice, Christie was awake instantly. She flashed a time/date stamp vid inside her head and saw the time was 3:19 a.m. Sitting up in bed, she reached for her pistol and her jeans. She recorded the phone call out of habit, spinning it into the computer in her head and backing it up with her office machine.

"I'm awake," she answered, pulse beating at her temples. "Is something wrong?"

"No." Dalton hesitated. She heard pain in his voice. "Yeah. Something's wrong. A lot's wrong."

"Michael?"

"He's fine. Asleep."

A knot of tension inside Christie loosened. "Then what?"

"I… I need to talk." Dalton let out a long breath, like a great weight had been lifted from his shoulders by the admission.

"How did you get my private number?"

He chuckled but he didn't sound as cocky as he might have under other circumstances. "You're not the only one capable of magic tricks, Chace."

"I'll keep that in mind. Where are you?"

He didn't answer for long enough that she started to think he'd hung up on her.

Finally, he said, "The ball field. Come alone or we don't have anything to talk about." He broke the connection.

Christie stood and dressed, using her Enhanced night vision to see. She slipped her nightshirt off, then pulled on the jeans and took out a T-shirt, not bothering with a bra because she was in a hurry. She didn't want Dalton to change his mind about talking to her. After listening to him, she knew the situation could go either way easily.

"What's going on?" Lorna asked from the other bed.

"Nothing," Christie said, remembering that the other agent couldn't have heard the phone ringing in her head. "Can't sleep."

Lorna rolled over in bed. "Girl, I told you that you had man problems."

"Keep telling yourself that if it makes the posting here a little more entertaining."

Lorna laughed softly.

Grabbing her pistol, Christie clipped the pancake holster to her belt at the small of her back. Then she headed for the ball field. The weapon made her feel a little safer. It wasn't that she was afraid of Dalton, but she knew she needed to be afraid of whatever had compelled him to call her.

Chapter 11

A gentle wind blew across the ball field under a quarter moon. There was just enough light—without Enhanced vision—to turn the white chalk lines of the diamond to silver.

Dalton sat in the home dugout behind the third base foul line. He wore jeans and a T-shirt, too. And his Braves hat.

Christie approached him slowly, her thumbs hooked into her jeans pockets. She couldn't help thinking that he might run if she walked toward him too fast.

"Night vision?" Dalton asked from the shadows. "Or did you hear my heart beating?"

"Neither. Just knew where you'd be." Christie stopped at the rail in front of the dugout. "You've got a tough call to make and the home dugout gives you the best view of a play that's going down to the wire at the plate. You gave me the impression that's what this was all about."

"I love baseball," Dalton said. "Always have. That was the one thing my dad and I had in common. Not much else. But we both loved the game."

Christie waited, knowing he had to talk himself through it. She was certain any prodding or pushing on her part would cause him to clam up.

"You get all the rules in baseball, you know," Dalton said. "When to run, when to slide, where to throw the ball." He paused. "When to sacrifice. But that's all for the good of the team. And at the end of it, even though you've sacrificed, you still get to be part of the team. I guess that's part of why I loved being a Ranger so much."

"Because they have rules, too."

"Yeah. Be good at what you do. Stand tall. Don't leave a man behind."

Slowly, Christie walked around the railing and stopped in front of Dalton. A chill ghosted through her, but she knew it was more from being in front of the man while he was in such a raw, emotional state than from the wind.

He looked up at her and the pain etched in his face nearly broke her heart. "You know why I came here, don't you? I mean, the story was in my military profile, right?"

"Yes. Your friend. Captain Reynolds."

"He was the best man I ever knew," Dalton whispered. "No one braver. No one wiser. No man I ever knew had more heart." His throat caught. "I loved my old man, too. He was hard and tough and fair, but there just wasn't very much of him to go around. He had all he could do some days just to hold himself together."

"He must have done all right. He raised you."

"Yeah. I guess he did. But Mac, Captain Reynolds, he taught me more about how to be a man than my father ever could have. Mac taught me how to be a good soldier, too. I'd never have kept my sergeant's stripes if it hadn't been for him. He taught me self-discipline, taught me how to be part of a team."

And his son taught you how to love, Christie thought.

Goose bumps raised on her arms and her eyes burned a little.

"He was the most giving man I ever knew, too. Always there to help. He shouldn't have died. Grace and Michael needed him here."

Christie sat silently, not believing he was telling her this much. She felt guilty now for looking forward to the encounter. She'd had no clue it was going to be this hard for him.

"I didn't bring Mac back," Dalton said. "I promised Grace that I would. I failed her. I failed Michael, too, but he doesn't remember that I promised to bring his dad back."

"That wasn't your fault, Dalton. You couldn't deliver on a promise like that. Not considering the work you two did."

"I know that now. But it was done. After he was killed, I came here to help Grace and Michael." Dalton bit his lower lip. "But you know that."

"I do. I think it was a very noble thing. Michael idolizes you."

He stood, and for a moment Christie thought he was going to leave. It took everything she had not to try to intercept him.

"I'm in a bad place," Dalton said. He took a deep breath and let it out. "In order to protect the people I love most in this world, I'm going to lose them."

"I don't understand," Christie said.

"Grace told me if I revealed to anyone what I'm about to tell you, she would make me go away. That she wouldn't ever let me see Michael again."

"She wouldn't do that."

He grinned crookedly, trying to mask the hurt that he

had to have known was showing. "That just goes to show that you don't know Grace. She meant every word she said."

Christie waited, barely breathing. What Dalton had to say was hard and he couldn't be hurried.

"They threatened Michael," he said finally.

"Who?"

"The Bronze Tigers."

"They've contacted her?"

Briefly but thoroughly, Dalton told her how he'd found out about Sammy Bao, how he'd had Katsumi Shan ID the man and how he'd come to be at the warehouse the night Arturo Gennady was murdered and over half of her FBI team wiped out. Then he told her about the satellite phone Grace had found in her office.

"The security here is compromised," Dalton said. "I can't protect Grace and Michael. She doesn't want to see that. But I know. And that makes all the difference."

"That phone didn't come from one of my people," Christie said a little defensively.

"It didn't come from mine either," he replied. "But it got here somehow. No one new has been through security since your people arrived."

They let that hang for a moment.

"You don't know what Grace was told?" Christie asked when he finished.

"She didn't tell me. She didn't have to. The prototype of the Seek-n-Fire hardware arrives tomorrow. So does all the research Gennady had done on the project. You want to guess what they want?"

"We don't have to worry about that," Christie said. "With your testimony and the images of Bao talking to Dr. Reynolds, I can get the DARPA section chief to have Dr. Reynolds and Michael evacuated from this lab within the hour."

Dalton shook his head. "I can't let you do that."

"Why not? Your testimony is all I need. The DARPA section chief knows I came down here looking for a link."

"If you call DARPA before I'm ready, the deal's off," Dalton threatened. "I won't corroborate your story, and I'll tell Grace that you're lying when you say I talked to you."

"She won't believe you."

"I'll make her believe me. I'll tell her you bugged the house. We talked about this problem tonight. I'll tell her that you heard about it then."

"You could do that anyway," Christie suggested. "You could get yourself off the hook. I don't mind being the bad guy here. In fact, I can plant a bug in the house tonight."

"No."

"Why?"

"Because there's a chance that Grace might still believe that I had something to do with this."

Christie hesitated a moment. "Dalton, you're going to save them. Even here, they're exposed, vulnerable. On-site security is compromised. The delivery of the satellite phone proves that." She paused, a little hesitant about advancing the scenario any further. "You saw what happened to Arturo Gennady."

"I know. That's why I'm having this conversation with you tonight. But I've got to talk to Michael. I've got to let him know what's going on and why his mom is sending me away."

"She might not do that." Christie saw how desolate the ball field was. It was almost like a premonition of things to come.

"Grace…" Dalton took a deep breath and let it out. "Grace isn't herself, Christie. She's still good at her job, but she's not centered. Losing Mac has left her scared and broken. Maybe she can figure out new Enhanced systems and design them, but she's barely holding herself together. I think she'd even regret sending me away, but she'd do it because she felt she had no choice. Because she told me she was going to. She's… she's struggling to have some kind of control in her world. She wants to know that she can have a cause-and-effect relationship with the world. And I don't know how Michael will react." He looked at her. "I don't want to lose Michael. Not without giving him an explanation. Maybe that's selfish, but that's how I feel. And that's my deal. It's the best one you're going to get."

Seeing him standing there in the darkness of the dugout, Christie felt how vulnerable he was in that moment. She crossed the short distance between them, then put her hand on his face, looking deeply into his eyes.

"We'll do it your way, Dalton," she said. "Until I feel like I have no choice. Don't get me in that position and it'll go down just like you say. I give you my word."

He nodded and started to turn away.

She put her hand on his shoulder, intending to tell him everything was going to be all right. But when he turned, she reached for him and pulled him into an embrace. Desire burned fever-hot within her and she couldn't pull away from it. She leaned up and kissed him. Then, just when she was certain he wasn't going to react and that she'd made one of the dumbest mistakes of her life, his lips came alive and sought hers hungrily.

His arms wrapped around her, pulling her to him. He growled deep down in his throat and his breath grew short. Christie knew her own breath was coming short now, too. There just wasn't enough oxygen in the air. Her hands slid down his back onto his hips and pulled him against her. She felt the challenge of his erection against her taut belly even as his callused hands slid under her T-shirt and cupped her breasts. Her nipples tightened instantly, filling her with an aching need. She turned molten at her center. He kissed her more deeply, taking her breath away.

Dalton drew back, looking at her. "This is a bad idea."

"Yeah." Christie took a ragged breath. "I was thinking the same thing."

"I think it's been in the back of my mind since I met you."

"Me, too."

"Probably we should go." But he made no move to pull away.

"You try to leave, Dalton," Christie warned, "and I'll run you down. I'm faster than you, you know. Enhanced speed."

He put a hand behind her head and pulled her close, cupping the back of her head as he kissed her deeply. His hands cupped her breasts again, finding her nipples and flicking them with his thumb. Christie knew they couldn't have gotten any harder. Pressed tight against him, she was convinced that he couldn't have gotten any harder either.

He pulled away. "You've got Enhanced strength, too. Are you sure this is going to be safe for me?"

Just when she was starting to think he was serious, he grinned. Then he swept her off her feet and carried her to the dugout bench. There wasn't much room to work with, but they made do. Their shirts came off in record time, allowing them to press flesh against flesh. They hung their pistols side by side on the dugout railing.

She tried to loosen his belt, but Christie could never remember fumbling so much or being so awkward. Thankfully, Dalton was just as graceful as she'd ever fantasized he would be. He tugged her shoes and jeans off, kissed her breasts and the hollows of her thighs, then, when she tugged on his belt, he surrendered and finished undressing.

He hesitated, awkward, then reached into his fallen jeans and brought out a foil pack.

"You always carry a condom around with you, Dalton?"

"Just since this morning."

"Why this morning?"

"Because when I saw you in that batter's box in those shorts and that T-shirt, hitting ball after ball, I realized I've never seen a sexier woman. Once the prototype was delivered tomorrow, I intended to take you out to dinner, talk about your dad and baseball."

Christie laughed. "We could still do that. Want to wait?"

"No," he growled.

She took the condom from him, tore it open, then sheathed him. He trembled, caught up in his own desire, and she teased him unmercifully till he grabbed her shoulders and pushed her back on the dugout bench, moved in and slid his hard length against her, rubbing against her instead of penetrating her. The slippery friction of the condom and her own wetness drove her crazy, pushing her right to the edge but never driving her over into the sweet abandon of release.

Nearing frustration, she reached for him. He didn't make it easy, leaning in to press his lips against hers and opening her mouth to plunder it once more. Then she had him where she wanted him, taking him in deep, surprised at how large he felt even though she was more than ready for him. She bucked up against him, igniting his desire, meeting his burning hunger with her own, till he could no longer hold back.

Christie crested and tumbled over into an abyss of pure pleasure. She came back to her senses just as he was about to reach his own climax. Using her Enhanced strength, she pushed him off of her and almost laughed at the surprised look on his face. Before he knew what was happening, she pushed him back down onto the dugout bench on his back, threw a leg across his lean hips, and pulled him inside her again. This time, firmly in control, she didn't stop surging against him until he exploded within her, triggering another spasm that racked her.

Later, when they had their strength back, Dalton held her tightly against him. She felt his heart beating inside his chest. The night air felt cool against her sweat-soaked body. She shivered, but it wasn't just from the chill.

"Help me save them," he whispered into her ear.

"I will," she said. "It's going to be all right, Dalton." She kissed him, then was surprised to find his hunger rising within her again. She met his passion with her own needs.

Christie yawned, barely getting a hand up to her mouth to cover it.

"Trouble sleepin', huh?" Lorna shot her a glance filled with mocking innocence.

"Yes." Christie sipped her coffee and hoped the caffeine would kick in soon. One of the coming Enhanced packages included stim-packs that could be stored inside the body and accessed through the onboard computer, an auxiliary subsystem to the adrenal pump she was now equipped with. A full range of stimulants, from caffeine to endorphins to system-wide antibiotics and painkillers, were going to be added. She had been resistant to that at first glance, but having that kind of control over her body—especially the waking up part—was becoming more and more attractive.

"Well," Lorna said, "that walk you went for must have done you a world of good, sugar, because when you came in last night I swear you were asleep before your head hit the pillow."

Grateful for the sunglasses she was wearing because they kept the other agent from looking into her eyes, Christie felt embarrassed and cocky at the same time. "Must have been the night air. They have great night air out here."

"Yeah, I bet. Well I just want you to know that I never seen night air that would make a person look so smug. And I just want to warn you that I hate secrets. I always find out what I want to know."

Christie enjoyed the bantering, enjoyed the glow she had somehow maintained after last night and would have enjoyed baiting Lorna, but she also dreaded what Dalton planned to do this morning.

She finished her coffee, nibbled at a bagel and wondered how Dalton was going to handle his talk with Dr. Reynolds. Either way it went down, she knew things were going to be hard on him. But both of them knew it was the only way to save Grace Reynolds and her son.

The DARPA shipment arrived at the compound at 10:07 a.m. by helicopter. The transfer between the cargo guards and Dalton's team went off without a hitch. The Seek-n-Fire prototype was delivered inside a time-locked security container coded to release a strong acid followed by an incendiary device for self-destruction if it was intercepted. Only Dr. Reynolds had the passcode.

The technology on the box was top-notch. And even if the Bronze Tigers—or anyone else—had succeeded in intercepting the prototype, Dr. Reynolds's research was necessary to make stealing the tech worthwhile. After that, the device and the bio-linking technology could be reverse-engineered by whatever company was undoubtedly bankrolling the Chinese Triad.

Without a doubt, the tech would be reverse-engineered at some point, but the difference between now and then could mean billions of dollars. On top of that, many of the Enhanced systems—including ones that Christie had embedded—were safe-coded to fail out and destruct if tampered with. As soon as a cracker had gotten past a system's defenses, new security was encoded or implanted, and new systems replaced old ones quickly. Being Enhanced was a constant process of being upgraded.

After the delivery took place and the cargo helicopter departed, Christie anxiously waited an hour for Dalton to tell Dr. Reynolds what he was going to do.

Finally at 11:19 a.m., she saw Dalton striding from the Reynoldses' home with a suitcase. Christie fell into step with him as they walked toward the parking area in back of the house where Dr. Reynolds and Dalton kept their private vehicles.

Dalton was grim, locked in tight behind his wrap-around sunglasses. He hadn't shaved that day either, which was totally out of character for the spit-and-shine image he generally wore. He wore jeans, square-toed motorcycle boots, a black muscle shirt and a brown bomber jacket. A Braves baseball hat shadowed his face.

Not exactly going for the professional look today, are we? Christie thought with some annoyance. He also didn't look like he was ready to take up where they'd left off last night. Either on the intimacy or the stand he was going to take with Dr. Reynolds.

Dalton opened the door of the powerful shortbed 4x4 midnight-blue pickup he drove when he wasn't riding his motorcycle. He tossed the suitcase in and started to climb in after it.

"Dalton." Christie caught his arm. For a moment she thought he was going to brush her off. He froze like a deer in headlights, not even looking at her. "Talk to me."

"Nothing to say." Dalton tried to pull himself into the pickup again, but she restrained him, using her Enhanced strength this time.

"Talk to me," she said, feeling bad about what she was doing and what she was going to say.

"Let go of my arm. I'm leaving."

"You're not leaving until you talk to me." She searched his face and saw the pain and fear there. Maybe most people wouldn't have seen those things, but she had been paying attention to him and getting to know him. Her voice tightened and she knew she was risking whatever trust he'd found in her last night when she went on. "If I have to, Sergeant Geller, I'll put you under arrest. Don't you think for a second that I won't." She took her hand back, releasing him, but she was sure both of them knew he wouldn't be leaving without her assent. Even if he got past her, she had guards on the gate, too.

An Important Message from the Editors

Dear Reader,

Because you've chosen to read one of our fine romance novels, we'd like to say "thank you!" And, as a **special** way to thank you, we've selected <u>two more</u> of the books you love so well **plus** an exciting Mystery Gift to send you — absolutely <u>FREE</u>!

Please enjoy them with our compliments...

Pam Powers

Peel off seal and place inside...

How to validate your Editor's "Thank You" FREE GIFT

1. Peel off gift seal from front cover. Place it in space provided at right. This automatically entitles you to receive 2 FREE BOOKS and a fabulous mystery gift.

2. Send back this card and you'll get 2 brand-new *Romance* novels. These books have a cover price of $5.99 or more each in the U.S. and $6.99 or more each in Canada, but they are yours to keep absolutely free.

3. There's no catch. You're under no obligation to buy anything. We charge nothing—ZERO—for your first shipment. And you don't have to make any minimum number of purchases— not even one!

4. The fact is, thousands of readers enjoy receiving their books by mail from The Reader Service. They enjoy the convenience of home delivery...they like getting the best new novels at discount prices BEFORE they're available in stores... and they love their Heart to Heart subscriber newsletter featuring author news, special book offers, book reviews and much more!

5. We hope that after receiving your free books you'll want to remain a subscriber. But the choice is yours— to continue or cancel, any time at all! So why not take us up on our invitation, with no risk of any kind. You'll be glad you did!

GET A *Free* MYSTERY GIFT...

SURPRISE MYSTERY GIFT COULD BE YOURS **FREE** AS A SPECIAL "THANK YOU" FROM THE EDITORS

The Editor's "Thank You" Free Gifts Include:

- *Two BRAND-NEW Romance novels!*
- *An exciting mystery gift!*

Yes! I have placed my
Editor's "Thank You" seal in the
space provided at right. Please
send me 2 free books and a
fabulous mystery gift. I
understand I am under no
obligation to purchase any
books, as explained on the
back and on the opposite page.

393 MDL D39C   **193 MDL D39D**

FIRST NAME   LAST NAME

ADDRESS

APT.#   CITY

STATE/PROV.   ZIP/POSTAL CODE

(ED2-SS-05)

Thank You!

DETACH AND MAIL CARD TODAY!

© 2003 HARLEQUIN ENTERPRISES LTD.

Offer limited to one per household and not valid to current MIRA,
The Best of The Best or Romance subscribers. All orders subject to
approval. Credit or debit balances in a customer's account(s) may be
offset by any other outstanding balance owed by or to the customer.

® and ™ are trademarks owned and used by the trademark owner and/or its licensee

The Reader Service — Here's How It Works:

Accepting your 2 free books and gift places you under no obligation to buy anything. You may keep the books and gift and return the shipping statement marked "cancel." If you do not cancel, about a month later we'll send you 3 additional books and bill you just $4.99 each in the U.S., or $5.49 each in Canada, plus 25¢ shipping & handling per book and applicable taxes if any.* That's the complete price and — compared to cover prices starting from $5.99 each in the U.S. and $6.99 each in Canada — it's quite a bargain! You may cancel at any time, but if you choose to continue, every month we'll send you 3 more books, which you may either purchase at the discount price or return to us and cancel your subscription.

*Terms and prices subject to change without notice. Sales tax applicable in N.Y. Canadian residents will be charged applicable provincial taxes and GST.

Dalton let out a pent-up breath. "There's nothing to tell."

"The suitcase means there's plenty to tell."

"Grace—Dr. Reynolds—fired me this morning."

That surprised Christie. She let him go. The pain in his face, that she *felt* in him, was raw.

Chapter 12

A pang of sympathy burst inside Christie as she heard the hurt in Dalton's announcement, but she shoved her emotions away. That had to have been hard for Dalton, but she had a job to do. "Why did Dr. Reynolds fire you?"

"She heard me talking to Michael, telling him what I was going to do. That I was going to come clean with your office and tell them about her contact with Sammy Bao and the Bronze Tigers." Dalton took another breath. "She went ballistic. Fired me on the spot just a couple minutes ago."

"You expected that. You can still testify and get her and Michael out of here. We can put them beyond the reach of the Bronze Tigers."

"No, we can't."

"Why?"

"Because while we were figuring out how we were going to finesse this situation last night before we got…distracted, we didn't think of what Grace could do."

"What did Grace do?"

"She told me if I try to betray her—and that's her word, Special Agent Chace, *betray*—then she was going to deny everything I said and tell the DARPA chief that what I said was all bullshit and the talk of a disgruntled employee."

"You work for the military, Dalton. You're not a disgruntled employee."

"That's not how she's going to tell it." He turned his dark-lensed gaze on her. "She's also going to tell my commanding officer that I made improper advances on her."

"But you didn't."

"Hell no. She's my best friend's widow. Michael's *mom*."

"They won't believe her."

"Belief doesn't count with the military. There'll be an investigation. Even when—and really I should say *if* because living there inside that house with them leaves me compromised—Michael will hear all about it." His voice tightened and he couldn't speak for a moment. He shook his head. "I'm not going to have Michael go through that. He's been through enough."

"But you didn't do anything wrong. His mother—"

"His mother is scared, Special Agent Chace. Her son has been threatened. She'll do anything she feels she has to do in order to protect him."

And so will you, Christie thought. Confused, she searched for a way around the situation. Couldn't find one.

"Even if I'm cleared of the charges, I'm not going to be in a good place with the Army," Dalton said. "I've got a lot of years in with the Rangers, even counting the duty here. The military has been a home to me longer than this place. I don't want to lose everything." He took another deep breath and let it go. "And I'm not going to have Michael deal with the fallout from this situation." He looked away from her, swinging his gaze back to the pickup. "*Now* can I go, Special Agent Chace?"

Feeling guilty, Christie stepped back. Her mind reeled and she faulted herself. She should have remained professional. Both of them had deserved that. Dalton had been on an emotional roller coaster with everything that had been going on for weeks. She should have kept her head.

She folded her arms across her breasts and kept her game face on. She could be professional now. Maybe it was a little late, but she could do that. "Sure," she said.

Dalton climbed into the truck and started the engine.

"Sergeant Geller," she said.

He looked at her. His face was clean of emotion, as smooth and hard as Kevlar armor.

"I'll put in a good word with your commanding officer. You ran a tight operation here. I can back that up. Maybe it will help."

He nodded. "Thanks."

Christie felt cold and distant inside. Part of her, she knew, was pissed at him. They'd been intimate last night, now there was no mention of it. He could have at least been a little more—*tactful*—about that and not so much with the *Special Agent Chace*.

"No problem," she said. She watched him drive away, checking through the security that he'd set up around the compound. In a few moments, the pickup disappeared around the tree-lined road and into the forest.

Lorna radioed for her over the Enhanced telecom/recording unit inside her right jawbone. "Hey, wasn't that the night wind I just saw leaving?"

"That," Christie said, "was Sergeant Geller departing. Evidently he's been relieved of command here."

"Oh." Lorna sounded embarrassed. "Is there anything I can do?"

"No." Christie couldn't be still anymore. She started walking, and she wasn't surprised when her steps took her toward Dr. Reynolds's office.

Standing outside Dr. Reynolds's office, Christie buzzed the video intercom inset in the wall beside the door. The screen cleared almost immediately. Dr. Reynolds sat at her desk studying a 3-D holograph of a complicated array of wiring and computer strands threading through a human spine.

Seeing images like that, knowing she carried a lot of the same hardware inside her own body, sometimes made Christie uncomfortable. She never felt the Enhanced equipment that allowed her the special abilities she had, and the pain of the surgeries was long forgotten. But seeing the systems and subsystems jarred her.

"Special Agent Chace," Dr. Reynolds said. "You're interrupting my work time. I don't tolerate interruptions."

"I understand, Dr. Reynolds." Christie forced herself to remain polite. It was hard to do knowing that the woman had fired Dalton and threatened to keep him and Michael apart. The two needed each other. Only an idiot would not see that. "I wanted to talk to you briefly."

"About what?" Dr. Reynolds stared at her through the screen.

"Sergeant Geller."

Dr. Reynolds steepled her fingers. Her face was as much of a mask as Dalton's. "Sergeant Geller no longer works here."

"I know that. I thought that we could talk—"

"Any concerns you might have about the security of this compound should be taken up with Gerald Abrams. Mr. Abrams is the new chief of security here."

Well that didn't take long, Christie thought sarcastically. *Throw out your husband's best friend, the guy who's been raising your son while you've been too busy, and just slip someone else in.*

Gerald Abrams was the number two man in Dalton's group. An ex-cop with an impressive record in Ohio who had gone into government security work. His promotion was a no-brainer. But it was immediate and bloodless, and damned cold.

"I'm sure you'll find Mr. Abrams a suitable replacement for Sergeant Geller," Dr. Reynolds stated crisply. She used a laser projection glove to touch points on the holograph, opening three-by-five card representations in the air by the image.

"I'm sure," Christie began.

"I've got a lot of work to do here," Dr. Reynolds said. "If Mr. Abrams can't help you with whatever it is you want, we'll talk at a later time."

The screen blanked, leaving only glassy ebony that held Christie's reflection.

Sure Abrams is going to be a good security officer, she thought bitterly, *but who's going to pitch Michael's batting practice?*

Christie walked, marshaling her thoughts and checking her options. What she'd wanted to do was kick down Dr. Reynolds's office door and tell the woman what a big mistake she'd made and how wrong she had been hurting Dalton.

And how unfair it was to the man and her son.

Cursing to herself, Christie reminded herself that *fair* rarely ever entered the real world. Memories of last night warred with batting practice and seeing Dalton playing in last Sunday's game, and they mixed up with how driven and deadly he'd been in the warehouse the night Arturo Gennady had been killed by the Bronze Tigers.

He was like no one else she'd ever met.

Before she knew it, she'd ended up at the empty ball field. Standing in the sun, she looked at the batter's box and the pitcher's mound.

Dalton's words from the previous night haunted her as much as his kisses and the feel of his hands on her body. *You get all the rules in baseball, you know. When to run, when to slide, where to throw the ball. When to sacrifice. But that's all for the good of the team. And at the end of it, even though you've sacrificed, you still get to be part of the team.*

The ball field didn't look the same without Dalton and Michael there.

When to sacrifice.

The feeling that something was wrong nagged at Christie. She tried to figure out what it was. Something about Dalton?

She closed her eyes and replayed the video that automatically recorded while she was on the job, giving her access to hands-on memory and automatic uploads to her case files unless she erased them. She saw Dalton walking again, carrying the suitcase.

The suitcase.

If he were leaving, would he be able to pack all his belongings in a single suitcase? Would he give in without fighting?

Only he hadn't fought because he hadn't wanted Michael to have to deal with repercussions. He was thinking about Michael first, putting the boy first.

Suddenly, Christie's eyes opened. She stared out at the ball field. Where the hell was Michael? She hadn't seen him all morning.

Christie's phone rang inside her head as she jogged back to the Reynolds's house. Caller ID opened a window in the vision of her left eye. The caller was Dalton Geller. The number wasn't one she had listed for him.

"Dalton—" she said, intending to take control of the situation immediately. She hated being played the fool.

"Not Dalton," a deep male baritone informed her. "I'm a friend of his."

Christie immediately executed a trace-back protocol with a GPS locator on the incoming call. "What friend?" she asked.

"We don't have time for a lot of horseplay, Special Agent Chace."

The trace-back bounced back with an immediate answer. According to the information the computer came up with, Dalton Geller was calling from inside the house here on the compound. She didn't believe the finding and immediately ran the program again.

"The trace-back is only going to give you the information you see," the man went on.

The trace-back program was FBI encrypted. If the man talking to her had spoofed it, then he was good.

"You're another minute behind," the man said. "You put together that Michael was missing. I'm impressed. Dalton said you were good. That makes me feel a little better about what we're doing because he left a lot hanging in the balance for me. And you."

"You've got my attention," Christie said, turning and looking around the compound.

"I'm not there, Special Agent Chace. I've been watching you via satellite since this morning."

A satellite recon? Christie was even more impressed. "Where's Dalton?"

"Making the drop with the Bronze Tigers."

Christie accepted that immediately. There could be no other way. "He's got the Seek-n-Fire prototype."

"And Dr. Reynolds's research, yes. They told Dr. Reynolds that they would kill her son if she didn't give it over. After they killed Arturo Gennady last week, Dr. Reynolds believes them."

Christie believed them, too. The Chinese Triad had concentrated on making believers with that strike at the scientist and her team. "What happened?"

"The Bronze Tigers had two men inside the operation here."

"Two of Dalton's men?" Christie had trouble believing that. Dalton was good and no one would have easily gotten past him.

"Not Dalton's guys. Two of Dr. Reynolds's lab assistants. Neither of them had previous criminal records so they checked out clean. Maybe this is their first time, or maybe they've always been clever in the past. They grabbed Michael this morning."

Accessing her onboard computer, Christie opened the security post checkout sheets. Two men, Wesley Baird and Ray Dooley, had been checked through at 6:53 a.m. that morning. Another brief cross-check showed they'd put in for the morning off weeks ago.

She called up video from the guardpost, coordinated it with the lab files and discovered the two men had left in Baird's custom van. The van offered plenty of room to hide a ten-year-old boy.

"Don't notify your team, Special Agent Chace," the man said. "The compound is under surveillance. The Bronze Tigers have already broken into your communications link."

"What about yours?"

"They can't get to me," the man said. "I'm one line of data-stream in a place loaded with them. Plus, I'm coming at you straight off a satellite bounceback rather than through the on-site systems or your government communication crap."

"That's what you say."

"If I say wrong, Dalton and the boy are already both dead."

"What happened?"

In terse details, the man relayed how Dalton had come home that morning only to find Baird and Dooley waiting on him. The two men had already penetrated Dr. Reynolds's security and taken the scientist and Michael into custody. Michael had been sedated. Once Baird and Dooley had explained how the arrangement with the Seek-n-Fire prototype was going to shake out, they'd tranquilized Dr. Reynolds and Dalton. They'd waited till the shipment had arrived, then staged the show for Christie's benefit. Dalton had explained her involvement in the situation and how she would have to be finessed.

"Have you had contact with Dalton?" she asked when he finished.

"Of course not. There was no way. I'm good, but I'm not that good."

"Dalton had you set up as a backup play."

"Yeah. From the moment he met you. You complicated things, Special Agent Chace. Presented too many variables on the field. Dalton would have been able to keep Michael and Dr. Reynolds safe if you and your team hadn't arrived."

"You don't know that."

"He foxed you and the Bronze Tigers," the man said. "I'd say he was covering his bases pretty well."

"So why did you contact me? Just to warn me away? Because if you or Dalton think you're going to be able to take on the Bronze Tigers, by yourselves, then you're—"

"Dalton told me to contact you. He's depending on you for the save." The man hesitated. "He said you impressed the hell out of him the other night at the warehouse."

By losing Gennady and nearly getting all of my team killed? Christie forced away the recrimination that had constantly lurked inside her mind since that night. The guilt jerked, twitched and occasionally wriggled like a live thing.

"You're Enhanced, Special Agent Chace," the man went on. "But you're going to have to decide if you can handle what you're about to face."

"I can get a team—"

"And they'll kill Dalton and the boy."

Christie thought frantically. She was at her best when she was thinking on her feet. "It doesn't have to be a team from here. I can get another team."

"By the time you convince your superiors you know what's going on, it'll be too late."

He's right, Christie realized grimly. Even if she'd left at the same time that Dalton had, she might be too late.

"You waited too long. They've probably already killed Dalton."

"No," the man said calmly. "Dalton has an ace up his

sleeve. He walked into the meeting with the prototype and a bomb. If he has to, he'll negotiate Michael's safety—"

"And sacrifice himself," Christie said, knowing Dalton would do exactly that.

"He said you had a choice to make, Special Agent Chace."

"What choice?"

"He said to tell you that you're the clutch hitter. You can wait outside till he sends Michael to you for safe-keeping, or you can swing for the fences."

"Do you know where Dalton is?"

"On the move at the present. He's already gotten through his initial meeting."

"How are you tracking him?"

"Satellite link on his heartbeat signature. We scanned him into the recognition system. Visual tracking backing that up."

Christie was familiar with the tracking ops. She'd used them before. "You've got some high-end tech."

"I'm all about the tech."

"Me, too," Christie said. "And when I've had the chance, I've always swung for the fences."

Chapter 13

Sammy Bao was not a happy man.

Dalton stood in front of the Bronze Tiger lieutenant and listened to the barrage of Chinese invective Bao unleashed over the Enhanced communication link the Triad man carried inside his head. Whoever was on the other end of the connection wasn't happy either.

Standing in the center of a circle of armed men felt alien and strange to Dalton. Enemies actively seeking his life had surrounded him on the battlefield before, but there had always been terrain to work with, other Rangers he could count on. Now, there was nothing, only the empty expanse of the fifth floor of the building presently under construction near Washington, D.C.'s downtown area.

Dalton stood with the suitcase he'd carried from the lab compound. His left hand felt almost numb with the weight, but he felt better for it. The Seek-n-Fire prototype didn't weigh all that much, but the plastic explosives he'd filled the rest of the suitcase around the device did.

The building's fifth floor, where he stood, was just a shell. Interior work to subdivide the floor into quadrants with an intersection of hallways had begun, but skeletal walls occupied the space under the rooftop. The building was on a tight deadline for completion. This morning, however, the construction crews had been kept away to give the Bronze Tigers a chance to complete their transaction.

But time was working against Dalton and he knew it. He spoke over the rapid-fire Chinese. "Bao."

One of the nearest Triad members hit Dalton for daring to interrupt his boss on the phone. It was a conditioned response, one brought about by years of showing similar instant punishment for demonstrations of disrespect. Instantly, Dalton captured the man's wrist in his free hand, then rolled sideways and delivered three stunning sidekicks to the man's head, breaking his nose and driving him backward.

In a heartbeat that was carefully measured by the monitoring device that Kirk Brandt, the cybercafé owner in Roanoke, had designed, half the Triad members had their weapons trained on Dalton, who stopped in his tracks and released the man who'd attacked him. But the other half of the gun-toting Chinese Mafia enforcers aimed their weapons at the man Dalton dropped nearly unconscious to the ground. All of them had seen the electronic trigger chemically adhered to Dalton's flesh over his chest. He was shirtless, and the movement had shifted his jacket to reveal the surprise that he carried. They obviously had experience with them, judging from the sudden unease they showed.

Dalton wiped blood from his mouth. "Bao," he said again.

Bao glared at him. "What?"

"I'm not going to wait much longer."

"The deal goes down when I say it does."

"It goes down," Dalton said, keeping his tone neutral

through years of experience even when he felt naked and vulnerable and was worried about Michael, "when whoever is at the other end of that connection says it goes down. Tell whoever that is that I'm not going to wait."

Bao stared at Dalton from behind the wraparound sunglasses. "And instead of waiting, what do you think you're going to do?"

Dalton walked toward the man. "I wouldn't shoot me," he said. "The explosive inside the suitcase with the prototype is set to detonate if my beats per minute drop below anything that allowed me to remain conscious." As long as he could remain conscious, there was also a manual detonation switch. The autodetonator precluded getting killed as well as getting tranquilized out of his mind.

The guards, having no choice, went with him. Bao, wanting to save face, stood his ground.

"If I get tired of waiting," Dalton said, "I'm going to believe that you've already killed the boy and that you're stalling, trying to figure out a way around that. And I'm going to detonate the bomb to kill you as well as the men up here. When the metro police find out who I am through DNA and that I brought the prototype here, which someone will recognize from the pieces, Dr. Reynolds will be pulled from her lab immediately whether she wants to be or not. You won't get another chance at this technology. Your boss won't get another chance at this technology.".

Bao took a deep breath, his face hardening with anger. "You're in no position to give demands—"

"I'm in no position," Dalton said, "to do anything else." He paused, locking eyes with the man. "You put me there."

"You would do this? Even if it means the boy's life is forfeit?"

"For all I know," Dalton said in a wintry voice, "Michael's already dead and you're treading water trying to come up with an alternative plan."

Bao was quiet for a time. "The boy is alive. He is just now arrived."

"Then show him to me."

Speaking quickly, Bao ordered that Michael be brought up. A moment later, the elevator dinged its arrival. Turning slightly, keeping Bao in his vision, Dalton watched Michael, herded between two enforcers with machine pistols from the elevator cage.

Michael looked terrified. Big tears leaked from his eyes and down into the cloth gag that kept him from talking. Disposable plastic handcuffs bound his thin wrists. He wore jeans, sneakers and his Atlanta Braves jersey.

"It's going to be all right, Michael," Dalton said, and hoped he sounded convincing. "I'm going to get you out of here."

"All right," Bao said, "let's deal." He took the pistol from his shoulder rig and pointed it at Michael's head. "Or I kill him and you get to watch before you blow us up." He smiled mirthlessly. "I've seen very few men willing to commit suicide the way you plan to, Sergeant Geller."

Christie stood in the cargo area of the small utility helicopter and peered down at the ten-story building under construction that Dalton Geller's unknown partner had identified as the place where the kidnap ransom was staged to take place.

The helicopter bore the identification markings of one of the large number of taxi-helos that handled arrivals and departures to and from Dulles Airport as well as outlying areas. Important political figures and corporate lobbyists didn't want to deal with the Washington, D.C. traffic.

Dalton's mystery partner had arranged a phone call from the Georgetown hospital that informed the lab security people that her father had been admitted for chest pains. A quick phone call to her father had set that up, and he actually was in the hospital at that point undergoing stress evaluation. The ruse had gotten Christie clear of the compound in minutes.

The taxi-helo had picked her up in Roanoke. She'd thought she'd get to see Dalton's partner, but the aircraft was remote-controlled. The cargo area had also been filled with enough firepower to outfit a small special forces unit.

Christie had skinned down to underwear on the twenty-minute trip to Washington, D.C. and replaced her outerwear with combat BDUs and Kevlar armor that protected her chest, midsection and hips down to her thighs, boots encased her feet. A Kevlar helmet with a full faceshield that would deflect everything but a full-on shot protected her head.

The combat harness supported six S&W forty-caliber pistols. Two were snugged in shoulder leather, two more at her thighs in counterterrorist drop holsters just above her knees at the sides, and the final two behind her back in pancake holsters. She'd never been loaded with this much gear before, but with her Enhanced strength, the weight was no problem to carry.

Extra magazines for the pistols, all of them in the extended thirty-round sizes currently in the pistols she carried, rested in the pockets of the combat harness.

She also had a few flash-bang grenades designed to create smoke to foil normal and night vision, and red-hot embers to throw off thermographic capability. Kevlar boots just her size encased her feet.

"Everything fit?" the man asked over her comm-link.

"Yeah." Suited up now, knowing that she was about to step into a whipsaw, Christie felt nervous. She blew her breath out and tried to relax a little. That was a joke.

"It's not too late to back out," the man told her.

Christie used her Enhanced vision to scan the target building. A huge crane hung beside the structure and hills of dirt and piles of steel girders occupied the broken land around it.

"I'm not backing out," she told him. Somewhere in that building, Dalton and Michael were negotiating for their lives.

"Your heart rate and respiration are up," the man said.

Christie damned the Kevlar armor's built-in system read-out. Those features had been layered in to help special forces teams monitor their members in case of injury.

"I'm fine," she said. "Bring me in."

The helo banked slightly and zipped toward the building. The rotor strained overhead and the pitch in the thunder filling the cargo space changed.

"What's the maximum drop you can take?" the man asked. "Fifty, sixty feet?"

"Closer to one hundred," Christie said.

"Never fully geared, though."

"No."

The helo shifted to a steeper decline. "Today we'll go for forty. Remember—when you hit, they're going to be gunning for you."

Christie pushed her breath out and gripped the sides of the cargo door. The wind shot by her, cool and crisp. The helo had a direct line to the building now, closing fast. Its distinct shadow fell onto the building as they came out of the sun to give her a small but precious edge because the men looking into the brightness wouldn't be able to see her and might impair their vision for just a few precious seconds.

"Ready…" the man said, "…and—go!"

Without hesitation, even though it looked like she was going to miss the building, Christie jumped from the cargo door. There was an instant of free fall, then she was dropping like a rock.

She hit the roof in a parachutist's roll, hands up to protect her head and control the direction. She pushed off the rooftop, charging into an all-out sprint, her Enhanced speed making her fleet as a deer despite the weight of the gear she carried. She ran back in the direction she'd come, knowing the men inside would have heard her hit.

Reaching the building's eastern side, she pulled a piton from the combat rigging and slammed the tip down through the metal with a shrill impact. She flipped the climbing rope from her shoulder, affixed the D-ring at one end to the piton, and threw the coil of rope down the side of the building.

She rappelled down, facing the ground below as she ran along the building's side. The rope burned along her gloves as she slid down it. At the fifth floor, she paused and took out the specially shaped plastic explosive she'd been given, affixed it to the wall, set the electronic detonator, and kicked back from the wall.

At the apex of her swing, made even wider by her Enhanced strength, Christie detonated the plastic explosive. Constructed as it was, the explosive blew inward, taking out a five-foot section of the wall. Christie swung toward the wall, aiming for the opening, then released her hold on the rope and shot inside.

She skidded across the floor, riding a wave of debris torn free from the wall, getting a knee folded up under her like she was stealing second base clean and free. She spotted Triad gang members all around her inside the big area. Dalton and Michael were to her left.

Reaching into the combat harness, Christie took out the WAM-ball—Wide Area Matrix—and threw it toward the nearest walls. Coated in superimpact-resistant rubber so that it bounced immediately and propelled by her Enhanced strength, the WAM-ball ricocheted from the wall and bounced at crazy angles around the room. Outfitted with a miniature digital video camera, the WAM-ball fed images of the room directly into Christie's onboard computer. As soon as the feed began, her vision split into two inside her head, giving her a whirling view of the room from the WAM-ball's perspective as well as her own vision.

Even before she skidded to a stop, Christie raked the forty-caliber pistols from her back and extended them in two separate directions. She started firing as she got to her feet, putting two rounds through the head of one Bronze Tiger and three rounds into the chest of another.

Through the video connection in the WAM-ball, Christie saw Dalton lunge toward Michael, taking the boy to the ground in a bear hug and covering him protectively.

"The bomb's shut down," the male voice said inside Christie's head. "It's all up to you whether the three of you walk out of there alive. I've called the police."

One of the Bronze Tigers lifted an assault rifle as Christie ran at him with both pistols blazing, aiming at him as well as other nearby targets. The shotgun blast caught her in the chest and knocked her backward. Although the Kevlar stopped the double-aught pellets from penetrating, the armor didn't stop the blunt trauma. Her breath left her lungs in a rush that left spots in her vision.

Throwing away the empty pistols, she stayed on her feet, then leaped up and flipped as more Bronze Tigers fired at her. She gripped the pistols snugged in shoulder leather and yanked them free even as she turned upside down. She started firing at once, hitting targets she saw as well as ones identified by the WAM-ball. When she came down, she landed flat and didn't try to stand. With both arms extended before her, she rolled toward the wall where the door to the hallway was.

Bronze Tigers fell all around her. Some of them were Enhanced and some were not. None of them were expecting the moves that she was showing them. It was one thing to get Enhanced, to have greater strength and speed, but training to use those things was a different matter. She'd worked diligently in her martial arts classes as well as on the shooting range holographs to get the most from her abilities.

By the time she reached the door, her second set of pistols had blown back empty. But three-quarters of the Bronze Tigers inside the room were down and out of the play.

Christie got to her feet and dashed into the hallway. She dropped into a crouch with her back to the wall, then threw away the second set of pistols. She took a deep breath, feeling her lungs scream with the agony of the unconscious movement for the first time since she'd been shot point-blank with the shotgun.

She stripped two flash-bang grenades from the combat harness, pulled the rings and tossed one into the door she'd just come through. She lobbed the other grenade ahead, getting it through the door at that end of the hallway like a shortstop picking off a runner going for first on a red-hot grounder. The grenade hit the wall inside the room, then ricocheted into the room.

Accessing the video feed from the WAM-ball, she saw the two grenades bounce into the room, scaring the Bronze Tigers back, then detonate one after the other. Pools of black smoke and blazing embers spewed into the air, creating dark masses that glowed with an inner light.

Drawing her final pair of pistols, Christie went back into the door she'd just left. The view she'd gotten from the WAM-ball indicated that most of the Bronze Tigers believed she would be coming through that door.

Inside the helmet, Christie felt like she could barely breathe. The bitter smoke slammed into her lungs with her first breath, biting deeply enough to make her cough. She triggered the adrenaline pump inside her body then, and the world suddenly got slower as her movements sped up.

She targeted the Bronze Tigers standing outside the billowing smoke clouds. Once she was immersed within it, even her Enhanced vision—night vision as well as thermographic—would be useless. She fired, aiming for head shots. Part of her, the part that would later regret the violence she'd unleashed, screamed. But she silenced the voice, knowing that Michael and Dalton would be dead the minute that she let up.

If they weren't already dead.

Once the pistols blew back empty, she stepped inside the swirling smoke. The WAM-ball came to a rest near the middle of the room, still providing Christie with a three-hundred-and-sixty-degree visual of the room as the vid-cam spun inside the resilient rubber housing. She judged her position as she reloaded the pistols by feel, slamming home two more extended magazines.

Using the information given to her by the WAM-ball, Christie fired at targets that stepped outside the two smoke clouds. Walking through the cloud revealed other targets when she bumped into them. She used the pistols and her knees and elbows to take out everyone she came in contact with. She shot those she could, but crushed larynxes, shattered temples and cheekbones to cause unconsciousness and concussion and grabbed heads to bring her knees up into them and stun or kill the Bronze Tigers.

The WAM-ball told her Dalton was still covering Michael, but Dalton was bleeding from at least three wounds. Evidently he'd caught stray rounds or the Bronze Tigers had guessed the bomb he'd used to hold them at bay was now disconnected.

Christie felt the adrenal pump strong within her now. Even her lungs opened up and she felt like she was breathing easier, but she knew that was a lie. Her lungs were filling up with smoke that would later have to be coughed out and the payback to her system would leave her devastated.

Sammy Bao had stepped into the smoke cloud as well, obviously deciding that was the safest place for him. Christie moved warily, knowing the smoke clouds were already starting to disperse. She blinked, waiting for her vision to return.

A shadow moved in front of her, getting more visible as it neared her. A moment later the man stood revealed in the shifting smoke. He had a hand over his mouth, coughing, eyes streaming tears. He saw her and lifted his weapon, aiming at her and firing.

The bullet cut the smoke-filled air and slammed into Christie's faceshield. With her adrenaline-spiked senses, she saw the bullet slap into the bulletproof polymer, hoped that the round wasn't dead-on and fired her own weapon at the man's hand covering his mouth. Her head snapped back, driving her backward a step. When she recovered, she looked around for the man and saw him still falling, a hole in his hand and blood rushing from his mouth as his eyes glazed.

Sirens shrilled out on the street, letting her know that the Washington, D.C. PD had arrived in record time. Christie figured maybe her dad had alerted some of his buddies to be prepared to roll immediately.

Then, over the WAM-ball view, she saw Dalton lurch to his feet unsteadily and get Michael moving toward the door. Evidently he'd decided to get the boy clear before anyone thought to use them against Christie.

One of the Bronze Tigers stepped through the smoke, saw Dalton escaping, then raised an alarm and his assault rifle. Turning instantly, Christie lifted her pistols and fired at the man, chopping him down before he could shoot. Two more Bronze Tigers stepped clear as well, and Christie killed one of them with head shots before her weapons blew back empty.

Gathering herself, she ran and leaped, delivering a flying kick to the man that snapped his neck and sent him down. She rolled and got to her feet as Sammy Bao emerged from the swirling smoke.

Stains from the smoke coated his electric-blue suit and his face. Dust coated the lenses of his wraparound sunglasses. He lifted his pistols and fired at her.

Suppressing the instinctive urge to duck for cover, knowing she was the only thing standing between Dalton and the boy, Christie ignored the thundering thumps that hammered her chest and faceshield, tilting her head so the chances of catching a bullet full-on was practically nil. Her faceshield shattered, holding together but filling her vision with cracks.

Bao's pistols blew back empty before she reached him. She threw herself forward into a slide, choosing to stay low rather than go into the air where Bao's greater size and strength could give him an advantage. She took his feet out from under him with her legs, spilling him to the ground.

She rolled, coming up at once as Bao did the same. The sirens continued screaming outside.

Circling to the right, keeping her hands up in front of her face, careful not to step on any of the dead bodies surrounding her, Christie watched Bao.

"It's over, Bao," she said.

"Not over," he spat. He reached under his jacket and took out a knife, flicking it open with quick movements to bare the blade.

"You lost," Christie said. "You lost the device and your hold on Dr. Reynolds. You lost face, too."

Bao smiled at her. "Then I'll wear yours." He lunged at her, swiping at her throat with the blade.

Instinctively, she dodged back. When she did, she stepped into a spinning sidekick that felt like it took her head off her shoulders. Recovering, she found that the faceshield had broken into pieces and the Kevlar helmet had slid sideways on her head. Still backing away, she loosened and removed the helmet, holding it by the straps. When Bao lunged again, she sidestepped and swung the helmet, catching his arm and knocking the knife from his hand.

Then he was on her, punching, kicking and blocking with his legs as she tried to hold him back. He was too big, too powerful and as quick as she was. For a few seconds, it was everything she could do to simply stay alive. And time was running out. She knew the adrenal pump was running out and would leave her defenseless.

Bao wouldn't care if she were unable to protect herself. It would only make her easier to kill.

The only thing she had going for her was technique. Bao was used to using his size, his speed and his strength, against opponents. Christie blocked a head punch with a forearm sweep, then jabbed him in the face, rocking his head back. She countered a leg sweep, danced out of the way and caught him with a round-house kick to the back of the head. Again and again, she managed to break his attack and sting him, but she might as well have been a mosquito for all the damage she was able to inflict. In time, she'd wear him down, but time was working against her. Once the adrenal pump emptied, she was finished.

Bao growled angrily, deep in his chest, and rushed in with his arms thrown forward. In the WAM-ball, she saw herself picked up and thrown back against the wall. Cracked plaster rained down around them, tainting the smoke-laden air with white dust.

He locked his hands around her throat and squeezed. She started choking at once. Spots filled her vision till she was blind. She turned her full attention to the WAM-ball feed and saw Bao choking the life from her, on the verge of snapping her neck as he forced her head backward. He'd wedged his body between her legs, forcing her back against the wall so she couldn't kick him or gain any real leverage, using his greater strength and size for all that it was worth.

She clapped her hands against the sides of his head, bursting his eardrums. But he didn't release her even though blood streamed from both ears. Curling her forefinger over her middle finger, stiffening them both, she brought her right arm beneath his left, then struck as hard as she could.

Her fingers penetrated Bao's left eye. Blood covered her hand.

For a moment she didn't think even that was going to stop him. He remained locked on to her. Then Bao toppled, dead before he hit the ground.

Christie tried to catch herself and remain standing, but her legs didn't work and she fell in a heap. Feeling the payback in her system already beginning, she managed to force herself into a sitting position with her back against the wall. She sat in front of Bao's corpse, with a room full of dead Bronze Tigers all over.

She was still there when the Washington, D.C. S.W.A.T. teams arrived to take charge of the scene.

Movement caught her attention at the corner of her eye. She lifted one of the pistols, holding it in a trembling hand.

"Chace!" It was Dalton, barely managing under his own power. His face was grim, smudged and bloody.

She put the pistol down as Dalton stumbled for her. She knew he wasn't going to make it. Forcing herself

up, she caught him as he started to fall. Only her Enhanced strength kept them from toppling.

"Knew I could count on you," he whispered. Then he
exhaled and went limp.

Tears filled Christie as she laid Dalton on the floor
and started C.P.R. *Damn you, Dalton!* she thought.
Don't you die on me!

She kept at it till the EMTs arrived and pushed her
away.

Epilogue

Still bruised and battered, sunglasses and a Braves baseball hat concealing some of the damage, Christie sat in the lower deck at the Atlanta baseball field along the third baseline. Three days of healing, and a constant series of interrogations and follow-up investigations, and she still looked like hell. The bruises were starting to fade, though. And D.O. Fielding, instead of writing her up for attempting the rescue solo, had ordered her to take a few days off.

Dalton sat beside her. Like her, he was dressed casually, wearing jeans, a pullover and tennis shoes. His right arm was in a sling and he limped on his right leg. He'd worn a Kevlar vest to the ransom meet, but he'd still suffered four bullet wounds. His doctor hadn't wanted him moving around much, but Dalton was Dalton and he decided he was fit enough to attend the game.

"Regretting being the tough guy?" Christie asked. "Thinking maybe you should have stayed in the hospital or checked into a hotel room?" The baseball game had been his idea, just to get outside once he was released from medical. Personally, she thought he was pushing it, but during the past few days of visiting him in his hospital room, she'd learned that he was an incredibly resilient guy.

And part of him, she felt certain, hadn't wanted to be alone while he faced losing Michael. Neither of them had been able to get in touch with Dr. Reynolds.

"I'm not the tough guy," Dalton said behind his wrap-around sunglasses. "You took out Bao and his guys. I just picked up your slack."

"You kept Michael safe."

Dalton frowned, and the expression pulled at the bandage on his face. A plastic surgeon had had to put his left cheekbone and face back together. "I shouldn't have ever let him get that vulnerable."

"That wasn't your fault. You did what you could." Christie stopped herself from telling him that if anyone was culpable in the boy's kidnapping, Dr. Reynolds had been. Since she'd gotten her son back safely three days ago, Dr. Reynolds had agreed to relocation. Christie still didn't feel overly charitable toward the woman. Grace Reynolds hadn't come to see Dalton while he'd been in the hospital. Neither had Michael.

"Still haven't found out who hired the Bronze Tigers?" Dalton asked.

"Not yet. We will. It's a matter of time. The Bronze Tigers, though, have become persona non grata. They're all in the process of being rounded up and bounced as undesirable aliens. That will help level the field. For a while."

Dalton craned his head around with difficulty, searching back up in the stands.

Christie took his hand in hers and squeezed gently. "It's going to be all right," she whispered. In the past few days of being around him, of talking about Michael and Mac and the other things he'd talked about while on painkillers, she'd gotten closer to him. Whatever was going on between them, even though she was afraid of putting a name to it, it was real and solid—the beginning of something wonderful. She didn't know how far it would go, but she was willing to go the distance.

Dalton felt the same way. She could see it in his eyes, and feel it—like now as he held her hand—in his touch. He just didn't trust life as much as she did. But that was fine because she was patient.

"I thought your dad was going to join us," Dalton said. He'd gotten to meet Wallace Chace in the hospital.

"He is," Christie said.

"He'd better hurry or he's going to miss the opening pitch."

And then Christie saw her father coming down the steps. He towered and stood out among the crowd, something he'd always done. With his size, he made the small boy at his side look even smaller.

Michael Reynolds, dressed in his Braves uniform and wearing his baseball hat, looked anxiously through the crowd as he held on to the big man's hand.

"Michael," Dalton whispered, pushing up from the seat. He had some difficulty with the wounded leg.

Then Michael saw him and came flying down the steps. In another heartbeat, Dalton had his arms wrapped around the boy's shoulders. After a moment, when Michael released him, Dalton looked up at Wallace.

"I found him at the airport wandering around," Wallace said. "I couldn't very well just leave him there, now could I?"

"You managed this?" Dalton asked.

"I still have a few strings I can pull now and again," Wallace said. "And I came from a big family, raised a big family." He shrugged. "I know how to negotiate when it comes to family. I talked to Dr. Reynolds and pointed out that Michael needed you. My daughter thought you did. And I thought so, too." He smiled. "You and Michael will get to see each other on a regular basis. Who knows, maybe Dr. Reynolds will decide she needs her security chief back when he gets on his feet."

They sat and Dalton looked at Christie in surprise. "You kept this a secret."

"I," Christie told him triumphantly, "keep the best secrets." But it had been hard.

Dalton took her hand, squeezed it warmly, then leaned over and kissed her. She kissed back, lost in the moment and the excitement she felt in him.

"Dalton," Michael whispered on the other side of Dalton, "is she your girlfriend?"

Dalton pulled back and looked at Christie, smiling. "Yeah. She is."

"Cool," Michael said.

Christie sat next to Dalton and snuggled in close when he wrapped his uninjured arm around her shoulders. His breath felt warm against her hair. Seconds later, the announcer asked the crowd to stand for "The Star-Spangled Banner" and she stood with Dalton with their caps over their hearts. Before she could sit down, Dalton turned her to face him.

"Thanks," he said. "For being here."

Then he leaned in and kissed her, tilting her face up to meet his. She wrapped her arms behind his neck and held on to him, surprised at his strength and the intense way he made her feel.

"Guys," Michael whispered. "This is a baseball game. Uh…guys? Everybody's staring."

Looking away from Dalton, Christie saw that one of

the audience cams had locked on to them. They stood embracing and kissing for the whole ballpark to see on the holograph above centerfield.

"Well, that's embarrassing," Christie said.

"Do you think so?" A playful smile pulled at Dalton's wounded face.

Before she could say a thing, he took her into his arms and kissed her again. She fought back, but it wasn't much of a fight.

TOTAL RECALL
Vicki Hinze

Dear Reader,

I am so thrilled to have the chance to visit with you again through the pages of "Total Recall." As you can see by the ties I have to the story and to the challenges of perfect recall, this story has special meaning to me and I hope that comes through and it will be special to you, too.

I watched Darcy Clark struggle to create a life for herself in circumstances that most of us don't ever encounter, and to draw courage she didn't know she had from within to do it. I came to admire her immensely for that, and I so wanted her to be successful.

Writing this book was challenging, because I could but imagine her trials. After getting to know Darcy, it is my most fervent wish to have done her justice. I was so happy when she took that leap of faith to try what she most feared. When she trusted. When she leapt. It was a joy. One I hope touches your heart as it touched mine.

Blessings,

Vicki Hinze

Chapter 1

Colonel Sally Drake was not happy. "General Shaw, surely you aren't suggesting that we disclose the unit to this man. This—" she checked her scrawled notes "—customs agent, Benjamin Kelly?" Sally frowned. For national security reasons, less than two hundred people in the world knew her unit existed. That was a significant fact for him to remember.

"I'm not suggesting it, Sally," the general said. "Secretary of Defense Reynolds and I are ordering it."

"But, General—"

"Just do it." His tone sounded sharp. Evidently, he wasn't at peace with the order either, and he went on to confirm it. "Look, I know all your objections and ordinarily I'd agree with them. But when you wear a military uniform and the Secretary of Defense and your commanding officer say jump, you don't even ask how high. You just follow the order. So follow the order, Drake."

Sitting in her office chair, she leaned forward over her desk and dragged a hand through her short, spiky hair. She did indeed wear a U.S. military uniform—air force—and as much as she hated it, General Shaw held authority, so she accepted the edict—if not with grace, with bitter resignation and a great deal of concern. There was only one Secret Assignment Security Specialist in the S.A.S.S. unit who had the unique qualifications for the mission he'd assigned, Captain Darcy Clark, and while she had extraordinary skills, she did not come without special challenges. Would Darcy willingly take on this mission? *Could* she take it on—willingly or not?

Sally's stomach churned and knotted. Forget feeling confident. She'd gladly settle for having a clue. That she didn't had her concern plunging into worry. "Yes, sir. We'll be expecting Agent Kelly within the hour."

"Keep me in the need-to-know loop," the general said. "I've got a bad feeling about this entire situation, and I don't want to be blindsided—especially knowing the secretary is going to be watching closely and reporting to Homeland Security and the president."

He had a bad feeling? She swallowed a grunt. This mission had all the makings of a disaster, and it'd be her ass and rank on the line, not his. When a mission failed, generals were rarely sacrificed. The fallout flowed downhill to the lower-ranking commander—that's who got the axe—regardless of who issued the orders. "Yes, sir." Sally hung up the phone and grumbled. "Typical. Just freaking typical." Secretary Reynolds dumps the mess on General Shaw, and he hadn't missed a beat in dumping it on her.

She swiveled her seat to a windowless wall and stared deeply into a garden mural, wishing for two seconds she could disappear in the foliage and just catch her breath.

You're the S.A.S.S. commander, Sally. You wanted this job, remember? Competed toe-to-toe with Colonel

Gray, the egotistical jerk, to get it. Well, these are the perks, hotshot. Handle them.

"Oh, shut up," she told herself, kicking off the floor to turn her seat back to her desk. She picked up a memo from Darcy, who assimilated Intelligence from all the reporting agencies, compiled it and then briefed the unit. Significant chatter had been intercepted on GRID—Group Resources for Individual Development—the terrorist group that was, by presidential edict, S.A.S.S.'s top priority and, by nature, its albatross. *What were they up to now?*

Darcy had penned a note on the margin. "Colonel, the pattern is intact and consistent. Brace. Kunz is gearing up for GRID's next attack."

Thomas Kunz, a German American-hater, ran GRID with single-minded authority and had made it the leading authority and broker of U.S. intelligence, technology and personnel. His goal was to take the U.S. down by any and all means possible, but he preferred economically. GRID and S.A.S.S. had butted heads and matched wits four times so far, and so far the S.A.S.S. had been successful. Unfortunately, the wins had been surface clutter. The S.A.S.S. hadn't destroyed Kunz's operation, only ticked him off and stiffened his resolve.

"Maggie?" Sally depressed the intercom button on her phone.

"Yes, ma'am."

"Could you get Kate and Amanda to my office ASAP, please?"

"I'm on it, Colonel."

"Thanks." Sally again looked at the report. Katherine Kane and Amanda West had firsthand experience with GRID. Both had survived the encounters. But even after taking out four GRID compounds worldwide, believing Thomas Kunz had been killed twice and arrested and convicted and parked in Leavenworth once, the truth was, the S.A.S.S. hadn't touched him. The men killed or arrested were all Kunz's body doubles, positioned to fool the S.A.S.S. into believing they had gotten Kunz. And the S.A.S.S. had believed it—if only short-term.

Most worrisome to Sally and her entire unit was that they had no idea exactly how many more body doubles or compounds Kunz had in operation. Worse, they had only identified thirty of the estimated ninety body doubles Kunz had substituted in high-level government positions around the globe to access classified information. He'd substituted medical and dental records, X-rays and biometric scans, successfully undercutting all preventative security measures. Worse, the real government employees were being held hostage—*somewhere*. Most likely, in several obscure locations. Less than a dozen had been rescued to date. And so sensitive, classified information continued to funnel out of top secret locations and minds and into Kunz's greedy hands, and the government employees he'd had body-doubled remained Kunz's hostages.

That worried Sally most of all.

Kate and Amanda shuffled in; Amanda wearing a crisp blue skirted uniform, and Kate in her habitual slacks, which told Sally that Kate's laundry was done. Only if it wasn't would she wear the skirt that required nylons and heels—both of which Kate considered to be devices created by men for the sole purpose of torturing women. "Sit down," Sally said.

They took the seats opposite her desk, and Amanda

hiked her chin. "Is this about Darcy's memo on GRID, Colonel?"

From their expressions, both of her top-notch covert operatives were having a tough time swallowing the report. She couldn't blame them. After the previous GRID encounters, neither of them could be eager for another confrontation. Amanda had been held captive for three months and Kate nearly had lost her life. "More or less." Sally leaned back in her chair. "We're getting a visitor in about half an hour."

"A visitor?" Stunned, Kate grunted. "Here?"

"I know." Sally held up a staying hand. "It's General Shaw's runoff straight from Secretary Reynolds."

Kate shook her head, clearly as baffled as Sally by the edict. "Not good."

"Secretary Reynolds isn't a fool, Kate." Amanda looked over at her. "If he's sending someone here, I'm certain he has good reason."

"Whatever." Kate grimaced. "But it's our asses he's putting on the line, not his own, Amanda. You might want to remember that."

"Excuse me," Sally interjected, and then waited until she had their full attention before going on. "Foolish or wise, it's happening. Accept it."

Amanda smoothed back a long lock of dark hair. "So what exactly is going on, Colonel?"

"It's GRID, of course," Kate answered, then swerved her gaze to Sally. "Isn't it?"

"Naturally." Sally cocked her head. "Intel suspects Thomas Kunz is planning to smuggle radioactive waste into the U.S. It also suspects he has a sleeper cell of GRID operatives already positioned somewhere within our borders who will use it in bombs targeting…" she paused to refer to her notes for the exact wording, "an undisclosed but significant, high-priority, densely populated site." She looked back to them. "Perhaps more than one site."

Amanda absorbed the news in silence. Her expression didn't alter or reveal her reaction—excellent attributes in a covert operative.

Kate's demeanor changed significantly. No longer challenging or defiant, she homed in and focused intently. "Kunz is pulling his usual."

"What usual?" Amanda asked.

"Wanting to inflict as much short- and long-term destruction as possible."

"Yes, and what's terrifying is that he's damn good at it," Sally said. "Radioactive or 'dirty' bombs have a relatively small kill zone—a few city blocks, typically—but the long-term impact on health… Well, suffice it to say that the ramifications are significant."

"How significant?" Amanda instinctively looked to Kate. Explosives and weapons of mass destruction were her areas of expertise.

Kate frowned, but answered Amanda. "You have the kill zone, but the damage doesn't stop there. Think of it like a wave that ripples outward from the explosion site, carrying with it health challenges like radiation burns, an increase of various types of cancer, severe birth defects." Kate grimaced. "How far the ripple extends from the blast depends on the strength of the explosives used, of course, but it's certain to be wicked. We'll see significant increases in health challenges for years."

Amanda frowned. "So at the outer ripple rim of those impacted, it could take time for symptoms to appear."

"I hate to say it, but it's even worse than that." Kate explained. "For every challenge we see, there'll be a half dozen with tentacles that we don't. Challenges medical professionals will tag 'etiology unknown.'"

Sally's skin crawled. How any terrorists could attack civilians like this and justify it as rational was beyond her. *Sick bastards.* "Intel considers July 4th Kunz's likely target date."

"Independence Day. Hoping to make us dependent." Amanda clenched her jaw and shifted on her seat. "Kunz does love to pop us on dates significant to us."

"Apparently," Sally agreed. He'd done it twice already. "This time we have a kicker to keep things really interesting."

"A kicker?" Kate asked.

"The man that Secretary Reynolds is sending here is a U.S. customs agent named Benjamin Kelly. He's a chief inspector and entomologist on the U.S.-Mexico border."

"The visitor and GRID are connected?" Shock riddled Amanda's tone, and she didn't bother trying to hide it.

"Homeland Security thinks so," Sally said, tapping her pen on her desk blotter. "If Kelly's story is as compelling as General Shaw claims, it's going to require drastic measures."

Kate nodded. "So what do you want us to do, Colonel?"

"There's nothing you can do." Sally wished there were. *If* there were, she wouldn't feel this sense of impending doom.

"Me, then," Amanda said.

"There's nothing you can do either—outside of support roles, which you'll both have to do."

Kate let her head loll back. "Colonel, I *know* you're not considering Maggie for this mission."

"Not yet," she admitted. "Maggie needs more training but, when the time comes, she'll be an excellent field operative, Kate."

"No doubt, ma'am, but that time damn sure isn't now. Not on this."

Kate had little patience with new recruits to the unit, and Maggie had been with them less than three months. She showed infinite promise, but she hadn't yet gotten past sticking strictly to the rules. In the S.A.S.S., that tended to get operatives killed. Yet with time, risks and a few narrow-miss attempts on her life, she'd adjust. "No, not on this. It isn't yet Maggie's time. Not yet."

"Then who?" Amanda asked. "Max, one of the other guys?"

Sally hedged, took the circuitous route. This news would be less popular than assigning Maggie. "We need to insert an operative as a customs agent on the border between Texas and Mexico—at the entry station at Los Casas." Now came the hardest part of this. "I'm assigning Darcy."

"Darcy? You can't be serious." Clearly distressed, Amanda stood up, her mouth drawn and tight. "Colonel, Darcy can't do this mission. She can't even stand being around other people. Since the fire, she's been incapable of any kind of fieldwork, much less a mission of this magnitude."

"Dr. Vargus disagrees. He says she can do it—if she will."

"*Can? Will?* Good God, Colonel Drake, the woman lives like a monk to avoid hyperstimulation attacks." Kate shot out of her chair. "She can't go to a shopping mall without getting knocked to her knees and you want her to do this? She works in a vault with old furniture and files because she can't take being around us. You can't throw her into the field at a busy border crossing." Mutiny filled Kate's eyes and a warning filled her voice. "She'll lose it, Colonel."

"Kate's right, Colonel," Amanda said, agreeing with her for the first time since they had entered the office. "Do this and the S.A.S.S. will fail on this mission. She'll try—Darcy always gives a hundred percent—but she will fail. She just can't handle it."

"She will handle it, Amanda. Damn it, she has no choice." Sally stiffened, motioned to the chairs. "Sit down. Both of you."

They did, but rebellion rippled off them in waves.

Sally ignored it, because inside she was rebelling, too. But, damn it, Darcy was the only operative who could do what must be done to stop this attack. "Now, listen. I know Darcy's challenges. I also know Dr. Vargus's professional opinion on Darcy's challenges. He's a hundred percent certain she *can* learn to shield herself from the sensory input."

"Not to dispute the good doctor or you, ma'am," Kate said, her voice droll. "But this mission doesn't sound safe enough for anyone to use it as a training ground to learn anything."

"Do we ever have safe training grounds?" Sally countered.

"Valid point, Colonel," Amanda said. "But Darcy would have better odds of success learning while on vacation or in some situation where she could control her exposure without consequences to others."

"Uh-huh. Totally logical, Amanda, but also unrealistic." Sally cocked her head. "She's had five years to do that and she hasn't. Regardless, our backs are against the wall now. We have no choice, which gives Darcy no alternative." Knowing that grated Sally's nerves raw. "The bottom line is that the S.A.S.S. needs her to stop Kunz from killing a lot of innocent Americans. The buck can't go beyond there. So if Darcy has to face demons in unfavorable circumstances to make that happen, then she's going to have to face them—and I expect both of you to help convince her she can."

Kate had mutiny in her eye. "Permission to speak freely, Colonel."

She had been speaking freely since entering the office. But she either didn't realize it due to being upset, or she'd been holding her harshest opinions in check. Sally dared to hope it was the former. "Go ahead."

"You're coming across like these hyperstimulation attacks are all in Darcy's head, and they damn well aren't. She needs that self-imposed isolation to function and avoid the attacks. I've seen her have one. She suffers, Colonel. She gets little warning, can't see clearly, loses control of her muscles—they totally lock down on her. I've seen her collapse and lay there unable to move so much as a finger. The whole time, she was in intense pain. This mission isn't something she can just do anyway, damn it. That's my point. You're demanding more than she can give."

"Kate's right, Colonel." Amanda chimed in. "The head injury she suffered in that fire wasn't a walk in the park. She was in a coma for three weeks. Normal noise and activity are sheer hell for her." Amanda chewed at her lip. "She'll try, but she won't last five minutes at a busy border station."

"You two haven't said anything I don't already know," Sally admitted. "Do you think *I've* been in a coma? Why do you think she works alone in a vault? Why do you think I approved her waiver to live outside the twenty-five mile radius to headquarters? It's a requirement for all of us, but I let her move to Rainbow Lake because she can be isolated and at peace there. As her commander, why do you think that I know I have this ace operative in her and yet I never assign her to missions in the field—and that's not to diminish the value of what she does here. God knows, she's saved our asses many times, piecing together seemingly unrelated bits of Intel. But she was an ace in the field, and I could use her there. Yet I don't." Sally paused, but Amanda and Kate realized the questions she had asked were rhetorical and didn't respond.

Silence fell between them. They all wanted to protect Darcy. In a very practical sense, she'd already forfeited her life for the S.A.S.S. and none of them wanted to ask her for more.

But Sally had no choice.

That truth crept through her. "I've done as much as I can, but I can't protect her now. Not this time. I have an obligation and a responsibility to protect Americans. And Darcy Clark *is* my best means of protecting them. I have to assign her to this mission. Let me say this again. *Only* she can do what must be done."

"I caught that when you said it before. But, Colonel, what can she do that Amanda or I can't?" Kate asked. "We've gotten the same S.A.S.S. training and we might not be aces in the field, but we damn sure aren't slouches. If Darcy can do it, we can. You know we can."

"No, you can't, Kate," Sally insisted, and then gave

in to her own frustration about this. "Neither can I, or I'd do it myself."

That surprised them. Amanda recovered first and asked, "Why can't we do it, Colonel?"

Sally frowned. "Because none of us has total recall. Darcy does and we need it because we can't bring in equipment and remain undetected." The bluster in them deflated and resignation slid into place on their faces. Sally captured a shuddery breath. "That's why only Darcy can handle this mission." She cleared her throat. "Now, we're all worried—and that's justified—but we must move forward and stop this attack. I support Darcy and I expect you two to support her—and to help reassure her that she's capable of tackling this mission. Dr. Vargus says that support will help, but only if it's genuine."

Amanda stood up. "Colonel, how can we do that? We just gave you all the reasons we *don't* think she can do this mission. How do we convince her we think she can?"

Sally stood up, looked them right in the eyes. "Get genuine. That's a direct order."

Knowing an exit line when they heard one, the two stood up.

"Dismissed." Sally waved them out.

They left her office without a word, though the mutiny in Kate's eyes had now spread through her entire body, judging by her stiff gait and ramrod spine. But Amanda would talk her around.

Grateful for that, Sally collapsed back into her chair, hoping to hell she hadn't just made a decision that would kill thousands of innocent Americans *and* Darcy Clark *and* Ben Kelly.

If what General Shaw said proved true, this Kelly had guts and grit, and his coming forward gave the S.A.S.S. the opportunity to save thousands of lives. And he'd done so knowing that if Thomas Kunz or his GRID goons ever learned of it, he'd be murdered.

Guts and grit. She admired that.

Ben Kelly stopped the Honda Pilot he'd rented at the Okaloosa Regional Airport on the dirt road at a metal gate. He was out in the middle of nowhere. *This couldn't be the right place,* he thought, and mentally retraced his path.

He'd taken Highway 85, passed the turnoff for Providence Air Force Base, taken a right on the dirt road exactly twenty miles north on the odometer. Secretary Reynolds had given him the instructions and he'd been very clear that there were no landmarks, just bent and twisted pines—victims of former hurricanes that had ripped through northwest Florida—and dense underbrush. He squinted against the blazing sun. Still, this didn't resemble any unit's offices he'd ever seen. There wasn't a building in sight.

His arm propped at the open window, he looked from the heavy-duty metal gate down the six-foot wire fence. Every eight feet, a posted sign read: Use of Deadly Force Authorized. That could be typical of a dormant bombing range, he supposed, but why wasn't there a guard at the gate?

"Drive on through." A woman's tinny voice echoed through a speaker attached to the gatepost, and the gate swung open.

Not exactly a warm welcome, but something in her tone appealed to him.

You've been alone too damn long, Kelly.

He grunted. At least they seemed to be expecting him. He tapped the gearshift into Drive, hit the gas and checked his rearview mirror. The tires lifted a cloud of dust. They'd likely seen him coming since he'd turned off the main highway.

Ben drove about a mile and came to a second wire fence. This one was topped with razor wire. Again, he stopped at the heavy metal gate blocking the road and glanced off to the right. In the distance, among tall weeds, he saw the telltale signs of an artillery battery. Definitely abandoned but obviously still protected.

The gate opened—this time, without benefit of the woman's voice.

Driving a short distance through the woods, he spotted a dilapidated shack. A beat-up trailer was parked behind it. Nothing but trees were in sight. It was hard to believe this was the elite S.A.S.S. unit's headquarters, but it stood exactly as General Shaw had described it. Pulling in front of the shack, he parked. The cut engine ticked and noonday sun glared off the hood of the Honda. Someone had put a little wooden sign above the shack's cracked door that read: Regret.

Before he could decide what he thought about that, a woman walked out, looking mutinous. She was tall and lean; her hair short, blond and curly; her jaw set firm.

She stopped six feet from the car. "Who are you?"

"Ben Kelly." It didn't occur to him not to tell her. She was armed and looked ticked off enough to shoot him rather than ask twice.

"Let's go." She took yet another step back from the car.

Ben got out and his knees cracked. His legs were stiff
from spending so many hours in the past two days on
planes and in cars. He'd left Los Casas and driven to
Corpus Christi, where he'd flown under an assumed
name to Washington. He'd briefed Secretary Reynolds,
who'd listened and then shuffled him to Homeland Security. They'd listened and then shuffled him to Intel,
who'd listened and shuffled him to the Office of Special Investigations, who'd shuffled him up the ranks to
General Shaw who, with Secretary of Defense Reynolds, listened again and then shuffled him here to meet
with the S.A.S.S. commander, Colonel Sally Drake.

Along about three shuffles ago, Ben had cursed himself as a fool for reporting anything, and then for not
just going direct to General Shaw, since they had a history. But that was weariness setting in. Ben had done
what he'd had to do because it was the right thing to do.
It had been right then and, though it had also been a
royal pain in the ass, it was right now—regardless of
how tired he was of repeating his story.

He followed the blonde into the shack and then, surprisingly, into a very modern and new elevator. When
the door closed behind them, she issued him a warning.
"If you want to live, forget what and who you see here."

She was dead serious and not exaggerating at all.
Certain of that, Ben nodded.

The door opened into a mass of offices. The blonde
stepped out. "This way." She hung a right in a hallway
lined with photographs of men "Most Wanted" by various government agencies. Scanning the line of them,
Ben's gaze lighted on the face of Paco Santana, the
man who had brought him here, and he slid to a stop.
Anger burned in his stomach, but he squelched it and

kept walking, kept following the blonde, who motioned him into a conference room. In stark contrast to the falling-down shack and banged-up trailer above, everything below ground seemed barely used or new.

"Sit down," the blonde said. "The colonel will be with you in a minute." She moved back to the door. "Don't touch anything, Agent Kelly. For the record, you are being watched."

What was there to touch? Six chairs and one table were in the room and not another thing. Nothing was on the white tile floor, no paintings lined the glaringly white walls, and not so much as a trash can or a pad of paper had been added or forgotten in here.

Minutes later, a petite redhead about forty walked in. "Agent Kelly." She thrust a hand in his direction. "I'm Colonel Sally Drake."

Ben shook her hand. "Ma'am."

"Please, sit down," she said, then dropped into her chair at the head of the conference table. "Before you tell me your story, let's make sure you've been briefed on the ground rules here."

"You don't exist, ma'am. The people working here don't exist, and this place doesn't exist. S.A.S.S. isn't an elite air force unit assigned to the Office of Special Investigations. Sass is when you talk back to your mother and usually get your backside busted or your face slapped for doing it."

"I see General Shaw was candid." Colonel Drake smiled. "Good."

The door opened and someone walked in behind Ben. "Sorry I'm late."

Recognizing the voice of the woman who'd opened the gate, he turned to look back at her and his breath hitched in his chest. She was a captain in uniform, trim with a dark brown mass of curly hair that brushed her shoulders. She glanced at him and intelligence burned in her green eyes. *Beautiful* came to mind and stuck. Not a conventional beauty, but a kind all her own. Very personal and very distinct.

"Agent Kelly, this is Captain Darcy Clark," the colonel said. "Darcy, this is Agent Ben Kelly, customs chief inspector and entomologist."

Darcy hesitated, and then took his hand. "How do you do, Agent Kelly?"

He closed his fingers around hers. "It's Ben."

"Darcy." She nodded, shivered and then stepped away and took a seat at the table opposite him.

He didn't know whether to be pleased or repulsed by that shiver, but he was certainly captivated by the woman. There was something different about her. He tried to peg it and couldn't. Whatever it was, she had it buried deep inside, and he couldn't repress a persistent curiosity about why.

"So tell us why you're here, Agent Kelly."

He looked from Darcy to the colonel. "Didn't General Shaw go through this with you?" He'd repeated the story so many times already.

"I want to hear it from you," she said, dispelling any hope that he'd get out of rehashing it yet again. "Please."

Resigned, Ben fixed his gaze on Colonel Drake—looking at Darcy Clark unnerved him for some reason—and started at the beginning. "I'm a crossing guard, so to speak, at Los Casas down on the Texas/Mexico border," he said. "It's my job to verify identities and inspect shipments of food and products coming into the country." That was simplifying the matter, but these were enlightened women. They'd know that. Hell, they probably knew what he ate for breakfast most days. "Three days ago, I witnessed my supervisor, Station Chief Lucas Wexler, cut a deal with a member of GRID at our point of entry."

"Excuse me," Colonel Drake cut in. "Two questions. One, how do you know about GRID, and two, Wexler cut a deal with which GRID member—specifically?"

"A little over a week ago, Homeland Security put out an alert on GRID," he said. "I read the bulletin."

"The alert report is accurate, ma'am," Darcy said. "Though it was on June 16th—eleven days ago—or it will be at 2:30 p.m."

Ben gave her a strange look, then shrugged. "The GRID member I saw is on your wall out there. Paco Santana. I recognized him from the photo, though he crossed the border wearing dark glasses and a hat."

"But you're absolutely sure it was him."

Ben nodded. "When I overheard the conversation between him and Wexler, I knew bad things were in store. So I waited until Wexler went home for the day— he always works the day shift—and then I reviewed the security tapes. Santana entered the U.S. on business as an agent for TNT Incendiary Devices, Inc."

Darcy's blood chilled to ice, but she sat still, watching Colonel Drake scribble notes.

Ben went on. "Frankly, finding that scared the hell out of me, so—"

"Why?" Darcy asked. She hadn't meant to, but the question popped out of her mouth before she realized she had asked it.

He swung his gaze to meet hers. "Because the name of the company nagged at me. I'd heard it before. I couldn't remember where or why, but getting that bad feeling, I checked it out on the Net. They manufacture fireworks in Mexico," he said.

Darcy grasped the connection. "And last October 10th, that company won the contract awarded for the July 4th fireworks celebration."

"That's right," Ben said, clearly surprised she'd made the connection without first researching.

Colonel Drake picked up on the high tension, stopped scrawling and stared at Darcy. "What celebration? Where?"

Darcy and Ben locked gazes, their worry shooting back and forth between them. Ben, not Darcy, answered the colonel. "The White House."

Chapter 2

"The White House." Colonel Drake sat back in her chair. "Oh, God."

Darcy nodded. The deduction was logical and terrifying. "GRID is using the fireworks display as a front to bomb the White House spectators."

Colonel Drake looked from Darcy to Ben, then back to Darcy. "The president will never cancel the fireworks. Never. It'd be perceived as giving in to terrorists."

"Listen," Ben said. "I don't know what to do about this. I know if Wexler or Santana figure out I know anything, I'll be murdered and buried in the Mexican desert. But it seems to me that GRID's already got this thing set up inside the U.S. Santana brought in a truck pulling double trailers. Whatever was on that load went somewhere within our borders. Anything I can do to help stop them, I will."

Darcy liked him. This Ben Kelly. He was gorgeous: about thirty with black hair and cool gray eyes, a little remote but not cold. His passion and outrage simmered just below the surface; she sensed it as clearly as she saw the thin scar slashing across his right cheek whiten. It took a lot of personal control to hold in that much outrage and appear calm and collected. She respected that discipline. And, these days, she envied it. "Where does Wexler think you are right now?"

He slid her a sidelong look. "Charter fishing a hundred miles out in the Gulf of Mexico—which is where I would be if I hadn't heard that conversation."

"You're sure he has no idea you aren't there?" Colonel Drake asked.

"Positive," Ben said. "Captain Jason Quade owns the *Twilight's Last Gleam*. He's a good friend. If anyone calls for me, he'll handle it without letting them know I'm not on board." Ben lifted a hand. "Don't worry. Jason has no idea why I'm not there, only that no one else must know it."

"And that was enough for him?" Darcy asked. It wouldn't be for most people. They'd want some sort of explanation.

"More than enough."

Ben didn't expound, and Darcy didn't feel the need to push. He was being straight with her. She had a sixth sense about that with people—another *gift* since the fire, like her total recall. "Good friend."

"Yes, he is." Ben stared at her a long second, clearly seeing far deeper than she would choose to let him or anyone else see, and then he added, "We served together in Iraq before I left the military. You know what combat is like, Darcy. You learn quick who to trust with your life and who not to trust to avoid losing it."

Far too perceptive. She didn't respond or look away, but holding his gaze took everything she had. The muscles in her chest were in revolt, and her backbone tingled from base to nape. Why did he affect her like this?

It was…odd—and damned unwelcome. She fought the urge to shake off a warm shiver.

"So your cover is intact. Excellent." Colonel Drake sized Ben up and apparently approved of all she saw in him. "Ben, we have reason to believe that GRID is going to use radioactive waste in the bombs they detonate. We think there could be more than one target—provided GRID gets the explosives into the country. So you can see that our concerns aren't topical or general interest. They're specific. We fully expect an attack, and it's the S.A.S.S.'s job to stop them. That means, we dig for information and, unfortunately, that includes information about you." She paused to give him time to absorb that, and then continued. "Now, General Shaw has vouched for you and, to be perfectly blunt, that's highly unusual. Why did he do it?"

"You'd have to ask him that question, ma'am. I'm no mind reader."

"I'm asking you for your opinion," the colonel persisted. "Not for an answer set in stone, just why you think he might have put his reputation on the line for you." She propped a hand on the table and leaned closer. "Before you answer, I'll tell you that the consequences of his being wrong could get a lot of people killed. People under my command." Warning sharpened her tone. "I'm very protective of my people, Ben."

"Every commander worth a damn should be protective, so that's good to hear." Ben hiked his chin. "You have nothing to fear from me, Colonel. Captain Quade and I served under General Shaw in Iraq. He's familiar with me and my motives." He hesitated a second, glanced down then back at the colonel. "I know S.A.S.S.'s mission, Colonel. At one time, I was invited by the general to join the unit. I declined."

"Why?" Darcy asked, surprised by this. She'd seen nothing anywhere in the history of S.A.S.S. to back up what Ben was saying.

"Because I was damn tired of getting shot at," he said. "That wasn't the main reason, however. I got married." He shrugged. "S.A.S.S. assignments might be given to the best and brightest, but its missions are hell on marriages. I didn't want to be another statistic."

A strange look crossed Colonel Drake's face. Darcy understood it. Her husband had been killed by terrorists. They used him, trying to find out what she knew. They failed, but he died, and she lived every day since, knowing that if he'd married anyone else, he'd be alive.

The colonel looked at Ben's left hand. "But you ended up as a statistic anyway," she said more than asked. "What happened?"

Surprise lighted in his eyes.

Darcy explained how the colonel had known he was no longer married. "No wedding ring. No telltale white skin rimming your finger. You've been without her for a while." She knitted her eyebrows. "I'm sorry—about the statistics."

"Rainbows and rain. Every life gets both."

"So why did your marriage end, Ben?" Colonel Drake pushed.

He frowned, clearly uncomfortable with the intense focus on his failed marriage, and clearly troubled because it had failed. "Diane and I divorced two years ago. I have this quirk. I like my women sober." He shrugged and blew out a breath. "Simply put, she liked tequila more than me."

"You make it sound simple, but I know it wasn't," Darcy said softly. Her instincts screamed it.

He looked her straight in the eye. "Nothing about it was simple. Being married to an alcoholic was three years, three months and four days of hell."

"I'm sure it was, Ben." Colonel Drake's tone softened, signaling she had ended this line of questioning. "On your own merits and General Shaw's recommendation, I'm going to trust you. Because you came to us with this, I feel that trust is well placed. Don't disappoint me."

"If I intended to do that, ma'am, I'd just have stayed home. I live here, too, and I'm not going to stand by and watch GRID or any other terrorist group blow our people to hell and back. Not without trying to stop them."

"I'm grateful for that because I do need your help." She paused and swung her gaze to Darcy. "And your help."

"Of course, Colonel." Odd that she would ask. Darcy participated on all missions in an intelligence-gathering and disseminating capacity.

"I want the two of you to work together on this mission."

Ben nodded. "Whatever I can do."

More and more odd. Darcy swiped her hair back from her cheek. Why did she have a weird feeling something was different about this mission? "Positively, Colonel," Darcy said.

"Excellent." Colonel Drake stiffened. "Darcy, I'm going to insert you as a customs agent in Los Casas."

"What?" Darcy nearly fell out of her chair. Shock shook her to her toes and she broke into a cold sweat. "But, Colonel!"

"What's the problem?" Ben asked, obviously thinking her objection was to working with him.

Darcy wanted to reassure him, but her throat muscles locked up; she couldn't talk. She moved her mouth, but couldn't utter a single sound.

Colonel Drake ignored him, stared at Darcy. Her voice was firm but not without compassion. "I know working this mission won't come easy to you, Darcy, but it's essential. Duty first, right?"

Clammy. She was slick with sweat and clammy. Her stomach roiled. *God, please don't let me throw up!* "But—but—"

Ben stood up. "Look, if she objects to working with me so much it's making her green around the gills, just forget it. You guys handle this without me." He pushed back and his chair's legs scraped the floor. "I'm going fishing."

"Hold it, Ben." Colonel Drake stood up, poured water over a tissue and passed it to Darcy. "This has nothing to do with you, and everything to do with Darcy."

"I'm sorry, Ben." Darcy finally found her voice. She dabbed at her face and throat with the wet cloth. "It's me. Not you. It's all me."

Frowning, he turned a hard glare on Darcy, but clearly recognizing her upset, his features quickly softened and he sat back down. "Darcy?" He pulled his chair closer to the table, and gentled his voice. "What the hell is wrong?"

"You explain," Colonel Drake said, looking in Darcy's direction. "I'll have Amanda cut your orders." Colonel Drake stood up. "Ben, who's the nosiest agent at Los Casas?"

"Fred Burns."

"Fine. We'll put him out of commission."

Shock elevated Ben's pitch. "You're going to kill him because he's nosy?"

"Of course not." She sniffed, affronted. "I'm sending him out on sick leave."

"But he's not sick."

"He will be." Colonel Drake left the conference room and shut the door.

Gape-jawed, Ben swerved a worried look to Darcy. "She's not going to hurt him, is she?"

"Not really. He won't feel well for a bit, but he'll be fine." Darcy swept her hair back from her face. Her forehead was soaked. "I can't do this, Ben."

"Why not?"

He hadn't argued with her. Probably saw little sense in it. Her skin must still have a green-to-the-gills cast to it. "I have residual challenges from an injury sustained on a mission five years ago. They're…substantial."

"Talk straight to me, Darcy. I deserve it."

He did. "I was trapped in a fire and the roof caved in on me. I got a severe head injury."

"I'm sorry." He looked confused. "But what has that got to do with this?"

She'd have to give him more sordid details. God, but she hated recalling them. Reliving them. Seeing Merry's face in that fire. Her muscles clenched. She would *not* talk about Merry. With all of this going on, she just couldn't take the added stress. She just couldn't. *I'm so sorry, Merry.*

"Darcy?" he prodded. "Talk to me."

She turned her attention to him and answered. "I stayed in a coma twenty-one days, Ben. When I woke up, I was…different."

"Different?" Perplexed, he furrowed his brow. "How?"

She lowered her gaze to the conference table— smooth and slick and gleaming light. It didn't look back or judge or see a person's flaws. Its reflections were soft, and Darcy needed the forgiveness in those blurred edges. "I sense things now," she said in a whisper. "And I have total recall."

He looked up at the white ceiling, at the bald and bright fluorescent lights. "Are you an operative, Darcy?"

"I'm the chief intelligence analyst for the S.A.S.S."

"That's a cagey response." He looked back at her.

"Not intentionally."

He grunted his opinion on that, and thumbed the edge of the table. "You said you were on a mission then. Were you a covert operative?"

No answer. She was, but she couldn't admit it then, and she couldn't admit it now. To do so was paramount to treason. And if he'd been offered a S.A.S.S. assignment, he damn well knew it, which meant this was an ethics test.

"So since the fire, you can't do field work anymore?"

She shifted on her seat and debated on what she could say that was both true and ethical. This was one of those times when combining the two proved difficult. "I can't stand to be in a room with more than two people for longer than a few minutes. Going to the grocery store is sheer hell. Forget dropping by a club or seeing a movie—and a shopping mall?" She rolled her gaze. "They're torture chambers." She steadied herself and released a little held breath. "I can't even go to a restaurant for dinner, Ben."

"You're afraid of crowds?"

"No, no, no. I'm not afraid," she said impatiently. "You don't get it."

"I'm trying, Darcy." He swiveled his chair and propped his arm on the table. "This is new to me, okay? Cut me a little slack."

She stood up, leaned across the table toward him. "I have total recall, Ben. That means I process everything I see. I hear everything. I smell everything. *Everything,* Ben."

"So in a group, you're bombarded by everyone's input, and it makes you a little nuts, right?"

"A lot nuts." She sat back down. "Totally nuts." Darcy wrung her hands. "I can't function. It paralyzes me. My muscles go into such deep spasms that I lose control of them. I'm helpless." Not to mention humiliated. "Sometimes the attacks are so severe that I can't see or even stand up on my own."

He looked up at her, his face changing from all hard angles and planes to ones softened by compassion. "I'm sorry you have to go through that, Darcy."

"Me, too." The understatement of the decade, that.

The skin between his eyebrows wrinkled. "So you isolate yourself most of the time, then."

Was he being critical, or just curious? She studied him and decided he wasn't being either, just trying to get an accurate understanding. "It's essential for me to stay on an even keel, so I rarely interact with other people." She let out a humorless laugh. "Actually, I've spent more time with you today than I have anyone else in months."

That revelation surprised him. He sat completely still for a long moment that stretched between them. Then he did the oddest thing—a thing she couldn't have expected or appreciated more.

He reached over and clasped her hand. "I really am sorry this happened to you, Darcy. Living apart…well, it's got to be hard."

A rush of heat swept up her arm from her fingertips to her elbow. He had great hands. Steady and large but not overbearing. Gentle, but definitely a man's solid touch. "My own company isn't that bad, but I'd be lying if I didn't say I get tired of it." Why was she telling him this?

"I'm sure you do. Who wouldn't?" He looked into her eyes and let her see inside him. "I spend a lot of time alone, too. Los Casas is pretty isolated. But I can go to Mick's bar for a beer when I get tired of hearing myself think."

"Lucky you."

"Yeah." He searched her face. "I didn't realize it until today, but you're right. Lucky me."

He let go of her hand and straightened his back. "Well, under the circumstances, I guess we're done." He started to push off the table to stand up.

"Are you leaving?"

"Well, yeah."

"Wait." A flutter of panic lighted in her stomach. "You can't go."

"Excuse me?"

"We have to work together to stop the attack."

He looked baffled. "Darcy, we can't work together. You just gave me all the reasons why."

"But—"

"But, what?" He looked at her as if she'd lost her mind. "Just talking about taking this mission on has you close to fainting and throwing up."

"I know, but, Ben, the consequences…"

"Darcy, listen." He softened his voice. "Your courage is inspiring and your intentions are admirable. More than admirable, considering the personal costs. But realistically, how are you going to handle being at a very busy border crossing? Los Casas isn't a little place with just a few tricklers strolling over every now and then. It's remote, yes, but it's also the third most active border-crossing in the State of Texas."

"Oh, no." Darcy blinked hard against the spots blinding her eyes. "I really can't do it, Ben." Anguish lighted in her eyes, tugged at the corners of her mouth. "I wish I could—I know the consequences of not stopping the attack—but…but I just can't do it."

"With utmost respect for you, I'd say all things considered, it'd be crazy for you to even try."

"Crazy it might be." Colonel Drake left the door and walked across the room to them. "But, Darcy, not only will you try," she said with steel in her voice, "you will succeed."

Ben intervened. "Take a look at her, Colonel. There's no way she can handle this mission."

"She'd better find a way." The commander cut loose a tone, revealing a temper as fiery as her short, spiked red hair. "We can't use surveillance equipment. With the security improvements made since 9/11, any device we install will be detected. If Wexler so much as sniffs a whiff we're involved, then he'll blow off GRID. They'll just activate an alternate route—one we're not privy to—and GRID will succeed. Maybe we prevent the attack on the spectators at the White House, maybe not. But they will blow up something, and somewhere in this country, people are going to get sick and die." She held her gaze on Darcy. "We must track GRID from Los

Casas to pinpoint the targets. There's no secondary path to them." Swinging her gaze, she added, "And, Ben, remember this.... Without Darcy's perfect memory, we'd be forced to rely on other means—any of which have high odds of being discovered. Remember, too, that discovery does not offer a positive outcome for your personal future."

He shoved his hands into his slacks pockets. "They'd kill me."

"They would." Darcy groaned. GRID never left loose ends or potential witnesses. Minimizing risks through attrition was a steadfast rule with them.

"Glad you two get the full picture." Colonel Drake passed Darcy an envelope. "Your power of attorney—Maggie's up next on the recipient's list—and your last will and testament. Review them both, complete the POA and make sure any changes you want are incorporated in your will. Have them ready by the time your orders are cut."

Typical premission protocol, but one that had fear cutting through Darcy like a sharp knife. Swallowing hard, her hand unsteady, she reached for the envelope and lifted her gaze to Colonel Drake. "You realize I'm going to fail."

"I realize no such thing," she said, her expression and voice flat and unwavering. "You realize that if you fail, thousands of innocent people are going to die on July 4th and many more, in the years to come, are going to suffer terminal medical crises and disease." Her jaw ticked and she looked at Darcy as if looking over glasses propped on the tip of her nose. "You can't just roll over and accept failure, Darcy. They deserve better."

"I know they do, Colonel. They deserve someone who can—"

"*You* swore to serve and protect them. They have every right to expect you to do it. I have every right to expect you to do it. And you have every right to expect it of yourself, Darcy. So just do what you're expected to do."

"I know my job and my duty. This isn't about that."

"What's it about?"

"Not being able to do my job. I'm a realist, Colonel."

Sally squared off on her. "You're afraid, Captain."

Anger sparked in Darcy's stomach. Anger and five years' worth of resentment erupted. "Hell, yes, I'm afraid. I don't want to kill anyone else, and I can't do this."

"You can," Colonel Drake shouted, then caught herself, and deliberately lowered her voice. She tugged at the hem of her blouse, pulled it down. "Dr. Vargus and I have spoken about your challenges at length, Darcy. He believes—and I agree with him—that your best odds of reclaiming a normal life are to suck it up and force yourself into hyperstimulated episodes until they become so common, they don't affect you anymore."

"That doesn't work." Darcy clenched her jaw. She'd tried. Damn it, she'd tried everything. True, they didn't know it, but it didn't mean she hadn't tried it on her own.

"Suck it up, Darcy." Colonel Drake moved back to the door, sliding Ben a cocked brow look that Darcy hated. "I've arranged for Fred Burns to be put out of commission. Maggie is taking care of inserting you as his replacement." The colonel looked from Darcy to Ben. "Brief her on operations at Los Casas. I'll be back with the orders as soon as we're good to go." She again walked out and closed the door.

Darcy felt her world spinning out of control, crashing down around her ears. "Suck it up." She grunted, stood up and parked a hand on her hip. "Suck it up."

Ben rolled his eyes back in his head. "Oh, hell."

She spun on him. "What?"

"I know that look. It says you're going into bitch mode." He let out a heartfelt sigh. "Can you wait until later? I've had about all the fun I can stand in the past two days."

"Not my problem." She lifted a staying hand. "I'm busy sucking it up over here." She walked around the table and stopped near him. "Of course, that equates to severe suffering that incapacitates me to various degrees, which could get me or you or others killed, but having no choice, I'll just suck it up and hope for the best."

Ben stared up at her for a long second, torn in internal debate. Finally, he made his call, stood up and put his hands on her shoulders. "Darcy, do you think Colonel Drake would put you in the field on a mission of this magnitude if she wasn't sure you could do your job?"

"Normally, no. But it's not like she has a lot of options, Ben. I'm the only S.A.S.S. resident with total recall. She's stuck."

"You really believe that?"

"It's the truth. Of course, I believe it." His hands felt warm on her shoulders. Warm and firm and far too pleasant. And he smelled good, too. She'd forgotten how good a man could smell when he'd been out in fresh air, earthy and tangy like summer.

"Then we've got a problem."

"I know that," she said sharply. "We've been talking about it for the last ten minutes."

"You don't understand." He shook his head, then turned even more serious. Serious and grim. "First of all, I don't believe Colonel Drake would insert you unless she felt you had reasonable odds for success. You don't believe it, and on this, we'll have to agree to disagree. But beyond that, if you've already decided to fail, I'm not going to work with you, Darcy. You can kill yourself, but I'll be damned if I'm going to let you kill me."

"I haven't *decided* to fail," she corrected him, prickly from his attitude and all the upset. "I intend to use all necessary means to succeed. But the odds aren't stacked in my favor, and that's just a fact, Ben."

"So you intend to succeed, meaning you are going ahead with this."

"I have to. I can't sit here because I might have an attack and watch people die because I didn't do anything."

"Okay, then. That takes care of that. And isn't going in with intentions of giving it our best—trying—all any of us can do?"

"Don't oversimplify, Ben." She crossed her arms. "We don't all suffer from hyperstimulation attacks." He was ignoring the parts he didn't want to hear. Typical male attitude. Damn it.

"The rest of us have our demons, too." The look in his eye turned remote.

She waited, but he didn't elaborate, leaving her to wonder what he'd meant. Regardless, his insight changed her attitude. "Okay, so we both fight our demons and do our best to accomplish the mission."

"That's about the best we can do." He shrugged.

He played her, but didn't manipulate her without letting her know what he was doing. Actually, to be fair, she had to admit he wasn't manipulating or playing her, just offering a shifted perspective. Whatever his demons were, he put them on par with hers. That saddened her. "We can do a little better," she said.

"I don't see how."

She parked her hands on his shoulders and looked him in the eye. "We can pray that if anyone dies as a result of my involvement, it's only me." She let her fear shine in her eyes, knowing he'd never miss it. "I like you, Ben Kelly. I don't want to kill you."

He swallowed hard and his Adam's apple rippled in his throat. "I don't want to kill you, either."

"Well, that's one point of agreement." She blew out a staggered sigh.

"Let's find another," Ben said, and backed away from her. "Let's put your Intel skills to work and trace ownership of TNT Incendiary Devices, Inc."

"Definitely, but where's your thinking on it?" Darcy shoved her chair up under the table.

"When Paco Santana and Lucas Wexler cut the deal, Santana was wearing this red shirt with the TNT emblem above the pocket. Call me skeptical, but I want to verify whose payroll he's on in addition to GRID's."

"That, I can handle. Come on." Darcy jerked her head toward the door. "We'll go to my office and take a look."

"What about Colonel Drake? Won't she look for us here?"

"She'll find us."

Darcy led Ben down the hallway. "You know whatever we find," he said, "won't be good news."

"Ha. Again, we agree." They were on a roll. She

shoved through a set of double doors that warned people to stay out. "But maybe, if we're lucky, what we find won't be deadly."

He grunted. "Care to bank on it?"

"With GRID mixed up in this?" She considered it a full second just for show. "Not a chance."

Ben looked to the left and right, then at Darcy's hub. "Unusual office."

Seeing the twenty-by-forty warehouse of unused furniture stacked in rows, and the shelves housing files that ran the full length of the area, and the hub where she'd carved out her workstation through his eyes, she had to agree that it was unusual. Her computer desk was clear of clutter, her desktop littered with piles of Intel reports and files on just about anything of interest to the S.A.S.S. She'd appropriated a drafting table and light where she mapped out areas of interest. To its right, she had placed a section of portable wall she'd snitched from the Providence warehouse. It was split into sections, each signifying a different S.A.S.S. mission. Every section was crammed full of tacked-up photos, reports and scraps of paper that bore pertinent notes written in her own personal shorthand no one else could decipher. Together, all the sections formed a cozy cubicle about fifteen-by-fifteen, which suited Darcy fine but would strike anyone accustomed to a normal office as unusual. More likely, she admitted, it'd strike them as weird.

"Quite a setup, Darcy." Ben strolled around the cubicle. "But definitely isolated."

"Yes." She shrugged. "On good days, I leave the double doors open to the outer offices."

He stopped and looked back over his shoulder at her. "Do you have many good days?"

The urge to squirm hit her hard. He was asking because he didn't trust her not to get him killed. She understood that, and yet a bitter part of her—the part that was still angry about the forced changes in her life—resented it. "Not many. An occasional hour here and there. Sometimes a little more."

"Very challenging." He didn't sound uneasy, and she didn't detect even a trace of pity in his voice, for which she was grateful.

"But, as you say, we all have bad days, don't we?"

"Yes, we do." Sadness etched his voice and shone in his eyes.

Was he thinking about his former wife? Regretting not taking the job with the S.A.S.S. that General Shaw had offered him, or something else? Darcy gave herself a mental shake. It was none of her business.

Okay, she gave in to that one. But the man was interesting. Handsome as sin and interesting, and he had ethics. She liked that a lot. Ethics were missing or something ignored by too many men these days. A shame, because they sure looked good wearing them.

She walked over and sat down at the computer. "Well, let's take a look and see who owns this TNT Incendiary Devices, Inc." She motioned to Ben. "Pull up a chair."

He sat on the stool at the drafting table instead. "There's probably stuff I shouldn't see here."

Darcy smiled. "Don't worry, Ben. General Shaw and Secretary Reynolds authorized your admittance to Home Base—that's here. Their authorization included your being cleared for all we do. Otherwise, they'd have had Colonel Drake meet you elsewhere."

"I see." He dragged the stool across the concrete

floor and sat beside her. "I have to say, I was a little surprised to see a woman installed as the commander of
the S.A.S.S. I figured with the nature of the missions,
the honchos would go with a big-gun guy."

"Colonel Drake has unique qualifications that make
her perfect to command the S.A.S.S.," Darcy said. Ben
wasn't being sexist, just speaking honestly, so she didn't
take offense. He wasn't questioning Colonel Drake's
abilities. "As it happens, she went toe-to-toe with a big-
gun guy—Colonel Gray, the Providence Air Force Base
Commander—and she won."

"Impressive."

"Yes. But also unfortunate," Darcy said softly. She
dropped her voice and leaned closer to Ben. "Gray was
not a happy camper about losing. He wasn't a good
sport either. Since he's the Providence base commander,
he's the S.A.S.S.'s host."

Ben put all the pieces together. "Which means Gray
decides what offices the S.A.S.S. gets, which explains
why you're stuck out in the middle of a dormant bombing range."

"He thinks we work out of the banged-up trailer and
shack above ground." Darcy chuckled under her breath.
"Tell him about the bunker and I'll have to shoot you."

Ben's eyes twinkled. "Your secret will go with me
to the grave."

A little dazed from the intimate moment, she winked
at him. "Your devotion leaves me breathless. Is it because
you think Gray's a pompous ass for sticking us out here?"

"Of course not. It's because you're my partner," Ben
said, his amusement touching his eyes. "And because I
like your smile." He cocked his head. "Playful suits
you, Darcy."

It did. "I used to be playful a lot."

"But that was before the fire?"

A shaft of sorrow arrowed through her, and she nodded. Avoiding it, she busied her fingers on the keyboard, flew through a few documents, quickly keystroked through a few more, following the paper trail on TNT.

Ben watched over her shoulder in silence. Minutes passed. Five, then ten. "The owner didn't want locating him to be easy, now did he?"

"No, he didn't. But persistence—" She keyed through documents on a fronting corporation and landed on a document that stole her breath. "Good God."

"What?" Ben picked up on the anxious turn of her tone.

She swung her gaze to meet his. "Broken Branch Redemption owns TNT."

"Is that bad?"

"It's damn sure not good," she said. "Broken Branch is a universal religious organization." She keyed in to get a list of the corporate officers.

"Who's at the helm?"

"Checking that now." She waited for the document to load. It finally appeared on the screen. "It's your man, Ben."

"Who?" He craned his neck, but still didn't have a clear line of sight to the screen. "Wexler?"

"No." She looked at Ben. "Paco Santana."

Ben frowned, dragged a frustrated hand through his hair. "So the jerk's working TNT on both sides of the border and working for GRID. That'll make the mission tougher, Darcy."

"More so than you think. Since the fiasco at Waco, the federal government has taken a hands-off approach on matters that could even remotely be considered an encroachment into the 'freedom of religion' domain."

Worry flitted through Ben's eyes that matched exactly what Darcy felt. "Are you telling me we've got to battle GRID *and* Broken Branch *and* TNT *and* your superiors?"

"I don't know if I'd say 'battle,' but you can bet Colonel Drake, General Shaw and Secretary Reynolds are going to watch every move we make. If we miss dotting an *i* or crossing a *t* on any step in any of the processes, we're going to be sacrificial lambs."

"So we'll have to verify, triple-check and verify again to make sure we haven't missed anything."

She grunted. "Ben, if you had any idea how challenging it is to do that kind of thing on active missions in the field, you wouldn't be so nonchalant about this. A hint of a misstep on our part will cause a public relations nightmare. A true misstep and people die."

"Drake, Shaw and the secretary won't be satisfied with anything less than unqualified success."

"With these stakes? No they won't," she agreed. "And they'll be brutal to get it."

"Then we'd better do what we can to minimize the challenges," Ben said. "You, no hyperstimulation attacks. Me, no nonchalant acts. Both are luxuries we can't afford."

She rolled her eyes heavenward. "Ben, I can't just will myself not—"

"We try, Darcy." Ben reached over and clasped her hands in his. "That's all either of us can do, okay?"

He did understand. She stilled. She should be

stunned, and she wasn't. She definitely wasn't. Why? And why was she confident he'd understood from the start—even before he'd been told Dr. Vargus's professional opinion?

"You watch over me," he said. "If I start getting careless, yank my chain." She nodded, still a little bemused, and he went on. "Now, tell me what I need to know to watch over you. What are your preattack symptoms?"

Damn. She'd really like for him to think highly of her—well, as highly as possible—but if she told him... Instead, she opted for her typical evasion tactics. "About what you would expect."

Silence.

She leafed through a sheaf of papers. But not a sound escaped him, and she accepted that a sound wasn't going to until she told him the truth. She stole a glance at him out of the corner of her eye. Yep, truth was what he was waiting for, all right. He stared straight at her. "What?"

"I expect nothing, Darcy. I have no frame of reference for this." He frowned, stirred on the stool, then hiked his knee and caught his heel on the lower rung. "I'm not just interested in everything about you, you know. And I'm not trying to invade your personal life. I really need to know the signs or I wouldn't have asked." He looked away, hesitated, then looked back at her, his expression frank. "Consider the possibility that I might just have something to contribute. Is it that hard for you to believe that I might be able to help save our asses?"

Oddly elated and disappointed and embarrassed all at once, she cursed herself as a fool. His interest in her was to keep his own neck out of a noose and do his part to stop the attack. It wasn't personal.

Disappointment took the lion's share of her reaction.

"I like you, Darcy," he said softly, dipping his chin to his chest. "If you think that sounds weird to you, I can tell you it's even more weird to me."

So his interest was personal, too. Enormously pleased, she bit a smile from her lips. "Because of what happened with your wife?" she asked. She didn't find it weird at all. For the first time since the fire, she felt a personal connection—a woman-to-man connection—and her body wasn't in full revolt or going haywire, threatening to kill her with a massive adrenaline rush. Could her reaction be that strong without positive receptive vibes from him?

Not believing so, she sat back in her chair, strangely content. These normal hormonal reactions had a lot going for them. They were a little scary, of course, but they were also exciting, enticing, even enchanting.

Until Ben, when she'd felt attracted to a man—there'd only been two—she'd had hormonal explosions. Those reactions had nothing good going for them. They were excruciating, excoriating and exhausting. Totally horrid. So after the second hormonal explosion, she'd sworn off men and resolutely avoided any who could possibly stir an attraction in her. Then along came Agent Ben Kelly…

"Because after my wife, I swore I'd never get close to another woman," he clarified. "I guess that sounds pretty weak. But I'll tell you, Darcy. When you watch someone you love hit bottom and they drag you with them through it over and again, it cures you of wanting another relationship."

"I can see that it would." She could see it. All the pain

and frustration and the sense of helplessness and hopelessness of watching his wife fall off the wagon time
after time and not being able to help her. In his way, Ben
was probably as bitter as Darcy.

She turned her back to the computer and faced him.
"I'd rather not talk about my problems, but you're right.
The odds of me having a hyperstimulated attack during
the course of the mission makes it imperative that you
know what to expect."

He didn't look pleased or disappointed that she'd
agreed to talk freely to him. More so, he seemed content to take what came in stride. "So what do I expect?" he asked.

"Like I told you. Since I awakened from the coma, I
remember every sight and smell and touch and sound
and taste. As long as I'm in a controlled environment,
and I limit the level of sensory input, I can live a pretty
normal life. But outside that environment, my brain
goes into overdrive and my body's stuck with enduring
it."

"So are you okay one second and hyper the next?"
He dropped a pencil back into a holder on the corner of
the drafting table. "Or are there preattack signs?"

"Blessing or curse, there are signs. The first one is
that my speech and brain function at different speeds.
I talk gibberish and sound like an idiot." Unable to sit
and disclose this to him, she stood up and paced a short
path in her hub. "As if that isn't annoying enough, my
chest gets tight and my muscles start twitching."

"Which ones?"

"All of them." She pretended not to see his surprise.
"If the sensory overload continues, I hyperventilate and
my muscles all lock down."

He winced. "All of them?"

"I try to avoid getting to that stage. It's pretty nasty. But the truth is, I don't know exactly what happens," she said honestly. "The pain gets so intense that I black out." She turned her gaze to the wall of photos and notes. "What I do know is that I wake up with one helluva headache from cracking my head when I fall— sometimes with blood and bruising and fanfare, and sometimes without it."

"Damn, Darcy."

"I know. It's awful." She lifted a supplicating hand. "But what can I do? This is my world."

He dropped his gaze, stared down at the drafting table and propped his heel on a stool rung. "This insertion won't work. You'll never make it at Los Casas without having those nasty attacks. You can't put yourself through that."

"I'm military, Ben. I don't get a vote."

"Nothing personal, but you can't risk this—not in your condition." He rubbed at his nape. "I can't agree to this, not knowing you'll be in that kind of pain. What kind of man could?"

Touched, her voice weakened to a thread. "Thoughtful, but you don't get a vote either."

He turned to look at her.

"You heard Colonel Drake. I have my orders and, considering the costs, I'd better work and work well." A piece of fuzz stuck to his shirt collar. Darcy absently reached over and removed it. "I'm high-liability, but I do have the assets we need—perfect memory. We will diminish detection risks by not using surveillance equipment."

"At your expense," he countered. "You'll be in pain and in danger, Darcy."

Caring. He was a very caring man. "This won't be my first mission, Ben. I have a few years' experience at this. I know the risks are high." Was she interpreting his self-concern as concern for her? His life would be on the line. That sobered her thoughts. She owed it to him to ask. Colonel Drake wouldn't approve, but this mattered more. If the current plan didn't work out, then the commander would just have to accept another plan. "Ben, I realize my challenges increase the risks to you. I want you to know that you're free to say no—regardless of what Colonel Drake says. This is between you and me." She drew back her shoulders and met his gaze. "Knowing what you do about me, will you work with me on this mission anyway?"

He pursed his lips, snorted and gave his head a good shake, as if he couldn't believe he was being put in this position, too, when he'd already taken on major risks just to come here. A minute ticked off on the desk clock. Then another.

"No, Darcy. I won't work with you *anyway*," Ben finally said. He sighed and snagged her hand. "But I will work with you." He gave her fingers a gentle squeeze. "If you're willing to take on GRID, Kunz and Santana in spite of your challenges, then I'm willing to bank on you." His eyes shone appreciatively. "I doubt all three of them rolled together have your courage, and that will take you places nothing else can."

She couldn't help it. She should be mortified by that remark—the responsibility—but instead she was thrilled from the marrow of her bones out. "Thank you, Ben."

The look in his eyes warmed—definitely attraction, and most definitely personal. "You'll thank me later."

Her breath hitched. "That could be interpreted as a threat or a promise, Benjamin Kelly." She wound her fingers with his. "Care to elaborate?"

He sent her a sly look. "Would I threaten a woman who knows hundreds of ways to kill a man?"

"I suppose not." Darcy laughed out loud. "So how do I collect on this promise and see what it really means?"

"Ah," his eyes gleamed, warm and wonderful. "There's only one way to find out."

"Just one." She thought about it, but failed to figure it out. "Okay, I'll bite. How?"

"Live."

Colonel Drake stood behind Amanda and Kate at the double doors, leading to Darcy's domain. "What are you two doing?" She tried to peer over their shoulders.

Amanda spun around, looking guilty as hell. "Nothing."

Kate didn't budge even to look back. "Not a thing."

Laughter rang out from inside. *Darcy?* Shock raked up Sally's backbone. "Is that really Darcy laughing?"

"Yes, ma'am." Kate smiled.

Amanda couldn't hold back another second. "This is the first time I've seen her laugh in over a year, Colonel."

"Nearly two." Sally shouldered her way between them to look inside. "So Ben Kelly has what it takes to make our Darcy laugh. Well, who would've thought it?"

Amanda watched Ben and Darcy verbally sparring with total delight. "You don't think we need to worry? He won't take advantage of her condition, will he?"

"Not if he wants to live," Kate said. "Look at her. She really likes him."

Darcy was glowing. "Mmm, interesting." Sally stepped back from the door. "Totally different reaction to him than to the two she liked before."

"Good thing." Amanda's eyebrows shot up on her forehead. "Liking them damn near killed her."

Kate clearly recalled the events, and shot Sally a worried look. "She couldn't chill out enough to sleep for nearly a week."

Checking Darcy again, Amanda reassured Kate. "She doesn't look hyped. She looks…happy."

Sally Drake smiled broadly.

"What?" Kate asked. "You know something."

"Nothing," she said in her best "damn right I do but I'm not telling" voice. "It's just interesting." Amanda and Kate would realize what was happening here soon enough.

And maybe, just maybe, this unexpected but oh-so-welcome event would do for Darcy what nothing else had. Maybe, with a lot of luck and a little divine intervention, it'd make her take back her life.

A man's face appeared in her mind. A man gloating. *Thomas Kunz.*

Fear clenched Sally's stomach, snapped her nerves tight. That is, if this mission against GRID didn't kill them both.

Or one of them.

That would be a hundred times worse. Being the survivor was a bitch—and no one knew that better than Sally Drake. She lived it every minute of every day.

"Colonel?" Maggie said from behind Sally.

Shaking inside, she turned. Maggie looked dog-tired. Her eyes drooped. "Yes?"

"Lucas Wexler just requested an immediate backup customs agent. We had Fred Burns call in with a family emergency. He'll be out on paid leave until further notice."

"That was quick." The FBI, who'd made the overt arrangements to pull Fred Burns off duty and have Darcy inserted as his replacement, and to recall Ben from his fishing trip to help train her, was on its toes. Of course, this mission involved GRID, and the FBI knew as well as the S.A.S.S. how dangerous and ruthless GRID was; it stayed on high-alert. Butterflies swam in her stomach. "Amanda."

"Transport for Darcy and Ben," she said, heading back down the hallway to her office. "I'm on it, Colonel."

"Colonel." Kate's voice sounded stilted, nearly as worried as she looked and Sally felt. "She's going up against GRID."

GRID. Thomas Kunz. The most feared and ruthless leader of the most feared and ruthless terrorist group opposing the United States. There was nothing GRID or Thomas Kunz wouldn't do, and both excelled at whatever they took on. Across the board, they had been sickeningly successful. Body doubles, undetected insertions into high-ranking government positions, intelligence interceptions, weapons sales, hostage-taking—the list went on and on. GRID and Kunz were the stuff of nightmares for anyone charged with the national security of the United States. "I know, Kate." Everyone in the S.A.S.S. feared GRID and Kunz for good reason, and everyone was terrified Darcy would fail to stop the attack.

But no one feared failure more than Darcy herself.

No one except Sally Drake, who was sending an impaired operative into this situation, praying Darcy's fears and her perfect memory would give her the edge the S.A.S.S. needed to succeed.

Sally stifled a shudder and prayed too that Dr. Vargus was right about Darcy rising to the occasion. If he was wrong, Sally would take him out on the range and shoot him in the ass. She'd told him so, and she'd meant it. He'd sworn that if he was proved wrong, he'd load Sally's gun.

Determined to hold him to that bet, she pushed through the double doors and walked past the stacks of unused furniture to Darcy's hub. Ben and Darcy sat with their heads together near Darcy's computer. She was listening intently to his every word, which led Sally to expect the chat was personal. Surprisingly, it wasn't. Ben was giving Darcy a detailed briefing on operations at Los Casas.

They saw her and stood up.

"As you were." Neither Darcy nor Ben sat back down. They knew the awaited word had come, and Sally didn't prolong it. "We've received Wexler's critical request for a backup agent. You two need to get down to Texas to Los Casas. Amanda is arranging transportation now."

Chapter 3

Los Casas wasn't what Darcy had imagined. Three lanes of traffic were allowed in each direction, each separated by a glass and metal stall protected from car bombers by concrete barriers and a chain link fence topped with circles of razor wire. It looked a lot like the fences at Regret. To the south of the fence lay Mexico. The hot wind blowing steadily over the dry, barren land stirred up enough dust to choke a horse. The agents likely spent a lot of time at the end of their shifts coughing to clear their lungs.

They wore uniforms of white shirts and navy slacks and stood outside the stalls, checking the new electronic laser visas on permanent residents or citizens of Mexico and identification on Americans. The stall roof's slight overhang didn't do much to protect them from the sun other than at high noon—the glaring light slanted on through, flooding the concrete under the roof.

"You doing okay?" Ben asked from beside her.

Surprisingly, she was. "So far, yes." She offered him a smile to thank him for asking then looked down the line of wilted people waiting in the walk-through lane. It was situated between the traffic lanes and a small cinder block building. In front of it, about a dozen cars were parked in the dirt in a neat slanted row.

"The walkers are mostly regulars with laser visas," Ben told her.

That explained the biometric scans and metal detection paces the people were being put through. "Mostly men," Darcy noted.

"In a couple hours, it'll be mostly women." Ben glanced over from the line to Darcy. Sweat beaded at his temples. "Different work hours."

"Ah." They walked over toward the building. The majority of the parked vehicles were Jeeps and trucks, which seemed prudent considering the U.S. side of the crossing station was fairly isolated. A bus sat with its engine humming about 300 yards inside the U.S. border, accepting passengers who had walked over. They most probably worked in or near Devil's Pass, the small town that had sprung up about ten miles north. There was literally nothing between the station and it but dry, cracked land, dirt and the occasional cactus that was too stubborn to die.

"Ready to meet Wexler?" Ben rounded the rear of a blue Trailblazer.

"As ready as I'm going to get." She fell into step beside him outside the cinder block building, swearing her knees weren't knocking out of fear; the ground was uneven. *You can do this, Darcy. You must do this.*

When she walked through the door, a cold blast from the air conditioner slapped her in the face. Welcoming it, she inhaled deeply. A water fountain was near the door, white tile on the floor, whitewashed walls, directives pinned up on bulletin boards everywhere. Two small offices stood off to the right. The first had a sign on the door that read, Private. The second door's sign read, Station Chief. Darcy assumed the blond guy in his mid-forties sitting behind the desk was Lucas Wexler. There was nothing remarkable or memorable about his face, which seemed to be a GRID requirement in recruits. *Definitely a pattern there.*

"I'll tell him you're here," Ben said from beside her. "Be careful around him, Darcy. He plays the devoted husband bit, but he hits on anything female. Not sticking my nose in your business, just preparing you, though I'm sure you've been hit on enough times to recognize the signs."

Protective. She could kill a man in a dozen ways without putting herself at risk and Ben knew it. Yet he was still protective of her. *Charming.* Darcy's heart skipped a beat, then thudded against her chest wall. "Hasn't happened lately," she confessed, "but I remember." She followed Ben over to Wexler's office and paused outside the door.

Ben stuck in his head. "Burns's replacement is here."

Wexler looked up from a report he was reading and saw Darcy. Surprise lighted his eyes and he slowed his gaze, giving her a leering once-over that totally ticked her off.

"Well, hi there." Wexler stood up. "You must be Darcy."

"Agent Darcy Clark," she said, holding her ground outside the door.

"Come in, come in." He sat back down. "Thanks, Ben."

Summarily dismissed, Ben reluctantly walked away. Darcy understood that. Ben didn't like leaving her alone with Wexler for a lot of reasons, not the least of which was saving his own neck. She wasn't yet steady on her feet, and Ben knew it. He had to be worried. What if she hyperstimulated and had an attack coming out of the gate?

"I'm glad you're here," Wexler said. "I was afraid it'd take a couple weeks to get a replacement for Burns." Wexler grinned and seemed innocent enough until she met his eyes, saw a predator's gleam. He launched into a briefing on his policies and procedures.

Darcy's stomach clutched and her anxiety level spiked. From the corner of her eye, she glimpsed Ben through the glass wall. He'd noticed Wexler's once-over and, gauging by his expression, was clearly irked. He grabbed a glass of water and plopped down at his desk near the window, where she supposed he caught about every third word of Wexler's lecture on how he ran his station.

A little brown book half-stuffed into Wexler's desk drawer snagged her attention. It wouldn't have, but all through Wexler's diatribe, he kept cutting his gaze to it. The repetition caught her attention. Later, she'd need to take a look at it.

Finally, a full ten minutes later, he finished. Her nerves were fairly frayed. The noise level outside the office hadn't knocked her off balance so much as the bull being slung inside. But she'd observed plenty in addition to the brown book. Wexler was affable, relaxed, a good old boy who kept his proverbial nose clean and spent more time chasing women than keeping up with his duties as station chief. That too made him a prime target for GRID.

"You sure you got all that, Darcy?" He searched her face. "You look a little pale."

She felt a half step from hitting the floor. Her stomach was churning, her head foggy and she felt clammy all over. "I'm fine, Lucas. Thank you."

"Don't worry. I know it's a lot to remember, and you're not expected to nail it all down now."

Tossing aside the extraneous material, she had two minutes of essentials. Even without total recall, it wouldn't have been a problem. "I'm sure I'll be fine." She stood up.

Wexler dragged a hand through his hair, preening. His left hand was bare, but the telltale circle of white skin was all too apparent. The jerk had taken off his wedding ring. "If you have any questions, my door is always open."

"Thank you, Lucas," she said then left his office and moved to her assigned desk. Ben was sitting at it. "Um, I'm supposed to be here."

"Take the desk behind me," he said. "It's less noisy."

It would be. It sat nestled between the two offices, which acted as a decent sound barrier. "Thanks."

Perusing a stack of reports, Ben didn't look up. "Did I hear you call him Lucas?" A muscle in his jaw ticked.

What was he angry about? "That's what he said to call him."

"Wedding ring was off, right?"

"Got it in one."

"Bastard."

"That'd be a fair assessment in my opinion," she said before thinking.

Ben looked up at her then. Their gazes met, and he smiled.

Wexler left his office. "I'll be back in about an hour."

When the door closed behind him, Darcy checked to make sure no one else was around. Mindful of the camera in the corner of the room, which recorded every word and action, she schooled her expression. "Ben, would you please show me one of the traffic stalls?" She lifted a sheaf of papers. They crackled. "Regional is asking questions on this monthly report I can't answer without the nickel tour."

"Sure." If he was perplexed, he didn't show it, just stood up and came around his desk.

Darcy walked to one of the booths with him, looked around, and then stepped outside. When they were in a "dead zone" for the monitoring equipment—far enough away from the stalls but not close enough to the building to be recorded—she asked, "What's this brown book of Wexler's?"

"I don't know. I've seen it," Ben said, "but anytime I get close to him, he stashes it."

He'd done the same thing with her. "I need to get a look at it."

"How? He's got it with him all the time."

"We'll figure out something. It needs to be soon." The proverbial clock was ticking. *Keep your friends close and your enemies closer.* The old axiom ran through her mind and she fleetingly wondered who'd first said it. Regardless, it was wise then, and it was wise now. "He's protecting that book, Ben. The prospect of anyone discovering its contents scares him."

"How do you know that?"

"Hypersensitive to input, remember?" She stepped closer, dragged a fingertip down Ben's face from his temple to his jaw, following a trickle of sweat. "His body language is a dead giveaway."

His breath caught. "Okay." He frowned and tilted his head. "For the record, is this touch personal?"

She looked up at him. "Does it feel personal?"

He hesitated, swallowed hard and let out a huff of breath. "Yeah, it does."

"Then it probably is." She shrugged, stepped away and walked back inside the building.

That afternoon around three, Wexler walked out of his office and stopped between Darcy's and Ben's desks. "Ben," he said. "I'm changing the schedule to take nights for a while."

"Nights?" Ben didn't bother to hide his surprise.

"Yeah." His eyes shifted. "Elizabeth is nagging me to go to the opera on Thursday. I can't get out of it unless I'm working, so I'm working." He shrugged, and then turned to Darcy. "Here's your cell phone. Keep your calls limited to work or I'll get chewed by Regional."

He didn't say it, but his expression warned her that if he got chewed, so would she. "No problem."

Nodding, he started to walk away, stopped and turned back to her. "Darcy, what are you doing after work?"

"Nothing." Her nerves stretched tight. He was going to move on her.

"Why don't you meet me after work at the Oasis? It's a local bar, just on the edge of town." He smiled. "I'd like to buy you a margarita to say thanks for helping us out in a pinch."

Right. Sure you would, you jerk. "Love to, Lucas." She smiled at the slime, pitying his poor wife, Elizabeth. How did she handle his flirtations?

"Great." Wexler strutted out of the station and climbed into his dusty red truck. When he backed out of the parking slot and took off down the road to town,

Ben stood up. "Darcy, would you come out to the stall with me? I forgot to show you how to reload the observation camera."

"Sure." She stepped around the desk and snagged her leg on a bent piece of metal stripping. It dug into her flesh. "Damn it." She tore the sliced fabric away from metal.

"Are you bleeding?"

"It's nothing." It wasn't. So why was her heart beating ninety beats per second? Why did she have that clammy-all-over feeling again? And why did she have chills racing up and down her backbone as if someone had just walked on her grave?

You're fine, Darcy. She walked outside.

Inside the stall, Ben reached up and opened a control panel on the observation camera. "You have to disengage the camera to change the tapes. So the first thing you do, is to get a new tape ready—so you minimize the length of time the camera is down." He did that and then continued. "Next, you push this button right here to shut down the system to make the switch." He pushed the button.

The stall system shut down.

"Listen to me." Though speaking freely, he still dropped his voice and spoke rapidly. "I put Wexler's brown book in your car under the front seat. I snatched it while he was in the john."

"He left without it?"

"Not exactly," Ben said. "He left with a blank one I bought that looks just like it."

Darcy frowned. "If he notices the difference—"

"If he opens it, we're screwed." Ben nodded. "I know. But I had the chance, so I took it. You need to look it over, get to the Oasis and switch them back."

"I'll do what I can."

He nodded. "And keep that cheat at arm's length. He comes across cool and laid-back, but he's got fangs and claws and he loves to use them."

"I can handle myself, Ben."

"Can you?"

There was no accusation in his tone, but there was uncertainty. She didn't like it. Yet under the circumstances, she couldn't complain. Hell, she felt more uncertainty than he possibly could. "Now, we've got to get back online." He reached for the button to reactivate the system. "The new tape is in, the old one you label and file in media storage and we're done."

"Where's media storage?" she asked.

"The office inside with the Private sign on the door."

"Okay. Great." She walked back to the building, grabbed her purse and rounded a corner to the front door. Beside it, someone had hung a poster for the July 4th Independence Festival being held in Town Square from 7:00 p.m. until midnight.

Darcy's stomach flipped. Everyone for miles around would be at the Independence Festival, making it an easy mark for a GRID attack—no doubt aided by Paco Santana and Wexler, though currently she had no hard proof of it, only Ben's word.

What was his word worth?

She watched Ben walk back into the building, take a seat at his desk. Instinct told her he was honest. And his gaze was clear. The truth hit her like a physical blow. She trusted him.

When had that happened? *How* had it happened? She, who had been taught since raw-recruit training as an S.A.S.S. operative, never to trust anyone; she, who had avoided personal attachments—hell, even interaction—with any man since the fire, trusted Ben Kelly implicitly.

Her head swam, her stomach revolted. Lights flashed colorful spots before her eyes and she broke out in a cold sweat.

In a near run, she slammed against the restroom door and barely made it into a stall before throwing up.

A mile from the station, Darcy pulled over and looked through the brown book. Every page was filled with numbers. Just numbers.

She thumbed through. Fifty pages, maybe more. She'd have to call it in to Maggie at Home Base on the way or she'd be late meeting Wexler.

Taking off, she pushed aside the phone Wexler had issued her and pulled out her own from her purse, then punched in the number for Home Base.

Nothing.

She checked the battery and tried again.

Still nothing.

Had to be in a dead zone, though there weren't supposed to be any. Resigned, she opened the book to the first page and began reading the numbers. Fortunately, the dirt road leading from Los Casas to the Oasis was as straight and barren as it gets—no houses, no businesses, not even a road sign for over five miles. In long stretches, the trail was pitted with potholes so deep she feared the rented tan Jeep might fall in and not be able to get out of them, even with four-wheel drive. When she wasn't rocking and rolling through potholes, she was stuck in ruts that'd keep a train on track. The potholes were a pain, but the ruts were helpful. Still, she could read a bit. About a mile out from the Oasis, she had covered nearly thirty pages of the book.

The sun hung low in the sky, streaking it pink and gold. Grateful for that sensory respite, she hooked a right into the Oasis parking lot and saw Ben's Jeep.

She pulled up alongside him. "I need help."

"What's wrong?"

"Can you keep Wexler busy for ten minutes? That's all I need."

"Sure." Ben hooked his arms on her door at the window. "Why the delay?"

"Cell phone's dead. I can't call in my findings."

"What's in it?"

"I don't know." She stuck her thumb between the pages to hold her place. "It's in numeric code."

"How long is the thing?"

"About fifty pages."

Shock stretched Ben's eyes wide. "You're going to remember the numeric sequences for fifty pages of code?"

"Yeah, if I can just read them once." She sighed. "I told you, Ben. Perfect recall."

"Yeah, but code?"

"Anything. Everything." They were wasting time she didn't have to waste. "Will you do it?"

"Sure."

"Then go." She shooed him. "Go."

He turned toward the door. "You're impressive, Darcy."

"Not me, my memory. It's not me."

"It's part of you," he countered.

He had her there. "Okay." She sighed. She couldn't help it. "Go, before he comes out looking for me."

She finished the book in short order, then exited the Jeep and went inside.

Dust filmed the darkened windows, but half-inch wide cracks let the weak sun slant inside across the wavy wooden floor. Red booths lined three walls and a long beautifully carved bar ran the length of the fourth. It looked totally out of place.

"Darcy." Wexler stood up from the booth in the farthermost—and, naturally, the darkest—corner. "Over here." He waved.

Totally predictable. She dusted the thigh of her navy uniform slacks and walked past a couple snuggling on the dance floor. At least the music was soft and low and not blaring, and there were only a handful of other people in the place. *She could do this. She really could.*

Forcing herself, she smiled and slid into the booth.

Wexler sat down, then yelled across the bar. "Hey, Mick." He twirled his fingertip. "Margaritas."

"You got it, Wex."

Apparently Wexler was a good customer.

Rubbing something beside his right leg, he leaned over, closer to her. "When Mick brings the drinks, tell him you like his bar." Wexler pointed to the ornate fixture. "He got it out of a place down south and brought it back up here by mule. It's his pride and joy."

Darcy nodded, more than a little perplexed. If Wexler was being genuine, then he was also being thoughtful. If he wasn't, he was softening her up. She wasn't yet informed enough to take a bet on which would prove true, though she leaned toward the latter.

Two margaritas later, Wexler excused himself to go to the bathroom. The little brown book lay on the cracked red vinyl beside a patch job done with a strip of silver duct tape. Darcy checked the blank book's exact positioning—this could be a test—then switched out the books, giving Wexler back his with the codes.

Double-checking, she nudged its placement to make sure she wasn't a centimeter off the mark. If she'd had more time, she could have had Maggie or one of the other S.A.S.S. operatives prepare a duplicate book with altered number sequences.

Risky, and truthfully it was a fanciful idea Colonel Drake would never approve. She *wanted* Darcy to follow the supply line to get them all, including the GRID thugs and, Darcy hoped, Thomas Kunz.

Wexler returned to his seat, and Ben, who'd been sitting on a stool at the bar, put his money down to cover his tab. "Might see you later, Mick."

Darcy stomached a flush of insecurity, and then one frustration-filled. He was leaving his options open to come back because he doubted her ability to handle this. She'd have laughed at that before the fire—dangerous missions had been her forte then. Missions with survival odds so slim they would have raised the hair on Ben Kelly's neck and scared the hell out of him.

But that was before the fire. And she was not the operative now that she had been then. She wasn't the woman now she had been then, either.

That had more frustration building inside her. And more fear.

"Yeah, come on back." Mick waved a once-white bar rag. "We got a DVD of the game."

"Last week's?" Ben asked, heading toward the door.

"Two weeks ago, man." Mick laughed. "Where you think you are? Corpus Christi?"

"If I can spare the time."

The minute Ben walked out the door, Wexler thumbed his book pages, saw what he wanted, and he scooted across the duct tape toward her. She tried to block out his sour scent.

He propped his elbow on the table and leaned even closer. "So, Darcy, who's the lucky man?"

"What lucky man?"

"Come on now. I'm sure a woman as pretty as you has a man waiting for her back in Seattle."

He'd read her trumped-up dossier. On it, her home was listed as Seattle. "There isn't any man. Not anymore," she said, offering him a watery smile. "He dumped me for a chef with two kids and a high-end restaurant."

"Stupid man." Reaching over the table, he dragged a fingertip along the shaft of her forearm. "Well, I'm glad you're here."

Jerk. Not so subtle in the coming-on department. His poor wife must hate him—if she knows what he's doing. In small towns, people hesitate telling what they know when it includes infidelity. *Keep your enemies closer.* "Me, too."

"So," he gave her a slow blink, "how long have you been without a man?"

This was definitely a topic that should be out of bounds between a station chief and an agent. Wouldn't he love knowing it'd been five years? "A while, Lucas." Playing this demure, she lowered her lids.

"There's a little cabin out back." He dropped his voice, deep and husky, deliberately going for sexy. "We could have a little privacy." He stroked her arm.

Her skin crawled. "That would be—" She checked her watch, rocked her arm so the light winked off it and he didn't miss it. "Oh, sorry." She sighed her disappointment. "I've got an appointment about a rental and I'm late." She slid out of the booth, touched his cheek. "Maybe next time."

Wexler leaned back against the red vinyl and sighed contentedly. For the moment, pacified. "I look forward to it."

She bet he did, the sorry jerk. "Good night, Lucas."

"'Night." He thumbed the little brown book.

Darcy turned and walked out of the Oasis. Passing the bar, she called out. "Good night, Mick."

"Later, Darcy." He waved with the bar rag.

She stepped outside into the cool, dark night. The security light mounted on a pole near the edge of the building spilled amber light on the parking lot. No shine, sheen or reflection of the light shone on the cars. Too dusty.

"Darcy."

Startled, she spun around to see Ben. The man had no faith in her. None. She frowned. "Look, I know you're worried about me, but I'm holding up fine. So there's no need for you to check on me every time I move. It's annoying as hell to fight all this and—"

"Calm down," Ben cut in. "Why are you pissed off at me?"

"Because you came back to check on me." She slung her purse strap on her shoulder and folded her arms. "And because you have no faith in me."

"Let's set the record straight." He glared into her angry eyes. "I lack faith in Wexler, but I have faith in you—enough to put my damn life in your hands—and I'm not checking up on you."

Right. "Then why did you come back, Ben?"

"Because right after I got back to Los Casas, Paco Santana crossed the border. I followed *him* here."

Darcy's mind raced and her heart rate kicked into high gear. "It's happening."

"What's happening?"

Fear rammed through Darcy's chest, caught it in a vise. "GRID is bringing in the explosives."

Chapter 4

"I can't go back in there, Ben." She was already edgy from the elevated level of sensory input. She needed a little peace and total silence to recuperate and regain full balance—not that she wanted Ben to know she'd been impacted. As bars went, the Oasis *was* calm. "I told Wexler I had an appointment to look at a rental."

"You made it, you got it and you're squared," he said succinctly. "You can stay in the guesthouse at my place."

Surprised, she hiked her purse back up onto her shoulder. The stars were out. With a lot of sky and few lights, thousands of them winked up the night. *Pretty.* "You have a guesthouse?"

"Yes, I do," he told her, walking to the bar's door. Pausing just outside it, he grabbed hold of the worn knob. "Kitchen, bath, living room and bedroom. Fully furnished. Six-fifty a month. No security deposit—we work together." He raised an eyebrow, which whitened the scar on his cheek. "Settled?"

What was left to say? Looking at the stars helped. Her insides weren't churning anymore and her head was clear. No spots, no fog. She could do this. "Yeah. Settled. But it's too soon for me to be back here. Open a window for me so I can listen in on the conversation."

"Okay." He waited for her to get to the corner then swung the door open and walked through.

Darcy moved down the side of the building and peeked inside through a window. Only three booths were occupied and Ben chose the one nearest the window. Wexler still sat where she'd left him. And a man pushing forty with black hair, dark eyes and a thick build sat across from him, facing Ben. He needed a shave and a haircut. Red shirt, emblem, yellow teeth.

The window stood cracked open two inches and sound from inside floated outside to her. She set her purse on the weedy ground. Wexler's companion was their man.

Ben leaned toward the window and whispered. "That's him. Paco Santana."

Twisting the catch on her purse, she lifted what looked like a tube of lipstick but was actually a high-powered camera. While Ben went to Mick at the bar to get a drink, she snapped off a few photos of Paco Santana and Wexler.

Ben came back with a soda and sat down in the booth. "Why aren't they talking?"

"Santana's looking at Wexler's brown book," she whispered back. "Wexler's drinking—heavily."

"Attack of conscience, I guess." Ben shrugged. "Womanizing aside, he's a pretty good man, Darcy. He paints houses and mows lawns for people who can't do them anymore, and he fixed Sarah Jacobs's roof. She's a widow."

"Another conquest?"

Ben smiled. "Not that one. She's about ninety. She taught him English in high school and she still calls to correct his grammar on his quotes published in the newspaper."

"So why do you think he's gotten mixed up in this?"

Ben shook his head, looked down at the table and then lifted his gaze to Darcy's. "Greed." He dropped his voice even more. "Lucas grew up here. His folks lost the home-place when he was in high school. He swore that one day he'd buy it back. Last year, it went up for sale, but he didn't have the money."

"He was bitter." Darcy could almost feel his frustration, his hopelessness and that overwhelming sense of failure. Had Elizabeth put him down, reinforced all those negative feelings? Was that why he went after other women? Or was he just one of those men who thought monogamous relationships were good and right, but their strictures only applied to women.

Ben nodded. "He felt as if he'd lost it twice."

She stomped down weeds scratching at her ankles. "I can see where that would be important to him, but important enough to do this?"

"He's so self-absorbed, Darcy, he probably doesn't even realize what *this* is. Lucas is all about Lucas. He always has been."

Darcy chewed on that a minute, then asked, "What would he do if he did know?"

Ben's expression, already serious, grew darker. "Nothing."

"Really?" That didn't seem to fit with all the other things Ben had been saying about him. He helped others. Surely he wouldn't continue if he knew he'd be killing thousands.

Stiffening, Ben looked around to be sure no one was within earshot or paying attention to him. "He bought out the folks on his home-place a little over a week ago, Darcy. It's taken him half his life, but he's gotten back his home. He's not going to do a damn thing to jeopardize that. I told you, it's all about him."

Land over people. It made her sick. Her chest went tight, her stomach roiled, and a dull throb started at her temples.

"What are they doing now?"

"Still reading." She glanced from Santana to Wexler, eased the camera back into her purse. Little white spots formed before her eyes, and she blinked hard. "Still drinking."

"Good," Ben said. "This is good."

"Why?" She didn't make the connection.

"They're still planning or he wouldn't need the book."

Mick walked over and set down a napkin and then a glass filled with something dark on the scarred table. It looked like cola. "Ben, you need to talk with Darcy about keeping better company." He nodded toward Wexler and spoke from the corner of his mouth. "Somebody needs to warn the girl to watch out for that one. He's trouble."

Darcy hunkered down under the window, surprised by the warning, but touched, too.

"Yeah," Ben agreed. "I should've talked to her already, but you hate to dump that kind of stuff onto someone new, you know?"

"New or not, warn her. He's got his eye on her, and that's not good." Mick walked back to the bar.

"Well, I'll be damned," Ben whispered, took a long drink from his glass. "Odd, Mick warning you about Lucas. They've been best friends all their lives."

Interesting. "Maybe Mick doesn't like something Wexler is doing." Darcy pulled a listening device and earpiece from her gear and seated the earpiece.

"Santana?"

"My guess is Elizabeth. I watched him when I was in here earlier. Mick likes women but he respects them, too. Actually, he's adorably protective."

"He was in love with Elizabeth before she and Lucas hooked up. They had a spat and Lucas stepped in and married her before she could change her mind."

"Ah, that's it then." Wexler was cheating on the love of Mick's life. He wasn't protecting Darcy, he was protecting—to the extent he could—Elizabeth. "She should have married Mick." Darcy passed the disc-shaped listening device in through the window. "Get that to the booth next to them so I can hear."

Ben took it, slid out of the booth and walked over, propping a hand on the back of the target booth. He let the device slide down its back to the seat. "Mind if I join you? I hate drinking alone."

"Sorry, Ben," Wexler said, looking rattled. "We've got a private discussion going on here. A family situation we need to resolve."

"No problem." Ben went on to the restroom, then returned to his booth. "Is it working?" he asked Darcy.

"Yes, it is."

Santana passed Wexler the brown book.

He opened it on the table and then pulled a pen out of his shirt pocket. "Okay."

Santana downed a healthy swallow of something pale amber, then reeled off a series of numbers.

Panic lighted in Ben's eyes and he stiffened.

Darcy smiled. Adrenaline was gushing through her veins, she was edging on being hyperalert, but she was getting it all. "It's okay. We're doing fine."

Mick turned on a big-screen TV and inserted a DVD—a football game. Dallas Cowboys, of course.

Santana dictated a full three minutes. Between it, two guys in a dart game hurrahing and booing each other, three men at the bar disputing each play on the ball game, and the jukebox playing for the sole delight of the one couple still on the dance floor, she was approaching overload. Fast.

Santana shut up.

But it was too late for Darcy. The gushing adrenaline combined with her fear of teetering on the limit, and she tumbled headlong into an attack. "Ben, the fixture is warbling. My mother said so."

"What?" Startled, he stared at her through the window, perplexed.

"She was a heart patient. Her wind chimes were stained glass."

Ben left the booth, hurried outside to where she clenched the windowsill. "Darcy," he said softly. "You need to let go." He touched her fingertips, curled on the wooden sill.

She tried to focus, tried to make sense of his words. What language was he speaking?

He peeled her fingers back, held her hand in his. "Breathe deeply. Focus on me. Just on me, Darcy. It's just me and you, and your hand in mine."

She darted her gaze to his fingers, watched them close around hers. "The aorta ruptured and the roof caved in."

"Darcy, focus on me." He spoke in a barely audible whisper. "Look at me, Darcy."

Her heart thundered, banging against her ribs. *Look. Look at Ben.* She grabbed the thought and held on hard, struggled and finally met his gaze. He was calm. Totally calm. His hand didn't tremble, there was no panic in his eyes. He wasn't rattled or worried or upset.

"It's just you and me," he whispered. "Just you and me, Darcy."

His tone was so gentle, so silky smooth and soft. Tender. Calming. Her heart rate slowed, then slowed again to nearly normal. The fog in her mind parted and the throbbing at her temples eased. The blood pounding in her ears faded, more and more faint until the noise totally disappeared. It seemed the worst was over, but she didn't dare to trust it. She took in a huge shuddery breath, then let it out slowly, testing, gauging. The worst *was* over—and she was still upright!

"Are you okay to leave now?"

She nodded, still a little shaky.

Ben held out a hand to her.

Weak in the knees, she held on to him. For a second, she saw stars. *You can do this. You stayed conscious. You stayed upright. You can walk to the Jeep under your own steam.*

Ben snagged her purse then circled her waist with his arm and they walked over to the parking lot together.

The cool breeze revived Darcy a little. "We need to see where Santana goes."

"We'll wait in my Jeep." Ben led her to it, then seated her inside. "You need silence for a bit."

"Yes." She didn't bother to deny it. It would have been futile.

Ben climbed in and let down the windows. "Give me your feet."

"Excuse me?"

"Take off your shoes and stick your feet up here." He patted his thigh.

She toed off her black flats—more out of curiosity about what he intended to do than anything else—

twisted, and put her feet in his lap. It was such an intimate thing, but he didn't complicate the matter by saying a word, just clasped her foot in his hands and began massaging it.

She leaned against the seat and closed her eyes. Never before had anyone succeeded in talking her down. Never before had anyone witnessing an attack reacted so calmly. Even Maggie, Amanda and Kate went into a near panic because they didn't know what to do. To Ben, knowing seemed to come naturally. Maybe that's why he'd been successful. Or maybe it was because Darcy found him extremely attractive and she wanted so much to be "normal" in his eyes. Regardless of the reason, she was grateful. Grateful, delighted, surprised and definitely intrigued.

Ben Kelly was revealing himself to be an extraordinary man.

Twenty minutes passed in total silence with Ben rubbing her feet and hands.

Darcy let out a contented sigh, feeling the remnant weariness of an attack, but not the usual fallout that took about three days from which to recover. Actually, she felt nearly normal. *Amazing.*

"Better?"

"Definitely." She cranked open an eyelid. "How did you do that?"

"What?" He thumbed circles into the ball of her left foot.

She paused. She couldn't explain this; she wasn't sure she understood it herself. She couldn't express how different this attack had been in a way that would do the contrast justice—he'd never before seen her during or after an attack. "Nothing."

He didn't push, just ran his fingers along the arch of her foot.

"Thank you, Ben." She closed her eyes again and enjoyed the moment. Her and Ben. Her foot in his hands. Relaxed. Content. *Total peace.*

Tears welled in her throat. It was the first time since the fire that she'd known peace. The very first time.

"Darcy?" He sounded pensive.

"Hmm?"

"I didn't know what it cost you to do this until now." His hand stilled. "I'm sorry I asked it of you. I—I—"

As the attacks went, this one hadn't been bad. He seemed so contrite. She hated that, and yet it was impossible to explain. "You didn't ask anything of me, Ben. You've only helped me do what I need to do."

The bar door swung open, and Paco Santana walked out.

"Time to roll," she said, reaching for her own cell phone in her purse. "I need to report to Home Base." She frowned. "Do you sweep your Jeep for bugs?"

"Every time I get in it."

She thought a second. "Not bugs as in critters you swipe out with a whiskbroom. Listening devices."

"Oh." He grinned. "Yes, Darcy. Since this started, I check. The Jeep's secure."

She let out a little laugh. Considering that somewhat miraculous, she dialed Home Base.

Maggie answered.

"It's me, Maggie."

"Darcy. It's Darcy," she shouted to someone in the background.

Imagining the entire S.A.S.S. unit standing around wringing their hands, worried that she was going to blow this mission, put a frown on her face. "Santana is in the U.S. We're following him. I need to report that coded text. I've gotten a look at it. Open the overflow, Maggie. There's about fifty pages and I'd guess another four or five that got entered in tonight."

Ben grunted in disbelief.

He got it, but he still didn't get it. "Ready?" She motioned out the window. "Go, Ben. Santana's on the move."

Ben put the Jeep in Drive and followed at a distance. There was little between him and Santana, so there was no fear of losing him and he'd assume someone else had left the bar. No big deal when there was only one road to town.

"Overflow's on, computer input is ready, direct link to Langley is engaged and operational and backup-recording is running," Maggie said. Then she set the parameters of who was reporting and added the mission number and code, fulfilling the typical prereport matter requirements. When she'd finished, she told Darcy, "Proceed with input, Captain."

Darcy began transmitting the contents of the book, pulling the numerical sequences from memory. She included when to start new lines and new pages. Those specifics could be imperative to accuracy in the decoding process. Between potholes and ruts, the ride was rough, but with Ben doing the driving and Santana puttering along fat, dumb and happy, she could forget worrying about him being suspicious. There was only one road into town, so them following was a given. And that left her free to focus entirely on relaying the code.

Ben gave her numerous curious looks, but he didn't interrupt once. He just drove the Jeep down the winding dirt road, choking on Santana's dust.

* * *

In Devil's Pass, Santana pulled into a hole-in-the-wall hotel with a pink neon sign out front. Traveler's Inn. The parking lot was pretty full, so Ben looped around the two-story white stucco building, turned off the Jeep's lights and then drove out and parked on the far end.

With a perfect view of the entrance, Darcy finished her report to Maggie. "I'll transmit the photos as soon as I can."

"Great," Maggie said. She paused, clearly hesitant, then added, "You are doing okay, right?"

"I'm fine." At least she thought she was. She looked over at Ben, hiked a shoulder, checking with him.

He nodded.

"Yes, I'm fine." She ended the call and dropped the phone into her purse. "Great view of the entrance," she told Ben. "I can see why General Shaw wanted you in the S.A.S.S. Do covert tactics come naturally to you, or were you trained?"

He didn't answer. "Santana's got company."

Darcy swung her gaze to the porch in front of the entrance. Two men in dark clothes approached Santana. She grabbed her camera and snapped off shots of each of them. Red shirts. *Interesting.* The trio talked briefly, then the two men walked back toward the hotel entrance.

"Do you recognize them?" she asked Ben.

"No, I don't." Worry edged his voice. "Who do we follow?"

Santana was walking back to his car. "Santana." The two men likely were hotel guests; easy to pick up on later.

But Santana didn't leave. He grabbed a suitcase and walked back to the entrance, then into the hotel.

A feeling Darcy often had gotten on missions awakened inside her. A feeling that all the puzzle pieces had gathered in one place and she didn't have enough eyes to watch them all. She hated to call in overt backup without first verifying specifics—but this mission was too important. Later, she'd prove she could handle her job. Now, too many lives were at stake. Her ego would just have to take the hit.

Again, Maggie answered the phone at Home Base.

Darcy quickly explained the situation and Colonel Drake got on the line.

"Darcy?"

"Yes, ma'am."

"I'm up to speed on this. I have Kate requesting overt resources to tag Santana and his friends. Get those photos to us ASAP, and as soon as backup is on-site, you concentrate on Wexler. Nothing's going to cross that border without him being there to let it in."

"Yes, ma'am." She stared at yet another Independence Festival poster taped to the hotel's front wall. They were plastered all over town.

"It'll be a couple hours. FBI," Colonel Drake said, tagging the type of overt backup that would be arriving.

"No problem."

The colonel's tone shifted, turned less strident. "Darcy?"

"Yes?"

"You—you are all right? I mean, all pretense aside."

Though her teeth ached from clamping her jaw tight, she held back a snapped response. They were justified in their concern. Still, if they were that damn worried, she shouldn't be here. "Yes, Colonel. I'm fine."

"Of course." Her sigh of relief blew static in Darcy's ear.

Less appreciative of their concern and more irritated by it, Darcy glared out the window. "Colonel, do you doubt I can handle this mission?"

Silence.

"Do you?"

"I don't doubt you can, Darcy. I'm concerned that you doubt you can."

"Well, I don't. Okay?"

"Okay."

Darcy hung up without a goodbye. Then what she'd done hit her and she nearly stroked. "God, I've lost my mind."

Ben's eyes stretched wide. "That's an overstatement, right?"

"Not by much." She glanced over and answered honestly. "I just yelled at and hung up on my commanding officer."

Ben grunted. "Almost like the old days, huh?"

Shock bolted through Darcy and the truth hit her. "Well, yeah. It was." And why knowing that made her feel infinitely better, she had no idea. In the old days, Colonel Drake had threatened to fire her ass at least once a week.

She looked back at Ben.

"It feels good to be treated normal." He winked.

Darcy grunted. It did.

Chapter 5

Two hours later, two backup male FBI officers arrived. Colonel Drake officially passed the torch of watching Santana and his two cohorts to them, and then turned Darcy and Ben loose.

Ben drove by Wexler's house on Palafox Street. His red truck sat parked in the drive. Weary to the bone, Darcy got out and checked the hood. It was cold, and all the lights were off in the house. He was down for the night. Just in case, she attached a magnetic tracking device under his rear bumper and activated it to Home Base. If the truck moved, they'd notify her. Done, she slid back into the passenger seat in Ben's Jeep.

His hand on the gearshift, he asked, "Where to?"

"Home." She needed sleep. More than needed it, she craved it.

Ben stopped at the intersection, then turned right and made his way to Dove Cove. At the far end of the cul-de-sac, he pulled into his driveway, and then cut the engine. It ticked loudly in the silence. "The guesthouse is back there," he said, pointing beyond the end of the drive and the back of his two-story home. The white clapboard looked inviting, and the house had a yawning front porch. One heavy rocker sat near the front door. *Since his divorce, a loner like me.*

"Come on. I'll walk you back and show you around."

"What about my Jeep?" Darcy climbed out of his.

"You can ride to work with me."

"But my things are there."

"Didn't think of that." He looked abashed. "I'll get you settled and run over and get them. That'll give you a little more downtime."

Thoughtful. "Thanks." Truthfully, she needed the downtime too much to object. While she wasn't suffering her normal posthyper symptoms, she was weary to the bone and needed respite.

The cottage was white like the house with sun-yellow trim. Pink roses grew on a lattice trellis outside the door. Inside, the cottage was calm and comforting in soft creams with splashes of blues and greens. "Very pretty."

He stood in the small living room attached to the kitchen and pointed out the amenities. "Bed and bath are down the hall. Basics like coffee and tea are in the pantry. Fridge is nearly empty, but there are canned goods and juices. Make yourself at home." He backed out the door. "I should be back in about an hour."

An hour. "Wait." She'd forgotten it was so far from Devil's Pass to Los Casas. "If you can spare a T-shirt, I can make do until morning without my things."

"Sure. There's a couple in the bedroom dresser. Feel free to use anything else around, too."

"Thanks, Ben."

He stood there a long moment, just looking at her, as if he felt torn between staying and going.

Odd to feel much less admit, but she wanted him to stay. Heat rushed up her neck to her face.

"Will you be all right here?" He licked at his lips, leaned against the open door. "You seem to be feeling okay. Are you?"

After the incident at the bar, she couldn't object to his asking. Again, his worry was just. It was kind of everyone, but she sure was getting weary of all the concern. It made her feel even less able than she already felt. "I'm fine, Ben." He was worried, not attracted. Damn it. "Just a little tired. I'm going to transmit the photos to Home Base and then sleep awhile."

"Do you need a computer?"

"No. I have a satellite-based transmitter." She pulled it from her bag. "It's much more secure than a computer or phone line—at least until Thomas Kunz gets his creepy hands on the technology. Then he'll have GRID sell it to anyone who wants to destroy us."

"It's sick to live with so much hate."

"The things he does? It's even sicker, Ben. Trust me on that." She set up the transmitter, connected the camera, and transmitted the photos.

"Maggie said you're really wired after an attack. But you don't seem wired."

"I always have been, but tonight I'm not," she confessed. He'd never before been around to talk her down. Odd. A man she'd known such a short period of time had so quickly come to mean so much. "You changed things for me."

"Me?" He walked back to her. "How?"

She looked up at him, touched a finger to his jaw. "By being you, Ben."

His eyes shone. "It's personal, isn't it, Darcy?" He cupped her chin in his hands. "For you and me."

The unsteady crackle in his voice proved he had mixed emotions about that. Well, so did she, so they were in good company. "Yeah, it's personal," she said, then lifted her gaze from his chest to his eyes. "At least, it is for me...."

"For me, too," he said straight out. "I don't like it, and I doubt you do, either. But it's there. It's been there since I first heard your voice—outside Regret, when you cleared me through the gate."

"Wow," she said, a little breathless, a little stunned and starry. "Since then? Really?"

He nodded.

She watched his mouth, his lips, the softening of the look in his eye. He was going to kiss her. It had been over five years since she'd been kissed, and excited and fearful of what her reaction would be, she welcomed and shunned it.

He didn't move. Just held her face in his big hands and looked into her eyes. Desire shone in his own, desire and uncertainty. He was worried about her reaction, afraid he'd do something to send her over the edge. Would it be okay? She had no idea. She could lose it. Could be wired for sound for three days. Could suffer all the horrible symptoms she'd suffered on other attacks that had knocked her to her knees.

Or maybe it wasn't her reaction but his own that worried him. He'd made no secret of it that he'd avoided women since being burned so badly with Diane. In his own way, he was every bit as fearful of entanglements as she.

A full minute passed. Then another. And still another. Darcy inwardly cringed. One of them had to take the leap. Could she? Hell, if one was going to be taken, she supposed she'd have to do it. He'd be afraid of sending her reeling. Should she?

She definitely should not. Not with everything else going on. Yet he looked so… She slid her hands at his waist. And he felt so… She inhaled deeply. And he smelled so…

Oh, to hell with it. No guts, no glory. She pressed her lips to his. Her senses wide open, she captured every minute detail, took in every nuance, got lost in sensations born in attraction and tempered into more like steel by fire. Deliberately firm, he gentled the kiss to tender and hinted at passion, though cautious and controlled. But the kiss demanded more, deepened, and caution disappeared, control surrendered questing to be swept into the desire assaulting the senses in battering waves. Heat swelled and spread through her chest and settled low in her belly, tingling, seeping into cell and pore, awakening her body from its long, lonely sleep.

Swimming in sensation, she wound her arms around him, splayed her fingertips on his broad back; felt his fingertips glide dancingly down her spine from nape to waist. He tugged her to him until their bodies aligned and his heat crept to her through their clothes.

He eased his mouth from hers, his breath rough and uneven. "Darcy, is the sensory input too much for you?" He looked worried and a little baffled. "I didn't mean to let things get so intense. I'm not sure how it—it just…happened."

The transmitter beeped, signaling it had finished forwarding the photos of Santana's cohorts to Home Base. It returned photos of the FBI agents so Darcy would recognize them.

Ben jerked, startled. He pulled back to better look at her, and grimaced. Slowly, hesitantly, he released her and stepped away. "I think we're in trouble here."

She blew out a hot breath, half-expecting to see steam rolling off them both. "Definitely."

He might not like it, but he wanted to touch her; he clasped her hands and the grimace left his face. Despite an obvious attempt to be neutral, hope burned in his eyes. "Do you mind, Darcy?"

She should. She'd like to. She wished she could. Life was so much simpler without relationship entanglements that *always* led to complications, and her personal challenges damned her and her partner to even more of them. After what happened to her friend Merry in the fire—as a direct result of being Darcy's friend—it was only right that she should mind. Yet truth was truth. "No, I honestly don't. It's selfish not to mind—if I had half a brain I'd run like hell, but I'm not going to run, Ben, and I really don't mind. So if there's running to be done, you're going to have to do it." Fully expecting him to do just that, she held her breath.

He ignored that aspect of what she'd said, and focused on another. "Why is it selfish not to mind?"

She tilted her head back to look up into his eyes. He wasn't joking. That made her frown. "The fire where I was injured…" She paused, awaiting his nod. When he gave it to her, she went on. "It was my house that burned. My friend, Merry, died in it, Ben." Her voice faded and she pushed strength back into it. "She died because the terrorists thought she was me."

"I'm sorry, Darcy."

"Me, too." He had no idea just how sorry—no one did.

"It's their fault, not yours." When she looked up at him, he added. "It's written all over you that you feel guilty about this."

"I feel responsible—and guilty."

"You're not. You didn't start the fire."

"There's more, Ben."

"What more?"

"You know I spend a lot of time in isolation. I have to do it. Anyone with me would, too." She rubbed his thumbs with hers. "I don't think that's fair to ask of anyone else—to ask of you. I shouldn't do it."

He grunted and rolled his gaze heavenward. "Hell, Darcy, think. Where do I spend most of my time?" He ticked off his own response. "Los Casas. Here at home. At Mick's, at church, rocking on the front porch—and once a year, at the festival. I *like* isolation."

"You do, don't you?" Relieved and excited, Darcy smiled.

"Yeah." He pulled her to him. "Come here."

Darcy walked into his arms.

Long hours later, Darcy's cell phone rang.

Ben rubbed her arm, wrist to elbow, unwrapped his leg from hers, letting it fall from the sofa to the floor. "It's yours."

"Aw, I don't want to move." Snuggled back against his chest, his legs on either side of her hips, her arms folded over his at her waist, she felt totally relaxed and too comfortable to consider moving.

He pressed a kiss to the side of her neck. "Don't."

Boy, would she love that. "Have to, but hold my place for me."

"You got it, sweet stuff."

She rolled off the sofa, where they'd sprawled and dozed off, then grabbed the phone from her purse. "Hello."

"Darcy, it's Colonel Drake. I've just upgraded your mission to a Code 2."

Darcy's heart thudded. Code 2 missions signaled imminent threat. Wide-awake now, she asked, "Why?"

"The photos you sent in—the two men with Santana—they reside at the Broken Branch Redemption compound. We think it's a front for GRID."

"Santana owns TNT and runs Broken Branch. He cuts a deal with GRID and hides the explosives at Broken Branch, knowing we won't go in due to the 'freedom of religion' complications. I'd say it's highly likely, Colonel. Do we have any more details on these men? They could be GRID operatives as well."

"Maggie, Kate and Nathan, and Amanda and Max are on it."

Five Class-A operatives. Darcy thought a second, reviewing their collective expertise. "You might want to get Jackson Stone from Task Force 123 on it, too, Colonel. He's got a mind like mine only his is a lot more full. He's been this way since birth." Darcy shoved her hair back from her face. "I'm guessing the supersleuths at Langley are still trying to break the code."

"Ever since you relayed it." She sighed. "So far, no luck."

Perplexed, Darcy stared at the window. "So why are we upgrading to a Code 2?" Something had to spur the urgency.

"The tracking device you put on Wexler's truck is active. He left home about five minutes ago, heading back to the Oasis."

Darcy grabbed her shoes and started shoving them on her feet. "I'm on my way, Colonel."

"You are holding up—"

"I'm fine." She'd spoken sharply—far more so than was warranted. The question irritated the spit out of her. It shouldn't, but it did. Her problem, not the commander's. She sighed. "I'm sorry, Colonel Drake. I know you're just concerned. Everything really is going fine."

"I'm glad, Darcy."

God, she felt like a heel. "Thank you for asking and for caring. I mean that."

"It's okay."

"I'll keep you posted." After ending the call, she grabbed her purse and told Ben, "Hustle. Wexler's on the move."

It was three in the morning. Neither of them had to say what they feared he could be moving.

Inside the Oasis, Mick sat behind the bar, his elbow bent, his chin propped on his hand, and eyes closed. The place was empty except for Wexler and a man who had his back to Darcy. They stood at the pool table and the man was taking a shot at the purple four ball. He looked out of place, wearing a suit. Wexler wasn't in uniform. He had on faded jeans and a cotton shirt.

Darcy sat down at a table near them, and half-turned away to better hear them. Ben went to the bar and snagged two sodas.

"Ben!" Wexler snagged him. "Who's that you're with?" He cranked his neck to look her way. "Darcy?" His affable expression faded. "What are you doing here?"

"Darcy's renting my guesthouse," Ben said. "Her car broke down, so I came to help her out. Since we were close, we figured we'd drop in for a drink."

The man sank the four ball.

"At 3:30 in the morning?" Wexler frowned.

Ben looked at Darcy. "Took me longer to get it running than we thought."

"Yes, it did." Darcy nodded, then glanced at Wexler.

Whether he was ticked that she was there with Ben or ticked that either of them were there, she had no idea. The man holding the cue stick turned around to look at her.

Needle.

She caught herself before reacting. Needle was a known GRID operative whose photo had been on Home Base's wall for six months, two weeks and four days. Both Amanda and Kate had had run-ins with him on previous GRID missions. That he was here with Wexler, and that he was wearing a red shirt under his suit's jacket, acted as heavy-duty verification of Intel's suspicions about another attack and Ben's assertion that Wexler was involved in it.

"Who are they?" Needle asked Wexler.

"They work for me at Los Casas." He subtly signaled with a negative nod that Needle had nothing to worry about from Ben and Darcy.

Ignoring them—which suited Darcy just fine—he turned back to his pool game, and took aim on the orange five.

Ben returned to the table and sat down. They worked to appear lost in conversation, seemingly uninterested in Wexler and Needle, but Darcy hung on their every word. After they finished the game, they walked back to Wexler's favorite booth in the far corner. He pulled out his brown book and passed it to Needle.

Darcy's skin crawled.

Needle reviewed it for a short minute, and then passed back the book and began spewing numbers, which Wexler hurriedly wrote down.

Darcy looked at Ben and saw his worry. She smiled to reassure him. "Drink your soda. This isn't a challenge."

With a little grunt she nearly missed, he reached for her hand and gave it a gentle squeeze. Grounding her, she realized. Just in case.

Vintage Ben, she thought. He didn't make a big deal out of anything. Just stepped up and did what he considered needed doing. She loved that about him.

Actually, she loved many things about him.

Needle's litany lasted longer than Santana's. At least twelve pages worth, Darcy estimated. Within minutes of finishing, Wexler closed the book, and Needle left the Oasis.

Darcy considered following him but instead excused herself. In the restroom, she called Home Base for backup. The FBI could intercept Needle at Devil's Pass as he went into town.

When she returned to the table, Wexler was gone and Ben looked furious.

"I retrieved the listening device." He passed it to her.

Almost afraid, she asked, "What's wrong?"

"The pompous ass just ordered me to back off from you. He's got dibs."

And Ben didn't like it any more than Darcy. "What did you tell him?"

He slid out of the booth. "It's not fit for a lady's

ears." Circling her shoulder, he tucked her under his arm and led her to the door. Locking it, he closed the bar, leaving Mick sound asleep, sitting at the bar.

"You take my Jeep," Ben said. "I'll drive yours."

"Why?" She walked over to his, swept it to make sure it was free of bugs or tracking equipment, and then let him seat her inside.

"Wexler saw us holding hands earlier. He was pretty hostile about you and me being together, and his getting shut out." Ben tapped the heel of his hand against the car door. "I half expect an ambush on the road to Devil's Pass. He wants to get your attention."

"Then you should go first in my Jeep."

Ben nodded. "If he tries to force you off the road, just go around him. I'll take care of him, and be right behind you."

Protective. She didn't need it, but that he wanted to protect her was endearing. She liked that about him, too. Yet the last thing she needed was a war between him and Wexler. "I'll see you at the house."

About halfway, her headlights shone on Wexler's red Jeep, stopped on the road. If he tried anything, Ben would beat the man to a pulp and that could create serious mission challenges. *Intercession required.*

She hooked the wheel, pulled right up beside Wexler, and stopped. Her headlights shining in onto his front seat, she stuck her head out her window. "Lucas, is everything okay?"

He got out of his car. "What are you doing driving Ben's Jeep?"

"Mine was running hot. He's driving it, and I'm sticking close in case it breaks down again. You having engine trouble?"

"No." He frowned down the road at Ben's lights, going haywire from him bouncing through the potholes. "Just stopped to, um, have a smoke before going home. Elizabeth hates it," he confided. "Everything is great. Just great."

He wasn't smoking, but the excuse worked for her. "Okay, then. See you at work tomorrow afternoon."

"No!" he shouted.

"No?" She slid him a puzzled look.

"You're off tomorrow."

"I am?" Damn it. She didn't like the feel of this.

"Yeah. Get settled and everything."

"Okay. Later, then." He waved and she drove off, then watched in the rearview mirror. He stood at the edge of the dirt road and glared as Ben drove past.

One war avoided.

But instinct warned her there would be another. She retrieved her cell phone and called in Needle's codes to Home Base. Kate took the call, and after the data had been recorded, she told Darcy, "Langley has made some progress on breaking the code, but they're having a hell of a time with part of it."

"Maybe Needle's latest will help them. So far, I'm coming up dry, but I haven't really had time to give it full focus."

"We can but hope. Everyone around here is getting really edgy. We feel GRID closing in. You know what I mean."

"Yeah, I do."

"Darcy?" Kate paused, her tone turned pensive. "I hate to ask but I need to know. Are you feeling okay?"

"I'm fine, Kate." Darcy resisted irritation. Her friend was worried. Her colleague was terrified. "Really. It's weird, Kate," she confided in her. "Being here and working with Ben. It's like having a buffer between everything and me. I still take it all in, but it's different."

"Different, how?"

"I don't know." She really didn't have a clue. "It's all there. Every bit of it. But it doesn't sink in as deep or something. I can't explain it. But I really am okay."

"Stronger emotions filling the space?"

What the hell. She knew it, and lying to Kate wouldn't make it less true. "It could be. Ben's pretty special. A lot like me."

"Okay, then."

Odd response. Shoot. "Is the colonel standing over your shoulder?"

"That would be an affirmative, Darcy."

"I'm off then."

"Good. Get some rest. We've got backup standing by on Wexler."

"Who?"

"Overt. As soon as our friends," Kate said, speaking of the FBI, "heard GRID mentioned, they swarmed us with offers to assist. We accepted."

The FBI had lost several agents to GRID, too. "Awesome."

"The colonel says to get some sleep. We've got you covered."

"In that case, I'm on my way."

Chapter 6

Darcy couldn't sleep.

Seeing Needle at the Oasis had rattled her, and while she wasn't hyperstimulating to the point of an attack, she was alert. Far too alert to sleep.

She made herself a cup of tea and sat down at the cottage's distressed kitchen table with a pen and pad and wrote down a segment of Needle's code. Why that specific segment stood out in her mind, she had no idea, but her instincts had been honed as an operative. She respected them. And so she'd follow them now. Assigning each numeral a letter, she went for the obvious vowels first.

At 6:00 a.m., she showered, cleaned up in a fresh uniform, and drove over to Traveler's Inn for breakfast and to check out, now that she had Ben's guesthouse. Starved, she turned her nose up at her usual banana and bran muffin and gorged on bacon and eggs, toast with homemade strawberry jam, blueberries and nearly half a container of yogurt. While eating, she read two newspapers, less the sports sections, and drank three cups of coffee. In her mind, she continued to work on the segment of code.

A rhythmic sequence hit her with a jolt. She played

and replayed it, assigning the known and adding the possible, then she mentally switched to another page, one of Wexler's first, and assigned it the same values.

It fit.

Excitement burned low in her belly. She returned to Needle's segment, deciphering it, and an important piece of the GRID mission puzzle fell into place. A piece that explained Wexler's sudden interest in working the night shift—and it had nothing to do with Elizabeth or the Independence Festival opera.

She rushed to her Jeep and then phoned Home Base, keeping watch on the Inn's dining room through the huge plate-glass window. As soon as Maggie answered, words spilled from Darcy's mouth. "Quick. Get the colonel on the line."

"You got it, Darcy."

Seconds later, Colonel Drake said, "What's up?"

"I got part of the code." She gave the colonel the rhythmic sequence, values assigned and data decoded. She'd pass it on to the S.A.S.S. operatives working it and to Langley. "Needle." Darcy named the source. "Same means as last time. One of three shipments is coming in tonight."

"Where are the other two?"

"I don't know," Darcy admitted. "They could already be here, or still be south of the border."

"Okay. Okay," the colonel said. "We'll chase that from here. Good work, Darcy."

"There's plenty more to be decoded. Maybe it will help us find out what we need to know."

"I pray it will." The colonel issued an order to Maggie to relay the information to Langley, and then again spoke to Darcy. "Monitor the shipment, but don't interrupt it. After we determine the location of the other two, then we'll have the FBI intercept and arrest all parties. Did you get the photos of the agents?"

"Yes, I did. Maggie sent them last night."

They were following standard operating procedure. The S.A.S.S. unit didn't exist, therefore it worked totally covert operations. Anything overt went to overt agencies at the time of the arrest and then they mopped up from there.

"I realize it's risky to let this play out so far, but Secretary Reynolds issued our orders," Colonel Drake said. "He wants us to confiscate all the radioactive material designated for use in the attack and facilitate the arrests of all the terrorist thugs GRID designated to use it. Hopefully, this time we'll get Thomas Kunz himself."

Darcy wouldn't bank on it. "He'll hide and let his minions take the risks. He always does."

"I know." Colonel Drake grunted. "But a woman can dream."

Darcy returned to the dining room and waited. Finally, the two men from Broken Branch Redemption came out of the bank of elevators and walked toward the little restaurant.

Darcy tucked her wallet back into her purse and asked the waiter for a newspaper.

A busload of teens streamed into the restaurant, laughing, squealing, talking across the tables. The Broken Branch men didn't seem to mind the noise, and Darcy tried to ignore it, but she just couldn't take it. Her chest went tight, her temples throbbed and the telltale warning spots formed before her eyes.

Get out of here, Darcy. Now.

She reached for her purse and looked up—just as her

FBI counterparts walked into the restaurant. But it was the man walking two steps behind them who had her in a full-blown attack.

Thomas Kunz.

The head honcho of GRID looked like anything but the chief of a major terrorist network. He was around forty with short blond hair—and, she recalled from memory, blue eyes. Amanda and Kate had reported that he looked like a sunny kind of guy—confident, controlled, casual but elegant—and Darcy had to agree. Even knowing what she knew about him as fact, it was difficult to reconcile the ruthless killer he was with the man walking across the restaurant.

He was familiar with the S.A.S.S. Would he recognize her?

Go! Go! Go!

She dropped a bill on the table, walked to the closest door and went outside. Twisting her purse clasp, she snagged her phone, palmed it and pulled it free. The spots in her eyes blinded her. *Damn it, damn it.* She dialed the phone by feel, and slid into her Jeep.

Maggie answered, and Darcy gushed out the news. "He's here—in the restaurant at Traveler's Inn. Right now."

"Who, he, Darcy?" Maggie sounded worried. She'd definitely picked up on Darcy's anxiety.

This time, the worry and anxiety were more than justified. "Kunz."

Someone tapped on her window. Startled, Darcy's muscles locked down. She couldn't move.

"Darcy?" A man moved around her, into her line of vision. A spot-speckled Mick. "Hey, what's wrong?" He shifted a paper bag from his left arm to his right. "You look scared to death."

Her heart still banging against her ribs, she didn't trust herself to speak and not spout gibberish, so she pulled her lips back from her teeth in what she hoped would pass as a smile, rolled down her window and gave him a negative nod.

"Here for breakfast?"

She nodded that she was, pointedly looked at her watch then grimaced, waved and cranked her engine.

Mick walked inside, and she launched into the relaxation techniques Dr. Vargus had taught her, then ran through the tests to make sure her senses, mind and speech were all functioning on the same speed. When they were, and the spots hampering her vision had subsided, she phoned Ben.

"Hello." He sounded fuzzy.

"You're still sleeping?" She thumbed the blinker, stroked the steering wheel.

"We were up late, Darcy," he reminded her. "You okay?"

"Not exactly."

"What's wrong?" Fully alert now, he went on. "Where are you?"

"Traveler's Inn." So far, so good. She swallowed hard. "Ben, can you get over here now?"

"Sure. I just need to call Bobby Meyers and see if he can come in a little early at work. What's up?"

"Thomas Kunz is here. He's meeting now with the two guys Santana was with last night. The FBI agents are here, too, but I can't listen in—Kunz could recognize me."

"Is it really Kunz, or is it one of his body doubles?"

"Good question." Unfortunately, it was also one she couldn't answer. "But it doesn't matter. They do his dirty work. I need for you to be my ears."

"On my way." He grunted, obviously rolling out of bed. "Did he see you?"

"No. He was too focused on Santana's men. If he's pegged the FBI agents, he could scrap the mission."

"If he seems suspicious, replace them. That's all you can do."

"As soon as I'm off the phone with you, I'll call and get their take. If they've been outted, they know it."

"No, use the cell Wexler gave you. I want you to stay on the line with me until I get there. General Shaw briefed me on Kunz. He's beyond dangerous."

He was. At the present time, he was hands-down the United States' most dangerous adversary. "I've worked dangerous missions most of my career."

"Not up close and personal. Not since the fire." He sighed. "I know you're tired of hearing that, and I mean no offense, but things are different now and backup is a good idea."

He was right. Being asked constantly if she was all right and being reminded of the fire irritated the spit out of her—worse, it undermined her confidence—but he was totally right to ask. His neck was on the line, too.

"For the record, you amaze me, Darcy. Not just your memory, but the scope of your skills. You're better now than before the fire. Then, you were doing what came easy to you. Now, you have to do those things in spite of your mind and body putting on the brakes every time you turn around. It's tougher work. But you do it anyway." He talked in spurts, obviously brushing his teeth. "Hold on a sec." Spitting noises, then gurgling followed.

The normalcy in his actions calmed her, and what he said made her feel great about herself—something she'd not felt, she realized, in a long time. Since the fire, she'd become a shadow of her former self—at least in her own eyes—and not a force for doing what she did despite the hardships. Why hadn't she given herself credit? Why hadn't she even seen what she'd been doing? Instead of looking at what she could no longer do, she needed to look at all she was doing *anyway*.

Once again, Ben brought things into perspective. He calmed her, helped her focus. He intrigued and excited and attracted her. Damn it, she just might be falling in love.

"You did sweep the phone Wexler gave you, right?"

"I'm not a rookie, Ben." She'd discovered the bug before leaving the parking lot, but left it intact so Wexler wouldn't know she was aware of it.

"I know. But it doesn't pay to consider him a lightweight. Not when he's keeping such heavyweight company."

Static filtered through the line. "What's that noise?" She tilted her purse and pulled out Wexler's phone.

"Power lines. I'm on my way over. They always screw up the phones and radios through here. It's a shortcut that shaves off half the time. I'll be there in about two minutes."

She snapped off the back of the phone. It was bugged. "Ben, are you talking on a Wexler-issue phone right now?"

"No."

Relief washed through her. "Don't."

"Gotcha." He paused, then added, "Wanna know what I was thinking when the phone woke me up?"

The shift in his tone from professional to personal was blatant. "Maybe." She was teetering on the brink of love. If it was bad, she didn't want to hear it. "Am I going to like it?"

"Good question," he tossed her words back at her. "It was damn pleasant from where I sat. Want to risk it?"

If he found it pleasant, it couldn't be awful, could it? "Why not?"

"I was thinking I liked falling asleep on the sofa last night with you in my arms." He dropped his voice, deep and rich and tinged with a hint of uncertainty. "I was thinking I'd like to do that again."

Her heart felt full, expanded, and she smiled at the dashboard. "Me, too, Ben." Them, together, felt so right.

"Ah, good." He let out a sigh that crackled in her ear. "That's good."

"I need to ask you something personal," she asked.

"Okay."

"I know you had a god-awful experience with Diane—"

"Yes, I did."

"So since then, has there been anyone else—seriously, I mean?"

"No."

Now what? Did she push? Right or wrong she was going to; this was her heart, and she needed to know whether to try to protect it or open it to him. "So you've turned against love."

"Yes," he said quickly. "Well, no." Frustrated, he cursed. "The truth is, I had, but I'm not anymore." Exasperated, he sighed. "It's personal."

"What's personal?" She'd need a map to track his thoughts this morning. "Your feelings about love?"

"You and me, Darcy. This…thing…between us. It's personal."

He loved her. Or he thought he did. Or he did and didn't want to love her. Something.

Movement beside her had her darting her gaze through the car window.

Ben pulled into the parking slot beside her, cut the engine and looked over. "It's very personal."

Even through the glass, the look in his eyes warmed her. Defining very personal could wait. For now, that look said more than enough. "We need to switch phones." Hers transmitted to Home Base and had been equipped with a more powerful microphone.

He got out of his Jeep and came around to her car window.

She opened it. He reached through, grabbed her and kissed her hard. Darcy let him, then returned his kiss, replacing commands with tenderness, raw emotion with compassion, matching passion with passion.

He pulled back and stared at her, a little speechless and a lot off balance.

She resisted the urge to giggle—of all things. But Ben Kelly off balance, starstruck by her kiss was an empowering feeling, a magnificent feeling. "Sit near them, eat breakfast and just put my phone on the table." She passed him her phone. "I should be able to pick up what I need."

Without a word, he dipped his chin and turned to go inside. At the door, she heard his voice. "You amaze me, Darcy."

Her heart skittered, her breath caught in her throat and she got that unspeakable "he's everything I've ever wanted" feeling that makes women think and act crazy.

Okay, she admitted it. She was a little amazed, too.

Forcing her mind back to work, Darcy filtered out the

background noise and focused on the conversation between Kunz—or his drone—and the two men from Broken Branch.

Quickly, frustration built in her stomach. They were discussing weapon specs, hunting, fishing and the history of the festival, which was a typical celebration of harvesting crops. There wasn't a rhythm or a cadence or any other signal detected that the men were passing coded messages. In her experienced opinion, this was exactly what it sounded like—a normal conversation.

Which meant they'd already done what they needed to do.

The planning was complete.

The players were all in place.

And the shipment would be moving in through Los Casas tonight.

Chapter 7

Within minutes, the FBI had replaced the two male agents with two women and reassigned the men to new locations. A third agent, a lone male who looked more like a nerdy kid than *any* kind of government employee, was tasked with tagging Kunz. He arrived on a skateboard, wearing baggy shorts, a worn-out T-shirt and a black baseball cap. Its brim rested at his nape.

Long after they were all in place, and the FBI agent on Wexler reported that he'd gone to Los Casas, Ben headed to work to help cover him. Technically Wexler wasn't due at work until 10:00 p.m. His showing up at 3:00 p.m. didn't do much to put Darcy's mind at ease.

Since it was her day off, she cruised around Devil's Pass, looking for any other known GRID members. By 5:30 p.m., she'd run into plenty of excitement about the July 4th festival but no other known terrorists. That both heartened and disturbed her.

In the past, GRID members had worked in teams, and so far, she'd only identified Needle. But maybe things were different on this leg of their current mission. They certainly could be. GRID could be just traveling through Los Casas on the way to another destination. Yet all Kunz needed was a safe place to park the firework bombs until time for his minions to set them off. No better place existed than Broken Branch Redemption's compound. Unfortunately, the damn place was perfect.

Her skin crawled. It was remote. It was secure. It functioned under the protection of the "freedom of religion" edict, and all that made her job not only difficult, but nearly impossible. There was no way she or any government authority could legally get in to take a look around, and Colonel Drake would never approve of Darcy making an illegal attempt. Not with these stakes.

Irked at being hamstrung, Darcy left the open-air theater where an opera rehearsal was scheduled for tonight. Dozens of eager people ready to party now took to the streets in a prefestival celebration. Ben had warned her that half the county would start celebrating today and be in the streets until midnight on the Fourth. Darcy couldn't imagine anyone in their right mind intentionally partying for four days and nights straight. But more than a few were already three sheets to the wind and the stench of beer and booze was strong on the street.

She stopped at the grocery store, picked up a few items and then took them back to the cottage.

After storing them, she fixed herself a sandwich and grabbed a soda from the fridge. Too many honchos were in town for a simple pass-through. Santana and Kunz.

And Kunz had broken the cycle. He had not been wearing a red shirt.

Did that mean he was authentic, or a Kunz-clone? Did it mean anything at all?

Feeling her anxiety level spike, she sat down in the middle of the living room floor and meditated. There was nothing left for her to do but wait until dark, then stake out Los Casas and observe the shipment.

At 8:00 p.m. Ben phoned.

"Time must be getting close. Wexler just shut down two lanes going in each direction and gave me the rest of the night off. He said he'd take the incoming."

"Can he conduct your inspections?" Darcy mentally reviewed Wexler's dossier. His expertise was in management, not specific to entomology, like Ben. With the amount of food imported, someone with Ben's expertise as a chief inspector should always be on duty.

"Normally, if he runs into anything suspicious, he just calls me in to come take a look."

It was what he wouldn't call Ben in for that worried Darcy, and judging by his tone, Ben worried about that, too.

"I'm on my way there."

"Better let the colonel know." Ben sighed. "This feels like it and Wexler's got a narrow window. He's only scheduled to work until 11:00."

It did feel significant, but then often when the instincts were on high-alert, an operative got that sensation and it proved false. She'd contact Home Base on the first hard sign. They had already been given a heads-up, and with the FBI being on-site, that's really all she had to give them at the moment. "Why did Wexler really want to work tonight?"

"He said he didn't want to take Elizabeth to the opera. It's true that he hates it, Darcy. He bitches every year."

"But he goes."

"Normally, yeah."

"So why not this year?"

"I don't know."

She couldn't imagine Lucas Wexler liking opera. So without Needle's decoded segment—which Langley had not yet verified as decoded accurately—Wexler's working tonight really didn't prove a thing. To avoid the opera, if they had one, he'd likely volunteer for a stint in the Foreign Legion.

Darcy scanned the Jeep for listening devices or explosives—just in case Kunz had seen and/or recognized her—but found none. She pulled out her hotline-to-Home Base phone and put it on the seat beside her. Her nerves stretched tight, preparing for what could come. She cranked the engine and blew out a long, steadying breath.

Watch it, Darcy. You don't have much wiggle room on the nerves. Keep it cool and calm. Just observe, and if they bring anything across the border, hang back and see where they go with it.

She turned right and pulled onto the dirt trail that led to Los Casas, her tires kicking up a dust devil behind her.

Every instinct in her body warned her the last of the fireworks would come in tonight and that Kunz's GRID goons would take them to Santana at Broken Branch Redemption. It was the logical place for the other two shipments to already be stored. Kunz certainly hadn't been in contact with anyone else around here, and it'd be atypical for him to wait until three days before he intended GRID to use the bombs to position them inside the States. That left just too little time to flex if their plans hit a snag.

Former missions proved Kunz liked lots of flexibility and always had at least two backup plans.

About a third of the way to Los Casas, Darcy heard her phone ring and answered.

"You almost here?" Ben asked. "Wexler is acting really edgy. I'd say they're due to arrive."

"I'm on my way. Watch him closely. Whatever is done, he'll be in the middle of it." She swept a wind-blown lock of hair back from her eyes. "Who else is working tonight?"

"Mick. Bobby Meyers is on the schedule now and coming in later."

Bobby Meyers had been at Los Casas for about five years. His dossier was clean. "Did you say Mick? The Oasis's Mick?"

"Yeah. He fills in when someone's out sick. James Grady was on the schedule until nine, but he's down with the flu. Frankly, I think he wanted an excuse to miss the opera rehearsal, too."

What was wrong with these men that they just couldn't say no? "Is Mick qualified to be there?"

"He's been filling in since long before I got here, Darcy. No clue what his qualifications are, but when I've worked with him, he's always been on the ball."

Something didn't feel right. Something just didn't feel right. Ben was saying something but he was breaking up. She was hitting a dead zone. Probably trouble on his end. She was on satellite—good almost anywhere. "You're breaking up, Ben. We'll talk when I get there."

"No, Darcy! Land…"

"What? I didn't get that."

"Land…"

The line went dead.

What had he been trying to tell her? She hit a rut that jarred her teeth and dialed him back. Her phone was dead.

Landline. Ben had been talking on a *landline.* It was her phone that was out—and now it was dead.

She checked the phone. It appeared to be fully operational. So why was it dead?

Her chest went tight and blood pounded through her temples. She hit the ledge of a deep rut—

And the rear right tire went flat.

You're going to miss the shipment, Darcy. You're going to fail. Colonel Drake blew it, trusting you with this. Thousands are going to die…just like Merry.

She fought the voice inside her head, fought the bitter memories but they wouldn't go away. Darcy with Merry in their dorm room at college. Darcy standing as maid of honor at Merry's wedding. Merry showing up unexpectedly at Darcy's house right after Darcy had been pulled by emergency extraction from a mission that had gone south. Two FBI agents had died and Darcy had gone home to mourn. In her mind, she saw it. Merry's silhouette shining through the windows, leading the terrorists to believe she was Darcy. The bomb crashing through the window, shattering the glass, landing at Merry's feet. The explosion that killed her instantly. Darcy, running into the thick smoke and fire to try to save her, only to realize that she was already dead. The huge wooden beam falling, hitting Darcy in the head, knocking her out.

The darkness.

The fury.

The guilt.

Tears flowed down her face. "I can't fail again. I can't...fail again." She fumbled for Wexler's phone, tried Ben, but couldn't get through. Her phone was still dead. This phone of Wexler's was dead. Dead like Merry. Like all the people who would be killed with GRID's bombs.

"I can't fail!" she screamed.

You can do this, Darcy.

Ben's voice. Ben's calm, quiet, gentle voice.

You amaze me. Then, you were doing what came easy to you. Now, you have to do those things in spite of your mind and body putting on the brakes every time you turn around. You can do this....

"I *can* do this." Darcy gritted her teeth, willed her heart rate to slow down. She wasn't the woman she had been then. She was wiser, stronger, more disciplined. She'd learned to compromise, to improvise, to do what she had to do to make it through tough situations. She'd learned to struggle and persist and, God knew, she'd learned to endure.

"I *will* do this." She reached for the car door, half climbed, half fell out of the Jeep. "I *will* change the tire. I *will* get to Los Casas before Santana and GRID take off. I *will* succeed in this mission."

Steadier now, she walked to the back tire and took a serious look, blinking hard until the spots obscuring her vision left her eyes. The tire seemed to be intact. She checked the valve. "Damn it." The stem had been tampered with so the air would leak out.

First the phone from work was bugged, then dead; clearly service had been cut to it. Now her tire was flat. Someone wanted to make damn sure she didn't make it to Los Casas.

Had to be Wexler. He'd given her the phone. He had the book. He took down the coded messages and relayed them to others. Had to be Wexler.

Or Thomas Kunz.

Chapter 8

Officially off-duty, Ben lingered outside the cinder block building at Los Casas and watched Wexler work the incoming traffic. He'd taken over the stall about thirty minutes ago to give Mick a break. Mick had gone inside to grab a cola from the fridge.

Something niggled at Ben. Something he couldn't yet grasp but which just didn't feel right—in addition to his worrying about Darcy. He again checked his watch. *9:00 p.m.* She should have been here ten minutes ago—and her damn phone was out. That could be incidental; there had been static on the line, and she'd been fine when it had gone out.

Likely, anticipation and dread just had him edgy. He wasn't confident she'd hold up when things started coming down, and not holding up when confronting GRID could get her killed.

Mick walked back outside, a thermos in his hand. "Coffee," he said. "Figured I needed a healthy jolt of caffeine. Lucas and his buddies kept me up too damn late at the bar last night for me to be doubling back here tonight, pulling a graveyard shift. It's going to be a long night."

It would be for all of them. "Bobby Meyers will be

in shortly to relieve you," Ben assured him, then leaned back against the building, propped his foot against the blocks and watched a Lincoln Navigator pull in, turn around and back into the slot at the far end of the parking lot.

No one backed in around here except cops.

"I ran into Darcy outside the hotel this morning. She looked...upset."

"Tired, I expect." Two guys got out of the Lincoln. Santana's cohorts from Broken Branch. Ben looked back down the road but saw no lights. So where were the FBI agents supposedly tagging these two jerks? Adrenaline shot through Ben's veins, and his worry deepened. They'd somehow ditched the agents. *This had to be it.*

Santana's cohorts stood near their vehicle. Mick glanced their way, clearly noticing them, but didn't comment on their presence. "I expect she was tired. Heard her car was acting up and you two were out late last night."

"Yep, pretty late." They were watching Wexler's stall.

"So are you two—"

"Yeah, we are." Ben swung his gaze to Mick's. "Definitely."

He smiled, wrinkling the skin under his eyes. The lines alongside his mouth became grooves. "Glad to hear it. You had me worried there for a while. It ain't normal for a man your age to go without a woman for years at a stretch."

"Waiting for the right woman. That's all." After Diane, he'd needed a break. She'd dragged him through hell and the last thing he'd wanted was to risk it again.

"What about you? You've been on your own a hell of a lot longer than I have."

Mick hiked his eyebrows. "Who says I ever been without a woman?"

Ben frowned at him. Mick had been in love with Wexler's wife, Elizabeth, his whole life. He'd never even been seen with another woman. The truth slammed Ben between the eyes. "You're still with Elizabeth?"

"You know, Ben," Mick said softly. "When a man's got her at home, he ought not be stepping out." Mick shrugged. "If he does, someone who appreciates her is sure to step in."

So while Lucas was out playing around on Elizabeth, she'd renewed her relationship with Mick. Surprised, Ben grunted and looked back to the stall, wondering which had come first: Lucas's extramarital ventures or Elizabeth's. Either way, Ben had to give it to Elizabeth and Mick. They'd been discreet. He'd bet money that no one in Devil's Pass suspected a thing about them, while everyone knew in intimate detail all about every one of Lucas's affairs.

"Why are you hanging around here?"

Ben looked at Mick, who was taking a sip of steaming coffee and squinting at him over the rim of his cup. "What else am I going to do tonight? You're here—the Oasis is closed."

"What about Darcy?"

"After last night, she's wiped out." True, if not the truth.

Mick snickered. "Ride 'em hard and often, I say. They'll always come back for more."

An eighteen-wheeler pulled into Wexler's stall, pulling a trailer with no markings on it. Was this it? Ben stole a glance at the two men, who'd perked up, paying attention. This was definitely the GRID shipment carrying fireworks laced with radioactive waste. *Dirty bomb-loving bastards.* "Excuse me."

Ben walked back inside and tried again to phone Darcy.

Still no answer.

What was he supposed to do now? Wexler was giving the paperwork a cursory glance. In minutes, he'd put the truck through. *Damn it.* Ben had to follow them.

"I'm not feeling good, Mick," he said on rejoining Mick outside. "Guess I picked up James Grady's bug. It hit me like a ton of bricks—all of a sudden."

"Did you drink water out of the cooler?" Mick frowned.

"Yeah," Ben lied. "A little while ago."

"Damn it, I told Wexler to change out that bottle. I think it's contaminated and that's making everyone sick."

"Tell him again. It's got me."

"Sorry to hear it." Mick looked him over, genuinely concerned. "Go ahead home, buddy. I'll take care of this until Bobby Meyers gets his ass in here to relieve Wexler—and I'll let him know you're down."

"Thanks. I think I'd better do that." Ben headed toward his Jeep, stopped and turned back. "Mick, get rid of that damn water, will you?"

"You got it."

By the time Ben cranked the engine, Wexler had backed off and the truck pulled through. Raw terror struck Ben in the stomach. Terror and fury—and fear that GRID would succeed with its plans and successfully attack White House spectators at the fireworks celebration.

Determined that it wouldn't happen, Ben tried yet again to call Darcy, but still got no answer.

Santana's cohorts pulled out in the Lincoln and followed the truck. Ben pulled in behind them, and someone fell into line behind him. Who, he didn't know, and their lights blinded him. He couldn't even make out the type of car. Fortunately, they were all heading toward Devil's Pass, and fortunately there were no other roads leading to it. No one should be suspicious about being followed.

Though, if all General Shaw had told him about Thomas Kunz and GRID proved true, Ben would never be so lucky.

Kunz and GRID suspected *every*thing.

Where the hell were those FBI agents?

Darcy whipped into Los Casas's parking lot. Wexler's truck was gone. Ben's Jeep wasn't in sight, either. He'd followed them!

Her blood chilled. He wasn't equipped to deal with Kunz or his GRID thugs. At least, so far as she knew. And if he wasn't, he was going to get himself killed.

She drove up alongside the concrete barrier at the open stall. Mick stood outside, under the overhang. "Hey, Mick," she shouted out. "Where's Ben?"

"He left about fifteen minutes ago," he said, not seeming to be surprised to see her. "He wasn't feeling well."

He *was* in pursuit. *Damn it!* She stuck out her hand and bent her fingers. "I need your cell phone. Mine's broken."

Mick frowned. "What's wrong, girl?"

"Oh, I left the damn iron on and I'm scared to death

I'm going to burn down Ben's cottage. He'll never forgive me."

"Long as you keep coming back, he'll forgive you just about anything." Laughing, he passed her the phone. "Get you one of them irons that shut off automatically."

"Next paycheck. Thanks, Mick." Hitting the gas with a little more force than she intended, she left Mick standing in a cloud of dust.

She hadn't passed them on the road to Devil's Pass, which meant they'd cut cross-country to Broken Branch. There was nowhere else for them to go out there. The odds were slim to none, but she tried calling Ben at home on the off-chance he really had gone home sick.

No answer.

She tried again—this time, his cell.

Listening, she didn't hear it ring, but there was activity—noise, actually. She focused hard, bumping across the barren terrain. Faint voices sounded in the background. Shouting. Cursing. Scuffling. More cursing. The voices grew louder, then louder.

"It's happening!" Ben shouted. "It's happening!"

A huge thud crackled in Darcy's ear. Someone hitting Ben? *Oh God!* Someone throwing his phone? *No! No!*

Grunting. Smacking. Something even more distant, more muffled caught her attention. Horns. Party horns and…music.

Darcy didn't believe her ears. Was she really hearing what she thought she was hearing, or had her senses and her ability to process sensory input accurately parted ways?

There were no party horns at Broken Branch. She'd learned enough about their strict disciplinary ways to know better than that. Yet she hadn't seen or heard anything that precluded them from music. Was Ben there, or somewhere else? If somewhere else, then where?

Think, Darcy. Think. You can't fail again. You lost Merry. You can't lose Ben, too!

Another man's shout came through the phone. "No, don't shoot him!"

Thomas Kunz's voice. She was certain of it.

Certain? How can you be certain of anything?

Damn it, it was him. She recognized it from the Intel interceptions. Every known torture he'd ever committed ran through her mind, and terror, stark and cold and unrelenting, seized Darcy.

The bastards had Ben.

Chapter 9

Darcy hit the brakes hard, swerved to a stop, grabbed her satellite phone from the seat beside her, and ripped into it. She'd repaired it before and, by God, she would again.

She pulled the schematic from memory, compared it to what she was looking at on the phone, and spotted a loose connection. She fumbled with her purse, snagged a penny, and used it to tighten the loose connection, then snapped the casing back into place.

She got a tone.

Grateful, she dialed Home Base, and when Maggie answered, her words came out in a rush. "They've got Ben. I need a locator put on his phone." She reeled off the number. "And I need it now. Kunz has him. GRID, Santana and Kunz—they're all together and they have Ben."

"Okay, Darcy, we're on it. Give me a minute. It's seeking," Maggie said. "How did GRID get Ben?"

"I don't know. Wexler—someone—tampered with the stem valve on my tire. I got a flat out in the damn middle of nowhere. The shipment had gone through by the time I got to Los Casas."

"How do you know that?"

"Wexler had already left. One of the other guys, Mick, said Ben went home sick. I figure he followed the shipment and they snagged him."

For fear of taking off in the wrong direction and putting more distance between her and Ben, Darcy stayed put, waiting for the locator to work its magic and tell her where to find him. "His phone is active," she said, more to reassure herself than Maggie. "There was fighting and party horns in the distance, and music."

"Sounds like a party."

Darcy gasped. "Not a party, a festival. He's in town, Maggie. They didn't take the fireworks to Broken Branch. They took them somewhere in Devil's Pass. I heard music. There's an opera rehearsal at the open-air theater tonight. He has to be somewhere around there." She hit the gas, made a sharp turn for town, and then stomped the accelerator.

"Definitely in Devil's Pass, Darcy." Maggie confirmed it. "Downtown, but off Main Street. We're getting a specific address on it now."

"I know Colonel Drake wanted to wait and monitor all three shipments, but I've been working on the code and I think at least one is already here."

"Intel confirmed that about ten minutes ago."

"We can't wait, Maggie. They could already have the third, or go without it. We need immediate FBI intervention or we risk losing Thomas Kunz again." They'd lost him before, thought they'd killed him twice and put him in Leavenworth once only to discover they'd never had him, only his body doubles.

"Colonel's briefing General Shaw and Secretary Reynolds now."

Darcy came to the edge of town. People stood crowded in the streets, dancing, laughing, drinking. It was a huge block party—only it went on forever. Frustration and fear stacked and spread in Darcy. She'd never find him.

"Warehouse, Darcy. Third and Main."

"I know it." She steered around a group of teens, sitting in the street, their heavy metal screeching, setting Darcy's teeth on edge and fraying what was left of her nerves. And then she felt the snap. The tight chest, the scattered thoughts she couldn't seem to grasp, and those telltale spots that blurred her eyes. Having no choice, she whipped into a parking place and slammed on the brakes.

Not now. She bent forward, leaned her head against the steering wheel. *Not now, please. Please, not now.*

Her thoughts ignored her, sped ahead to what could be happening to Ben. The rest of her tried to keep up but she just couldn't do it. She was functioning a few beats behind, and clammy with sweat.

You can do this, Darcy. For five years, you've done damn near everything a few beats behind. You can do this that way, too. You have experience at it, lots and lots of experience at it. Just do what you have to do, Darcy. Just do it!

She snapped her phone to her black slacks, concentrated hard and checked her weapon—ready to fire—then got out of the car. *Okay. Okay, where are you?*

Slowly, she turned around and spotted the flag and wide stone steps. *The courthouse. You're at the courthouse. Three blocks to the warehouse.*

She started out on foot, winding between the throngs of people, humming to minimize their input into her senses. She held her nose to block out smell, kept humming and moved quickly—too quickly to grasp impressions. Ah, move quickly!

Run, Darcy. Run!

She focused hard to get her feet to work in rhythm with her brain, sideswiped people and just kept running, shouting, "Sorry. So sorry. Sorry." She ran two blocks—and took in nearly nothing on impressions. Then she ran headlong into Mick and a petite brunette, dancing in the grass above the sidewalk. "Sor— Mick?" She'd left him at Los Casas, working. How had he gotten here so quickly?

"James Grady came in to help out Bobby Meyers."

Odd. Ben had said James had the flu.

"I'm keeping Elizabeth company. Elizabeth Wexler, meet Darcy Clark."

Lucas's wife. A pretty brunette with doe eyes and full lips. Darcy nodded. "Have fun," she said, because it was easier than explaining anything, then she rushed on.

The crowd thickened. The tightness in Darcy's chest felt like a vise, and someone wrenched it a half hitch. The crush of people squeezed and her feet lifted off the ground. Her back and neck muscles twitched, locked for seconds in little spasms, warning of bigger ones to come. She could barely breathe. The hyperstimulation was strengthening….

You can't fail. Not again. Not Merry and Ben. You can't do it, Darcy. Die if you have to, but don't fail.

"Ben, please be alive," she muttered to herself. "Please be near your phone. I need you!" She snaked toward the building, pushing and shoving, bit by bit making her way out of the crush. A man grabbed her shoulder, spun her around and kissed her. She pushed away, looked him in the face. He was drunk. Harmless and drunk.

"Come on, hon. Let's go party. I'll bet you're one hot mama under those tight pants."

Darcy didn't have time for this, and she damn sure didn't have the patience for it. When he grabbed for her again, she popped him with a right cross that knocked him back off his staggering feet. To the laughter of the men, and gasps and cheers from the women right around them, Darcy took an exaggerated bow and then walked on.

She didn't have time for this, but the last thing she could afford while others watched her was to appear panicked. She looked back and saw Mick looking her way. He shot her a big grin and a thumbs-up.

Why was he watching her? Why was he with Elizabeth Wexler?

Regardless, it was time for Darcy to disappear. She wound through the crowd and around the back of the warehouse. Finally, she touched the building's cool metal. Its windows were dusty, the door padlocked. For all intents and purposes, it appeared empty.

She double-checked with Maggie on the phone. "Are you getting the same location on my phone as Ben's?"

"You're right on top of each other."

"Get me some help, Maggie. Now."

"On the way. It'll be a few minutes. They were staked out at Broken Branch."

"That'll be ten minutes, at least." Ben could be dead in ten minutes. So could she.

"At least."

It was too little, too late.

Handle it.

He was here. No. No, his phone was here.

Darcy lifted her leg and pain shot through her spine up to her nape. Her knees collapsed and she crumpled to the ground.

Her muscles were in lockdown.

You can do this, Darcy.

I can't move! I can't defend myself, much less fight to defend Ben. How can I do this? I can't freaking move!

You can. You can, Darcy. Breathe deeply. Relax. You can do this. I swear, you can.

She heard Ben's voice, heard Dr. Vargus, Colonel Drake. They all believed in her.

Merry. You can't fail again like with Merry. Get on your damn feet!

Drenched in cold sweat, Darcy slid up the building to her feet. She took her gun from her purse, folded her fingers around the grip. She wasn't steady. Hell, she wasn't even sure she could aim much less shoot. She stumbled along the perimeter of the building to the side door. It wasn't padlocked. Did she dare to just walk in?

Ten minutes. Did she have a choice?

She slid inside, into a darkened doorway. She heard muffled noises from across the warehouse. In her vicinity, nothing stirred. Deliberately, she brought Ben's voice to mind, focused on his soothing tranquility, his gentleness, his tenderness.

With a shake and a giant shudder, she regained some of her control. Swiping her slacks at her thighs, she dried her soaked palms, gripped her gun tightly and then stalked the warehouse, looking for Ben.

Darcy moved with stealth through the dark warehouse toward the bald yellow light shining in its center. Wooden crates stacked ten or more feet high formed barricades. They were marked as canned goods, but her heightened senses disagreed. Darcy sniffed a crate and smelled a trace of gunpowder.

The bombs? Probably, but they should smell stronger. Maybe her senses weren't as attuned as usual because her focus was slivered. *Something* was off.

She scraped her back against the rough wood, checked for signals that she'd been spotted, but she perceived none. Silently, she peeked around the corner of the crates—and saw Ben in the center of a circle of wooden boxes stacked far above his head so that no one outside could see what was going on inside the building.

He hung suspended from metal rods, tied a foot off the floor with heavy ropes, his arms stretched wide, his legs pulled apart. Sweat-soaked, pain had his face haggard, and his head lolled forward, chin to his chest.

Her heart nearly ruptured. *Don't do it, Darcy. Not now. You can handle this.*

"Why were you following us, Ben? Who told you to follow us?"

Needle. Darcy recognized his voice before he turned and she saw his face. He picked up a syringe. He'd drugged Amanda. She'd lost three months of her life! Darcy's stomach twisted and churned.

No answer. Ben didn't so much as grunt.

"We have the means to make you tell us everything," Needle warned him.

They did. Oh, God, but they did.

"Spare yourself the pain and just tell us, Ben."

Darcy swallowed hard, looked around. Needle couldn't be here alone, yet she saw—

Thomas Kunz walked into the light, paced a short

path before Ben, looking up at him. But when he spoke, it was to Needle. "Anything?"

"Not yet."

Kunz turned his attention to Ben. "Agent Kelly, I admire your loyalty, but it's severely misplaced. You will tell me what I want to know. The only question is how much pain you'll endure between now and then, and that is totally up to you."

"Go to hell, you sadistic son of a bitch." Ben spit at Kunz. The strain on the ropes had his wrists bleeding.

"Soon enough." Kunz stepped back. "You'll of course join me there." He turned back to Needle. "The authorities are too late to affect the mission. The S.A.S.S. blew this one. Unfortunately, pressing matters call and I don't have time to play with our friend, Agent Kelly," Kunz said. "Kill him."

Shaking, her muscles spastic, Darcy gritted her teeth. She couldn't follow orders and watch Ben suffer. She wouldn't watch him die. *Not him, too!* She lifted the gun, struggled to hold it up and aim at Thomas Kunz's broad back. He was the most valuable target in GRID. Without him, the terrorist network wouldn't collapse, but it would be disorganized and give the S.A.S.S. time to run down its components. Her grip slipped.

She caught the gun in midair, now shaking like a leaf. *You can do this, Darcy. Damn it, you will do it—now!*

The barrel of the gun lifted. She took aim and fired, dropped and rolled to the next line of crates.

Grabbing his shoulder, Kunz dove into the darkness. Santana, whom she'd not seen, stepped out and aimed at the crates where she'd been standing. "Come out. We've got you."

The hell they did. He wasn't shooting. He *knew* what

was in this warehouse and he wasn't going to blow himself up. But she couldn't get a clean shot at him.

Needle cut Ben down.

Santana snatched Ben from Needle and disappeared into a hallway near two rows of low-ceilinged offices. She had a clear shot at Needle and took it.

He dropped to the floor.

Certain Kunz had departed—he never hung around for the fight—she started toward the offices, to where Santana had disappeared with Ben. Her legs didn't want to work. Her mind was already there. *Damn it! Can't I get just one break here? Just one?*

Her left arm went numb.

She couldn't move it.

Acknowledge and accept the pain, Darcy. Dr. Vargus's voice. *I promise you, if you acknowledge the pain, you can overcome it.*

You'd damn well better be right, Doc. She gripped the gun in her right hand tighter, entered the narrow hallway, knowing she'd be wiser to avoid it. Odds were high Santana would ambush her here, and she had no cover. But blood smeared on the wall insisted she go on. Ben's blood.

He was brushing the walls deliberately, leaving her a trail.

Behind her, something crackled. Seconds later, she smelled sulfur then heard the hiss of fire.

Fire.

She turned and saw the flames sweeping across the warehouse. Kunz, the bastard, had set a charge to burn it before running out—and Needle no longer lay on the floor. He'd been winged, not mortally wounded.

It's just like Merry. It's your fault Ben's here. Your fault he's going to die. Darcy, it's all your fault.

Her entire body in full revolt, Darcy fought hard. Fought the guilt, the fury, the fire she most feared. None of Dr. Vargus's techniques worked. None of her own techniques worked. *Her damn feet wouldn't move.*

Ben. I'm sorry. Tears stung her eyes, fell down her face. *I'm sorry…*

"Darcy!" Ben's shout. "Darcy!"

Too late. He's going to die, just like Merry. You failed, Darcy.

Rage swelled in her and erupted into the thick smoke. "Shut up!" She screamed at the voices in her head, lifted her left leg and then the right one. "You *will* work. You *will move!*" She lifted them, alternating left to right again and again, and then her right leg lifted on its own. She moved. *She moved!*

The building burned in earnest. The smell of charring wood, the hiss and crackle all proved it. And Darcy knew one thing as fact—there were no fireworks in those crates or by now they would have exploded. She wound through the hall, through the maze of stacked crates on the other side, looking for spots where fiery debris wasn't crashing to the concrete floor and flames weren't flaring floor to ceiling. "Ben! Ben!" she called out, blindly seeking him in the thick smoke.

"Darcy!"

His voice rang out above the roar of the blistering fire. Dropping to a crouch, she yelled back. "Keep talking, Ben. I can't see."

He heard her, and responded, calling her name over and again. Eyes and lungs burning, tears streaming, knees cracking, fire and flames and intense heat encompassing her, she moved methodically, fearful he'd be a mere foot away and she'd never know if she just missed him.

Something snagged her ankle. She turned. "Ben!"

"I'm cuffed." He lifted his arm and the chain clinked against the metal beam. "My leg's messed up, too."

"Broken?"

"I don't think so. But it's pretty useless."

Darcy looked up. A huge beam above Ben was about to fall. Nightmares, flashes of the fire danced before her eyes, threatened to again paralyze her. *Not this time. Not again.*

She forced herself to look away. Spotting a fire axe on the wall, she grabbed it, swung and chopped the chain binding Ben to the metal beam. He pulled himself upright. "Let's go, let's go!"

Her arm around his waist, she helped him hobble out of immediate danger.

Behind them, the beam crashed to the floor, spewing sparks and fiery embers that now fell harmless. "Where's the door?" She couldn't see six inches beyond her nose and was totally disoriented.

"I don't know." Ben grimaced and shifted his weight, leaning heavily on her. "Santana went this way."

They moved straight ahead and Darcy brushed against a burning crate. Her slacks caught fire. She let go of Ben, stopped, dropped and rolled, jerking out of her slacks—and the crushing memories of the first fire, the one that stole Merry's life *and* Darcy's, bore down on her with brutal force. A full-blown attack seized her. She couldn't move. Helpless and hopeless, Darcy screamed.

Ben clasped her face in his hands, stared into her eyes. "Darcy. Darcy look at me."

Gasping, her chest heaving, her eyes watering from the smoke and heat from the fire singeing her skin, she fought for control to focus.

"Darcy, look at me. Only me," Ben insisted, calm amid the turmoil, gentle in the chaos.

She caught the thought, held it, breathed deeply and finally met his gaze.

"You can do this, Darcy. Get me out of here."

She wanted to—oh, how she wanted to, but she couldn't do it. "Ben, I can't—"

"You can." He shook her. "You can, Darcy. I'm crazy about you. I don't want to die in this inferno. I want to live and even try again to love. I want to be with you and see what happens for us, Darcy. You can do this. You can give us that chance."

In his eyes, she saw certainty and faith. He believed it—every word he was saying. He believed in her.

The fire crackled and hissed, rebelling against her growing strength, asserting its power over her. It was stronger, meaner; she couldn't win against it.

All Ben had said to her—she wanted those things, too. And she wanted them more than she feared the fire. She wanted to put the devastation of the past—her fears and regrets and guilt—to rest. She wanted a life, with all the good and bad and ups and downs and love. Oh, how she wanted love. She wanted Ben.

Her lungs felt scorched; her throat, raw. She darted her gaze left and then panned right. *A window!* Blackened with soot and hard to see through the billowing smoke, but it was there. She scanned the area between them and it. No flames. Smoldering embers, but no flames. She grabbed the axe and held on to Ben. "This way."

She led him to the window, then let go of him. "Stand back." She lifted the axe and swung hard.

The glass shattered.

Darcy stepped forward, felt the blast of fresh air and used the blade to knock out the sharp shards of glass. "Come on, Ben." She looked behind him, saw the creeping flames, the fury of the fire eating through a major support beam overhead. "Hurry."

He hobbled over, and she made a lift with her hands, then shoved him through the window. She couldn't make it without a boost—she spied a small crate against a wall not yet in flames. She shoved it over but the chains keeping it on its wooden pallet were too short. The crate wouldn't reach the window. "Damn it."

"Darcy?" Ben shouted from outside, his voice a shade shy of panic. "Darcy?"

She judged the distance between the crate and window. She could make it. "Move away, Ben," she shouted, backing up as far as she dared. She heard a loud pop—a sizzle—and knew the beam was going to come down. She ran full out, vaulted over the crate and dove through the window.

Her shoulder hit the ground first, stinging, and she tucked and rolled on the grass, then up onto her feet, winded and feeling the jolt of the landing, but no worse for the wear. "Ben?"

He limped toward her, opened his arms.

She walked into them, felt him close around her, and buried her face at his neck. "I did it, Ben." Her voice cracked and five years of tears and guilt and regret found vent. "I faced the fire."

He pressed his lips to her temple. "Yeah, baby, you did." Ben splayed his broad hands across her back and squeezed her to him. "Damn right, you did."

Chapter 10

Darcy and Ben kissed, and kissed again.

"Darcy?" The lone FBI agent walked up to them, pushing frameless glasses up on his nose.

She pulled back, saw he was wearing a suit, and hardly recognized him. The skateboard and ball cap was a better fit. "Baxter, right?"

"Yes, ma'am." He frowned. "We picked up two men coming out of the warehouse." He slanted a nod to the curb where two female agents cuffed the men.

"Santana's buddies," Ben said.

She nodded. "Where's Kunz? Santana?"

"No sightings on Kunz or Santana," Baxter said. "I take it the shipment was brought here."

"Yes," Ben said. "But it wasn't fireworks."

"Figured. No explosion." Baxter shifted his weight on his feet. "We've checked and we're not picking up radioactivity, but we're clearing the area, just in case."

Darcy hadn't even thought of radioactivity. She'd been so busy trying to keep a lid on the attacks and so focused on the fire that it hadn't dawned on her.

That was it. Until she got these attacks totally under control, she was done with field work and this was her last active mission as an operative. Colonel Drake would just have to accept it and leave her in her hub at Regret.

"Put an APB out on Thomas Kunz and Paco Santana. They were both in the building," she told the agent. "They can't have gotten far."

"If they've got any sense, they're heading to the border," Ben said, keeping an arm around her shoulder for support.

"You need a doctor?" Baxter asked.

"No. It's not broken." Ben glanced down at his leg.

"I'll brief the locals," Baxter said, then walked away.

Darcy scanned the crowd for Kunz. It'd be just like him to mingle and watch. With his sunny good looks, no one would give him a second thought. But she saw no sign of him.

Disappointed, she turned to look at Ben—and glimpsed Paco Santana walking away, watching her over his shoulder.

Darcy pulled her gun and ran.

Santana took flight, shoving his way through the re-treating crowd. He rounded a corner, knocked down an old man pushing a shopping cart, cut through an alley and disappeared in a cemetery.

Darcy stayed with the chase, weaving and ducking between the tombs. She stopped, her back against a rough cement wall, her chest heaving, trying to pull oxygen from the windless air. He was close. She felt it in her bones. Stilling, she opened her senses, blocked out the hustle and noise of the people on the street. She waited, listened, willing herself to stay calm, to control her fear, to home in on just him.

The past threatened, and she squelched it. She'd faced it fully. It was time to put it to bed. That was then, and this was now. Now, she had suffered and endured and survived.

The fire had changed her life.

But no longer would she permit it to claim her life.

Her fear dissipated to a healthy level and her reclamation took hold. The spasms in her neck and back ceased, and she no longer fought spots, her vision was clear. She ran a quick mental test and passed. Her mind and senses were attuned, working perfectly.

For the first time since the fire, she was in crisis and in full control.

Something crackled—a snapping twig.

Santana.

The urge to move assaulted her, but she rebuffed it, stayed hidden in the shadows between the tombs, gripping her gun, checking her earpiece and sliding her lip mike into place, preparing to aim and fire.

Gravel crunched.

He'd moved again. Quickly, she spun out.

Caught in the moonlight, he dove behind a tomb. But he was too slow. She fired.

He fell, dead before he hit the ground.

"Baxter?" Darcy summoned him via her lip mike.

"Yeah?"

"I've just killed Paco Santana. I need a retrieval," she said, then added directions on her location.

"Darcy?"

Hearing Ben, she turned and saw him coming toward her, putting some weight on his injured leg. It definitely wasn't broken. Winded, he looked at Santana, lifeless against someone else's grave. "Are you okay?" he asked.

"I'm fine."

"Thank God." He hugged her to him. "I couldn't get here. I tried, Darcy."

Just as she'd tried with Merry. "Shh, I know, Ben. It's okay. Everything is fine."

Baxter came up on them. Darcy had him in her sights, and when he realized it, he shouted, "Whoa, Clark. It's Baxter."

She let out a sigh of relief. "Santana's over there."

"Any sign of Kunz?" he asked.

"Check the tapes at Los Casas," Ben said. "I'm sure he's hotfooted it to Mexico."

"No doubt." Darcy frowned. "He's very good at leaving others behind to take responsibility for his dirty work."

"Don't worry," Ben told her. "We'll take one battle at a time until we catch him."

"That could take a while," she said. "I'm sure Kunz has at least a dozen body doubles. The S.A.S.S. has already gone up against four."

"Okay, so it'll take a long while," Ben said. "Wars are won one battle at a time, Darcy."

She left Ben with Baxter and Santana, got her Jeep and then retrieved Ben. When he slid onto his seat, she said, "I thought about what you said—about the battles."

"We did win this one, Darcy," Ben insisted, clicking his safety belt into place.

Leaving Baxter with Santana to mop up, Darcy drove away.

"Kunz and Santana won't launch that July 4th attack. The White House will have its fireworks—and they won't be radioactive."

"It can't be this easy, Ben. With Kunz and GRID, it's never this easy. We're missing something. Trust me on this. I've studied this man intensely. It just can't be this easy."

"Okay. So what do we do now?"

"First, we think and get your leg checked out."

"It's not broken."

"Great. Indulge me, then and let the doc take a look." She drove on toward the hospital, wondering why things weren't clicking into place. "Where's Wexler?"

"I phoned Bobby Meyers a while ago. He says Wexler's home in bed with the flu. Apparently, he left a few minutes after I did. Bobby says it hit him hard."

"Bull." She looked over at Ben. "Wexler lied to Bobby. He took in the shipment."

"I don't think so, Darcy. Bobby says he got sick as hell all over the pavement. He has to be really sick. Mick swears the water's contaminated in the cooler. He's putting in a fresh bottle."

Interesting. She filed that tidbit of information. If Wexler was really sick, then maybe he was being gotten out of the way, too. Maybe he wasn't the one accepting the shipment. He couldn't have been—unless GRID was done with him and wanted to wipe out the connection between them by taking Wexler out. Still there had to be someone else involved. But who else—

Mick.

His name came to mind and wouldn't let go. He'd been at the bar when Needle and Santana's cohorts were there. He'd been at Los Casas when the truck had come in. He'd been at Traveler's Inn when she'd spotted Kunz there. And he'd been outside the warehouse with Elizabeth.

He'd been in all the right places to be doing all the wrong things. Question was, had he actually done the wrong things. All the evidence pointed to Wexler.

And what if that was by design?

She asked Ben, "Did you see Mick tonight?"

"Yeah."

"What color was his shirt?"

"Damn, Darcy." Ben grabbed hold of the dash. "Slow down. You're going to kill somebody. My leg won't be any more broken in five minutes."

Darcy ignored the turn for the hospital, took the one for Los Casas and slammed her foot down on the gas. "It might be if you don't answer my question. What color was Mick's shirt?"

In the bar, it had been red. Outside the hotel, red. Tonight, red. "Damn it, Ben. It's not just Wexler. It's Mick, too!"

"No, Darcy. Not Mick." Ben shot her a look that she was way off base. "Wexler's taking the numbers and passing them on. We heard and saw it firsthand."

"Why would he do that?" She asked herself more so than Ben, yet he answered.

"Mick's having an affair with Elizabeth. Lucas meets his women at Mick's. It's a neat little arrangement."

"And Lucas Wexler doesn't want that screwed up. So he takes the numbers for Mick and shoots a little pool. Kunz and Santana think they're dealing with Wexler, only they're not. They're dealing with Mick. It's protection. Mick knows anonymity is all that will keep him alive when GRID is done with him. Wexler hasn't got a clue what he's doing."

Darcy saw more clearly. "Mick gave them something to make them sick—Grady and Wexler," Darcy said. "He wanted them out—away from Los Casas."

"Oh, hell. The first truck was a decoy. He's not yet put through the real shipment." Ben motioned. "Faster, faster."

"Get me the phone. I need to call this in."

Ben scrounged through her purse, pulled it out and passed it to her. Moments later, Maggie was on the line. "Code One, Maggie. Get forces to the border. Mick is working with GRID and Santana and blackmailing Wexler, who probably figures Mick's running numbers or some other type of gambling stint. Santana's dead."

"Are you sure? With GRID, we have a lot of corpses turning up to fight another day."

"I shot and killed him," Darcy said. "He's dead."

"Verified. Hold on." She was gone a second, and then returned. "Colonel Drake and General Shaw are on the line with me, Darcy."

"Darcy?" It was Colonel Drake's voice, and she was severely worried. "Rank it."

The colonel ranked everything on a scale of one to ten. "Ten, ma'am. Quick upshot. The shipment we followed was a decoy. It burned at the warehouse. Not radioactive, not filled with bombs, not even with fireworks. Grain would be my guess. I smelled it when I first entered the warehouse. I got one whiff of gunpowder. I figure it was the charge Kunz later set to facilitate his escape."

"Where's the real shipment?"

Good question. "One moment, ma'am." She told Ben, "Call Los Casas. If Mick is back out there, then the shipment isn't in yet. Who's working graveyard?"

"Bobby Meyers."

Darcy grunted. "I've got ten that says he's gotten the flu and Mick's been called back in to cover for him."

"I won't be taking that bet." Ben dialed the phone. "Los Casas."

"Mick?" Ben grimaced. "Is that you?"

"Yeah, Ben. What's up, buddy?"

"Nothing. Just checking to see if Bobby needed any help tonight. I'm feeling a little better."

"He's sick with the crud, like the rest of them. Called me while I was downtown. Hey, did you hear the warehouse on Main caught fire?"

"No, I didn't know that," Ben lied. "You need help out there?"

"Naw. It's deader than dirt tonight. Ain't a soul crossed in the last hour. Just marking time."

"Okay, then. I'll see you in the morning."

"'Night." Ben disconnected, then looked at Darcy. "You win."

Darcy relayed to Colonel Drake.

"Why is the border open this late?" Colonel Drake asked.

"Commercial interests only. It's so hot here that the loaded trucks overheat during the day. They travel at night for safety reasons—it's strongly recommended for flammables."

"Fireworks are that," the colonel said. "So what's your ETA?"

Darcy checked her watch. One-twenty in the morning. "I estimate a 1:35 a.m. arrival at Los Casas, ma'am."

"The shipment has to be coming across the border at any time," Ben said. "Remember, we're closed from two to three."

Darcy couldn't risk it. "Ma'am, they've got a fifteen-minute window before we arrive. And they've got a twenty-five-minute window after we arrive. Then the station closes for an hour to do a daily security sweep. You'd better get overt forces down there now."

"They're already in position, Darcy." Colonel Drake let out a sigh fraught with relief. "When you called for backup, we included Los Casas in the equation."

"Did Kunz get to Mexico?"

"We're told no."

Darcy didn't believe it. Not for a second. "Is he at Broken Branch Redemption?"

"Definitely not. We've had them under surveillance since you left here."

Where the hell had Kunz gone, then? "Anything else, Colonel?"

She hesitated.

Darcy waited, and then realized what Colonel Drake wanted to know but didn't want to offend Darcy by asking. "I'm fine, ma'am."

"Oh, good." She cleared her throat, but her relief stuck in her voice. "Of course you are, Darcy. Of course."

When they arrived at Los Casas, the FBI had seized control of the border crossing. Mick stood against the cinder block wall, his hands behind him in cuffs. An unmarked eighteen-wheeler pulling two trailers was pulled past the stalls and onto the open dirt road. The two men who had been in it were being loaded into the backseat of an unmarked sedan. Darcy recognized one of the female FBI agents she'd seen at Traveler's Inn.

"Stay in the Jeep, Ben."

"Why?"

"No sense in testing your leg. It's done."

He looked through the window at Mick and sadness filled his eyes. "Mick set it up to look like Wexler had done it all. He wanted to get rid of him to clear the way for Mick and Elizabeth."

"I guess so." Disgusted, Darcy walked over to the agent, identified herself, then went to Mick.

"How did you know?" He didn't bother denying his part in the attack.

"Your red shirt," she answered honestly, though the reasons had been far more in number than she'd disclosed.

The whole truth was that something had warned her. Something so nebulous she couldn't begin to describe or explain it, though she knew exactly when she'd first felt it. It had come to her with the first fire, along with her total recall.

And tonight it had worked to save thousands of lives.

For someone who had so often in the past five years felt cursed, at the moment, she felt decidedly blessed. She glanced over at Ben; saw him watching her through the Jeep's passenger window. Decidedly blessed.

Winning on all fronts would have been fabulous. But in this war on terror, it was unrealistic. Like Amanda, Kate, Maggie and the rest of the S.A.S.S., she'd have to be content to take her successes where she found them— one battle at a time—and to pray for many more victories.

Along the way, she'd be grateful. She had enjoyed some personal gains on this mission, too. She'd faced her guilt, her fear of fire, and reclaimed her life. She'd rediscovered the power of love to overcome even the greatest fear.

Those were pretty significant gains she never again wanted to forget—and since she had perfect recall, she wouldn't.

Smiling to herself about that, she walked back to the Jeep and got in beside Ben. "I guess we'd better see about that leg."

"Only if you're through saving the world."

"I am." She sniffed. "For tonight."

He laughed and rubbed her shoulder. "You amaze me, Darcy Clark."

She tried not to, but she couldn't help herself. She laughed with him. "Tell me that twenty years from now, and I might just believe it."

"You got it." He turned on the radio. "And that, you can commit to memory."

"I will." She already had. Darcy smiled. "Finally, a personal perk in having total recall."

Everything you love about romance...
and more!

Please turn the page for Signature Select™
Bonus Features.

Bonus Features:

BONUS FEATURES

smokescreen

Conversations with the authors
of SMOKESCREEN

Doranna Durgin

Tell us a bit about how you began your writing career.

4 At the age of three, when I wrote and illustrated (and bound!) my first book. Or at the age of 12, when I wrote (and illustrated and bound) my first novel. After that, the words never stopped flowing. I did stop binding them, though.

At 12, I received my first rejection from Paramount (Hey, who knew you had to be agented? Or write in actual screenplay format?) and at 14 my first short-story rejection. At that point the adults in my world decided I was weird, and I went more underground with my writing (but never stopped or even slowed down). Finally, just out of college and living in a remote area where I couldn't use my degree or indeed get any job at all (or even meet anyone for the first six months...), I decided I'd try to publish again. Didn't let anyone discourage me this time. Took a while, though!

Was there a particular person, place or thing that inspired this story?
Not this time. Just a whole bunch of little things that came together into a whole with that synergistic power the muse sometimes wields.

What's your writing routine?
I work on a page quota, seven days a week. Sometimes life happens instead, but not so often that you'd need all your fingers and toes to count the days per year. Usually I have music going in the background, but sometimes I need to quiet my brain and then I don't. I write on a laptop in Rough Draft and pull it all together in Word Perfect. And I often burn scented candles (sugar cookie, yum!). What time of day I write depends on the weather, season and Other Things Going On. I use a recliner or I stand; I don't sit at a desk. My only hard and fast rule—aside from that page quota!—is that I don't actually hold myself to any particular routines. If I feel like doing something different—a different kind of music than ordinarily inspires me, two work sessions a day instead of one, etc.—then it's no big deal. I know someone who has to have a dozen sharpened pencils at the desk (even when work-ing at the computer). This is not me.

How do you research your stories?

Extensively. Overextensively. I get lost in research. I love the Web, I love my Internet community and their vast collection of knowledge, and I love research books.

Excuse me. Must go build another bookshelf now.

How do you develop your characters?

They develop themselves. That's trite, I suppose, but I often don't truly have a good handle on my characters until they've gone through a couple scenes and have a chance to play off each other and events. If I need to go back and tweak things to suit, then I do—because sometimes characters grow into something else than I expected (if I'm smart enough to pay attention). Even when I do have a character down cold at the start, I usually discover more about them as I go along.

I don't do any of those exercises that one can do, involving index cards and character interviews and the like. I do stop and go off to ponder things now and then.

When you're not writing, what are your favorite activities?

I have four dogs who are in training for various activities—one Cardigan Welsh corgi matriarch, two Cardigan agility dogs and a young beagle now in breed competition who's starting agility basics; we all go to shows. I also have a Lipizzan whom I ride dressage and who lives on the property. (Lots of pictures on my Web site, [www.doranna.net].) That pretty much keeps me busy!

What are your favorite kinds of vacations? Where do you like to travel?
I'd love to see all sorts of places—Australia, South America, Europe, our very own national parks—but I don't travel well at all (this is an understatement), so for the most part I see tiny bits of the world through nearby dog shows or convention locations. As for actual vacations... define those for me again?

Meredith Fletcher

Tell us a bit about how you began your writing career.

I've wanted to write since I was in third grade. My fourth- and fifth-grade teachers often caught me working on stories during class. Instead of chastising me (I was fortunate to be an A and B student in spite of my extracurricular activities in the classroom!), those teachers read the stories to the class. I've written on a regular basis, mostly for myself and to learn the craft, then had the opportunity to begin my career with Harlequin. I've got several more books and novellas in me that are dying to come out!

8

Was there a particular person, place or thing that inspired this story?

I love tech. Sweet and simple, I know, but I really do. I'm constantly fascinated with the computerized world we live in (which most people never seem to notice, or just take for granted), with the medical reconstruction that physicians can do, and with the resiliency of the human body and spirit.

What's your writing routine?

I write every spare minute I have. Usually early in the day and late at night are best for me. I'm active and like to do things with the rest of my day.

How do you research your stories?

Usually I have an idea and jot it down, kind of get the feel of it. Once the characters and action hook me (which means I can't stop thinking about the story!), I begin preliminary research. I read every chance I get, and I've got a mutant ability to remember a lot of what I've read and definitely where I read it. When I do intensive research, I begin with children's books. They're absolutely the best for getting the biggest amount of information in a short span of time. Tech books even have a glossary! And books about people and places have tons of photographs! They're amazing! It's a wonder more kids aren't brainiacs. After I have the basics down, I decide where I need to invest most of my time. Rather than studying a particular field, I study parts of a field as they apply to the story I want to write. Or a certain area in a country. Then I look over my notes and see if my additional information lends itself to changes or developments in the characters or plot sequences.

How do you develop your characters?

I start by figuring them out. What do they want? What experiences have they had that will make a mark on the story I'm trying to tell? What is her greatest fear? Once that's done, I audition them on the page by writing scenes that may or may not make it into the story I'm writing. I write lots of dialogue. I have to hear them to truly "get" them. Once I have them down, I start over and write the story from beginning to end.

When you're not writing, what are your favorite activities?

Love reading. Love research. Love gardening (it gives me something to do with my hands while my mind is sorting out a knotty problem!). I love to travel. I'm an amateur photographer, cutting-edge tech whiz, and hobby borrower (if I see someone doing something I think is interesting, I do it, too, till I learn it or get bored).

What are your favorite kinds of vacations? Where do you like to travel?

I love the impromptu vacation, the one when you just get in the car and go. I've found more delightful out-of-the-way places and people in this manner than any "planned" vacation. Structure is all right to get you there—sometimes (even that I find arguable!)—but I like to throw the itinerary out the window and go exploring. Caves are awesome. Every time I vacation where there's a cave, I go see it. I don't know what that says about me, and probably I don't want to know. I love going to the Yucatán Peninsula. There's something about the history of the place, the slow and easy manner of the days, the quick light showers that scatter baby crabs across the beach and vanish just minutes later and the cool blue of the water that is just so relaxing.

Do you have a favorite book or film?
The Princess Bride, in both book and film. I just love it when Westley says, "As you wish." Both mediums are such a delight.

Any last words to your readers?
Happy reading! And if I write something you like, or you have questions, please contact me at MFletcher1216@aol.com. I hope to have a Web page up soon. I'm still working on that.

Vicki Hinze

Tell us a bit about how you began your writing career.

In 1984 my mother introduced me to romance novels. In particular, to Harlequin Presents®. After the first novel, I was hooked. Trouble was I read faster than they were printed. But since I enjoyed those novels so much, I began looking at other romances—Harlequin Superromance, Silhouette Special Edition. I loved the positive roles of women in them, and the heroines' ethics in dealing with so many of the challenges we all face with family and friends and work/home.

Like many others, I read hundreds of these books. I'd fill a tall kitchen trash bag with them and then ship them to my mother to donate and share with her friends. We were living in Illinois and the weather turned foul. Snow, ice, freezing rain. My husband, a military officer, was away again, and so the kids and I were limping along as military families do. The simple truth is I loved the books so much I wanted to write one. And so I did. It was awful! A heartwarming story, but buried in a tomb of mechanical errors so deep, the story was lost. So I wrote another. And another.

They were awful, too. Not that it stopped me from submitting them, I'm sorry to say. And I got the most kind rejection letters from editors who had to be pulling out their hair at trying to read them. Finally, one of those dear souls who is still with Harlequin today, wrote: "Vicki, if you're really serious about writing, why not take a course?"

Notice that by this time, we were on a first-name basis—which should have been much to my shame, but wasn't. I was too driven to write books to have decent judgment. But I bless her for making that suggestion most days of my life. (Can't be expected to on the days I'm fighting for every word that goes on the page. But "most days" is an excellent average!) Anyway, I took her advice and took a course. And another. And another. And I kept writing. Fifteen books and I have no idea how many partial books. My problem, by this time, wasn't that my stories were still mired in those tombs, it was that my books didn't fit anywhere on a bookshelf. Simply put, I wrote odd stories: contemporary novels that read like historicals, time-travel novels (before there were time-travels in romance), and reincarnation stories (before there were paranormal romances). I was just a couple years ahead of myself. But I loved them all.

That's always been my criteria in writing a book. I must love it. Totally and completely and without reservation. However, after having written 15 books, I also wanted one that someone other than me, a dear friend, my mother and the editor who rejected it would read! So I invested in studying the market, and I discovered a new line where a type of story I loved would fit. That line was Silhouette Shadows®.

Needless to say, I was thrilled to pieces. I wrote the entire book, which became known as *Mind Reader,* and sent it in to my agent. She was doubtful because the heroine in the novel was an empath and that sort of thing wasn't being done. So she agreed to send it to Silhouette Shadows® but was very clear that if it didn't sell there, she just didn't have another publisher to send it to that would be open to a heroine who was an empath. I said okay, and held my breath. Okay, truth is, I prayed, too. A lot.

14

Two weeks later, I got "the" call. An editor wanted to buy it—but not for Silhouette Shadows®, for Intimate Moments!

I'm laughing at myself here. Because I was so thrilled—(after six years and all those books, wouldn't you be?)—I told the editor it had been my goal for many years to write for Harlequin.

Today, that doesn't seem like such a bad slip. But then it was a horrible one. Silhouette was under the Harlequin umbrella but they were competitors in those days. (*Open floor and suck me down!*)

The editor understood, bless her, and I survived it—if with a red face for a long time. But I learned that day that while you might not hit the target you're aiming at, you well might hit the one next to it. So I've imagined a row of targets rather than one when I write, and I stick only to one rule: Love the book. Totally and completely and without reservation.

So far, it's working out.

Is there a particular person, place or thing that inspired this story?
A person and a thing inspired this story, actually. My dad had a photographic memory, which was an asset in many ways, but it made living with those who had an imperfect memory challenging for him at times. He was empathetic, as well, which created special challenges for him, particularly when in crowds or large groups of people. At times, he'd grow so overwhelmed by the sheer volume of sensory input, he would get wicked migraines. I wanted to do a novel that expressed understanding of those challenges and the extra effort required to live a "normal" life when you're enduring them.

The thing that inspired this story is the national focus on our borders and the conflict between retaining that openness and the terrorist vulnerabilities that come with it. It is, to say the least, a delicate balance. One that is, at times, doomed to swing too far to either side, but also one by our very nature we are obligated to continue to attempt.

What's your writing routine?

The truth is I don't really have one. I believe that if you lock yourself into doing anything— especially something you love—one way, then it becomes easy to convince yourself that this one way you've defined is the only way to do it. Life has too many interruptions and detours for that! My writing hours vary. The way I go about writing a novel varies. Everything about the process and fitting writing into my life varies. Often, I'll start my writing day at 2:00 a.m. Other days, I start at 10:00 p.m. This makes it sound as if I lack discipline, but the truth is, I usually write until I either fall asleep at my desk or I get stiff-shouldered because I've been at it far too long. I write everywhere—in the park, in the backyard, in my recliner, at my desk. But when I get stuck, I always go to the kitchen table. My father once told me that 99% of genius is created at a kitchen table. So I've always done that—gone there when stuck. It's always worked.

How do you research your stories?

I do a lot of background work in the library or on the Web. Books, magazines, newspaper articles. More comes from medical or scientific studies, governmental agency reports and diaries. When I'm familiar enough to know what to ask, and where I'm going to focus, I seek out professionals or subject-matter experts and speak with or interview them, depending on what I need for the story. Early on I was writing a thriller and needed specifics on how a person being murdered would react to specific tactics used to kill him. I called a doctor I knew and put the questions to him. He went silent, stayed silent. Finally, in this wee voice, he said, "Vicki, where is Lloyd?" Lloyd is my husband. The doc was worried I wasn't speaking hypothetically! I learned right there and then not to assume that anyone *knew* I was a writer and to *always* specifically state that I am before asking the first question.

How do you develop your characters?
This is going to sound a little wacky—and maybe it is, but it works. I interview them. I pretend I'm sitting across a table from them, and I listen to them tell me their life story. Without fail, what they tell me drives the story events and their reactions to those events. Many times I've had in mind to write one story, but the characters led me to write another. They know what matters most to them and why. I just have to listen.

When you're not writing, what are your favorite activities?
I love to do remodeling. There's something empowering about knocking down a wall or tearing up a tile floor and replacing it with a new one. And I'm crazy about power tools. My

husband doesn't fear me running loose in a clothing store, but he quakes in his shoes when I go into Home Depot or Lowe's.

Could you tell us a bit about your family?
Delighted. My husband is an artist. He does realistic wildlife woodcarvings. Prior to this, he had a very different career as a U.S. Air Force officer in Special Operations. We have three children—two sons and a daughter. One is an electrical and computer engineer married to a nurse; the other son has a degree in environmental studies, owns a boating company and is married to a newspaper reporter. They're expecting a baby as I write this. My daughter is a teacher who had the great sense to marry a brick mason who is hands down the world's greatest son-in-law. They have a daughter who is the joy in my life; my sun, moon and stars. And we have a hundred-plus-pound Weimer (Gray Ghost), my faithful sidekick, who has no idea she's a dog and never lets the rest of us forget it.

What are your favorite kinds of vacations?
I'm a simple woman and I have simple tastes. Open the gates to a water park anywhere, and I'm very happy. One of my favorites is in San Marcos, Texas. I love the slides and the rafting. It's a kick—and I get a license to act like a kid again.

Any last words to your readers?

It's hard to verbalize this, but I'm going to try. Writing requires so many sacrifices. Yet I love it and I can't imagine my life without it. The truth is that it's my readers' support that grants me the gift of being able to do it, and I am very grateful. I read their letters and I'm so touched. I can't begin to tell you how much I cherish them, but I do. I save them all, and when times get tough, I pull them out and reread them, and I remember why I do what I do. Many readers write and tell me how much my books help them. I want them to know that they help me, too.

Marsha Zinberg, Executive Editor of Signature Select, spoke with Doranna, Meredith and Vicki in the winter of 2005.

Author's Journal
by Doranna Durgin

We asked Doranna Durgin to tell us a bit more about the heroine in CHAMELEON. Here Doranna discusses the heroine's abilities and talks about the point at which the heroine knew she was different. 🖎

Samantha Fredericks: nine years old, sobbing her pillow wet at the latest brutal honesty from her parents. *You'll never be pretty, so get used it; you're not smart enough to aim high, so get used to going low.* Samantha Fredericks, escaping into her own mind. She imagined she was a princess.

She didn't ever imagine she could actually make it so.

You're nine years old and you want to be anyone but who you really are. So you haul out your imagination and pretend that it's so. You're a princess. Maybe even a warrior princess. With hair that gleams. *Tame* hair. And you imagine it night after night, perfecting the details. Until one night you look in the mirror and—*whoa!*—it's not you in the reflection.

Welcome to Sam's world.

Of course, turning into a warrior princess overnight is bound to attract some attention. And since attention was the last thing Sam wanted, she set about being unremarkable: she controlled her hair, softened her young features. Even at nine a girl can study magazines to refine her fashion imagination.... But for Sam it wasn't enough; once she realized this was something she could do, really *do*, she set about exploring her limits. She investigated different skin colors, different shapes, different sizes. She even experimented with changing her apparent sex—and turned it into her first undercover adventure by checking out the boys' room at school, which wasn't nearly as interesting as she'd hoped...except for the ultimate excitement of pulling it off.

Over time she grew and stretched her startling talent, and by the time she graduated, had used it to suss out the dark secrets of her high school, including several anonymous tips that led to drug busts. The last skill she conquered was that of going *unseen*, and she tries not to rely on it too much; it can be too difficult to manage, and has left her cornered once too often.

Sam's skill doesn't encompass actual physical change, but is as complete as a psychic experience can be. Those who perceive her guises do so visually and tactually—and because of that, she's limited in what she can pull off. She can change her skin color, but not radically. As a freckled, fair-skinned woman, she cannot present herself with deep black skin tones—chocolate is as dark as she gets. As a short, slight person, she can only gain a few inches and perhaps fifty pounds of mass, whether in muscle or jiggle. And when she changes to a male form, she can appear as wiry and slender with little effort, but has trouble with beefy and barrel-chested.

Then again, she's still young...who knows what she'll learn next!

TIPS & TRICKS

Six Tips To Improve Your Memory
by Vicki Hinze

Everything we sense is fed into the subconscious part of our minds. It never forgets anything. But the subconscious takes everything literally, and that's where we get into trouble remembering. The subconscious can't differentiate truth from fiction, doesn't interpret right from wrong. If we sense it, we store it. But—and here's the trick—we remember best that which engages our senses.

FOCUS

It is as we sense that our conscious minds do the interpreting and make value judgments on what we're sensing and taking in. If we're half listening and half hearing, glimpsing rather than really looking—preoccupied—then that sensory input gets jumbled up. If you want to remember something, as you're sensing it, focus intently on it. Then you're filtering truth from fiction, making those value judgments as you sense.

An example. My children used to deliberately wait until I was at the computer, writing, to ask me for permission to do things they knew I wouldn't approve of them doing. They'd ask, and I'd respond with an "uh-huh," and later when I'd ask them why they'd done whatever thing they'd done, they'd say, "But you said I could." That led to the inevitable "When?" Canned response: "When I asked. You were at the computer." To that I had no defense, because I vaguely recalled a glimmer of that "uh-huh" and knew that, preoccupied, I very likely had given permission for whatever had been done.

Focus. Focus intently. It not only improves memory but also eliminates the embarrassing incriminations you earn at the hands of your children.

FOOD
Some scientists say tea, gum-chewing and/or vitamin supplements can improve your memory. Others disagree. But there is consensus that a balanced diet helps give the brain what it needs to function well.

EXERCISE
Muscles and the brain are said to have a common bond. Exercise them both and they're stronger and stay stronger longer. Activities that make you use your imagination and really think

about what you're doing or imagining—like reading—are great exercise for your memory. Exercise will also help in other areas that have a major impact on memory, such as stress, high blood pressure and high cholesterol.

REPETITION

If there is something that you want to remember, you have to get it from short-term memory to long-term memory. Much of short-term memory is fleeting and lost within the first day. To get that information from short-term to long-term, focus and repeat the significant portion of it to yourself multiple times. Now, an hour from now, five hours from now, when you're in that twilight sleep: almost sleeping but not quite. According to the experts, if you perform this repetition for three days, you will have committed the information to long-term memory.

ASSOCIATION

Some find that association works well to enhance memory. Using a child's birthday as a security code. Using the name of your first pet to jog your memory of a password. Associate a needed series of numbers with a string of birthdays, or with birthstones. Association is effective in helping us remember, provided we use analogies that are significant to us.

GET CREATIVE

If you're trying to remember a list of items, get creative and use what you've got to help you. Ten fingers, ten toes. Two feet or hands or eyes or ears. Associate the number of items with a body part. Say, for example, you're off to the grocery store. You need five items. Five items equals one hand. If when you're shopping, you remember the hand, you'll be less apt to leave the store short an item.

There are a lot of tips on bettering your memory. Some are by well-respected authorities and some are by elementary school children, who learn a lot by rote and repetition. Practical tips are all around us. We simply must open our eyes to them—and then focus on them long enough to grasp them and put them to use.

RECOMMENDED READING

Memory Prescription, Gary Small,
ISBN: 1-401-30066-9, Hyperion.

Brain Power: Practical Ways To Boost Your Memory, Creativity and Thinking Capacity, Laureli Blyth,
ISBN: 0-760-73231-0, Barnes & Noble Books.

The Memory Bible, Gary Small,
ISBN: 0-786-88711-7, Hyperion.

Total Memory Workout: 8 Easy Steps to Maximum Memory Fitness, Cynthia R. Green,
ISBN: 0-553-38026-5, Bantam.

TOP TEN

Technology-Based Action Movies
by Meredith Fletcher

1 MATRIX.

No doubt about it, this mind-bender featuring
Keanu Reeves started moviegoers everywhere
talking about what is and what could be. Filled
with near-tech and Japanese-style action, MATRIX
delivers a double-fistload of provocation and
violence.

2 HACKERS.

If we all agree that the actual computer work and
accompanying dramatization of the same was
incredibly wrong, this is still a fun film and can be
enjoyed. This movie also opened a lot of eyes to
what young people might be doing with their
computers instead of homework.

3 SNEAKERS.

Starring Robert Redford and Sydney Poitier (two leading men for the price of one!), this movie was a more cerebral approach to cyberchaos in today's world. A lot of fun and a peek at the world that was coming.

4 THE SIX MILLION DOLLAR MAN.

Posing as a full integration between man and machine, Steve Austin (played by hunky Lee Majors) starred as a secret agent ("I'm about to raise your security level.") equipped with bionic limbs. THE BIONIC WOMAN was a spin-off series featuring Jaime Sommers (Lindsay Wagner). Both series are reportedly coming to DVD soon.

5 THE NET.

Sandra Bullock plays a computer-savvy virus hunter who ends up taking on a murderous cyberphreak after the program he created could cripple the United States. A great popcorn-and-ice-cream movie. In addition, a limited television series based on the film exists that further extrapolates Angela Bennett's run for her life.

6 TRON.

Although aimed at the younger set, TRON nevertheless intrigues film watchers interested in the what-if of virtual reality.

7 BLADE RUNNER.

Harrison Ford stars as a burnt-out cop chasing Replicants, artificial beings that have learned to kill in order to preserve their lives. The peek at this dark future world as well as the very human lives trapped within it is great.

8 GHOST IN THE SHELL.

Probably the hottest-selling anime movie ever. Motoko Kusanagi is a cyborg chasing a computer hacker known as The Puppet Master. A definite influence on THE MATRIX and the whole cyberpunk movement.

9 T2.

Although some might disagree with the choice and the exclusion of the first Terminator film, T2 really stood apart not only in the tech department regarding the action and what-if scenarios (and the chilling depiction of the T-1000 by Robert Patrick!) but in the special effects, as well.

10 WAR GAMES.

This chiller starring Matthew Broderick kicked off the artificial intelligence examinations by the film industry. Although intensely dated these days, the movie nevertheless sets forth the idea of a sentient computer judging the world.

Yes, I know I probably left some of your favorites off the list. And I probably included some that you don't agree with. I'd be happy to entertain discussion at MFletcher1216@aol.com. If you haven't seen all of these movies, you really should.

Cool Technology
by Meredith Fletcher

Anyone who grew up reading science fiction knows that we're now living in a world that's really far beyond anyone's expectations based on the technology of twenty and thirty years ago. The sheer immensity of how much technology has invaded our everyday world is only matched by the unbelievable casual disregard for it.

Microwave ovens, television remote controls and video games (remember Pong? Or Space Invaders?) were all in their infancy. Computers weren't thought of as a household necessity, and few people believed their kids would be doing their homework on them or be able to check their school grades by simply accessing a Web page. I've got a friend who has wired his computer system throughout his house. Using just his voice while sitting in his easy chair (as long as he's able to speak into a microphone to the computer), he can turn the lights on and off, change temperatures throughout the house, retrieve his e-mail messages and bring up the alarms that safeguard his house.

Here is a short, compact list of the coolest technology currently available on the market. The discussion about each is brief, but there is plenty of information about all of these items on the Internet—and in the library for those of you who haven't yet learned the intricacies of surfing the cyber world.

1. WiFi (Wireless Fidelity). Without a doubt, this budding technology is going to change the face of the world. Setting up a network at home that will allow you access to your online connection from your desktop computer, notebook computer and pocket PC (not to mention the kids' X-Box) is relatively simple. Everything you need comes in a kit and you can have it running within minutes and say goodbye to cables running throughout the house. Once the home network is set up, you can take your notebook computer out to the backyard pool and crunch numbers or write books while watching the kids frolic (or while watching that handsome hunk do half-gainers off the diving board!). WiFi allows a frequent computer user/Internet surfer to change surroundings easily, with no need for rerouting cables. Several bookstores and coffee shops offer WiFi hotspots with Internet access for free, and those numbers are growing every day. In 2004, Cincinnati, Ohio, was the first American city to go totally wireless.

2. Mobile Ad Hoc Network. An offshoot of the WiFi networks, a mobile ad hoc network relies on the availability of other network users. If a car going down the highway is equipped to receive the Internet from that city's hot points while on the go, the receiving car also acts as a sending station, theoretically pushing out as much information as it takes in. Therefore, like the individual pearls that make up a necklace, the Internet signal is pushed farther and farther by each computer accessing it. These networks will expand the potential of computer users.

3. BlueTooth. This wireless application is quickly replacing the need even for the nifty and ever versatile USB cables. Only a few years ago, every peripheral that hooked up to the home computer seemed to come with its own connection. Then USB came onto the market and all the peripherals started speaking the same language and being able to share com ports. With BlueTooth installed on two devices, such as a pocket PC and a cell phone or a pocket PC and a desktop PC or a PC of any kind and a printer, those paired devices communicate efficiently and without cables. BlueTooth enables hands-free operation of cell phones in cars, with recognition of up to five different cell phone numbers. The only drawback is that the paired devices have to be within 33 feet of each other. Simple encryption keeps others from intercepting your signals even out in public. If your devices (like the printer you use nearly every day) didn't come equipped with BlueTooth, you can add a USB plug-in (capable of being used by all your BlueTooth devices instead of a cable—er, plug-in—for each). Do away with the cable spaghetti in your office!

4. **GPS.** Everyone seems to take this technology for granted because it has definitely become so pervasive in society. GPS just rolls trippingly off the tongue. Even most users don't know how the technology works. (A GPS-equipped device passively contacts at least four of the 24 U.S. Air Force satellites kept in 12-hour orbits around the planet. But you knew that, right?) Many phones come equipped with GPS locaters installed for 911 calls so emergency teams or law enforcement personnel can quickly find them. Less climatic but no less stressful, many cars now come equipped with GPS and an onboard route mapper so the driver always knows where he or she is. If your vehicle doesn't have GPS and a mapping system built in, one can be quickly added for a modest price. Even

pocket PCs (like the IPAQ, discussed next) can be equipped with a GPS sleeve that allows communication with those space-based satellites that constantly know where you are. And the technology can be used for more frivolous purposes than simply having to ask the next convenience-store clerk how to get where you're going. One of my friends maps a golf course with a pocket PC program, then uses GPS to check the distance on his golf swing!

5. Pocket PCs. First of all, a PDA (personal digital assistant) is not a pocket PC. A lot of confusion exists on the similarity and function of each. A PDA basically keeps up with contacts, appointments, some math utilities, etc. A pocket PC on the other hand (like IPAQ's awesome device and Dell's new Axim) runs Windows-based products like Word, Outlook, Excel, Microsoft Money, MSN Messenger, Streets and Trips, etc. If a program exists on your desktop that you like, chances are that one exists for the pocket PC or is coming soon. In addition to handling your checking and travel arrangements, pocket PCs also take care of your e-mail and online needs when linked by BlueTooth to your cell phone. Recently, though, IPAQ has started manufacturing their pocket PCs with phones built into them, eliminating the need of carrying a phone while upgrading to a nearly full-on computer experience. Worried about managing your pocket PC on the go while juggling the same files you're working on away from home? Afraid that you'll mix them up? With the docking functionality (by USB cable, Blue-Tooth or infrared) the pocket PC communicates with the desktop or notebook PC and updates the latest information between both, including your expense account and changes to your projects as well as e-mail updates.

6. MP3. Despite getting a somewhat black eye over the music downloads that go on, MP3 format audio is—for the moment—the best tech going for those products. MP3 works by encoding digital audio data into a compressed format called a bitstream. The second part of the tech decodes it on your device (such as your computer, iPod or DVD/MP3 player in your home or car). I love to listen to audiobooks as well as music, but keeping up with all of those CDs gets problematic, and I've been known to lose or destroy a few. Now audiobooks are being manufactured on DVD in MP3 format. All on one disk. You could upload them to your iPod so you can take it with you wherever you go. Personally, I just dump audiobooks onto my IPAQ Pocket PC and play them through my car stereo. That way my originals stay in perfect condition. MP3 allows you to put 12 times as much audio on a hard drive, portable drive, CD or DVD. I don't know about you, but I can always use extra closet space!

7. TiVo. Absolutely an incredible product for those of us who are constantly on the go. I like television. It soothes and relaxes and entertains. But being busy sometimes means not being home to catch every episode of a favorite show (like *Buffy the Vampire Slayer, Alias, 24, Lost, Desperate Housewives, CSI, CSI: Miami, CSI: NY, House, Veronica Mars*—pick your own delish dish!). TiVo, with its season pass, records your favorite shows automatically when you're not there.

8. Bittorrent. Another cyber utility that is getting a black eye, Bittorrent allows video compression of files. Unfortunately, a number of movies appear on the Internet before being released on U.S. screens (because of the 12-hour time difference between China and other countries and the U.S.). Pirates with handheld recorders download the first-release movies then upload them to the Internet. However, I love Bittorrent for the simple fact that sometimes local television preempts one of my favorite shows (can't believe they do that) or a show is moved around and the season passes on the TiVo get into conflict (don't you hate when that happens) and I can go onto the Internet and download whatever episode I want to see. Occasionally, an episode gets chopped up by local events (news, weather, a Presidential speech) and I want to see it without those things getting in the way. A quick trip to my favorite Bittorrent site on the Internet takes care of that!

9. eBooks. Don't get me wrong, there's something *so* magical about holding a book in your hands and kicking back in a chaise lounge at the beach (with guys playing volleyball nearby). But when I'm on the go, I like the portability of the eBook. A simple download puts a book on your notebook PC or pocket PC (it really is a versatile tool and entertainment center all rolled up into one!) so you can read it on the plane, in a hotel room, in a doctor's office or at the beach.

10. MMORPG (Massively Multiplayer Online Role Playing Game). Okay, this last one is purely a guilty pleasure. Getting on the Internet and immersing myself in another world with people I meet online is just sheer fun. I get to be somebody else, anybody I want to be. MMORPGs had their beginnings in MUDs (Multi-User Dungeon) but have far outstripped anything that has gone before. In addition to playing really cool games in real time, I get to meet interesting people and form friendships that stay neatly within the game. Also, the games run 24 hours a day, so when I'm restless, I can pop in and see what's going on, exchange strategy or news with one of my buds and potentially save the world while I'm at it! It's a win-win situation. One of the grandest MMORPGs is Everquest, but my favorite for the past few months is Cryptic Studios' City of Heroes. I get to be a superhero, have cool powers and I look really great in spandex!

There you have it. A list of technology and gadgets that I think are the coolest around. Take a look and see what you think. If you want to compare notes, I can be reached at MFletcher1216@aol.com, if I'm not busy catching up on television or battling some archvillain!

Buzz on Bombshell

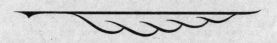

Recently, Associate Senior Editor Natashya Wilson gave us the scoop on the Silhouette Bombshell series that features empowered heroines, like the heroines in SMOKESCREEN, who take charge and save the day.

What are people saying about Silhouette Bombshell?
USA TODAY calls them "strong, sexy heroines who save the day and then pick their own man." The *Chicago Sun-Times* says, "when the pedal hits the metal, these ladies are at the wheel." The *Austin Chronicle* calls it "the first-ever fully realized line of action-adventure books for women." Get ready for the time of your life....

What is Silhouette Bombshell?
You're about to enter the high-stakes world of Silhouette Bombshell, where the heroine takes charge and never gives up—whether she's

standing up for herself, saving her friends and colleagues from grave danger or daring to go where no woman has gone before. Every Silhouette Bombshell story is a high-voltage, high-stakes suspense adventure in which the heroine saves the day—guaranteed.

If you like what you read here, we've got just the books for you. These three stories are shorter than a full-length Silhouette Bombshell novel, but they pack just as much punch! Every month, Silhouette Bombshell stands and delivers four fascinating, fast-paced reads about women you'll want to know, caught up in adventures you'll never forget. Multilayered, compelling and unpredictable...that's Silhouette Bombshell!

Who is the Bombshell heroine?

She may be a secret agent, a mother protecting her child, a military officer who stumbles into a hornet's nest. She could be any woman, seeking to bring some justice to the world. She's the bombshell of the new millennium: smart, savvy, sexy and strong. She's as comfortable in a cocktail dress as she is brandishing blue steel. She's everywhere in the media—on the big screen and the small—in movies such as *Kill Bill*, *Tomb Raider* and *Charlie's Angels* and TV shows such as *Alias*, *Crossing Jordan* and *CSI*.

She isn't perfect. She isn't immune to harm. But a Silhouette Bombshell heroine has smarts, persistence and an indomitable spirit, qualities that will get her into trouble and out again in an exciting adventure that will also bring her a man worth having...if she wants him!

Who are the Silhouette Bombshell authors?
They're writers from all walks of life—military, rescue workers, professors, psychologists, homemakers, pilots and much, much more. They're *USA TODAY* bestselling authors, award-winning novelists, veteran action-adventure writers and fresh new voices who create compelling stories featuring women you'll want to read about.

Look for Silhouette Bombshell books, available at your favorite retail outlet. Silhouette Bombshell...for the strong, sexy, savvy reader in you!

Here's a sneak peek...

CHECKMATE

by

Doranna Durgin

On sale June 2005 from
Silhouette Bombshell

Every month Silhouette Bombshell has four fresh, unique, satisfying reads to temp you into something new...

Here's an exclusive excerpt from one of this month's thrilling releases, the final Athena Force adventure, CHECKMATE by Doranna Durgin.

"Ambassador—" Selena Shaw Jones rubbed the bridge of her nose, right above the little bump Cole liked so much. *Don't think about Cole just now.* Fatigue washed over her in a startling rush. She closed her mouth on indiscreet words, a warning from the supersecret Oracle database—the alarming intel from the CIA, along with other military and agency listening posts with which an FBI legate such as Selena should have no direct connection. Word that the Kemeni rebels of Berzhaan were desperate in the wake of what they thought was U.S. support—that they had to grab power *now,* or concede it forever.

"Selena?" Ambassador Allori set his teacup in the saucer, brows drawing together. "Are you quite all right?"

And just like that, she wasn't. Her stomach spasmed beyond even her iron control, and she blurted, "Excuse me!" and bolted from the room, briefcase clutched in her hand. She remembered the bathroom as a barely marked door down the embassy hall and only hoped she was right as she slammed it open. *Thank God.* Most of the room was a blur but she honed in on an open stall door, grateful for the lavish, updated fixture—

Better than a hole in the floor. Been there, done that.

And when she leaned back against the marbleized stall wall, marveling at the sudden violence her system had wreaked upon her, the thought flashed unbidden and unexpected through her mind: *We were trying to start a family.*

No. Not here, not *now.* Not with Cole half a world away and an even bigger emotional gap between them. She knew he hid things from her; she thought she could live with that. *Maybe not.* Selena clenched down on her thoughts the same way she'd tried to clench down on her stomach, and stumbled out to the pristine sink to crank the cold water on full and splash her face and rinse her mouth. When she dared to look at her image, she found that it reflected what she felt: she looked stronger, less green. This particular storm, whatever the cause, was over.

What if she were pregnant in a strife-torn Berzhaan, her estranged husband not even knowing he was estranged? Theoretically he was still deeply undercover in wherever it was that he'd gone, unable to do more than send a sporadic e-mail or two. *Theoretically.*

Except she'd seen him in D.C.

Kissing someone else.

If she were pregnant…she'd have to stay here long enough to stabilize this new legate's office, in spite of the unrest. And then she'd have to go home…she'd have to tell Cole. To decide if she trusted him, or if she'd merely contribute to the long line of broken branches in her family tree.

And if this is any taste of things to come, I'll have to carry around a barf bag wherever I go.

The water still trickled; she scooped another handful into her mouth, held it and spit it out. Her eyes stung, sympathetic to her throat. It wasn't until she coughed, short and sharp, that she stiffened—and realized that the uncomfortable tang didn't come from her abused throat, but from the air she breathed.

Tear gas.

Trickling in from the street outside? From somewhere in the building?

Damn. Damn, damn, DAMN.

Listening at the bathroom door revealed only silence, and she went so far as to peek out. The smoke hung thickly in the abandoned hallway. Selena ducked back inside, took another deep breath—this one to hold—and eased out into the hallway, running silently to the waiting room she'd left the Berzhaani ambassador so precipitously only moments before.

Empty. Allori's teacup lay broken on the floor, tea soaking the priceless carpet.

Son of a bitch.

The door leading to the prime minister's office stood slightly ajar, and Selena made for it, her chest starting to ache for air. But breathing meant coughing, and coughing meant being found.

She didn't intend to be found until she understood the situation. If then.

Razidae's office proved to be empty, as well, the luxurious rolling office chair askew at the desk, papers on the floor, the private phone out of its sleek-lined cradle—and the air relatively clear. Selena closed the door, grateful for the old, inefficient heating system, and inhaled as slowly as she could, muffling the single cough she couldn't avoid.

All right, then. The building was full of tear gas, and the dignitaries were gone, and Selena had somehow missed it all.

48

They could have blown the building out from under you while you were throwing up, and you wouldn't have noticed.

Think, Selena. She pressed the heels of her hands against her eyes and calmed the chaotic mess of her mind. She could call for help from here—Razidae's private line might have an in-use indicator at his secretary's desk, but it wouldn't show up on any of the other phone systems, so she wouldn't give her presence away by picking it up.

But there was no point in calling until she understood the situation. No doubt the authorities were already alerted.

You still don't know what's going on.

Well, then, she told herself. *Let's find out.*

Selena laid her briefcase on the desk, thumbed the

token combination lock and flipped the leather flap open. She'd left her laptop behind in favor of her tablet PC, and the briefcase looked a little forlorn…a little empty.

Not much to work with. No Beretta, no extra clip, no knives…

Maybe she wouldn't need them. Maybe by the time she discovered what had happened, it would actually be over.

Nonetheless, she took a quick survey: cell phone, battery iffy; she turned it off and left it behind. A handful of pens, mostly fine point. She tucked several into her back pocket. A new pad of sticky notes. A nail file, also worthy of pocket space. Her Buck pocketknife, three blades of discreet mayhem, yet not big enough to alarm the security guards. It earned a grim smile and a spot in her front pocket. A spare AC unit for her laptop, which garnered a thoughtful look and ended up stuffed into the big side pocket of her leather duster. A small roll of black electrician's tape. A package of cheese crackers—

Selena closed her eyes, aiming willpower at her rebellious stomach. *I don't have time for you,* she told it. Without looking, she set the crinkly package aside. And then she looked at the remaining contents of the briefcase. A legal pad and a folder full of confidential documents. She supposed she could inflict some pretty powerful paper cuts. A few mints and some emergency personal supplies she wasn't likely to need if she was actually pregnant.

No flak vest, no Rambo knife, not even a convenient flare pistol.

Then again, there was no telling what she might find with a good look around the capitol. Almost anything was a weapon if you used it right.

Selena jammed the rejected items back in her briefcase, automatically locking it; she tucked it inside the foot well of Razidae's desk and checked to see that she'd left no sign of her presence, except there were those *crackers*—

She made a dive for the spiffy executive wastebasket beside the desk, hunched over with dry heaves. Mercifully they didn't last long. And afterward, as she rose on once-again shaky legs and poured herself a glass of the ice water tucked away on a marble-topped stand in the corner, she tried to convince herself that it was over. That she could go out and assess the situation without facing the heaves during an inopportune moment.

She dumped the rest of the water into a lush potted plant that probably didn't need the attention, wiped out the glass and returned it to its spot. She very much hoped that she'd creep out to find an embarrassed guard and an accidentally discharged tear gas gun.

A stutter of muted automatic gunfire broke the silence.

So much for that idea. Selena's heart, already pounding from her illness, kicked into a brief stutter of overtime that matched the rhythm of the gunfire.

"All right, baby," she said to her potential little passenger, pulling her fine wool scarf from her coat pocket and soaking it in the pitcher. "Get ready to rock and roll."

But as she reached for the doorknob, she hesitated. She could be risking more than her own life if she ran out into the thick of things now. As far as she knew, whoever had pulled the trigger of that rifle didn't even know she existed. She could ride things out here with her lint-filled water and her cheese crackers.

Or she could be found and killed, or the building could indeed blow up around her, or whoever'd fired those shots could succeed in their disruptive goal, and Selena and her theoretical little one could be trapped in a rioting, war-torn Berzhaan. Her mind filled with images of frightened students and dead capitol workers and a dead Allori. She closed her eyes hard.

It really wasn't any choice at all.

...NOT THE END...

Look for CHECKMATE by Doranna Durgin, on sale June 2005 at your favorite outlet.

Here's a sneak peek...

DOUBLE VISION

by
Vicki Hinze

On sale June 2005 from
Silhouette Bombshell

*Every month Silhouette Bombshell has four fresh,
unique, satisfying reads to tempt you into something
new...*

*Here's an exclusive excerpt from one of this month's
releases, DOUBLE VISION by Vicki Hinze.*

"Okay, Home Base." Staring through her diving mask, Captain Katherine Kane swam toward the rocks above the newly discovered underwater cave. Cold water swirled around her. "I'm almost there."

"Roger that, Bluefish." Considering the distance between Kate and Home Base, Captain Maggie Holt's voice sounded surprisingly clear through the earpiece. "I don't like the idea of you diving alone. The boss would have a fit."

The boss, Colonel Sally Drake, would understand completely. "Sorry, no choice." Captain Douglas and his tactical team had been diverted. "If we want to find GRID's weapon cache, then I've got to do this now—before they have time to move it."

Douglas and his men had assisted Kate on a former mission, intercepting GRID—Group Resources for Individual Development—assets, and when he'd summoned Kate to the Persian Gulf, she'd known he suspected a GRID presence and needed help. All the key players in the Black World community knew that pursuing GRID, the largest black-market sellers of U.S. intelligence and weapons in the world, was

Kate's organization's top priority. And it had been designated such by presidential order.

"I still think we should follow the usual chain of command," Maggie said. "If the boss were here, you know she would agree with me."

If Colonel Sally Drake were there and not at the intelligence community summit meeting coordinating the war on terror, Kate and Maggie wouldn't be having this conversation and there would be no debate. Kate resisted a sigh.

Maggie was new to their level of covert operations and still adjusting to tossing out standard operating procedure and assuming command in critical circumstances. But she had all the right stuff; she'd grow into the job eventually. Nothing taught operatives better than experience, and she'd get plenty in their unit. Still, for everyone's sake, including her own, Kate hoped Maggie adjusted and grew into it soon.

"Look," Kate said, speeding the process along, "ordinarily Douglas would have worked up the chain. This time he came straight to the S.A.S.S." Secret Assignment Security Specialists were the last resort, and Douglas respected that. "I know this man and he knows us. He's got a fix on GRID." Kate couldn't resist an impatient huff. "No offense intended, Home Base, but you've got to learn to trust your allies." That included Douglas, his team and Kate.

"Yeah, well. I'm gun-shy. You have to prove you deserve it."

That response surprised Kate. "How?"

"Don't get yourself killed today. Do you realize how much paperwork I'd have to do?"

Kate smiled. Okay, she'd cut Maggie a little slack. The woman was trying. "Waking up dead isn't my idea of a fun way to start the day, either, Home Base." She reached the finger of rocky land jutting out into the gulf and, treading water, removed the black box from her tool bag.

Stiff-fingered from the cold chill, she flipped the switch to activate the C-273 communications device and then affixed it to the rock just below the waterline. If this leading-edge technology worked as advertised, she would still be able to communicate with Maggie at Home Base via satellite. Supposedly the water would conduct the signal from Kate inside the cave to this box and then transmit via satellite to Home Base, completing the link to Maggie. Kate hoped to spit it worked. "Okay, C-273 is seated. We're good to go."

Looking up, she again checked the face of the rock above the waterline. Worn smooth *and* scarred by deep gouges. *Definitely signs of traffic.*

That oddity had caught her eye initially and led her to dive here for a closer look. Otherwise she never would have found the cave—and she seriously doubted anyone short of an oceanographer charting the gulf's floor would have, either.

"Bluefish?" Worry filled Maggie's voice. "The guys at the lab swear this device will work, but if it doesn't and we lose contact, I want you out of there pronto. I mean it."

"Here we go again. Trust a little. Remember, no guts, no glory." Kate adjusted her diving headgear, checked to make sure her knife was secure in its sheath strapped to her thigh, pulled her flashlight from her tool belt, turned it on and then dove.

"Glory?" Maggie's sigh crackled static through Kate's earpiece. "What glory? You're a phantom. Less than three hundred people know you exist."

The S.A.S.S. was a highly skilled, special detail unit of covert operatives assigned to the Office of Special Investigations and buried in the Office of Personnel Management for the United States Air Force. The unit didn't exist on paper, its missions didn't exist on paper—the unit's name even changed every six months for security purposes, which is why those who knew of the S.A.S.S. operatives referred to them by what they did and not by their official organizational name. If more than a couple hundred people knew S.A.S.S. existed, Kate would be shocked. "Personal power, Home Base." Kate had learned from the cradle to expect no other kind. "Doesn't matter a damn who else knows it as long as I do."

At the mouth of the cave, she paused to scan the rock. More of the same: worn smooth and deep gouges. Even considering tidal fluxes, too many deep gouges rimmed the actual opening. Water action alone couldn't explain them. She swam on, entering the cave.

"Are you inside now?"

"Yes." Snake-curved, the inner cave was about three feet wide. Kate swam close to its ceiling. Suddenly the width expanded to nearly ten feet. "The cave's opened up." She lifted her head above water, cranked her neck back and shone the light above her. "Now this is bizarre."

"What?"

"I dove a solid twenty feet to get to the mouth, then swam a couple football fields to get to this point. The water rode the cave ceiling the whole way. Now I'm seeing a stretch of wall that's exposed a good nine feet above the waterline." She stopped treading water and tested for bottom. Her fin swiped the sand, and she stood up. "Water level's dropped. It's chest-deep."

"I'm plotting your GPS," Maggie said.

"Good, because even considering an umbrella effect, this shouldn't be possible." Kate kept her diving mask on in case she was standing on a shelf or sand bar—false bottoms had proven common in her explorations—then looked down the throat of the cave. A diffused light emanated from somewhere far ahead, creating a haze. The rocks jutting out from the cave walls cast deep shadows. Must be reflections shining through the water, or cracks in the rock. Neither seemed possible, but the alternative... "Oh, man."

"What is it?" Anxiety etched Maggie's voice. "Bluefish?"

"This is more than we bargained for." Kate's heart beat hard and fast. "A whole lot more."

...NOT THE END...

Look for DOUBLE VISION by Vicki Hinze, on sale June 2005 at your favorite retail outlet.

MINISERIES

From _USA TODAY_ bestselling author

Marie Ferrarella

Two heartwarming novels from her miniseries The Bachelors of Blair Memorial

THE BEST MEDICINE

For two E.R. doctors at California's Blair Memorial, saving lives is about to get personal...and dangerous!

"Ms. Ferrarella creates a charming love story with engaging characters and an intriguing storyline."
—_Romantic Times_

Available in July.

Where love comes alive™

Bonus Features, including:

Sneak Peek,

Author Interview

and Dreamy Doctors

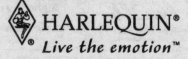

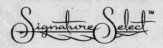

DORANNA DURGIN

Doranna Durgin obtained a degree in wildlife illustration and environmental education, then spent a number of years deep in the Appalachian Mountains. When she emerged, it was as a writer who found herself irrevocably tied to the natural world and its creatures—and with a new touchstone to the rugged spirit that helped settle the area, which she instills in her characters. *Dun Lady's Jess,* Doranna's first published fantasy novel, received the 1995 Compton Crook/Stephen Tall award for the best first book in the fantasy, science fiction and horror genres. She now has 15 novels of eclectic genres on the shelves and more on the way. Most recently she's leaped gleefully into the world of action-romance. You can find a complete list of titles at www.doranna.net along with scoops about new projects, lots of silly photos and a link to her SFF Net newsgroup.

MEREDITH FLETCHER

A true wanderer at heart, following her Sagittarius nature, Meredith moves around a lot. She can't say much about her earlier career (contractual obligations and some things that the U.S. government has expressly forbidden talking about), but she enjoys travel, technology, science and history. She's an avid gardener and even though she doesn't settle down, thankfully there are always people who need help. She has many hobbies and collects stories, which means her books and novellas are going to range far and wide. She can be reached at MFletcher1216@aol.com and looks forward to hearing from readers.

VICKI HINZE

Vicki Hinze is the author of over 20 novels, a nonfiction book and hundreds of articles published in over 40 countries. Many have won distinguished awards such as Best Romantic Intrigue, Best Suspense and Best Romantic Suspense Novel of the Year. She's recognized in *Who's Who in America* and *Who's Who in the World* as a writer and educator. More information on Vicki and her books can be found on her Web site at www.vickihinze.com.